Light in the Night

Lance Vaughn

Contents

Prologue

In the forest, the sounds of the waves stopped short. The initial wave of ferns opened up into a dark understory with a floor more root than earth. What little leaf litter still clung to the crevices rotted almost visibly. Taz pointed straight and a touch right. Of all of them, only he and Fletch didn't need the sun for directions. There was no sun here.

Before long, they were crossing the same streamlet the exploration team had found. Taz hit a slick rock and went down, soaking his fur.

"Don't groom," said Fletch.

"This is going to Rockwaters and Leswaters all over again."

"Lovely," grunted Firebrand as she too skidded. "Maybe we can make it all the way to Amatsu status this time. See how Iris would fare out here."

"She wouldn't," said Phoenix. "I'm okay, so it's too dry for her to survive."

His fur-glow was visible in the gloom. It faded around his paws, but barely.

"What do you do when it rains?" said Taz.

"Get lucky, mostly."

"Does it hurt you?"

"Only if I get soaked." Phoenix eyed the Rocklander, who was clearly struggling with this perspective. "It doesn't suck. How often do you ever get stuck in a storm?"

Taz shuddered. "Never, if we can help it."

"Exactly."

"Pitt-web," said Loki.

The plant-creature was up a tree this time. Brownish-green tentacles clung to the bark with suckers textured like moss and lichen. No part of it pulsed. Halo ogled at it until she ran into a root buttress. She leaped back as a piece of bark flapped away. The moth was as big as her face, and so perfectly camouflaged, it vanished as soon as it landed on the next tree.

Taz startled violently as a second moth shot up in front of him. His head smacked a woody vine and its bark exploded. For a heartbeat, the air was thick with moths. Creatures darted clear of the dusty cloud of wing-scales. Fletch hopped off a vine that moved when he touched it, but it only recoiled. Its white-tipped leaves folded into tubes all the way up a treetrunk into a flat, leaf-and-vine ceiling above them. A dead leaf fluttered down.

"It's awfully quiet here for a Lowland forest," said Firebrand.

"Please don't talk like that," said Taz, and got a comforting lick from his brother.

Sethral lost her footing and wound up belly-down over a root arch as thick as a Mountainair's chest. She swallowed her growl. It was quiet. There was no wind, no birds save for the odd trickling call, and almost no insects. She slid off the root and rolled onto her back. The vine ceiling two tail-lengths overhead didn't show a single gap. The structure of it was made of small and bizarrely flat-topped trees, strung through with the woody cables of vines.

These wove together into a net overgrown with hundreds of plants that did not seem to need soil. Roots trailed from everything that grew.

Fletch hauled her up by the scruff and set her back on her paws. They kept walking. Closer to the forest's edge, most of the trees' roots had been thick and tubular, mounded over each other into tangles taller than a Coppertail. Those thinned now, replaced by stilts, winglike buttresses, and trunks that split or bulged towards their bases. One ahead looked like it had melted into the ground. The vine ceiling was tall, but nowhere near tall enough to be even halfway to the top. Or thick enough to be cutting out this much light.

The afternoon wore on quietly, then darkened as the sun fell and the trees grew thicker. Silversand caught a lizard and shared it between all of the hunters: a bite for each. There was no sign of any danger, so the group walked until it was too dark to see, then found a hollow in the buttresses of an enormous tree.

"I'll take first watch," said Fletch.

"Second," said Silversand.

Everybody else lay down to sleep.

"Any luck?" said Sethral.

Whipper dropped to the ground and pounced on his fur. Small, yellow ants clung to him, biting ferociously. He yanked them out and hopped out of their crawl range, disgusted. "I can't get through. It's all either too dense, too slippery or too well protected. I've never seen so many biting bugs in my life, and I've been in a jungle." He hissed and went after an ant he had overlooked.

Silversand returned from another foray. "No luck?"

"None," said Sethral. "You?"

"No. Is Loki back yet?"

"Haven't seen him." Sethral beat her wings. Ants tumbled away from Whipper, picked themselves up and scuttled furiously towards him again. Sethral pulled him away.

It had been a day and a half. Past the lush and strange forest fringe, the Daemon's Outback had reverted to something eerily like the South Forest, save for the vines and the fact that the trees were the size of Rockhall's tunnels. The light was dim, the forest empty, and the soil almost devoid of vegetation. It was still very quiet. Lowland plants phased away as they traveled, but aside from that, it was hard to believe they were making any progress away from home.

The twins arrived with Firebrand close behind them. Sethral raised an eyebrow at the conspicuous absence of Phoenix.

"Don't look at me," said Taz.

"I thought we agreed to stick together."

"He's a satellite," said Fletch. "He's not obliged to listen."

"He is if he starts making trouble for us."

"Because he's the one who usually gets us in trouble," said Dusk under his breath.

Sethral rounded on him. "Want to say that to my face? Besides Iris, I seem to recall an incident on an island named Linderward. Or did our protracted visit there escape you?"

"If that was his fault, I find it funny that Iverae went so lightly on him. And you have no right to judge creatures by who's chasing them if you care at all about Jay."

"Don't you dare say anything about Jay!"

"Then you shut your sour mouth about Phoenix!"

"Why do you care?"

"Guys!" Fletch forced his way between them. "Calm down."

They fell silent, glaring at each other.

"Why do you care?" said Sethral.

"If I could add up how much of your business that was, it wouldn't fill a nut cap."

"Dusk, walk away," said Fletch. "We're not going to continue this."

Dusk left like Sethral had ceased to exist.

"Sethral, I don't want another word out of you," said Fletch. "This conversation is over."

Sethral lowered her wings. Taz was glaring at her worse than Dusk had been. Silversand was crying into Firebrand's shoulder and the Leslander looked sad.

"Umm..." said Loki. "Sorry if I'm interrupting something, but I found a place to spend the night."

The path Loki retraced quickly grew rockier than anything they had crossed since the cliffs.

Taz guided Wing around a small sinkhole. "How much worse is this going to get?"

"Not much. And it's worth it, trust me."

"What's that sound?" said Silversand.

Whipper stepped on an exposed outcrop and wrenched back. He backed away with fur fluffed protectively.

"Sorry, Fuzz," said Loki. "Forgot to warn you."

Whipper ran up a tree and hid on Wing's back. Sethral tossed him her blanket to burrow in.

The rumbling grew stronger the farther they walked, until everyone could hear what Silversand had: a deep roar with a hiss on top.

At last the forest opened up into a magnificent gorge. Creatures squinted in the late afternoon sunlight and shook their muzzles in surprise as mist from a six-tail-length waterfall stuck to their whiskers. The cataclysm poured from a hole in the rocks into a round pool occupying the gorge's dead end. Carved out on either side were flat banks, lush with vegetation and flowers. These tapered out where the water emptied into a swift, narrow river.

Loki pointed over the edge. A ledge ran down the gorge wall beneath them, to a cave entrance that was almost certainly part of a network. One by one, the renegades dropped to the ledge. Loki took them right down into the cave. The last two tail-lengths to water level were navigated through slippery tunnels and small drops, and just when everyone was getting sore and slimy and claustrophobic, they reached the exit. Silversand gave a cry of delight. They were behind the waterfall. The cozy alcove was lit by the curtain of sunset-burned water that made its far wall. The floor was a crescent of moss-pillowed land around a tongue of water that lapped at the polished rocks.

Loki followed a ledge right through the waterfall's fringe. He was back heartbeats later. "Who wants food?"

They pressed through the curtain after him. The ledge continued under the undercut cliff before giving way to sand, then soil. The renegades stepped from beneath the cliff into an evening garden. Flowers of all shapes and colours nodded in the spray that beaded their petals, then scampered off in rivulets to spatter the wet soil. Small trees clustered in pockets where the soil was deeper. Shrubs, ferns, thick grasses, vines, and leafy plants vied for the rest.

Firebrand shouted for the other Coppertails. Taz, Fletch and Dusk fell upon a bush the Leslander recognized from Benty's books as edible. From the water's edge came a simultaneous whoop from Loki and laugh from Silversand. Fish swarmed the shallows, seeking refuge from the currents created by the waterfall. The pair were soon up to their bellies in the water. Whipper and Sethral lay on the bank and picked off smaller fry.

Firebrand fought her way back through the vegetation to the exit ledge. "Going hunting? I know you usually hunt alone, but we might have a better shot here if we try together."

Ruatzi nodded. They set off together along the base of the vine-festooned cliff. Before a tail-length had passed, Ryatzi pointed up the wall. A lizard lay immobile in a loop of woody vine. Firebrand stalked it into pouncing distance, then lunged. The lizard exploded into fans and streaked up the cliff, but Ryatzi could jump like a Coppertail. They shared the catch and continued along the cliff base.

Chapter 1

Another three tail-lengths in, they found themselves in a small grove of trees. Firebrand held up her tail. A strange shuffling and squeaking was making its way though the plants towards them. It moved quite fast, but zigzagged back and forth, pausing frequently to snuffle at things. At the grove's edge, the vegetation caught it. The squeals spiked, and the creature thrashed and flailed until it plowed out into the grove.

The size of a plump Hollow, it was a brown-furred critter with short legs and a pointy snout. Lying flat all down its spine was a mass of thick, white quills. It must have scented them, for it froze at the grove's edge with its nose in the air. Ryatzi flew from hiding. The creature squealed loudly. Its spines shot up to form a prickly sausage the length of its back. It shook them until they rattled, and bared rodent's teeth.

Ryatzi danced forwards. The creature lunged, and they circled each other again. One paw shot out. Suddenly the creature was on its back, and a wild squealing pounded Firebrand's skull. Dirt and leaves sprayed everywhere. When the melee ceased, the creature lay dead on the ground. Ryatzi stepped back, lay down and began to lick one paw gingerly, parting the fur around the ends of two broken spines. He nipped each and pulled it out. "Glad I haven't completely lost my touch."

"That was amazing."

Firebrand skinned the creature while Ryatzi licked his paw until the bleeding stopped. She pushed the catch towards him. He pushed it back. They shared again. When Ryatzi had finished half his portion, he dropped the rest in front of Firebrand and fell asleep on her back.

Midway through her meal, a rustle made Firebrand glance up. It was nearly dark out, and purple shadows softened the grove. The rustle built to a crackle, paused, and crackled again. All at once, a dead leaf the size of Halo folded up and vanished into the ground. Firebrand stared. The rustle began again, on her other side. She looked just in time to see another leaf whip out of sight. She growled.

The grove stood silent. Firebrand gathered the rest of her meal and snuck towards the path she and Ryatzi had made coming here. A chewing sound made her look back. A plant at the grove's edge wobbled and fell over. Slowly, as if drawn by a string, it slid away into the grasses.

The cave, when she returned to it, was empty but for the sleeping forms of Dusk and Wing. Firebrand left Ryatzi with Wing and followed the sound of laughter to discover a set of stepping-stones leading out the cave's opposite side. She plunged through the waterfall on them. Before her opened a grassy bank like the one she had just left, edged by a small beach. Renegades tumbled up and down the far end of it, laughing and pouncing on things in the sand.

Whipper popped from the vegetation beside her. "Kick the sand!"

She scooped some up and flicked it at him. Bright blue sparkles lit up all through it. Whipper batted a wave of sand back. Tiny lights cascaded over Firebrand's paws. Together they romped up the beach, kicking sand ahead of them and dancing through the fleeting stars.

It was a sandy but happy group that collapsed into piles in the cave some time later. A near-quarter moon had crept above the canyon and the waterfall was bathed in silver, casting a faint glow through the cave. Loki woke with a grunt. Now he was paying for having swallowed so much water while snapping after fish. He extracted himself from the warm pile. The air was cold and damp out with the mist from the waterfall, and the moss squelched beneath his paws as he padded to the nearest exit. He darted through the waterfall, shook himself off, and froze.

Phoenix? How had he gotten down here?

The Pyrya stood poised on a spit of rock jutting out into the middle of the pool. From crest to tail, his fur was on fire. Flames raced as he lunged at the water, and Loki's throat went dry. Something enormous boiled back beneath the surface. Phoenix bared his teeth and screeched. He darted down the spit. Vortexes sucked the water as a fin the height of Firebrand rose and cut a sharp turn away. Phoenix jumped as a wave swamped the rocks. The fin appeared again, and this time carved the water that rolled and churned around it as it slid away into the gorge-bound river. Phoenix's flames went out. The glow that remained was blackened halfway up his legs, and he struggled to shore along the slippery spit. He lay down to watch the water.

Loki's bladder reminded him why he was here. He found a spot in the bushes and finished his business, then crept back to the waterfall.

Phoenix was gone. Was he dreaming? How could the Pyrya have gotten here anyway, if not by the spray-soaked ledge and caves? The pool gave no indication that a monster had been there. Legs still wobbly, Loki tiptoed back to the cave. He should get some more sleep.

Silversand was dreaming. She could tell it was a dream because all the trees were blurry, like they tried to run away whenever she tried to count them. She didn't mind, though. Her dreams were usually nice.

In this dream she was back at the Royals' camp, which was in a dip like Lockhaven instead of on a hill, but that didn't really matter. There were kits playing chase all around her, and running over her too. Their tiny claws pricked her fur. One ran at her face and climbed it, and Silversand sat bolt upright as a sharp pinch stung her nose. Tiny crabs tumbled off of her. She swatted the one now dangling from her muzzle fur. It landed in the moss and scuttled off with claws upraised. Through the cave marched hundreds if not thousands of nut-sized crabs. They scrambled over everything that lay in their path with the gusto of a first-wave Hyenar gathering. She could hardly believe no one else had woken up yet.

"Silver!"

She wasn't the first one up. Whipper was perched on a boulder beside the cave exit from which the crabs streamed. Judging by the pile of shells beside him, he had figured out how to get around their claws, and was having a fine meal.

"Catch!"

Something small and round sailed towards her. Silversand snapped it from the air and grinned as the flavour of crabmeat burst across her tongue. Whipper swiped another crab from the flow. In a flick he detached the claws and popped the top half of the shell off its body. He teased the meat out in one piece. She couldn't replicate that. Silversand cocked her head at the crabs. She trapped one under one paw.

"Yeek!"

She smacked it off her paw on a rock, then smacked it several more times for good measure. Her paw hovered in midair. The crab didn't move. Had she killed it? She poked it. Yup, dead. She snapped it up, spitting out the hard claws. The rest was soft enough to chew, and delightfully crunchy. When she had finished, she smacked another. Who knew food could be this easy?

By the time everyone was awake, the crabs had mostly vanished into the pool. Everyone but the twins and Dusk was licking their lips.

Dusk rubbed his eyes. He had been last to wake. "Where's Halo?"

The kit had disappeared overnight. Sethral shrugged. "Probably with Phoenix, trying to feed him or something."

Dusk left the cave. The twins followed him, and when the three of them had eaten, the renegades began the much more arduous journey back up the gorge.

Silversand pouted. "I wish we could stay there. Not actually, because we'd run out of food and we'd never find out how Radar controlled the you-know-whats, but I still wish."

"What's up, Loki?" said Fletch. "You've been quiet all morning."

"It's nothing." The Fisher turned his eyes away from the pool. He brightened. "Halo! Hey short stuff, you missed the crabs!"

"She says she doesn't like them," said Ryatzi.

Halo repeated the little dance that apparently meant she didn't like crabs, then jumped straight off the cliff to their ledge.

"Okay, bird morph," chuckled Ryatzi while Silversand squeaked at the three-tail-length drop. Sethral blocked his path with her wing. He rolled his eyes. "There are water morphs, too. That's it for the South Forest, I think."

"Most what fall into one or the other? Coppertails have types, not morphs!"

"You're serious? Hey Halo! Permission?"

Halo looked at Sethral, befuddled. A step to the side gave Ryatzi whatever answer he was looking for, and he started laughing at the look on Sethral and Loki's faces. "I can't believe you guys! Why do you think she doesn't talk? Halo's a Forestair!"

Halo cocked her head farther, like she still couldn't understand how they didn't know.

Sethral hurled herself on Ryatzi. "Yah, got anything else you want to tell us? You Drakon turd; we've been searching for moons for anything on Forestairs! You can't just spout stuff like that!"

"I thought it was obvious! Her horns are even coming in!"

"They're what?"

Loki put a paw to his face. "The cabin hatch. That's how she could headbutt it without concussing herself."

Halo cocked her head to the other side. There were two small knobs on top of her skull. At a glance, the fur ruffled by their presence just looked like an unfinished grooming job.

Sethral pinned Ryatzi and ruffled all of his fur, then sat on him. "Okay, tell me about the morphs."

"You're not getting anything like this."

She let him get up. Ryatzi sat down and began to groom his fur back into order. Sethral vibrated with impatience.

"Fine," said the Saberel at last. "The Forestairs in the South Forest fall into two groups: the bird morphs and the water morphs. I don't know much about either except that bird morphs like trees and make more bird sounds, and water morphs make more water sounds when they make noise at all. They prefer the ground too, I think, and I assume they can swim. They always brought me fish when I was recovering after escaping from Radar."

"Just fish?" said Loki.

"No, sometimes crabs or crayfish if they could catch them, but it was mostly fish. I guess they assumed I needed the energy."

"You probably did," said Sethral.

Loki had stopped walking. "What about Springfish?"

Sethral went stock still.

"Those too," said Ryatzi. "I couldn't catch them myself, but I guess they were good at it. Why?"

"Ratty," said Sethral. "Do bird morphs catch water things too?"

"Halo?"

The kit hopped and wove backwards.

"No, almost never," said Ryatzi. "They can't see underwater."

"How the heck did you get that from what she just did?" said Loki. "And Seth—"

"It wasn't her," said Sethral. "Loki. She didn't catch the Springfish you and Silversand got back in the Darkwood!"

"Or the fish Firebrand got," said Loki. "Spitfire, you weren't there. It was before you rejoined us."

"But after Halo, Dusk and Whipper did," said Sethral. "Great Drakon shit, Loki; we've been being followed by another Forestair."

Ryatzi looked down at the kit. "Did you know about this?"

She looked up at him and shut her mouth.

"What's that supposed to mean?" said Loki.

"That she's not supposed to tell."

Chapter 2

After the canyon, the forest was dark and almost startlingly drab. The Coppertails were up ahead, investigating a plant Firebrand had pointed out. Whipper was on Wing's back. Halo ran o   ff again.

A shot of ice went through Loki's body. "Spitfire, look out!"

Sethral lunged and Loki was smacked sideways as tentacles whipped from the dirt, swallowing her and Ryatzi in a tight ball of brown. Loki hurled himself at the ball, kicking and clawing.

"Let them go! Let them go!"

The tentacles scrunched tighter. Loki attacked their base, a fleshy disk from which the fat, tapered arms radiated. Nothing even made a mark. There was a ping, and Silversand was on top of the ball with her gauntlet on. Loki joined her and they savaged it together. The thing fell halfway between a plant and an animal like the Pitt-webs did; its camouflaged skin was rubbery and its body firm, but just squishy enough to absorb the power of Loki's kicks. Silversand managed to slice into the skin, but no blood welled out. The thing continued tightening, a slow, unstoppable death lock around the two creatures wrapped up somewhere inside.

A growl like thunder split the air. Loki and Silversand were knocked from their perch in a blaze of light. Phoenix had his teeth in the wound Silversand had created. His tail lashed. 'Dusk, help me!'

The Nightlock landed beside him and pressed against his side. The wound began to smoke. With a jerk, the tentacles unfurled. Taz and Firebrand darted in and dragged Sethral out; she had all four paws and both wings wrapped around Ryatzi. She groaned.

"You're alive!" Taz managed.

Everyone relocated to several tail-lengths from the trap. Silversand flung herself on Sethral, who gasped. "Ow! Silver—"

Silversand tumbled off again, her words a frantic jumble. "Are you hurt? What did it do? Where did it come from? Why is it—"

Sethral struggled to push herself up, defying Fletch's firm paw. "Where's Ratty? Please, is he okay?"

Ryatzi was coughing nearby, still unable to get up. "He's not hurt," said Whipper, finishing his check.

Sethral yelped as Fletch put down her wing.

"The good news is, it's not broken," he said. "The bad news is, you sprained it pretty badly. Sorry, Seth, you're grounded for a moon at least."

"How did you get us out?"

All eyes turned back to the trap. Across from the group, Dusk had curled up in a root hollow. Phoenix was standing beside him, watching the trap. Its arms were splayed across the ground, sinking almost imperceptibly slowly into the soil. The hub at their center remained flush with the leaves. Its texture and colour were identical to that of the forest floor.

Firebrand flicked her tail to the Pyrya. "I honestly thought you were a Mountainair when you showed up. I didn't know there were Coppertails that could growl like that."

"What's up with Dusk?" said Sethral suspiciously. "He looks exhausted."

"No shit, mossfur," said Phoenix. "He just gave up a day's worth of energy to save those two. Darkness strengthens fire, fire saps darkness. It's the only way I can burn things. He knows how it works."

Taz's fur went down again. Phoenix's gaze followed Halo as she bounded up to Dusk, twittering anxiously. She poked his muzzle with her nose, then started grooming his fur. Phoenix kicked the burn-scarred tentacle. It wasn't sinking like the rest. He spat on it and stalked into the forest.

"Looks like we couldn't keep up that travel pace for long after all," said Fletch. "We need to start being more careful out here."

"And figure out what the dangers are," said Firebrand.

"How? The hard way?" Sethral winced as Whipper folded her sprained wing and began tying it in place on her back.

There was a ping from beside Ryatzi. Gauntlet on, Silversand walked straight up to the tentacle-trap and smacked its center.

"Silver!" gasped Sethral. Tentacles juddered briefly, then fell back in their troughs.

"Like this," said Silversand. "Nothing is perfect. We know how to survive other places because we know how their things aren't perfect, so now we have to figure that out here. The only way to do that is to interact with things."

She smacked the trap again, then jumped right onto the trigger pad and sat swishing her tail, completely safe. "See? We wouldn't know this took time to recharge if I hadn't just done this."

Fletch turned and poked a striped, fountain-like plant sprouting from a root beside him. Its center cone rippled. "It's full of water," he said in surprise.

"So we all turn into poke-happy Silversands," said Sethral.

"If you don't admit she has a point, I will jump on that trap-pad after her," said Ryatzi, his voice still hoarse.

"Don't you dare."

Silversand was now scratching at the charred wound on the trap's arm. She purred as she discovered a cord-like structure within it that had been severed by the burn. Poking it made the tentacle's tip wiggle.

"That must be how it controls them," said Firebrand, giving it a poke herself. She flipped the tentacle over—it looked beastly heavy—and identified a second cord running the length of its translucent underside, just beneath the skin. She jabbed it and the tentacle-tip flipped downwards. Silversand poked hers and it flipped up. They took turns, making the tip dance all over the place. Ryatzi rolled over and started towards them, and Sethral admitted the cat had a point.

"Blackmailer," she said as he returned and curled up under her spare wing instead.

Silversand yelped as a drop hit her on the nose. The renegades fell silent. Whipper pressed his ear to a tree. "It's raining."

Somewhere beyond that flat, green ceiling and whatever canopies grew higher up, the clouds must have begun to shed a long time ago, and they hadn't even noticed.

The rest of the morning passed uneventfully. The rain passed, but enough water had trickled through the leaves to make all roots and rocks dreadfully slippery. The sun must have come out then. Slowly, the forest warmed. Whipper started panting as the muggy air thickened, concentrated in this windless, vine-capped lowest forest layer. The humidity soaked even Loki's waterproof fur.

"I can't do this," said Sethral at last. She dropped to the ground, spreading her good wing over the soil.

"I say we find water," said Loki. Everyone agreed. Loki climbed on Fletch's back and scanned the local topography. "Try that way."

They followed his direction. Before long, Silversand located a tiny streamlet flowing down the gradient Loki had identified. It joined a bigger rivulet, which met another and became a small stream.

"Keep going," said Loki.

They paused for a drink, letting the Fisher test the water first, then continued downstream, scrambling over rocks and tripping on vegetation. The stream made a happy gurgling sound beside them.

"I can hear it!" cried Silversand.

From the forest ahead came a rushing noise. Faint at first, it grew rapidly louder until they climbed the last ridge to find a crystal-clear forest river leaping over rocks through a carved-out watercourse. Downstream it widened around a smooth bend, where the water grew flat and lazy as the power was taken out of it. A pebble beach filled the crook.

Whooping and laughing, Loki and Silversand ploughed into the water. Tadpoles in the shallows wiggled industriously away from the disturbance, to settle only copper-lengths from where they'd started. Tiny fish sprayed outwards. At the base of the rapids, Firebrand spotted a slow-crawling creature on the river's rocky bottom. It looked like a dragonfly nymph, only four or five paw-lengths long. Ryatzi joined the party in the water. Even Sethral waded in up to her belly fur. Wing took a drink and walked back up the beach, where he lay down and closed his eyes.

Halo set about filling her mouth with water and trickling it over Dusk who, while unconscious, was still drawing dangerously close to overheating. When this cooling method proved slow, she dug trenches to the water level and set his paws and tails in them. Then she soaked herself and lay on his head.

"Thanks, Halo," chuckled Whipper.

A fight had broken out between Ryatzi and Loki in the deeper waters. Both could swim, and so had taken to dunking each other and attempting to get away unscathed, which of course never worked. Water sprayed everywhere as the Saberel pounced on his friend and they both went under. Their current knocked Silversand off her feet. Fletch retrieved her. Taz leaped over them and hurled himself into the fray.

It was midafternoon by the time creatures finally climbed back onto the bank, wet, cooled off, and thoroughly exhausted.

Sethral smiled as Ryatzi came to join her. "You don't look like a skeleton anymore."

With his fur slicked flat, it was evident the Saberel had gained a satisfactory amount of weight since they had left the forest. He shook himself, spraying her with water, and smiled back. "I've had some help."

Silversand finished stealthily arranging flowers in a sleeping Whipper's fur. Picking more, she sidled up to Dusk and began to repeat the decoration. Halo contemplated this with head cocked, then purred and joined in. Dusk looked cute with flowered fur.

Firebrand made her way gradually to the top of the beach. She lay down beside a screen of grasses sprouting from a long rock crack. Sethral, Ryatzi, Loki and Whipper were now heaped into a quadricoloured pile of fur by the water, asleep or getting there. Taz was stealthily picking flowers from Silversand's pile and placing them in her fur while she hopped around Dusk. Fletch was stealing them when they fell off, and dropping them on Taz.

Firebrand put her chin on her paws. When her silence convinced Phoenix she had fallen asleep, he began to lick his paws again on the grass screen's other side. They should have been clean long ago. This must be why the fur on his forelegs was thinning.

"Taffles, you've got bird shit on you!"

Taz ducked, but his twin was faster. Giggling, Fletch wrestled him down. "What did you sleep on? You've got a white spot. Right there."

"What, that? That's been there since last night."

Fletch scooped a pawful of wet sand and rubbed the patch. "Well, it's not from a bird at least. Here, try and wash it out."

Phoenix whimpered softly. The licking switched spots.

"Phoenix?" said Firebrand.

He startled violently and hissed. Before she could get to her paws, he had fled into the forest. Firebrand circled around the grass. The place where Phoenix had lain was sprinkled with strands of fur.

"What's up, Fibes?" Fletch trotted up behind her, a flower tucked artistically behind his ear.

"Is Phoenix sick?"

"Oh Shelha, I hope not." Fletch scanned the Pyrya's patch, then sniffed it cautiously. "It doesn't smell like it. Maybe he's just stressed?

That whole boat journey was awful for him, and the heat can't be helping."

Like Dusk, Phoenix was long-furred. Firebrand realized she didn't know where he was from.

Fletch tapped the scuffed plants. "Did you try and talk to him?"

"Yeah. He bolted."

The worry in the twin's expression redoubled. He closed his eyes and let out a deep breath. "Hope to Shelha he's not sick. I don't know any of the plants out here. In the meantime, we're thinking of staying the night beside the river. Not here, but maybe around the bend where it's quieter. Thoughts?"

"Isn't it a bit open?"

"We'll have creatures on watch. Also, we haven't seen hide or hair of a living thing capable of coming to find us yet, so I'm personally willing to take the risk. It'll be better to stay by water than to wander off and risk being without it."

The water vote won out. The renegades found a quiet hollow downstream of the beach and curled up together. Silversand perched herself on the hollow's edge. Her silver fur gradually vanished as the sun went down. By what was probably moonrise, the darkness was absolute.

Morning found the streambank and forest exactly as they had left it the night be- fore.

"Ready to keep walking?" said Fletch when everyone was awake.

"I'm hungry," said Silversand.

"Can we find food first?" said Sethral.

"There's not much to find," said Firebrand. "I haven't seen a prey-creature since yesterday and I hardly recognize any of these plants anymore"

"We can scout around, and if we don't find anything, we can eat on the move," said Fletch. "Put that to a vote?"

The vote was unanimous.

"Whip, want to try the trees with me?" said Sethral.

Whipper shuffled his paws. "I already ate."

"What? When?"

"Before you woke up." He pointed to the side of their hollow. "There were worms all over."

Sethral groaned. "I keep forgetting you're half insectivore. Loki, want to try the water?"

Together he, Sethral and Silversand returned to the river. A few stones overturned revealed crayfish and lots of wormlike creatures, likely the larvae of water-spawning bugs. Between the three of them, they found enough to make a meal.

The Coppertails had less luck. Plants along the waterway were sparse and increasingly inhospitable. Taz had numbed his mouth on an innocuous-seeming waterlettuce and Dusk was still spitting from a soft shrub that tasted fine but left a bitter aftertaste that intensified sharply when a creature tried to drink it away. Firebrand and Ryatzi had not caught so much of a glimpse of prey.

"'We have made three onshore forays for food; none have reported sighting any creatures or animals'," said Sethral. "That was in Salisetta's logbook, wasn't it?"

"Please don't," said Taz. "I'm trying not to think about that logbook."

"Wait," said Firebrand. "What came after that?"

"Something about birds." Sethral dug a tattered notebook from her satchel and flipped through it. "I took notes on what I remembered after we got back with Benty. Here. 'A few birds farther from the river.' Not that that helps the rest of you guys. It was the river that had all the plants."

"I say we just keep heading the way we're supposed to be heading," said Taz. "We can forage or hunt as we go, and if we start detouring now, we'll never get anywhere. Besides, I don't even know which way the river is anymore."

"And we might get too far off our path if we start following other directions," said Firebrand. "Taz, hold still."

Bobbing above the Rocklander was a translucent—almost transparent—pearly white bubble the size of his head. Feathery, fin-like appendages flapped up and down on top of it, the source of the bobbing motion. In front of them were a pair of pale green coins, and below these, a short, protruding tube.

"Please tell me that's not a creature," said Loki.

Sethral whipped a rock at the bubble, which rolled sharply out of the way. It tumbled like it had little steering or brakes, but eventually it found its way upright again. It was now bobbing over Wing.

"It's got guts," said Taz.

From this angle, pale pink, pearlescent innards could be seen folded back and forth across the bubble's inside wall. They were as see-through as it was.

"I don't like it," said Silversand.

"Then it's probably dangerous," said Sethral. She threw another rock. The bubble bobbed higher, almost to the leaf ceiling.

"It's got company," said Ryatzi. A second bubble was bobbing over Firebrand.

"Let's just leave," said Taz. "They don't look very fast."

They weren't. The renegades only had to walk to leave them behind. Sethral dropped back from the leading position she had taken up automatically. "Can I not go in front?"

"I'll go first," said Firebrand. "I'm pretty sure I'm too big for one of those trap-things to handle. Ryatzi, for Shelha's sake, just ask for a ride."

The Saberel tried to stifle a second yawn. It wasn't even midmorning and he already looked exhausted. He accepted Fletch's ride offer and fell asleep.

"Speaking of which, how are you doing?" said Fletch.

Dusk was up and walking, though he hadn't said a word yet today. He gave a noncommittal shrug.

Nobody stepped on any trap-pads, though Fletch had a very close face-off with a large, green snake partway through the morning. Silversand pounced on it as it uncoiled to slither up its vine. In short order, Firebrand, Ryatzi and Wing had been fed. The Saberel returned to Fletch's back.

"Taz, you okay?" said Firebrand as the Rocklander stumbled on a second root.

Taz leaned his head against a tree. "Yeah. Just tired."

"We both slept fine last night," said Fletch.

"Yeah, well, we all know you burn less energy on poorly handled stress." Taz pushed away from the tree and kept walking. "And you don't absorb everyone else's feelings."

The juxtaposition flashed as he passed Wing: one half the size of the other, but both with their gazes turned down. The weight sank in Sethral's stomach again. She forced away the tears as they pinched her throat. Not now. The time for worrying about Jay had ended when they had set paw in this forest. Here she needed to focus.

Dusk yelped shrilly. Creatures whipped around to see the Nightlock jump back with one paw tucked to his chest. A black spine retract into the dirt in front of him. A blood drop hit the leaves.

"Here, let me see it," said Fletch quickly.

Dusk wavered, then leaped the patch of ground on three paws.

"Loki, water?" said Fletch.

There was none nearby. None, that is, until Firebrand tapped a cone-shaped plant growing from the bark of a tree. "You mean this kind of water?"

The stab wound on Dusk's paw was washed and inspected. It was not deep, thankfully. His tough pawpads seemed to have spared him worse damage.

"How are you feeling?" said Fletch. "Sick or dizzy at all? Is it numb or tingling?"

"No, it just hurts." Dusk shook his paw like he was trying to shake something off it. "A lot."

Silversand sniffed around the spot where the spine had vanished. She reached out a paw.

"Silver, don't," said Sethral. "Not until we know it's not poison."

Silversand ignored her. Her gauntlet claws crept over the leaf litter, then hooked it and yanked a clump back. Beneath it was a bone.

"Dusk, lie down now," said Fletch.

"I feel fine."

Silversand whipped her paw back as the black spine shot from the dirt. She grabbed a long stick and ran it over the soil. Leaves lifted on a wave of thin, black blades. Silversand kept poking, uncovering more bones until it was clear the leaves were shrouding an entire skeleton. The spines, it seemed, responded mindlessly to touch, and repeated their attacks wherever her stick made contact with the forest floor.

"I'm fine," said Dusk again. He dodged around Fletch and turned to face him, standing steady even on three paws. "See?"

"You shouldn't be." Sethral backed away from the spine-patch as Silversand dropped her stick. The skeleton was now uncovered enough to discern its species. "That's a Coppertail."

"Maybe they're not poison?" said Firebrand. "The body could have been here first, and the spines just grew up around it."

"Well, I don't plan to find out." Sethral grabbed Silversand by the scruff and dragged her back as she inched forwards again. "If Dusk is somehow poison-immune, we'll see some reaction eventually; even Dustlanders have to sleep off a snake bite."

Dusk went rigid.

"Dusk?" said Taz. Fletch leaped forwards.

Dusk snarled and dodged him again. "I'm said, I'm fine! Sethral, say that again."

"What, even Dustlanders have to sleep off a snake bite?"

"Where's Phoenix?"

"What does that have to—"

"Where's Phoenix!"

"We don't know," said Taz. "We last saw him yesterday afternoon."

"What does he have to do with any of this?" said Sethral.

Dusk groaned. "Because I shouldn't be poison-immune. But Pyrya come from Dustlanders and Phoenix saved my life when I got Vipra-bitten. He took all my power and neutralized the poison."

"What in Shelha's name—"

"That works?" said Firebrand.

Dusk looked down at himself and back up again. "Well, I'm still here and the bite I got was lethal, so yes?"

"How?"

"I don't—"

"Charcoal!" said Sethral. "You had charcoal on the back of your neck when we found you. Did that have anything to do with it?"

"Well, that's where he touched, so probably. It burned like a freaking forest fire."

"But you weren't burnt."

"I don't know how it worked. I honestly thought I was hallucinating." Dusk looked around pleadingly. "I don't know..."

Firebrand was hopping. "Maybe his fire powers give him another kind of poison resistance that he passed to you."

"Assuming these spines are poisonous," said Fletch. "But if they are, are you saying this could be residual from the thing with Phoenix?"

Sethral smacked the dirt with both claws. "I've got another question. Dustlanders are from the East Desert. Just over the North Mountains from the North Flats and Plains."

"I knew he was northern," said Firebrand.

"Well, this is basically a game for us now, isn't it," said Taz. "What's he doing here?"

Fletch's voice was quiet. "No, I've got a better question. What's he doing here alone? Dustlanders live in pairs."

"Well, he's not from a pair, that's for sure," said Taz. "He's got the social skills of Liebling."

"The creeping winter probably drove him here," said Sethral.

"No," said Firebrand, "Dusk, you said it doesn't reach that far yet, right?"

"It hasn't," said Dusk.

"Well, Iris is chasing him, too," said Sethral. "Like the rest of us were so kindly informed about."

"Iris wouldn't survive in a desert though," said Fletch. "Phoenix said she probably wouldn't even survive here."

"So let me get this straight," said Sethral. "Fifi's from the north, wasn't driven out by the creeping winter, wasn't driven out by Iris, but for some reason made the migration to the other end of the world, is now the target of a mad water elemental, and has tacked himself onto the renegades despite appearing to hate every single one of us." She looked around at the group. "Because none of that is suspicious at all."

"But do you trust him?" said Silversand, speaking for the first time. "Because you're the one with the sense for that."

Sethral picked at the soil. "I don't know."

"Liar," said Dusk.

Rarely in her life had Sethral bothered lying. She had never needed to; open admission was a far more effective strategy, as it gave others nothing to hold against her. Not to mention that lying through her own lie detector was decidedly uncomfortable. It had probably shown.

"You do trust him," said Dusk, and now Sethral could feel the cold anger seeping off of him. "You just refuse to admit it because he's too much like you and you hate being shown how nasty you are. Well, I'll tell you something. One of the two of you has a reason to be the way they are, and it's not you. I stick up for Phoenix because I don't think he's ever had a creature who's treated him kindly, and because that's hardly changed here. I was the one who figured out Iris was chasing him, and Taz guessed when we got back, so I told him too. We didn't tell the rest of you because we knew this was exactly what would happen. Suck up your damn pride and leave Phoenix alone."

He was right. Everything he was saying was right.

Dusk stalked away. Fletch cornered him and got snarled at, but he didn't back down. Dusk was backed into a buttress hollow. He let the Rocklander bandage his paw. Sethral kept her mouth shut. If she kept talking, Dusk would talk back and it would only hurt more. She had told herself she didn't want to be like that anymore.

When Dusk's paw had been treated and Fletch was sufficiently persuaded that he wasn't dying, Firebrand took the lead again.

Sethral flung a stone at a bubble-creature bobbing a ways off in the forest. She trailed after the group.

They travelled in silence for the rest of the day. Silversand joined Firebrand in the lead and pointed out slight nuances in the forest floor—a rougher patch, a slight dip, a marginal swell—that Firebrand then steered around. The cat tossed a rock at each as they passed it. Once, Sethral thought she saw a mound shudder slightly. It was midafternoon according to the twins, but the forest was as dark as late evening. Whipper said it was raining again.

Dusk started to stumble hard as nightfall approached. Fletch questioned him constantly about how he was feeling, but 'tired' was the only answer he got until Dusk got irate and told him to screw off. They found a stream near evening. Loki tested the water. "No drinking."

Everyone groaned. Firebrand prodded Dusk, who dragged himself to his paws again and nearly keeled over. She supported him as Taz led the way upstream. It was almost dark out by the time they found the Pitt-web in the water. Loki sampled upstream of it. "It's fine here."

"Everyone drink," said Fletch. "We're all getting dehydrated."

"Firefly!" said Silversand.

A small, cheery yellow dot flashed far away in the forest. Another danced in another direction.

"'Nights are warm and full of fireflies'," quoted Sethral. "We must be near a canyon."

Shelter for the night came in the form of an upturned tree stump. Its roots made a jutting disk with a deep, slotlike hollow tucked against them. Ryatzi and Loki backfilled this partway, and creatures piled in. They barely fit.

Darkness fell again, so completely, Firebrand couldn't see her tailtip when she waved it in front of her face. She tried to find a comfy position and got jabbed by a root. She resisted the urge to twist again. As creatures fell asleep, the only sounds In the silence were the tinkle of the stream and her own buzzing brain. She tried to pinpoint what she was trying to think about, but it was all a mess. She flipped over again.

"Lie still, Fibes," grumbled Taz.

"You're still awake?"

"You haven't stopped writhing against my back since we lay down. Also, it's hot." He flopped over and squirmed. "I feel like the air is sticking to me."

The humidity was high still, but the air had cooled to a tepid body temperature. Firebrand touched her tail-tip to the Rocklander's flank. She could feel the heat through his fur. "No Drakon shit. You're burning up."

She kicked Fletch, who bolted awake, detected no crisis and relaxed again. "What?"

Firebrand poked Taz.

"I'm hot," said Taz in a smaller voice than before.

By the feel of it, it was taking all of Fletch's healer's training not to tense up as he repeated Firebrand's analysis. He licked his brother on the forehead. "Get some sleep, okay? If it's heat exhaustion, you'll feel better tomorrow. If not, we'll worry then."

Chapter 4

Sethral stirred as a feeling of something wrong infiltrated her consciousness. She kept her eyes closed and sharpened her other senses. A shot of ice swept all traces of sleep aside. Fletch was crying quietly and Firebrand was holding him. The twin sounded t e r r i - fied.

Sethral opened her eyes slowly. Dread crawled over her body like a fingered blanket. She checked for Dusk, but the Nightlock was awake and looked fine.

"What's going on?" she said.

Firebrand let Fletch answer.

"Taz is sick," said the Rocklander. "That white patch he had on his leg... it grew. He had a fever last night. He woke me up this morning and said he was scared it was contagious, and he was going to leave until it got better or..."

Firebrand shushed him and turned his face back into her shoulder.

"Where are Ratty and Silver?" said Sethral.

'Just seeing if they can figure out what direction he went,' flicked Loki. 'We don't think they're going to have much luck, though.'

Sure enough, the pair were back within a sun's paw-length. They relayed whatever they had found in whispers to Firebrand. Fletch didn't want to hear it. Sethral felt weaker than she should have and her claws weren't steady, but despite the hunger signs, she didn't feel hungry. Ryatzi and Silversand were now talking quietly.

"We're going hunting," said Silversand at last. "Anyone else want to come?"

"Do we want to keep guards here?" said Loki. Whipper was still pressed to Wing's back in the same position he had been in when Sethral had woken up. His eyes were closed and his paws were clenched tight in the mutt's fur.

"I'm staying," said Sethral.

"We can take turns, too," said Silversand.

"That would work better," said Loki. "I'd have a hard time keeping up with you two anyway. Seth and I can go after."

Sethral threw him a glare, which he ignored. She hoped he knew he had just sabotaged her plan not to eat this morning. Then again, given how she got when she went without food, that might have been the point.

When Ryatzi and Silversand were gone, Loki edged over to Whipper. "Fuzz? Do you want to talk?"

Whipper shook his head, then buried his face in Wing's fur. Loki reached out to stroke his back and he started crying. Hard. He looked like he desperately wanted a hug, but he wouldn't let go of Wing. Loki pried him loose and climbed onto the mutt's back as a compromise. Whipper was losing his second herd. Sethral focused intently on the bugs scurrying up the side of the hollow. If she started crying, Whipper would never stop. She had to not think about Jay. She had to not think about Taz. She had to not hear Whipper's sobs, or see the panicked grab he made for Wing's fur every time the forest made a sound. She closed her eyes but that left her with her other senses, which was worse. She went back to watching bugs.

"Sethral."

Loki kept his voice perfectly even, so she didn't tune in until he said her name again. "Sethral."

Sethral dragged herself back from the bugs and looked over mutely. Loki was backed against the root ball of the tree they were camped beneath. He had Whipper in a hug so the Forester could not see the rest of the hollow. Firebrand across from him lay perfectly still, still holding Fletch. There was a yellow-grey tentacle wrapped around her hind paw.

Very slowly, Sethral opened her bag. Her claw went automatically to the metal dish and her tiny knife, with the flint rock she had tied to it on a string. Her tinder pouch was beneath them. By the time a small fire smoked to life in the dish, the tentacle had wound its way halfway up Firebrand's leg. Sethral wrapped the handle of one of her Costar knives in her blanket and held its blade in the nascent flame. When she could feel the heat through the thistlecloth, she pressed the blade to the tentacle. It whipped into the soil so fast she dropped her knife. She snatched it before it tumbled to the hollow bottom. Still nobody moved. Loki pointed to Fletch's back.

Sethral jumped out of the hollow and crept around the edge. Her throat went dry. Splayed across Fletch's back was a rubbery yellow sheet branched into at least a dozen long, fingerlike tentacles. Sethral reheated the knife. The thing jerked when she pressed the flat of the blade to its base. Tenacles curled off Fletch as if in pain, and the whole thing drew itself back into the soil. Dirt showered down as the last tentacle-tips slithered out of sight. One of them had blood on it.

Firebrand leaped to her feet and dragged Fletch out of the hollow. His body was limp and shaking. They regrouped several tail-lengths away. Fletch was coming around, and whimpered as Firebrand ruffled through his fur. She turned him over. There was a bloody patch on his side.

"Shelha," murmured Sethral.

Just behind the twin's ribcage was a hole the size of a large berry. Loki and Sethral found water while Firebrand comforted Fletch. She pulled him down again as he tried, disoriented, to rise. His back leg gave out on him.

"Just stay still," said Firebrand. "Let it wear off."

Loki growled. A tentacle poked from the soil a tail-length away, probed around a blood spot, then withdrew. The soil moved half the distance closer. Firebrand pulled Fletch onto her back, and this time they ran. They didn't stop until they were back where they had found the stream, and found it sour, the evening before. The ground here was mostly rock.

"Fibes?"

Firebrand let Fletch down gently and curled around him. "Don't try to move. You got jabbed by a soil-hunter of some kind. Seth, can you treat the wound?"

They washed the blood off again.

"I can't feel anything there," murmured Fletch. He looked about to faint.

'Keep him down,' flicked Sethral. She pulled out thread and the suture needles she had once used to pick the lock on Ryatzi's PAON prison.

"You left your dish," said Loki suddenly. "There's still a fire in it."

"Take water."

The Fisher grabbed a large leaf and made himself a bucket. He snuck back the way they had come. Fletch's side hadn't stopped bleeding, and the blood ran thin like water. Sethral braced herself and poked a needle in the wound. It met something hard. Very carefully, she pried a long, thin spine from the twin's side.

He twitched. "Ow."

"I thought you couldn't feel anything there."

"I felt that."

"Well, I found out what was making you not feel, then." Sethral flicked the spine onto a rock and turned it over. It had been broken off at the base, likely when the tentacles startled at the burning knife.

Sure enough, by the time the wound was stitched, Fletch was feeling much better, and waas grumbling about how much it hurt. "Give me your bag," he said.

"I thought you used all your painkillers on everyone's headaches when we got bashed against the cliffs?"

"I can almost guarantee Halo has added more since then."

Sethral handed him her bag. He poked through it and came up with a small package wrapped in a red leaf. "See?"

"How do you know those are painkillers?"

"She colour-codes them."

He dug around some more. Sethral watched with a growing frown as bundles in light green, dark green, white-spotted, brown, tan, and yellow were lined up on the rock

"I thought those were yours. Where does she get all these?"

"No clue." He pulled several things from the packages and re-turned everything to Sethral's bag. "Probably talks to the locals. Though I also wouldn't be surprised if she knew them all herself."

"Does she know food, too?"

"I doubt it," said Dusk. "Otherwise she'd be feeding all of us right now. I think she can eat more things out here than we can, but she's not always sure what the overlap is."

There was a call from the forest. "Fletch!"

Sethral could have cried with relief as Ryatzi, Loki and Silversand bounded back to them through the trees. Loki handed back her dish.

"Did you guys eat?" said Firebrand.

"Kind of," said Ryatzi. "There were a couple of birds around."

Silversand set a dead bird in front of Wing, then shoved Ryatzi against Sethral's side. He dropped to the ground with a whine.

Sethral put a wing over him. "Go to sleep. I'll wake you if we go anywhere."

"We're not going anywhere unless we absolutely have to," said Firebrand. "We want to make it as easy as possible for Taz to find us again."

Fletch shuddered and curled up. Silversand joined Whipper on Wing's back, and Dusk pressed against the mutt's side. Loki paced around the group like he couldn't trust the ground enough to lie down. He stopped walking and cocked his head at it.

Sethral backed away. "Loki?"

He circled the spot, then lunged at the soil. Dirt flew. Everyone was on their paws as he dashed to another spot and stamped the ground in. "Silver, catch it!"

A creature shot from the first hole. Silversand was waiting. When the prey was dead, the panic calmed. The ground-creature was the size of a tailless squirrel, but its front claws were huge and its eyes looked half-developed. Loki carefully excavated the tunnel he had exposed at one end and blocked at the other. "I sensed it moving down here. Does it look dangerous?"

"No," said Sethral as Silversand turned the creature over. "It looks like a herbivore."

"Underground?" said Firebrand.

Sethral passed her the small corpse. The ground-creature had wide, flat front teeth and grinding back ones.

"Uncover more of that tunnel," said Firebrand.

This time, Loki and Ryatzi worked together. Loki ran up against a tree and called Firebrand over. At the tree's base, the tunnel ended. The root blocking its way was heavily gnawed.

Firebrand traced the damage. "This is what it eats. Look, it took off the root-bark and left the rest untouched. It it was trying to get through, it would have chewed deeper, or just gone around."

Ryatzi was still farther back along the unearthed tunnel, sniffing at something. They joined him to find a much smaller hole—mouse-sized—running across the big one.

Whipper grabbed Ryatzi's tail as the Saberel made to follow this one. "Dig there," he said, pointing off to the side.

Ryatzi obeyed. He was barely three paw-lengths into the soil when he leaped back. Loki reached out a leg and kicked the side of the hole. It caved in.

"This way, slowly," said Firebrand.

They backed onto the rocky streambank. The hole had exposed a cave-like pocket in the soil, large enough to comfortably house Wing. Sitting motionless in it was a mound of rubbery flesh and tentacle the same colour as the thing that had tried to take Fletch.

Behind this was a tunnel wide enough for it to crawl through. The renegades did not make a sound until they had retreated well up the streambank. They regathered on a patch of flat boulders.

"No wonder we haven't seen any surface life," said Loki. "It's all down there."

Firebrand was comforting Fletch and the Rocklander was crying again. Sethral stared at the flat, featureless ground. Taz was alone out there. Sick, probably stumbling, if not already fallen. The subterranean predators in this place weren't just stationary like the trap-pad or the black spines. Some of them could crawl. They could crawl fast. They could follow the vibrations of creatures moving over the surface and hone in on potential prey.

"We need to find Taz," she said.

"We can't," said Firebrand. "We need to stay here and trust him to come back. Especially if what he's got is contagious."

"No! We need to go find him!"

"Sethral."

Something pulled her back as she tried to run. She spun, ready to punch whoever it was. Her claw froze midway.

Ryatzi had his tail around her wing. "Listen to her."

"What—"

She clamped her mouth shut. The last time she had said that, it had gone badly and she regretted it to this day. And she had just been about to say it again, because she knew it hurt him. This was everything to him, as much as it was to her.

Ryatzi's face was expressionless; not angry, but calm enough to show he knew exactly what she'd been about to say. "This isn't a forest to mess around with. Taz did the right thing and finding him would undo the protection he's giving us right now. And I don't like it any better than you do."

Sethral started to cry before she could stop herself. Ryatzi let go of her wing. She sat down and rocked back and forth as fresh memories imprinted themselves on this place: Taz's letter saying he was leaving the renegades, Whipper not coming out the other side of the mountains, being told by Rose that Winter had taken Jay.

And then older memories, their details blurry but the emotion in them still stark. Being grabbed and carried with her face hidden while clan creatures shouted that the Drakons were coming. Two kisses on the head and 'I love you's, and someone else telling their child what her own parents weren't saying: a promise to be back. Hearing the warriors taking flight like the wind of a storm behind her.

Waiting, when the news of the battle's outcome didn't come, and then still didn't come. Brave messengers who finally decided to go find out themselves. Struggling to understand that the two creatures they returned with, both hardly recognizable and close to death, were the only two she would ever see again.

Sethral was scarcely aware of being lifted. She curled up and sobbed like the kit she was all over again, and it was hard enough to make breathing difficult, but she couldn't stop. When she was set down again, it was in a nest like Talin had always made for her with his body from the moment he could move again. She clutched the fur against her side and buried her face in it. Someone was grooming her. Talin had done that, too. She had fought it so hard at first, until she could accept that her parents wouldn't be coming back to do it themselves.

After a time, the grooming switched to someone else, then back to her. It continued to alternate. Sethral let every worry, every memory, and every scrap of the anger trying to form dissolve and fuel the tears until her entire body felt empty and washed out. Slowly, the sobbing dissipated. Sethral kept her eyes closed. The scent, touch and heartbeat of the creature nesting her wrapped her up and carried her somewhere calmer than the pit of memories. She was in a nest, but she was herself and not her kit self, though the creature grooming her was large enough to be Talin from back then. He shifted to let someone in beside her. Ryatzi's scent joined Whipper's. The Saberel was shivering. His Drakon-dasher instinct wanted to follow Taz, but he couldn't let it.

She still had two parents left. She still had Talin, and she still had Wing.

"Just tell them," said Firebrand's voice. She sounded tired, but a mix of amusement and tenderness laced the words.

Wing didn't answer out loud. He had all the younger renegades curled on or against him now: not just Sethral, Whipper and Ryatzi, but Loki, Silversand and Dusk, too. Very deliberately, he licked them each on the head and snuggled around them.

"There," said Firebrand. "Congrats, guys. You're all his kids."

Sethral hugged the mutt. Wing had to pick Whipper up and transfer him to an easier spot to reach as the Forester's crying spiraled abruptly out of control.

Chapter 5

It was reminiscent of the moment they had spent together just after Whipper and Loki had returned from under the mountains. A Hyenar had interrupted that one. Sethral wished this one could go on forever, but then Silversand stiffened.

"Don't move," she said to someone across the clearing. She got up slowly. Phoenix's scent reached them a heartbeat later.

Sethral lifted her head. The Pyrya stood in the shadows, but the glow of his fur was faded like someone had thrown ash on it. He looked like he hadn't groomed in days. He flinched as the small bird following him landed on his back and yanked out another tuft of his fur. Silversand moved like chain lightning. By the time she dropped the bird beside the dead ground-creature, Phoenix had faded back into the forest.

Sethral jumped as an upset chirr sounded beside her. "Halo!"

Halo's eyes made half moons as she glanced up, briefly after Phoenix, then back at the ground.

"Halo, what's up with him?" said Dusk. "You've been following him, right?"

Halo shifted. Half her stance was affirmative. The other half looked guilty.

"What do you mean, you don't know?" said Dusk. "You've been right there."

The guilt was eating up her body language. As all eyes turned to her again, she crouched against a tree. She crackled.

Dusk groaned. "Halo, if you can't go near him because he's fire, don't even try. It just makes him feel worse."

Halo jumped up and genuinely stamped her paw. A string of bird noises and little dances were loosed in such rapid succession, Sethral didn't think Dusk could possibly follow them. But the frown on his face didn't turn out to be incomprehension.

"Like he's starving?" he said when the kit took a break.

Halo took an affirmative stance.

"But he eats."

Another affirmative, and a dance.

Dusk turned to Fletch. "Apparently Pheo's eating all the time, but he's still wasting away. What does that to a creature?"

"Any number of things. I'd need to get closer to tell."

Halo lay on the ground and imitated Phoenix's snap.

"He's being aggressive," said Dusk. "He won't let her close."

There was a whimper behind them. Phoenix was back with another bird. He stumbled as he stopped beneath another tree. When Silversand came towards him this time, he backed away.

"Pheo, hold still," she said. "It's hurting you. I'll get rid of it."

She took another step and Phoenix hissed. He ducked and whimpered again as the bird dropped its latest haul in a vine curl and flew at him like a small, feathered arrow. Silversand lunged and caught it. Phoenix bolted. Silversand tossed the dead bird to Ryatzi, passed

Firebrand the first one, and swapped the one she had given Wing for the ground-creature. Wing didn't like eating birds.

They had scarcely finished their meal when Silversand screamed. A rubbery yellow tentacle-tip probed around the edge of the rock slabs they were gathered on. This time, even Firebrand looked scared. "Fletch, can Taz find you again by seventh sense?" she said. "How big is your range?"

"The size of the Lowlands, generally. Usefully, about two days."

"We need to leave."

Loki was pointing to the soil a ways off. It was ruffled where a portion had just shifted. Firebrand pulled Fletch up and made sure he could walk before leaping the stream. Everyone followed except Halo, who disappeared after Phoenix.

The forest had been empty for much of the last day, but now the undergrowth began to thicken again. Firebrand pointed out edible plants, which were quickly stripped bare. It was still not enough to eat. Sethral grabbed a stone and hurled it at a bubble-creature bobbing by the leaf ceiling, then gasped. "Whipper! There's a hole!"

On Wing's back, Whipper acted like he hadn't even heard.

The canopy ceiling was thinning. Sethral circled below the gap and tried to get a look at what lay beyond it. "I can see sunlight! Just a little, but it's there..."

Loki bulled into her as a small trap-pad whipped shut by her paw. Balled up, it was the size of her head. "Watch your step."

The plants got so thick they were soon fighting to walk. Sethral passed out her two longer knives, and the renegades took turns slashing through vines to clear a half-navigable path. The trees gave way to tall shrubbery, then to open, blazingly sunny sky. With everyone blinded, the canyon came up so fast, Loki nearly fell into it. Plants spilled down its sides on mats of vines until about halfway down, where suddenly the plants disappeared and only the long cords of the vines were left. They dissolved into the water in thick tangles of roots.

"Look!" cried Silversand.

Clumped in an eddy upstream on the other side of the river was a patch of brown disks. No paddle-runners dashed across them, but they were undoubtedly the same as the ones Watersinger had encountered.

"They come from here," said Sethral, realizing. "The floods probably washed them into the Lowlands."

"Is there a way to get down to them?" said Loki. "I'm starving."

They all scanned the canyon sides, but they were sheer and the water had no banks.

"Pity you can't fly," said Fletch.

"Don't remind me," growled Sethral.

"Wait, your hook, Seth," said Firebrand. "If we can get across, we could use one of those vines as a rope to fish one out."

"I think the problem here is getting across."

"Shelha, we're useless out here, aren't we," said Loki. "Hey, scat."

A bubble-creature bobbed nearby. Loki hauled back a sapling and released it; it whipped into the bubble, which careened into the forest. There were two more on the renegades' other side. They bobbed fearlessly close.

"I can't tell if they're curious, predatory, or just brainless," said Firebrand. She sat down, pulled out a notebook and began to sketch the bubbles.

"Is this really the time for that?" said Sethral.

"Well, nobody's proposing any canyon-crossing ideas and they're all occupied, so why not? Also, I promised Benty."

Silversand, Loki and Dusk were all head to head over a bug that looked like a very slow, very hard black worm some five paw-lengths long. It did not stretch like a worm, though. In fact, it seemed to be crawling. Sethral couldn't help herself. A peek over Loki's shoulder revealed the worm to be made of segments like a dragonfly's tail. It was indeed crawling—almost floating over the ground, it seemed, on a raft of what must have been hundreds of short, orange legs. Silversand poked it. It rolled over and curled up into a spiral, which tightened into a round black coin. Loki flipped it over, then hopped back.

"Yuck!" said Silversand.

They abandoned the worm, which had begun to emit a foul-smelling liquid from the cracks in its shell.

Exploring their immediate patch of vegetation revealed so many different plants and bugs that Fletch and Sethral eventually had to team up to make everyone keep moving. Firebrand was drawing everything she saw, and Silversand and Loki had begun a game, taking turns finding new species. Even after half a sun's paw-length, they had not slowed down. The group resumed their laborious trek, this time parallel to the canyon. The sun beating down on them was as hot as a live flame. Whipper and Dusk started panting heavily, and Sethral was about to suggest a move back into the forest when the sun disappeared.

She looked up. Thick clouds rolled across the sky, as dark as late evening. There was not a heartbeat of warning when they opened. Shrieks of surprise were lost in a thunderous downpour. Sethral was soaked to the skin instantly. She fought her way towards Firebrand, whose outline and colour she could still see. The Leslander was huddled under a bush with Loki, Fletch, Ryatzi and Wing. Sethral had to touch Wing's back to find Whipper. Silversand and Dusk had disappeared.

They couldn't even shout to each other to be heard, so the group stayed where they were until the rain stopped as suddenly as it had come. Immediately, Fletch jumped up. "Silver! Dusk!"

There was no answer from the surrounding vegetation. Firebrand scanned for smells, but it was like the ground had been scrubbed.

"All together," said Fletch.

On a count of three, they shouted the pair's names. Struck by a sudden idea, Sethral pressed her tongue to her teeth and whistled Silversand's name. The Long Night adaptation carried shrilly in the clear air. There was a return whistle from the forest. Silversand and Dusk fought their way back to the group, panting and excited. Dusk dragged a branch behind him.

"Look at this," said Silversand. "It fell through the canopy right beside us."

The branch was rotten and near-black with a sooty fungus. Lined up in rows along its underside were eggs. Buglike eggs, each the size of a small nut.

"I bet they're edible," said Silversand. She pointed to an offshoot of the main branch. Here the egg cache had been decimated by some predatory creature: several were ripped open and a series of circles on the bark indicated the absence of a number more. Sethral hooked one claw and slit an untouched egg. Everyone yelped as a tiny eel writhed out. Whipper snatched it and passed it to Silversand, who ate it. She shrugged. "Tastes fine to me."

Sethral might have felt bad about decimating the entire branch had she eaten well the night before, but she had not, and food in this forest was rapidly becoming a 'take what you can' affair. Judging by the fact that even Dusk partook, she was not alone in the sentiment. When the eggs were gone, Silversand and Loki scouted the canyon again. There was no sign of a way across.

The heat was unbearable when the clouds moved away, so the renegades fought their way back to the forest and trudged along clearer ground. Everyone was jumpy. Silversand found small-prey tunnels under piles of leaves, but despite the feeling that so long a walk must be punctuated by some ground-predator, nothing appeared. By midafternoon, everyone was so exhausted that Silversand started crying when she found dozens of bugs latched onto her skin beneath her fur. Creatures checked their own pelts. None of them had escaped unscathed. They lay together and spent the rest of the afternoon grooming each other, dropping the bugs in a leaf-bowl of water. Fletch had recommended against eating them. Dusk had collapsed again. Fletch checked his paw and found it aggravated from the day's walking, but the wound bore no sign of the poison they now strongly suspected the Nightlock had been exposed to. Fletch rebandaged it and left him to sleep.

With evening falling, fireflies began to appear in the distance over the thickets that blanketed the canyon's edge. Something in the forest crackled. Everyone lay still. In the silence, the crackling came again, slowly at first, then louder and sharper until it abruptly vanished into the ground. Another crackle began on the other side, then another farther off. In a hundred heartbeats, the forest was full of crackling and munching, never in the same place twice, never moving towards or away from the renegades.

"I've heard this before," said Firebrand. "Our first night here, down in that waterfall canyon. Something was pulling leaves into the ground."

Sethral and Silversand both gasped. Sethral grabbed the Royal's paw in the blackness. "Silver, do you think?"

"Mhm!" Silversand sounded squeakier than usual.

"What?" said Firebrand.

"You wouldn't know because you don't live in a forest," said Sethral. "There's something that does this back home, too, though it's way smaller there. It's worms."

There was silence.

"Sethral," said Firebrand, "the leaves I saw disappear were the size of a small Hyenar. That would take a worm bigger than my leg."

Silence again.

"And?" said Sethral. "Tell me you don't believe that's a possibility here."

Something slid past her tail. Very slowly, Sethral reach out and touched it. It recoiled, slimy and soft enough that the leaves stuck to it as it drew away. She kicked up a pile of dirt to block its way if it decided to come back. The crackling petered out into what might have been moonrise had there been a moon. One by one, creatures went uneasily to sleep.

It was early morning when Sethral was catapulted to wakefulness by Fletch's scream. She leaped to her paws to find that the twin had doubled.

"Taz!" Fletch wrestled his brother to the ground and pinned him there, sobbing hysterically into his fur. They were swamped by everyone else.

Taz fought off the mob, laughing. "Guys! Guys! I'm okay. Fletch, I'm okay." He curled up with his brother and groomed him until Fletch cried himself back to coherence and then to exhaustion, then simply buried his nose in Taz's fur. Taz checked that he was settled and looked up. He flinched as the bombardment of questions hit him again. "Not yet; no; yes; no, I'm all good now; no, yes. Look. See? I'll tell you after. Fletch, can you let me go for a heartbeat? Seth, I need you."

He fought his way to his paws and pulled her away with a meaningful look at Firebrand. The Leslander hauled Silversand back, recruited Loki to help block the other renegades, and took over comforting Fletch to keep him in place.

Taz took Sethral just out of earshot into the forest, behind the root mountain of a giant tree. "I need your help. That sickness was from that white patch I had, but there's an easy cure for it and we need to find it again before Phoenix figures out he's got four of those patches on his leg. Wing's got one, too."

Sethral grabbed the roots and peered between them. She had not even noticed Phoenix. Several tail-lengths from the other renegades, he was curled in a ball between the buttresses of a small tree. By the dirt and litter on his fur, he had dug himself in on purpose.

"Sethral, please." Taz looked harried. "Stay with me. It takes a day or two for the sickness to kick in, and I don't know how long those two have had their patches."

"Okay, I'm listening." Sethral let go of the roots and, with effort, turned her focus back.

"Thank you. You know those water pitt-webs? We need the stuff they leak into the water."

"Can we get Loki?"

"Yeah, bring him."

They briefed the Fisher, who promptly located a stream. It had the faintest hint of sourness. They followed it upstream for close to a sun's paw-length to find the pitt-web. Taz hooked one of its knobs from the water and asked for a leaf-bowl. When squeezed, the knob trickled a thin, milky liquid into the vessel. Taz repeated the process with each knob until they had close to a bowlful. They carried it carefully back to the other renegades.

"Silver, come here," said Taz.

The cat had a small white patch, too, almost invisible in her fur. Taz dipped his paw in the pitt-web milk and rubbed the patch. It melted away under the substance. Sethral handed the cat a bowl of water to wash out the milk. Taz was beside Wing now, locating and treating what turned out to be several white spots. Everyone else checked their fur. Ryatzi had a patch as well, even smaller than Silversand's. Everyone else was clean.

When he had confirmed this, Taz took a deep breath and approached Phoenix's nest. "Pheo? You awake?"

There must have been some response, because Taz flicked for the rest of the renegades to leave. They tiptoed out of earshot to look for food.

Sethral had no idea what Taz had done to win the Pyrya over, or whether he even had. But when the renegades reconvened, Phoenix no longer had white patches and Taz had disposed of the rest of the milk.

"I need to tell you guys something," he said.

They sat in a circle.

"Seth, you asked this earlier," said Taz. "No, I didn't figure out that trick by myself. I was rescued in the forest and you may not believe this, but it was by a Lowlander herd. There are Coppertails in this forest. Huge ones; as big as Rose. They took me up there." He nodded to the leaf ceiling. "It's got its own floor, and you can walk on it. I woke up there with the Coppertails all around me. They didn't talk out loud, and they had a totally different tail-talk, but I found out I could get my point across by drawing or pointing to things, and they showed me the cure. But they were also really suspicious of me and never really got over it, and I think I found out why. I know we all know Radar's been to this forest, but he's been here. And it was ages ago—they compared it to when I might have been a kit, so before most of you were born. Seth, does that fit with anything you know?"

Right before she had been born, Radar had been terrorizing the Lowlands. He had struck the clan groups and captured three Saggitayrii, one of whom had never been found again. Then he had disappeared. "That's in line with my clan's stories."

"And with Benty finding the skeleton had disappeared," said Firebrand. "So, were they suspicious of Radar, and that you might have been connected to him? Or just suspicious of you in general?"

"I couldn't figure out that much, but I think it was both," said Taz. "They seemed suspicious of everyone coming from outside the forest, but particularly of Radar. Either way, they knew of him and they didn't like him at all."

"Well, that's heartening," said Loki.

"Did they say which way he went?" said Firebrand.

Taz pointed southeast. "The same way as Salisetta."

Chapter 6

The group began to pelt Taz with questions again. Sethral was about to join in when something touched her paw. 'Don't move,' tapped Silversand. 'Pass it on.'

Sethral did, and in heartbeats the message had spread around the circle. Silversand's paw inched towards her neck chain. Sethral scanned the forest over and around and under them, trying to spot whatever the cat had. Dusk at her side went tense. She followed his gaze. Phoenix was still in his root hollow, but now his head was up and his whole body was frozen. In front of him was a snake as thick as a Mountainair's neck and as long a small tree. It was the same colour and texture as the soil it was stretched out along.

There was a ping as Silversand's gauntlet snapped on. The snake did not startle. As slowly as a vine growing, it was lifting its head to face Phoenix. Silversand began to move towards its tail. 'Get back,' she flicked to the rest of the renegades. 'Ryatzi, help me.'

Creatures moved in opposite directions. Sethral tried to catch Dusk's attention as he stayed in place. He was watching the snake with narrowed eyes.

'Dusk, don't!' flicked Whipper. 'It's too big; it'll take all of your energy.'

'Taz,' flicked Dusk. 'Is that a Dustlander reflex?'

'Drakon shit.'

That was a yes. Sethral glanced back at Phoenix. The Pyrya was so still it was eerie; even his breathing was almost invisible. Desert Coppertails dealt with vipers, snakes that saw heat and could strike faster than anyone but Silver could move. Moving made heat. Taz directed Firebrand in a wide arc around the other side of Phoenix's tree. The snake had lifted its head to Phoenix's head height, no more than a few paw-lengths from his face. It wove slightly, confused. Silversand raked her claws deep into its tail.

Sethral had never seen something so large move so fast. When she could see the snake again, it was doubled back with its teeth where Silversand had been, and now Ryatzi was at the curve of its body, teeth puncturing its scales. It looped into a circle, building itself up coil upon coil until it made a mound with no stray ends. Taz and Firebrand had dragged Phoenix to safety. Dusk leaped forwards and joined the Royal and Saberel in circling the mountain of snake. Loki followed him. The snake wavered. For a heartbeat its head drew back into the center of its coils, then it surged upwards. Steely coils bunched as its head plunged through the leaves. The whole snake drew itself up through the vine ceiling and out of sight.

"Let go," said Taz.

Sethral's whole body was made of jelly. She dragged her gaze down to see Phoenix with his teeth sunk deep in Taz's paw. The Pyrya was hunched up like he was ready to bolt, but he was shaking too hard to go anywhere.

"Let go," said Taz again. He kept his voice calm. "It's gone, Pheo. You're safe. I'm not going to hurt you."

Blood dripped to the ground beneath them, but Taz gave no indication that the bite hurt. Phoenix tightened his grip as Firebrand took a step forwards. Unseen by Phoenix and silent as a shadow, Dusk crept up behind him. He lifted a paw and tapped Phoenix's side. He must have given a substantial burst of power, because the coal-glow in Phoenix's fur rippled brightly around the point of contact. He gasped and let go. Fletch grabbed Taz's paw and staunched the bleeding. Phoenix backed away, but he was still trembling like a kimberleaf. He stumbled and fell, tried to scramble up and fell again. He lay on the ground, every part of his body shaking out of control.

The soil shifted two trees away. "Move, now!" shouted Loki.

Firebrand grabbed Phoenix's scruff and everyone ran. They plunged back into the plants at the canyon's edge and did not stop until they were deep in the greenery. Here the roots would be too tightly matted for a ground-predator to get through.

"Don't let go," said Dusk to Firebrand. Phoenix's eyes were half closed and he kept stumbling towards the canyon's edge. Sethral could not tell if it was intentional.

The sun was not yet overhead; they had a bit of time before the canyon sides got too hot for travel. Wordlessly, Fletch and Taz forged into the vegetation. They still had to find a way across the canyon, and they had to find it soon. If they stayed in one area, predators would find them, but if they moved too far, they would be off Salisetta's path.

"Up there!" called Ryatzi.

They wove carefully to the edge of the drop. A ways off, a ropelike structure spanned the canyon, dipping sharply off their side of it and cutting a gentle curve up to the other. They had to retreat to the forest again to reach it. The structure turned out to be a cord of woody vines thicker together than Sethral was tall. Several had long ago broken on this side of the canyon. Their dead weight stretched the rest until the bridge's end had sunk to its current placement, two tail-lengths down. Before anyone could say a word, Silversand braced to jump down onto them.

"Wait!" said Whipper. Sethral could not remember the last time she had heard his voice. "I'll go," he said, though he was very clearly not looking at the river below the vine bridge. "I'm less likely to break it."

"No," said Silversand. "If it breaks, whoever jumped will be stranded alone on the other side."

Whipper looked at his paws. Silversand dropped gracefully off the canyon's edge. The vines barely shuddered when she landed on them. The bridge was sound. Silversand found the flattest landing zone and clawed the bark to roughen it. Taz and Fletch made the jump easily despite Taz's injured paw, and scampered across the bridge. Loki landed less than gracefully, but stayed on. Ryatzi closed his eyes, took a deep breath, and followed him. Both made it across.

Firebrand still had Phoenix's scruff and Dusk hadn't taken his eyes off the Pyrya. Phoenix still looked checked out. Sethral had serious doubts as to whether he would try and catch himself if he lost his footing on the bridge.

'I'll jump with him,' flicked Firebrand. Sethral translated for Dusk, who nodded and looked marginally less tense.

Firebrand gave Phoenix full warning and counted down for both of them. Sethral half expected Phoenix to simply not jump, but he proved her wrong. The two landed together and began their slow journey across the bridge.

Whipper gripped Wing's fur as Silversand tapped her paws by the landing pad. Wing wove back and forth several times to get a handle on the sound. Sethral closed her eyes. She flinched as she heard the mutt jump, but a heartbeat later came the thump and creak of the vines, and Silversand's sigh of relief.

"You go next," said Dusk.

Sethral opened her eyes and her heart lodged in her throat. Of course she would have to cross, too. She couldn't fly. All of a sudden her heartbeat was punching her in the chest, and the world was narrowing to the bridge and the river far, far below it. She dragged her focus upwards, to the bridge alone.

"You can do it!" called Silversand.

But she couldn't. Her claws were slick on the stones and she backed away from the canyon edge. She was trembling. Since when was she this scared of heights?

"Want a ride?"

It took a moment to register that she was the only one left here besides Dusk; he was talking to her. The Nightlock looked as non-scared as the twins had, and they had been calm enough to make the vines look like a walk on the Rock Flats. Dusk tapped his back. Sethral could barely get on, so he crouched for her. She gripped his fur and squeezed her eyes shut as his paws left the stone and they fell, fell, fell...

And landed with a graceful thump on the landing pad. Sethral did not open her eyes as Dusk easily navigated the vines up the incline to the canyon's other side. Silversand's claws scritched the bark behind him.

"First canyon crossing, guys," said Taz. "Congrats."

Dusk did not object to her continued presence on his back, so Sethral stayed until they were back in the forest and everything about the canyon—the sound of the river, the heat of the sun, the smell of the scratched vines—was a memory. Loki found a stream and Fletch made everyone drink.

"You guys need to do this without me reminding you," he said.

"But I'm not thirsty," said Loki.

"You are, you just can't feel it because it's so humid out."

"I'm hungry," said Whipper in a small voice.

Silversand perked up sharply. Sethral dug in her bag for snacks. It was past midday now and they hadn't stopped for food since the morning. Even that had been brief. Whipper needed food more often than that.

She had no snacks left.

"Group up if you're going anywhere," said Fletch. "Nobody goes hunting alone."

Phoenix jerked away from Firebrand and she released his scruff. He stalked into the forest. Taz's face shadowed, but he said nothing.

"Where's Halo?" said Dusk.

"I don't know," said Sethral. All of a sudden, she was exhausted. Some combination of hunger, sleep deprivation, constant danger and residual fear sucked her energy like a leech, and there was no reprieve in sight. The group's hunters were now walking in circles, listening and digging for underground prey. Whipper poked through their dirt piles. Sethral prodded Dusk as Taz called his name again. He startled. He had been staring off into the forest where Phoenix had disappeared, but he also looked as tired as she felt.

'I'm not hungry,' he flicked to the twins. He tapped Sethral and she dropped off his back. In twenty heartbeats he was asleep under a tree. Loki was in a showdown with Ryatzi, who couldn't stop yawning. The Fisher won.

Ryatzi wandered over to Sethral. "You staying?"

Sethral lay down. Being under her wing was too hot, so Ryatzi curled up against her side and fell asleep with his head on her shoulder. She closed her eyes.

Someone was shaking her. Sethral opened her eyes to find the forest much darker than it had last been.

"Come on," said Taz. "We've found a place for the night."

Phoenix was back again, stuffed in a root hollow. Something glinted in the forest behind him. Sethral watched it vaguely while Taz roused Dusk. Dusk was capable of grumbling fit for Wing.

Ryatzi stirred at the sound. He wilted at the sight of the darkened forest. "Did I miss the whole afternoon?"

"Ratty, your eyes are sharper than mine. What's that off behind Fifi?"

"Hm?" He turned without lifting his head from her shoulder. Then he flew to his paws. "Phoenix, behind you!"

Creatures dashed together. An Aria-like creature stepped across the forest floor towards Phoenix. He struggled upright and limped to join the renegade cluster. The more Sethral looked, the more she realized the group was already surrounded. Small, thin-legged Aria with huge eyes perched up trees, among roots, and on the vine ceiling. More approached from all directions, in no apparent rush. Each took up a position at the same distance and then simply stood. There were dozens of them.

"They're not attacking," said Fletch. "Are we just a curiosity, or are they waiting for something?"

"I suggest we move," said Firebrand.

Together they edged in the least occupied direction. The Aria made no move to stop them. Instead, they followed. Darkness was turning the trees to shadows; Sethral could no longer see any detail of where she was putting her paws. She could smell the other renegades around her, but she could not see any except Phoenix.

Suddenly, Firebrand in the lead pulled up short. Or Whipper pulled her up short; he was on her back now. The soft scratches of Aria claws had circled in front of them. Sethral pulled out a knife and sat up with it at the ready. She could hear silk being strung between trees all around them. She located Silversand and made to shift closer to her, to find she couldn't move. Her back paws were trapped in vine-like tentacles so thin, she had not even felt them twining up from the ground.

Chapter 7

Time slowed down. Sethral's claws moved on their own, fumbling in her satchel. Loki broke his bonds with a kick. Ryatzi shredded his. Metal met stone in Sethral's claws. Around her, creatures shouted and screamed, their voices overlaid by the hisses of Aria kicked and smacked and beaten back. Thread-tentacles snapped and regrew at a terrifying rate. The ground around them was sticky. A spark flared into a flame. Sethral coaxed it to grow, shielding it from the gusts of battle all around. It got hotter and hotter, burning her claws, but she held it until she no longer could. Then she flung it at the ground.

Bright orange flame flew outwards. It shot along threads of flammable Aria silk and up trees and across the thin air. A net around the whole space was etched in orange light. The ground was aflame. Tendrils vanished. The smell of their burning fur and scorched Aria shell permeated the air. Sethral was snatched up by a Coppertail. Then they were running, tripping on roots, running into trees, every sense alive in terror of stepping on a black spine or a trap-pad or the den of some subterranean hunter. The Aria did not follow them. The group slowed when the fire was a distant orange speck. Sethral was set back on the ground and hugged by someone else; Silversand. A quiet flurry of voices gathered a ways off behind her. Sethral tried to look.

"Don't go over," said Silversand. "Pheo's having a panic attack."

"From what, the Aria?"

"Taz thinks it's the fire."

"He's a fire elemental."

"So?"

"You're a flight creature and you're scared of heights," said Dusk in the darkness.

Sethral changed the topic. "Where's Whipper?"

"With Wing," said Silversand.

"Have either of you got burns?" said Fletch, making the rounds.

Sethral lifted her claws. She had scorched them holding the budding flame, but it didn't feel like a proper burn. "I don't think so."

Silversand held out a paw for Fletch to treat. Sethral could hear Taz trying to coax Phoenix to breathe, but Phoenix wasn't responding. Dusk left to join them. The Pyrya kept spiraling and eventually made it to his paws. He fled into the forest. It was too dangerous to travel in the dark, so the group bedded down exactly where they were. Sethral remembered all the creatures who had foraged all afternoon while she had slept, and grudgingly volunteered to take first watch.

The ground here was never comfortable. Sethral shifted over and over, distracted first by Taz and Fletch talking quietly, then by a lone humming insect, then by the silence. A crackle made her freeze. The worms were pulling leaves into their tunnels again. She jumped every time one began. Then through the crackles she detected another sound: soft pawsteps, stumbling now and again, coming towards them. Her heart rate doubled in a flash. Sethral rolled to a crouch. There were fireflies back by the canyon again, but in the opposite direction, another light was approaching.

It was only Phoenix. Something told Sethral to stay still. The Pyrya crept back to the group and sought out a spot between the roots of a nearby tree. How many nights had he slept near them? Was this a first, or were Taz and Dusk hiding something about this, too? Sethral shook Taz as quietly as she could. She noted that he woke without any of his usual drama now.

'Fifi's here,' she tapped on his paw. 'Is that usual?'

'Yes.'

Sethral swallowed back a hot bubble of anger. First the snake, then the Aria had veered towards the Pyrya. It was pretty clear why: his ribs now showed, his fur was thinning visibly, and he could hardly walk straight. Fletch still had not gotten close enough to find out why. 'Isn't it dangerous? All the predators have it out for him.'

'Yes,' tapped Taz, and put his head back down.

Sethral waited for him to go back to sleep, then got up quietly. Phoenix was out for the count, but he twitched and jumped in his sleep, whimpering softly. He was shivering. He shouldn't be cold. Sethral reached out a claw but stopped halfway to his shoulder as the memory of him biting Taz resurfaced. She went back to her sleeping spot.

Phoenix was gone again the next morning. Sethral shunned her usual greeting for Taz and joined the other renegades in scrounging for food, and for Pitt-web milk to treat the white patches half of them had acquired again. This close to the lush canyon, they found both. Nobody spoke as they regathered, redetermined which way was southeast, and just started walking. The forest darkened over the course of the morning. Whipper couldn't hear rain through the trunks of the trees, and the darkness didn't go away. The air began to cool.

"Bets we've added another canopy up there?" said Loki.

"Fletch, you keep looking behind you," said Taz.

"So does Wing," said Fletch. "I keep feeling like something's following us."

They all stopped.

"Don't," said Taz as Sethral opened her mouth. The silence that fell instead was just as stifling.

"'Day thirty-two'," said Sethral anyway. "'Had the feeling of being watched again today.' And day thirty-six, 'We see strange lights at night. I don't think they are fireflies. The forest has gotten denser, with more vines. In the day it seems uninhabited, but now I am not so sure.'"

In the low light, the colours around them had been reduced to dark greens and browns. Thick vines looped across the vine ceiling and down to the ground. A firefly-like light sparked in the distance.

"How many days was that after Salisetta reached the Outback?" said Firebrand.

"Nine and thirteen. I think we're moving faster than they were."

Taz started walking again.

"Taz," said Firebrand sharply. "That logbook could help us avoid whatever happened to Salisetta; we're being idiots if we just ignore it."

Taz whirled. "And we're being bigger idiots if we stop moving out here! I thought we'd established that already!" He was trying to hide his fear, but his voice cracked.

Fletch caught him and hugged him. "Sorry, Fibes. The clawmarks on that logbook box are just freaking us both out."

"You didn't watch the creature you love most get caught by the chest by a Whitewing," said Taz, his voice muffled in his twin's shoulder.

"Fine," said Firebrand. "We can keep moving." She tapped her back and Sethral joined her. "Not fireflies, then?" said the Leslander in an undertone as they started walking again.

"I guess not."

"I found out why there are no plants down here," said Silversand.

They joined her beside the chewed-off stump of what had been a plant stem as recently as the night before. A slime trail led from it to a head-sized pile of worm castings. Sethral upturned them. The hole underneath was big enough for a Coppertail to break a leg in.

In the darkened forest, they had only their body cycles to tell the time of day, and only the twins' directional senses to tell them which way they were going. When everyone got tired and visibility decreased until only Whipper, Dusk and Silversand could see, they decided it was evening and made camp.

Phoenix was asleep on the ground—not even in a root hollow—very close to the group when Sethral woke up again. By the murmurs around her, she was neither the first one up nor the only one mildly alarmed. Loki tugged her away and they searched for food for what must have been half the morning. They found almost nothing. They returned to the group's spot. Phoenix hadn't moved.

Taz, Fletch and Firebrand were talking in whispers at the edge of the camp. At last, Taz took a deep breath and approached the Pyrya. "Phoenix?"

There was no response. Taz reached out and touched Phoenix's shoulder. He bolted awake with a hiss and collapsed, shivering. He had white patches all over his side, but this was different from Taz's fever. Taz lay down and reached out a paw. Phoenix shuddered as it touched his.

"Pheo," said Taz, "this has gone far enough. You need to tell us what's going on."

Another shudder wracked Phoenix's body. Taz beckoned Fletch, but as the other twin approached, Phoenix whimpered and pushed himself backwards, trying to sit up. He hissed.

"That's enough," said Taz. "We're fine if you follow us, and we want to help if you're hurt. But right now you're a target for all the predators here, and your sleeping close every night is going to start endangering all of us. If you want to stay, you need to tell us what's going on."

Fletch stepped forwards, but this time Phoenix made it to his paws. He hissed again.

"We can't leave you alone anymore," said Taz. "I'm sorry."

Fear swept across Phoenix's expression so visibly, Taz faltered. Now the Pyrya stumbled back. He bared his teeth.

"Phoenix, we want to help."

Phoenix tried to run as Fletch came towards him, but he fell. He scrambled backwards, suddenly screaming. He snapped at Fletch.

"Fletch, stop," said Dusk.

Fletch did. Phoenix started coughing and he didn't seem able to stop. His body was shaking violently now. Seizing.

Taz ran forwards and held him steady. "Fletch, find out what in Shelha's name is wrong!"

But before Fletch could take a step, Phoenix had thrown up on the ground and struggled out of Taz's grip. His eyes were wild and his breathing far too fast. He panicked as Fletch and Firebrand circled to cut off his escape routes.

"Stop blocking him in!" shouted Dusk. "Phoenix, please, stop. We're not going to hurt you. Please. Breathe."

Phoenix whimpered and fell. He screamed as Taz went to touch him, and Taz leaped back with a bite-slash on his paw.

Fury, hot and untempered, engulfed Sethral's body. "Take the help!" she screamed. "You little shit, you've done nothing but snap at us this whole trip; if you want to be a satellite, then act like one! Either you actually join us, let Fletch see you and then stay close, or you can get lost!"

Everything in Phoenix's expression crumpled. Before Taz could grab him, he made it to his paws again and ran. Not southeast or back to the Aria, but off their Salisetta trail. In the direction they were most trying to avoid. Taz sat stricken on the ground behind him.

Sethral was not thinking enough to move. She could not process soon enough to dodge as Dusk walked up and slapped her. She had never seen him look so cold.

"If that's how you handle a hurting creature, you shouldn't have taken me in either," he said. He walked after Phoenix. Taz bounded to block his way and he snarled.

Taz stood his ground. "We're going too."

His voice was too calm. Sethral looked around to see Ryatzi with his nose to ground where Phoenix had been sick. His eyes were closed.

"What is it?" said Firebrand.

"Moonworm."

By Fletch's look, it was not familiar to him.

"It's a northern parasite," said Ryatzi. "He must have been carrying it when he first came south. It usually stays low, but if it gets triggered by stress or sickness, it lays all its eggs and goes dormant. They all hatch a moon later."

"The ship ride made him sick," said Silversand.

"But it hasn't been a moon since we got on Watersinger," said Loki. The horror crept across his face even as he said it. "We left two nights before new River Moon. There's still four days left."

"Does it ever come early?" said Fletch.

Ryatzi shook his head. "This is just the eggs developing. He's got it bad." Sethral could see the fear, the Drakon-dasher instinct, clear in his face even after he'd closed his eyes and taken a breath to calm himself. He took a step back. "Halo!"

The shout echoed so sharply, everyone flinched. Ryatzi kept his eyes closed as ten heartbeats passed, then twenty. Just when he looked ready to shout again, a small blur bounded over a root mountain. Halo had grown a paw-length since they had last seen her. She skidded to a halt in front of Ryatzi, who slid one paw across the ground and started to dance. Sethral could see representations of creatures travelling and creatures interacting, and what was almost certainly the milder symptoms of what Phoenix was in. Halo watched every motion, rapt. When Ryatzi spun to a halt, she gave a quick dance of her own and shot off into the forest.

"She's going to try and find a treatment," said Ryatzi.

"There is one?" said Dusk.

"There's a few at the earlier stages. When it's progressed this far, there's one I know and the local Forestairs might know more. We need to find Phoenix."

Taz moved aside. Dusk took only a heartbeat's pause to locate the Pyrya's signature. He led the way off the renegades' southeast path.

Chapter 8

It was an eerie flashback to the Salisetta logbook. Once novel and full of intrigue, the Daemon's Outback forest had become haunted. Wing glanced constantly over his shoulder, and Fletch did too. Silversand, meanwhile, proved to be rapidly developing an ability to spot inconsistencies that might spell danger in the ground ahead. Dusk let her take the lead. Nobody said anything as they circled a churned-up patch where something had tried and failed to take Phoenix. Ryatzi jumped on Firebrand's back and curled up with his nose in his fur to suppress the urge to run.

In the silence, Sethral kept thinking she could hear things: strange calls, or rustles too close behind her. She knew they were her imagination—nobody else reacted to them—but the sounds increased and turned to whispers, then a voice so broken it sent daggers through her. It's 'almost like' I've got nowhere else to go. Dusk would no longer even look at her. Sethral got a sympathetic glance from Firebrand and almost one from Taz, though the Rocklander was so distracted he kept running into trees. But even though she had been right about a satellite's position, even though a satellite acting like Phoenix would have to make a choice, somehow Dusk's chilly resolution stung more than justification could soothe. Somehow, it was still Dusk they were following. Somehow, being right this time didn't count for anything.

Silversand stopped as Phoenix's trail swerved suddenly. The ground ahead had a wide depression in it, so shallow it was almost unnoticeable. Silversand went around it. The forest was so full of vines, they had to duck or climb over them with every tail-length they covered. Phoenix's trail jolted again, this time pulling up sharply, then jumping. His landing was scattered with blood. Silversand grabbed a limp vine and tossed it onto the patch he had avoided. Nothing happened. She dragged it across the soil, then flipped it over. Sethral swallowed hard. Sap leaked from a score of tiny, fresh holes in the vine's underside.

Firebrand's tail rested on her back. 'If it's poison, it won't hurt him.'

The reassurance rang hollow. It won't hurt him.

'Fibes, what should I have done?'

Firebrand didn't answer. It was hard to see her face in the gloom, but the tension in her step gave her away. Neither of them knew an answer.

Phoenix had a shocking amount of stamina left, given how close to collapse he had already been that morning. A new scene added itself to the torturous montage in Sethral's mind. This one was of Wing, forging through the snow long after he had run out of dispensable energy, undoing the healing a quarter moon in the herd's South River base had given him. It hurt to walk and not run, run after the Pyrya still running away from them, run to find him and stop him and take away all the pain that had been revealed when Sethral had revoked the group's support. The pain and the fear.

But they had to walk, and the forest dragged on and on, into the evening, then forcing them to stop for night. Phoenix's trail was still running. Dusk lay down apart from the group. Sethral wondered if he would sleep at all. Taz certainly didn't, and twice Sethral heard Fletch comforting him as he cried quietly. Taz was as sensitive to others' pain as Silversand, though he was less transparent and she handled it better. He was already driven to the edge just by being around Wing. Adding Phoenix must be unbearable.

Dusk kicked everyone awake again the moment the forest lightened enough for the nocturnal renegades to see. By midmorning, the part of Phoenix's trail they were on slowed. It deteriorated rapidly. At last it broke, weaving in search of a place to curl up in. They rounded a tree and Dusk choked on a gasp. The tree had buttressed roots like Phoenix always preferred. Two of them swooped close to make a nest against the trunk. The Pyrya's body only filled half of it.

Silversand crept forwards while everyone else stood rooted. She peeked over the buttresses. 'He's alive!'

Dusk almost started crying. Taz ran to the nest, but Phoenix still had the strength to hiss, and to bite when anyone attempted to touch him. Taz walked agonizingly slowly back to Fletch. It was another flashback: the twins failing to try to stop Wing from leaving the herd's base. If Phoenix was in this state and didn't want to be touched, they wouldn't touch him. One by one, creatures found their own corners. Loki and Firebrand crept away to find Pitt-web milk for the white patches everyone now suspected came from the soil they slept on. Ryatzi paced around and around the group, waiting.

Evening brought a distant chirr. Whipper leaped up. "It's Halo!"

The kit skidded back into their camp with something in her mouth. It was a fruit, small and round like a waterapple but uglier, its yellow skin flecked with brown like it had been dirtied on the way here.

"That's the one I know," said Ryatzi in relief.

"I thought those were toxic," said Sethral.

"They are."

Dusk's hackles went up.

"Not lethally," said Ryatzi. "At least, not if he can fight. Just enough to kill the eggs."

"And what if he can't fight?"

Ryatzi finally let his pain show. "Then it kills him. He's got one chance. If he doesn't take it, he dies in three days anyway, if he even lasts that long."

Halo tiptoed to Phoenix's nest and hopped inside. Creatures waited tensely. With an unhappy chirr, the kit leaped out again. She headbutted Taz, who tried instead. This time there was no biting. Sethral could hear Taz's murmur, then at last a shift in the leaves. Taz's expression crumpled. When he jumped out again, Fletch was waiting for him.

Taz buried his face in his brother's shoulder. "He won't take it."

He was crying again. Silversand walked to the tree and found a place outside the nest. Sethral knew that choice of placement, of position. She knew that intentionality. There were still stories about Royals. Royals were protectors, of the forest and of the creatures who lived in it. No matter whether they knew them or not, they would keep vigil beside a dying creature until that creature died.

Dusk stepped into the nook where the buttresses met, in the nest but no closer than Phoenix had wanted Taz. He was talking quietly.

Ryatzi met Silversand's eye and she gave a small, sad smile. Her tailtip flicked. Ryatzi copied her position on the other side of the nest. He looked less resolved than she did, but the gesture Silversand was making was both symbolic and practical, respect and a watch for predators who might bring a sick creature to a more violent end. It seemed a reassurance for the Saberel. His clan probably didn't have anything like this. He probably wished they had.

Sethral swallowed back the very sharp lump that had lodged in her throat and walked to a spot a respectful distance from Silversand. Loki joined Ryatzi. Fletch asked Taz if he wanted to join. Sethral couldn't hear the answer, but it was a no... not that he didn't want to, but something to do with Dusk. The Nightlock looked like he was settling in for the night, and like he fully intended to keep up whatever he was saying. Maybe Taz didn't want to intrude on the quiet exchange. He probably knew he was not going to be able to keep from crying tonight. Wing lay down far from the nest, curled up and went to sleep. Firebrand lay down to keep watch near him. Afternoon faded into evening. Evening faded into night.

Taz startled in the quiet forest as something touched his shoulder. Opening his eyes did nothing to the darkness; it was still the middle of the night. He could smell the creature standing beside him. There were no words exchanged. Shaking, Taz got up. Dusk led them back to the nest in the tree roots. This was it.

But the sound from the nest stopped Taz in his tracks.

"I can't touch him," said Dusk quietly.

Slowly, Taz put one paw in the nest, then the other. It wasn't the sound of a body in its last stage of giving out. It wasn't a sound he had ever expected to hear from the Pyrya. Phoenix was churring.

Only Silversand had managed to stay awake the entire night, though Ryatzi would probably have wanted to had he not still been working off a lifelong sleep debt. Sethral could have thrown up as the world came back with all its pain and guilt and apprehension. She couldn't look at Silversand. First she had screamed Phoenix into leaving, and now she couldn't even stay up to keep watch for him. She wanted Dusk to slap her again. It hurt more than doing it to herself.

"Mosshead!"

The whisper alerted her to the fact that Loki had already flicked her name several times. She could just see him over the buttresses, Ryatzi asleep on his shoulder. Loki was smiling. Silversand would not say a word until Phoenix either stabilized or passed away, but she too wore a cautious smile. She tipped her muzzle towards the nest.

Getting up broke the vigil, but Sethral told herself she wasn't a Royal and so didn't need to follow the rules. Dusk was asleep where he had been lying the night before. In the hollow between the buttresses, Taz was curled up, awake but pretending not to be. Phoenix was melted into the crook of his flank. The pips and stem of the fruit were scattered about his paws.

Sethral sensed more than heard someone trot up behind her. She turned to find Halo there with a large, dead moth in her mouth.

"Let her in, Seth," said Taz.

Sethral realized she was blocking the way into the nest. She moved. Halo hopped the buttresses and passed the moth to Taz, who de-winged it and nudged it against Phoenix's muzzle. Sethral stared. Halo hopped out of the nest again. Her eyes followed Sethral with a look that was not quite reproach. She sped up and vanished into the forest.

Moth wings were scattered about Taz's paws and there was moth fur on his shoulder where he offered the soft insects to Phoenix. Of course a desert creature would be an insectivore. The guilt in Sethral's body sank another increment. All this time he had been around them, and she hadn't even known what Phoenix ate. That was the most basic information about a creature.

Taz was waiting to catch her eye. 'He takes worms too, if you want to help,' he flicked. 'We're avoiding anything tougher than that for now.'

How Halo caught even one moth was a mystery. Worms weren't any easier. Also, she wasn't willing to stray out of earshot, which wasn't far. Returning for a periodic check-in, Sethral found Silversand on her paws, crouched and growling. Two bubble-creatures bobbed over Phoenix's nest. Sethral reached automatically for a rock, to find it was a small mushroom. The bubbles kept dropping lower, then rising again as Silversand twitched like she was about to pounce.

Sethral would have given a lot to have her wings back right then. Or to have a rock. She was spared the need for either by Ryatzi, who leaped from hiding and caught one bubble in midair. Its companion tumbled crazily away. The Saberel landed on the nest's other side and dropped a limp, pearlescent sack. His bite had punctured the creature, which seemed to have died immediately. Silversand poked it. Firebrand pulled out her sketchbook. They were all startled by a sudden, sharp whine.

It was Wing. On his paws, he faced the way they had come with a swish in his tail. He flinched back a pawstep, then returned and whined again. Sethral moved slowly to cover the nest. Everyone did. Wing went silent, though his tail kept swishing unabated. He was straightening up now. Then he growled.

Sethral could not see anything between the trees. There was not even a whiff of a breeze to carry smells, and the forest remained eerily silent.

Silent until Firebrand was dropped to the ground in a streak of blue.

It was over in heartbeats; there wasn't even a battle. Even Taz had his head slammed against the buttress roots before he could twitch. Dusk couldn't move. Every nerve in his body was on fire from whatever pressure point the blow had struck. He could only watch as Bluejay circled the only creature left standing. There was a restlessness in his steps, like he wanted to close in, but could not.

"Jay, please," said Wing again, his voice barely above a whisper. "Come back. I know you're in there."

Bluejay faltered, then shook his head so hard he stumbled. He backed away.

"Please," said Wing. "You can do it. You can fight him. I'm right here."

Fireflies.

Something moved around him, creature-sized and quick in the darkness. The fireflies bobbed in the air, a heartbreakingly beautiful dance that curled and twined, that moved in synchrony like it was puffed by a breathless wind, that seemed to pool over places on the forest floor. Something pricked his haunch, and Dusk tried to gasp. A tingling gripped his body. He had been unable to move already, but this probably made sure he wouldn't even be able to try.

The scents that swam in the air were nothing he knew. Dusk was vaguely aware of being lifted. Fireflies trailed after him. They trailed ahead, too. In a ribbon of lights, they guided a line that stepped softly in the darkness, a convoy of creatures as wordless as the fireflies, who did not seem to need light to know their way. Their smells mingled with those of the renegades.

The world would not stop turning. They were probably going straight, but for a moon's paw-length they were walking in circles, and then they were on a boat, and the boat was going in circles, too. It rolled over and over. Water echoed off of rocks and still the fireflies bobbed. They were still in a line. Like a ribbon, a scarf, an earthbound Silverpath. Dusk shut his eyes but the tingling wouldn't take him. The echoing grew louder, the spinning faster, and then they were in a cave, spinning and spinning until he was too dizzy to focus, and passed out.

Chapter 9

Her   satchel   was
gone.

Sethral fumbled beside her before she had gotten a grip on her consciousness; there was nothing over her shoulder, or beside her, and she never took it off. Being without its weight left her feeling acutely vulnerable. She was breathing hard before she could stop herself, and the world faded back into existence.

Her claws were scrabbling across a stone floor. Sethral jerked her head up. At her back was a stone wall. To every other side was a tail-length of space and a wall, of vines this time, woven tightly. The ceiling was almost impenetrable. It was nearly dark and no lighter outside. Sethral tried to get up, but her legs would only half obey her. She dragged herself to the front of the cage.

Her cage was one of many, lined up along a stone ledge that slanted away to one side. Past a narrow walkway past its front, the ground turned to air. Smooth, sheer stone walls plunged down to a canyon bottom webbed with rope bridges and platforms all made of living brown and muddy green vines. More vines climbed the walls, making ladders and hammocks, crossing the canyon as more bridges suspended in midair. Their walkways were sturdy and their railings were more like nets; a child could walk across one and not be able to fall off.

Still the canyon walls kept climbing, far, far above this ledge, but instead of flaring like a canyon should, they began to close in on themselves. Where they ended at the surface far above, they were separated by little more than a slot, if one still wider than twice her wingspan. It too was webbed over, crisscrossed by vines woven into a mesh as tight as the walls of her cage.

The whole slot canyon was filled with flitting shadows. Pale shapes moved up and down the ladders so quickly they seemed to be flying, or at least floating. Sethral tested her own body just to be sure, but the force that kept her tethered to the ground felt, if anything, stronger than ever. She tried to get a handle on the shapes. They darted over bridges, met and danced, and darted apart again. They seemed to come and go from nowhere, sometimes straight in and out of the walls. Sethral stared at one spot until her eyes ached, and in a hundred heartbeats she could start to make out the ghostly outline of a hole in the canyon wall. It was confirmed as a pale shadow darted out of it. There were caves.

Sethral stepped back from the cage front as her eyes started throbbing from straining in the gloom. She scanned the other cages in her row. The ones flanking hers were empty, but the two past that each had a motionless figure in them. Ryatzi was still out cold; he always curled up if he was lying down. Sethral ran to the other side. "Loki! Loki!"

He leaped in his skin and jumped up. He had been awake. "Sethral?"

"Over here!"

He ran to the near side of his cage. "I can't see you."

She was the same colour as the vines. Sethral exposed her wing's pale underside. "Can you see this?"

"Oh, there you are."

Sethral screamed as something hissed outside her cage. She backed against the stone wall. Gripping the vines was a Watermouse-like creature with pale, fluffy fur and a tufted tail. It bared sharp teeth at her, then vanished. Loki had a fright as it was suddenly outside his cage. It hissed at him too, then dashed across the path and plunged over the precipice.

"How long have you been up?" whispered Sethral across the empty cage.

"A couple sun's paw-lengths? Who's on your other side?"

"Ratty. Yours?"

"An empty cage and a wall. Are you hurt?"

Some part of her brain was blocking out what had happened leading up to the gap in her memory. Sethral looked down at her claws. They were still burned from the Aria encounter, but they were healing. And she had no white patches. "I think I'm okay."

"Sethral." Loki's voice was gentler than before. "It's okay. How were you knocked out? Are you hurt there?"

She was too scared to even tune into what her body was telling her. If she kept out all feeling, she could keep out the memories that would come with it.

"He didn't hurt me," said Loki. "Not seriously. Are you the same?"

Sethral hugged herself. The world had started to fracture. She took a panicky breath and pain rocketed up her back. She gasped.

"Sethral, talk to me. Talk it out."

"Where's Whipper? Where's Silver? And Firebrand? And Wing? Where are the twins?" The tears were falling now, dripping down her arms as she rocked back and forth. "Where are we? Why are we here?" She was struggling for breath again. She couldn't breathe. What had they done to her? What did they want with her and Loki and Ryatzi? Where was Dusk? And Phoenix? Was Phoenix okay? Was he alive? Would they kill him like the creatures on Linderward had tried to?

Everything was shaking, and she was crying and huddled up like a little kit against the stone, but its coolness just made breathing harder. Her whole back throbbed. The pain knotted in her chest and made her heart pound to try and fight it off.

"We're still in the Daemon's Outback," said Loki. How could he be so calm? "We're in a slot canyon, in a colony of some sort, and you, Ryatzi and I are together. They must have picked us up, so the others are probably here too. They almost certainly are. I'm not hurt, and it doesn't look like you are either, so Bluejay spared us. That means he probably spared the others, too. We're in cages, but that means nobody can get in either, so right now we're safe. And I'm here. Are you listening to me? I'm here, and I'm talking to you, and we're going to figure something out because the two of us at least are alive and moving and able to talk. As long as we're alive, we're going to be okay."

He had one paw reached out towards her, resting on the floor of the empty cage between them.

"Loki, I'm scared."

"I know. But we're still alive, and we're going to figure something out. Okay? We're going to figure something out."

Something banged the front vines of her cage. Sethral snarl-hissed as furiously as she could, trying to force aggression into the display to cover her fear. The white Watermouse stopped banging his long, sharpened stick against the vines. He glanced at his companion. The second white Watermouse placed her paws and took several quick, sweeping steps backwards. The first lowered his stick. With a piercing look at Sethral, he followed his companion back over the cliff.

Sethral ran across her cage and gripped the tough vine bars. "Ratty! Ratty! Are you okay? Wake up." Her voice caught and she choked out a sob. "Please."

He didn't stir.

"Sethral," said Loki. "Come back over here. He'll be okay; we're just bigger, so we woke up faster."

"No! What if he's hurt? Ratty!"

There was a hiss and a thunk. Sethral stared uncomprehendingly at the arrow buried in a vine a whisker from her face. There was a low chatter outside her cage. It sounded like speaking, but it was not any language she had ever heard. The white Watermouse who had uttered it had another arrow nocked to his bow, pointing at her. Sethral backed away from the bars. The arrow followed her. She lay down, closed her eyes and lowered her head. There was a creak as the bow was withdrawn. The white Watermouse spat something else at her, then ran up an empty cage and bounded away up the vines on the wall above.

"I think it might be dangerous to make too much noise here," said Loki in a low voice.

Sethral could still see the white Watermouse through the ceiling bars. He had stopped just shy of the canyon's woven ceiling and was ducking back and forth, scanning the forest outside. He had the arrow ready again.

There was a soft sound from the next cage over. Sethral nearly stabbed herself on the arrow shaft as she clamped to the bars. "Ratty! Ratty, over here. It's me. Look at me."

She could already see the panic in his body as he realized he was caged. He began to back towards the stone wall.

"Ratty, look at me."

His eyes darted to her.

"Loki's here, too," said Sethral. "We're both okay, and he thinks the others might be somewhere in this canyon. Listen, I need you to come to this corner. Yes, by the wall. On my side. Lie down and don't look outside. You're going to be okay."

He curled up and pressed against the stone. Sethral tried to determine if there was some way to get her thistlecloth to him, but there wasn't. Then she remembered she didn't even have her satchel.

"Just stay there, and I'll let you know anything Loki and I are thinking, okay?" she said. He nodded.

Somehow it was easier to focus when there was someone here handling this worse than she was. Sethral went back to Loki's side of the cage. "We need to get a message out so the others know we're here, if they are too. Any ideas?"

"Well, smell won't work. I can barely smell you, and you're right there."

"Yeah, the air's too still. I can't see past Ratty's cage either; the vines are too thick. And we can't call. I was going to risk a whistle, but they'd probably shoot me."

"I've still got my sling, but they took my rock pouch."

"They took my bag too. Are there any rocks around your cage?"

"No." He sounded glum. "I already checked."

She was about to answer when something skidded into a stone bump outside her cage. It was a piece of vine bark. Checking for white Watermice, Sethral crept to the front of her cage and fished it through the bars. Silversand's scent was all over it. Sethral flipped it over to find a message scratched on the smooth back.

Me and Whipper here. Your side?

Sethral rubbed the bark over her face, then scratched 'Ratty, me, Loki' below Silversand's message. 'You hurt?' she added along the edge, where there was still room. She climbed to the top of her cage and tried to gauge how far Silversand's would be. The bark was sturdy, so she threw it like a tiny javelin. It sailed out of sight. Less than thirty heartbeats later it skidded to a halt outside her cage again. 'No' was scratched on the last available corner.

"They're okay," said Sethral.

Loki breathed a sigh of relief. "Tell Spitfire."

He started testing the bark of the vines in his cage while Sethral relayed the message to Ryatzi. He didn't respond, but he was using the breathing techniques Talin had taught him, so he was awake and had probably heard her.

Another piece of bark skidded up. A white Watermouse stopped it with his foot and picked it up. He was the spear-creature from earlier. He scanned the message, then glared at Sethral, snapped the bark and tossed it into the canyon behind him. He was carrying a wooden bucket with a vine handle. From this he pulled a fat, leaf-wrapped packet, which he tossed into her cage through a gap in the vines. He went to Loki next, then backtracked and continued down the line of cages, dispensing packets to each of them here.

"What is it?" said Sethral when he was gone.

Loki had opened his packet. "Food, I think."

Sethral pulled the stems of the leaves free; they were woven into the packet, holding it tidily shut. She teased the top open. Inside was an array of scraps, none of which she recognized. There were a couple of leaves, clumps and crumbs of something with a texture like fungi, a slice of tuber, a hunk of something soft and rubbery, and what looked like a two-paw-length maggot. It was still moving slowly.

Loki had gotten the same things, it turned out, including the maggot. He sampled each cautiously. "Well, none of them taste bad."

Sethral plucked a leaf from the mix and nibbled it. It tasted leafy. She finished it and delved into the rest of the scraps, working her way from the least suspicious up. She was so hungry, though, that even the rubbery thing wasn't hard to choke down when she reached it. The maggot, meanwhile, proved surprisingly pleasant. It was mild and meaty, and by far the most filling of the bunch.

"Well, if they're feeding us, they probably don't plan on killing us yet," said Loki. "What do you think they want us for?"

"I guess we'll find out, won't we?"

He gave her a look. "You're the last creature who would actually give me that answer."

He was right, so they spent the rest of the evening trading theories and observations. Sethral wished Silversand or Whipper was near enough to talk to. Neither she nor Loki had night vision, so they had seen about the same things in the canyon outside. Loki, though, had been up longer than Sethral had.

"They came by to check on us before you were awake," he said. "Three or four of them; they kept jumping off the path and back, so it was kind of hard to tell. They stopped by each of our cages and it looked like they were talking about us."

"So they're got plans for us. Delightful."

"But they are feeding us, Seth."

"Long-term plans?" She wasn't sure how she felt about that. Long-term plans meant there was more guarantee they would be kept alive, and it gave them more time to collaborate and plan an escape. But it also meant they could be stuck here for some time. "We need to get out. We need to solve Radar's slave trade and get Jay back before Winter destroys him."

'Sethral?' came a small click.

It was Ryatzi. Sethral ran back across her cage. The Saberel looked calmer now, though he was still shivering. He managed a smile. Then, very carefully, he took hold of a small vine in front of him and pulled back on it. It was broken. No... he looked too pleased with himself for that. He let it spring back to apparent wholeness and bit another. Very slowly, he drove his teeth into it, then let go, moved a claw-length and bit again. Soon a ring of tooth-marks circled it like a bracelet. He must have bitten all the way around the first vine, too, weakening one part of it enough to be snapped.

"You're a genius," said Sethral. "Don't let them see you doing that."

"Is he getting out?" said Loki incredulously when she returned to him.

"He'll be able to get out by morning at this rate. It's not something the rest of us can replicate, though."

"No Drakon shit. Have you felt how tough these vines are?"

"I climbed them, fish-face. And I'm not light."

They talked until they couldn't see each other in the darkness. Sethral didn't want to stop and go to sleep. Her whole body took fright at every noise and her mind was whirring out of control. Every rustle made her heart pound.

"Loki?" she said at last, breaking the silence that had fallen between them.

"Yeah?"

"Will you still be here when I wake up?" Her voice was smaller than she had intended. She sounded like a kit, but she didn't care.

"I'll try to be."

Chapter 10

S omething was banging the vines, snapping at her in a language she didn't know. Sethral scrambled to the back of her cage. The cool stone wall did little to soothe the sudden, petrifying adrenaline. The white Watermouse from yesterday threw her a food package, then moved to Ryatzi's cage and lifted his spear to bang it too.

"Don't!" gasped Sethral.

Too late. The heavy wood slammed the vines, which were hard like trees and carried the tremors right through the cage. Ryatzi was on his paws in an instant. He backed against the wall with his hackles up and his mouth half open, showing his teeth and trying to breathe. The white Watermouse levelled the spear at him. Sethral ran forwards and pulled up short as the spearpoint was suddenly in her cage. Spear-knocker growled something at her in his language, then jabbed the point at her. She backed away. He repeated the short word and jabbed again. Only when Sethral was at the back of her cage did he seem satisfied. He withdrew the spear, angled it at Ryatzi again with what sounded like a threat, then walked down the line of cages towards Silversand and Whipper. Ryatzi collapsed against the wall. He had not been given a food package.

They were only half finished eating when white Watermice suddenly appeared all up and down the ledge outside. Several held ropes and collars of some tough jungle material, and nearly all of them had bows. There was a sharp word, and all the arrows pointed at the renegades. There they held. Sethral could not move. One twitch might be one twitch wrong, and all of those arrows would find their mark. She scarcely noticed the white Watermouse fiddling with the cage's outside until a round section of it swung open like a door. Bowstrings creaked tighter. A creature carrying ropes and a harness climbed inside, followed by a companion. They circled her so the arrows would still have a clear shot if she did something wrong.

The white Watermouse carrying the harness held up a loop of it that was undoubtedly a muzzle. Sethral stayed still. When he sensed she was cooperating, the creature slid the muzzle on, then slung a loop over her head and another around her neck. In a few deft movements he had secured things all down her back. Sethral yelped in pain as he yanked her bound wing. He turned to the creatures outside the cage and did a little backwards step-dance. Spear-knocker stepped back in reply. The creature beside her started undoing the straps Whipper had woven to bind the wing to her back. Sethral bit back tears as he pulled her wing open. Spear-knocker pointed his spear at both her wings and chattered sharply. Sethral beat the good one. Spear-knocker jabbed his weapon harder.

She couldn't. Even when she pressed through the pain and tried to move her sprained wing, it was too stiff to twitch. Sethral lay down and rested her forehead on her claws as a growing dizziness threatened to make her pass out. Spear-knocker's paws shuffled as he stepped a line back from the cage again. The creature beside Sethral refolded her wing across her back and replaced the straps.

There was more fiddling and tugging around the harness. When she could look up again, the two creatures around her had attached leads to several parts of it. Her good wing had also been bound. At Spear-knocker's command, one of the creatures tugged her upright. Several took the other ropes, and she was led out of the cage. Silversand and Loki were on the ledge outside, also harnessed and muzzled. 'Whipper?' flicked Sethral.

'They didn't try to catch him,' Silversand flicked back. 'He was being too aggressive.'

'Did he get food?'

'No.'

So they were trying to starve Ryatzi and Whipper into submission. Ryatzi would sooner waste to death than be put back in a collar, Sethral knew, but he could also last a lot longer without food than Whipper could. Their leads were tugged, and the three renegades were led down the long, slanting ledge. Sethral glanced as inconspicuously as she could at Whipper's cage as she passed it. The Forester was balled up in a back, upper corner. She could not see his face.

The line of cages ended at a rock outcrop not far past Whipper's cage, but the ledge kept going. Half the white Watermice were dismissed by Spear-knocker and bounded down vines on the canyon wall. Sethral squinted through the gloom. She could see no end to the slot canyon in either direction, just an endless cobweb of vines, vine bridges and low-slung platforms. The air was so humid, it felt like a creature could drown in it, but at least it wasn't hot.

The ledge ended in a precipice, but a sturdy vine bridge cut a right angle to the end of it and swooped away across the canyon. Sethral focused hard on the opposite canyon wall to keep herself from looking down. After a time, she dared to lower her gaze to the bridge railings, then out through their mesh. This was actually okay. These bridges had looked flimsy from a distance, but the vines they were made of were as tough and expertly woven as the cages. Even with their entire convoy on it, the renegades tripping on the slick, uneven woven floor, this bridge did not jiggle or sway. When she finally felt brave enough, Sethral looked down.

It was a surreal view. She felt like a spider in a huge web, all of it misty and brown or green, hung with skeins of fluffy plant material bearing a passing resemblance to moss. Soil-less plants like spiked fountains or ribbon-leaved cones sprouted from joints between the bridge vines, whose stingy bark was black with the damp where there was bark at all. The very bottom of the canyon was covered in vine nets. If she fell, she would almost certainly be caught unharmed. Sethral tried to see what lay below the nets, but it was too dark to tell until she spotted white Watermice hauling buckets on vine ropes up through a hole in the safety webbing. Water sloshed over the bucket rims.

'It's a river,' flicked Silversand ahead. Her ears were twitching.

At the end of the vine bridge was another, this one running along the canyon wall. At the end of it was a cave.

The temperature dropped as they stepped into the stone. The cave walls were slimy and reeked of algae and damp. Sethral had to deploy her claws to keep her grip on the floor. The white Watermice seemed to have no issue with the atrocious footing, and yanked their prisoners' ropes when the renegades stumbled. The tunnel began to cut a steep curve upwards. Soon Sethral was panting and scrabbling, and her claws felt ready to rip out of her fingertips. Her heart hurt from the strain of the climb. Up and up they went. Sethral was just debating what punishment she might get for 'slipping' and tumbling back down the slope when they rounded a corner and the exit appeared ahead. They emerged from the cave tunnel into a hollow tree. The light Sethral had seen was from a sizeable hole in the trunk, but it was woven over with vines. Tightly woven, as sturdily as the cage walls. Sethral looked up. A vine bridge spiraled up the hollow trunk, to another light far, far above.

Sethral could feel the moment they passed the vine ceiling separating the forest floor from whatever lay above. The light they were heading towards was nowhere close yet. She began to count the tail-lengths as they climbed up into the second canopy. At two, she could start to hear sounds outside, trickling through insect holes in the wood. At four, these became dominated by a loud, metallic buzzing, but then this fell behind. At six tail-lengths above the vine ceiling, it stopped altogether, and she suspected they had passed another layer. Then they were at the exit and the white Watermice were pushing aside the curtain that had shrouded it, and Sethral flung up a claw to shield her eyes.

Sun fell in patches across another mesh of vines: daintier bridges and dozens of small, hammock-like platforms. Dangling everywhere were the most extravagant, giant, fluted pitchers. Their green colouring—speckled with red—and attachment to the vines seemed to indicate they were plants. White Watermice as light-footed as birds tended to each of them. Some of the pitchers were full of soil; half of these had plants growing in them. Others swarmed with insects. Some stank, some oozed perfume. As Sethral watched, a white Watermouse dipped a net into one and hauled out a mass of wriggling maggots. They were the same maggots the renegades had been eating.

The renegades' escorts were unhooking something from the trunk's inner wall. They were pairs of narrow baskets, strung together by ropes. One was slung over Silversand's shoulders. When they were adjusted and secured, they hung down on either side of her back, their open tops to the sky. Before Sethral could examine them further, she and Loki had baskets dropped over them, too. Spear-knocker thumped his spear on the tree. In heartbeats there was a line-up of gardeners outside.

The baskets held a deceptively large amount of produce. Sethral had to brace herself under the weight by the time the last tuber, sheaf of plants and box of worms had been loaded. The renegades' escorts chatted amongst themselves for a moment, then untied she, Loki and Silversand's leads. Spear-knocker clapped his paws and pointed back down the hollow trunk.

Sethral could hardly walk by the time they were allowed back to their cages that evening. She had lost count of the trips they had made up and down the path to the gardens, carrying soil and water, composting food scraps and freshly harvested food. When the gardeners needed time to stock up more things to send down, Spear-knocker sent the renegades back and forth across the canyon. They brought water to upper caves, food everywhere, and soil and plant mulch to fungus gardens in the backmost tunnels. White Watermouse patrols from the forest brought in stone for arrowheads and sticks for arrow shafts, and they carried those too.

Sethral collapsed in the corner of her cage and tried not to cry as her back extended its pain to her whole body. She still couldn't tell where Bluejay had kicked her. It could have been anywhere for all she knew now. Loki hadn't fared much better. Sethral didn't try to talk to him. They both curled up in their smoothest floor corners and plunged into sleep. The next morning, Speak-knocker was banging on their cages again. The escorts with the harnesses at the ready were right behind him. This time, though, when Sethral struggled out onto the ledge with Silversand and Loki, someone else was waiting too.

Sethral stood rooted. A huge Saggitayria wearing little more than a collar stood beside Spear-knocker. He came up to the white Watermouse's armpit. As she stumbled to a halt on sore limbs that could hardly support her, he looked over. For a moment, they just stared at each other. The big Saggitayria's eyes narrowed slowly. Did he recognize her? She had no idea who he was.

Before she could flick a word to test if he knew tail-talk, Spear-knocker had banged his spear on the ground. The big Saggitayria lowered his head slightly and walked ahead of their guide. Sethral gasped. His wings were clipped. Each feather—he had six—ended in a straight slice, scarred where they had been cauterized to stop the bleeding. A wave of nausea swept over her. Before she could catch it, she had staggered to the precipice, then been sent reeling back by the butt of Spear-knocker's spear. She threw up on the path instead.

Clipped. That must have been what Spear-knocker had tested her wings for. Had she been able to fly, he would have clipped hers, too.

The white Watermouse was snarling at her, beating her with his spear. Sethral found her paws and stumbled back into line. With a final smack, Spear-knocker resumed his position behind the big Saggitayria. The Saggitayria was watching Sethral again, expressionless. He turned and kept walking.

That day was agony. The Saggitayria carried twice as much as any of them without a wince, and he wasn't even breathing hard after a full morning going back and forth to the gardens. His lip started to curl as he waited for them to catch up first once, then twice, then four times a trip. Spear-knocker belabored the renegades with his spearbutt, but it had little effect. Loki was the first to collapse. It was hotter out today than the day before, and the trip up the hollow trunk was especially stifling. The Fisher's panting was fast, shallow and ragged. This time Spear-knocker seemed to sense that a beating would not change the situation. He banged his spear against the wall in a pattern that brought several of his lackeys to the ledge. They dragged Loki away.

Sethral kept trying to get into a position to tail-sign to the big Saggitayria, but he was always ahead of them and if he looked back, she was too exhausted to do anything but catch her breath. One of these times she did manage to flick off a question-sign, but he didn't respond. She didn't know if that meant he didn't know tail-talk, hadn't seen it, was ignoring it, or if she had simply been too tired to be flick legibly. When they finally stopped for the evening, she thought she might get a chance. 'Do you know tail-talk?' she flicked as Spear-knocker's lackeys fiddled with whatever mechanism held her cage door so securely closed.

The big Saggitayria just watched her silently. Sethral's cage door clicked open. Spear-knocker pointed his spear at it. Sethral climbed up through the opening and fell to the ground on the other side. She lay on the stone and watched Spear-knocker and the Saggitayria walk away while frustration and helplessness rolled over her in hot, tear-pricking waves. She swiped away the tears and sat up. She could see Loki at the back of his cage, motionless but breathing, a bowl of water beside him. She had been left water, too. She drained it and inspected the bowl. It was the shell of some hard-backed creature; a giant crab, maybe. Sethral knocked it gently against the floor. It was lighter than wood but felt stronger than bone. She looked around the cage. The rock was smooth and barren, but the ceiling had several places where the tightly woven vines left slots just large enough to suit her purposes. She checked that nobody was watching, then climbed the wall and wedged the bowl into one of these.

The next day crawled by the same way as the first two, only now the soreness was either wearing off or so potent her body couldn't feel it anymore. Sethral returned to her cage that evening to find a fresh bowl of water; a wooden bowl this time. She checked the vine slot. The shell-bowl was still there. She let a smile creep across her face for the first time in days. She didn't know what she could do with the shell, but it was something and something was infinitely better than nothing. Spear-knocker was clearly the head of the colony's slaves, but several creatures worked together in no particular order to clean and maintain the cages. Whoever had left her water today must just have assumed someone else had taken the shell bowl away.

Chapter 11

Loki did not recover for several days. Sethral found she adjusted quickly to the daytime workload. Now able to focus on something other than making it to the end of her next step, she began to scan the canyon and memorize everything she saw, heard or smelled. The caves she had been to so far—fungus gardens, insect gardens, living spaces and an infirmary—had so far been dead ends, but there was a spot near the bottom of the canyon that intrigued her. There were several water-holes in the nets along the canyon bottom. When creatures dropped their buckets in most of these, the lines they dropped them on were swept taut by the river. One place, though, was different. For one, it was right near the canyon wall. For two, a bucket dropped here swept briefly away from the wall before succumbing to the dominant current. It was like there was a separate stream of water at the spot, emanating from a tunnel hidden   beneath   the nets.

She had still seen no sign of the Coppertails, but she caught Fletch's scent on a wall on the fourth or fifth day. He was not distressed enough to have lost his brother, so Taz must be okay, too.

"I told you," said Loki when she told him, though she could hear the tremble of relief in his voice.

"And if all of us so far have been here and uninjured, there's a really high chance we all are." Sethral closed her eyes. As it had for days, Phoenix's haunted face played across her vision. She faced it. It hurt, but she deserved that pain and she wanted to feel it. *You made him look at you that way*, a small part of her brain repeated. *Until you hurt as much as he does, you can't understand how he feels.*

Aside from the burns sealing the ends of the big Saggitayria's wings, she had seen no evidence of fire in the canyon colony, and there were plants that could have done the cauterizing. She wondered if the creatures even knew what fire was. In such a damp, thick forest, natural fires would be next to nonexistent. She wondered if the colony's ignorance had saved Phoenix's life, or taken it.

Loki had fallen asleep. Sethral rolled onto her back and listened as hard as she could to the silence, trying to detect anything in the sky above. But like the last days had all been, the night seemed clear. They had hauled twice the usual amount of water up to the gardens today. It must be a dry spell.

She was about to drift off when other noises echoed up the canyon, faint and far off at first, then louder. Then Spear-knocker's spear banged against her cage vines like a thunderclap. Sethral had never been able to not startle when he did that; in the near-darkness it nearly gave her a heart attack. She bounded upright. Spear-knocker grabbed the vines and squinted through them until he spotted her, then ran to Loki's cage and smashed his spear against it too. He always came to her first, though Loki was at the end of the cage line. Loki too was in his cage. The white Watermouse ran to the rest of the cages, repeating his check. At Whipper's there was shouting and more banging than anywhere. Whipper's screech-chatter cut it short. Spear-knocker left and shouted across the canyon. Nobody here ever shouted.

But what happened next was even more chilling. Sethral had to scrub her eyes to make sure she was seeing properly as a cluster of fireflies appeared on the opposite canyon wall. Then the cluster blossomed. Like the pulse of a heartbeat, the lights flowed from a cave and radiated outwards, moving in ribbons that dipped and swayed in eerie synchrony. It was like watching a giant, glowing spider spread its legs across the canyon wall. Then the legs began to fracture. Clusters of fireflies broke away and vanished into caves, then reappeared from them. They began to spread across the bridges. Soon the entire canyon was sparkling with disparate moving lights. One bobbed past Sethral's cage, then another. She gripped the vines until her knuckles cracked. She knew that bobbing.

Another light was approaching, a larger swarm behind it. White Watermice whispered and darted. One fumbled with the door of the cage between Sethral and Loki. When it swung open, a huge shape bounded inside and let himself be locked in. Sethral could not tear her eyes from the lights casting a cool glow over the white Watermice and the path. Bubble-creatures, the lights flashing from points in their centers and reflected around their globe-like bodies, bobbed in swarms wherever the white Watermice walked.

There were more creatures coming up the path. It sounded like they were being wrestled along, fighting every inch of the way. A shout sent one of Spear-knocker's lackeys to the cage between Sethral and Ryatzi. A Coppertail spat and hissed as he was flung inside. Sethral ran to the bars. "Taz! Taz!"

He bodychecked the door, but it had been hastily slammed and locked behind him. He spun around. "Who's there?"

"Me." Tears streamed down her face. No amount of speculation was the same as hearing and smelling him here, alive. The slam of a cage door past Ryatzi's was followed by Fletch's hiss.

"Sethral?" Taz found his way to their shared wall and reached a paw through it. Sethral grabbed it and hugged it and sobbed into his fur. On Loki's other side, another cage door banged. A storm of screeching and battering pounded it; the creatures outside held it shut and screamed for Spear-knocker. He came running. Firebrand darted out of range of his weapon and was locked inside.

"Where's Wing? And Dusk, and Phoenix?" Sethral could hardly speak, her body was shaking so hard.

"Wing's not here; I don't think they caught him. Dusk's disappeared. That's what all this fuss is about. He went down from heat exhaustion and they locked him in a cage, but they just found the cage empty. It probably wasn't; he probably hid in the shadows, then snuck out when they came to search it. Either way, he's gone and they haven't found him yet, so they're moving the rest of us in case he comes to free us."

"Where were you?"

"They tied us up as guards. Or bait. In the exit tunnels."

"Where's Phoenix?" The Pyrya glowed in the dark, and she hadn't seen them bring him here yet.

"He's locked up somewhere else." Taz's voice was tight.

"Is he okay?"

"No."

Sethral gripped his paw tighter. "What did they do to him? Is he hurt? Is it the Moonworm again?"

"No, he's gotten through that okay, but he's alone and they've had to drug him just to keep him from panicking. They've been using him to catch bugs."

"They've been what?"

"His fur attracts bugs. Especially moths. It's probably how he catches food normally; he's always out at night if he's healthy. But creatures here eat a lot of bugs too, so they've been dragging him out every night to use as a lure."

"But he's still hurt!"

"I know. They used to take him past my exit, so I at least got to reassure him when they came by. But then he started clinging to me and freaking out when they tried to take him away. Now they take Dusk's exit. Or did, anyway. So Pheo can't touch him."

That was just cruel.

"And is—"

She was cut short by a bang on the front of her cage. Taz flew at it with a snarl. He was forced to leap back as Spear-knocker thrust his weapon between the vines. The white Watermouse carried on down the cage line, banging Silversand and Fletch into silence too. Loki and Firebrand seemed to have taken the hint.

"Did he get you?" said Sethral as Taz stalked back to her.

"No."

The search in the canyon spread thinner as the white Watermice and their bubble escorts dispersed into its farthest corners. Like regular Watermice, they searched by sight, not smell.

"They're not going to find Dusk," said Sethral.

"I know. They missed their window of opportunity when they first opened his cage. If he's had this long to hide, he's long gone. Seth, who's locked up on your other side? Is it Fibes?"

"No, a Saggitayria who was here before us."

"Before us? Have you talked to him?"

"I haven't gotten a chance to face-to-face."

"Seth, do that! Shelha! If there's a Saggitayria here, he could have something to do with Radar!"

It hit her like a smack in the face and the lungs and the gut. A Saggitayria who had something to do with Radar. A Saggitayria caught by the slave trade but never making it to the chains; a big male from the twin groups, who had disappeared en route and never been seen again.

Sethral walked slowly to the other side of her cage. She could not see him in the dark, but she could hear him breathing. He was not asleep. "Buckthorn?"

Slowly, he stirred. "It's been a long time since I heard that name," he said. He sounded like he had not used this language in just as long.

"Did Radar bring you here?"

"The snake-face?"

He didn't say more, so Sethral said, "Yes."

Buckthorn gave a short, harsh laugh and rolled over.

"I'm from Nova," said Sethral, hoping to get him talking again. Top warriors across the clan groups always knew each other. "Icarus and Shaira were my parents."

"Upstarts," growled Buckthorn. "I don't talk to Nova."

Clearly being the first Saggitayria he had seen in twenty years was not enough to override what was probably a family grudge. Sethral collared the heat that seethed up from her stomach. "Well, most of the Nova you knew is dead now, if that makes you any happier."

He paused, then rolled over again. "Larcin and Tamarack?"

"I don't even know who those are."

"Huh." He did sound happy. Disgust made Sethral's lip curl.

"How quick did Zehran get to lead the clan group?" said Buckthorn.

"I don't know who that is either."

That made him pause. It gave Sethral more satisfaction than it should have. "Arcturus," he said, slowly, like he was explaining something to a winglet. "Zehran. Leader."

"Arcturus's leader is Blackbird. I don't know who Zehran is. He's probably dead."

Buckthorn rolled to his paws. Sethral checked that she was out of his claw-reach. She was. She didn't move.

"What, did Radar disappear the rest of the clan groups too?" said Buckthorn. He wasn't threatening her, but it felt like a threat.

"No, the Drakons. They got driven from the cliffs into the Far South by a cold winter, and they attacked everyone. It was three years after you left. Like I said, most of the Nova you knew is dead. So is half the Phinx you knew, a quarter of the Aldebaran, and a few warriors from Arcturus and Orion. Probably including Zehran."

"Who were your parents?"

"Icarus and Shaira." She knew he hadn't actually been listening to her before. "And Talin."

"If Talin had a kit, I'll be very surprised."

"He didn't. He adopted me when my first parents died."

"He didn't have kin."

"It wasn't official."

She had a feeling Buckthorn was watching her through the dark. She glared back where she knew he was.

"Talin was a good warrior," said Buckthorn. "Not cocky like most of the ones from Nova. I liked him better. Did he die too?"

"No, he survived."

"Still?"

"As of a moon ago when I last saw him, yes."

"Got himself a mate yet?"

"Yes. And a kit. Adopted with full clan approval."

"That's good."

Again he left it at that. Sethral turned the conversation back where she wanted it to go. "So Radar brought you here?"

"Yes."

"Why?"

"As a trade."

"For what?"

"He was going somewhere. He wanted directions."

Sethral's pulse sped up until she could feel it. "Where?"

"Don't know."

"How don't you know?"

"He never said it out loud."

"Then how do you know he was asking directions?"

"You've seen that little backwards dance creatures here do? They're talking. Snakeface talked to them in that. They pointed him on his way and he left me here and left."

Sethral groaned. "Okay. Well, which way did they point him to?"

His body shifted as he pointed in the complete darkness. She could hear him snickering.

"This isn't a joke," she said.

"Chasing Radar when you can't even survive out here? You're young naivety at its finest."

"Well, we're also the first thing standing between a tyrant and the annihilation of both the clan groups and most of the South Forest, so we figured it was worth the risk."

She was starting to really enjoy wiping that snide smile off his face. His truth-radar, clearly, still worked.

"One of our members just escaped from a cage here," she continued. "They're not going to catch him, and given that it gets this dark every night, he'll be able to walk around wherever he wants. We don't know how yet, but we're getting out of here."

Either Buckthorn had decided to ignore her now, or he was finally taking her seriously. "How did he get out?" he said at last.

"He's a darkness elemental. As long as there's shadows, he can basically turn himself invisible. And he can sneak like our best hunters. We think he never actually left the cage, then slipped out when they came to search it."

"Do you really think you can get out of here?"

Sethral couldn't tell if it was mockery or an honest question.

"Hey Seth," whispered Taz behind her. He sounded like he was grinning. There was a click from the back of Sethral's cage.

She gasped. In a heartbeat she had floored Ryatzi and clamped him in the tightest hug she could give without breaking his ribs. His voice wasn't back yet and he was thinner than before, but he was definitely smiling. 'Do you have any food left?' he tapped on her paw.

"No, I gave it to Whipper this time. Sorry. When did you get through my cage?"

'Last night. I have a link to Fletch's, too, and through Silversand's.'

"I love you so much. How are you doing? Does the spear-happy slave driver come and harass you in the day, too?

'Not really. I'm doing okay. Just hungry.'

"I'll save you some food tomorrow. You should get back to your cage before they see you here."

She gave him a final hug and he wriggled back through the broken vines. Sethral returned to Buckthorn. "I think we stand a chance."

"Then I'll help you if you promise to take me along."

The message was passed quickly up and down the cage-line now that all the cages were full. They had a consensus.

"Deal," said Sethral.

"That water-hole you've been watching?" said Buckthorn. "There's a tunnel in the wall there. They brought you all in by boat through it, but the water is too fast to go upstream in regular weather. But, it's the only entrance I know that's unguarded. And anytime there's a storm, this whole canyon floods."

"So the water backs up."

"If you got a boat down there at the start of a storm, you could ride the flood up the tunnel. I don't know what's past it, but I assume at some point it leads outside."

"Where are the boats? I've never seen one."

"They've got two. They're kept in a side channel down the canyon to our left. They're guarded, though."

That could be an issue; almost every creature here had a bow. But they stood a chance if they were out of the cages. "What's the mechanism on these cage doors?"

"That? That's not even a lock. It's only openable from the outside, though, and it takes fingers to do it. That's why they shut your friends in here when your Coppertail friend got out."

"Would anything else work?"

"If you had a knife, maybe. But these creatures don't."

Sethral could hardly keep from bouncing. She forced herself to stand still and take a deep breath. "Okay, two more questions. Actually, three. One, where do these creatures leave loot they've captured from creatures like us? Two, we've got a member locked up somewhere else in here. A fire elemental; a little red Coppertail. Do you know where he is? And three, how often does the canyon flood?"

Buckthorn grumbled, but answered in order. "They're usually suspicious of anything from outside, so they stash it in the equipment room. Your friend is down that way, on the other end of the canyon. That's where the other exits are, and they're keeping him close to those. The canyon floods periodically in the rainy season, and it's technically the rainy season now. It could happen anytime."

"Seth?" said Taz. "Ryatzi says there should be a storm tomorrow or tomorrow night. The dry spell's passing."

"So we need to be in the tunnel with Phoenix and a boat before it hits."

"Well, when you put it that way, it sounds next to impossible," growled Buckthorn. "Do you actually have a plan?"

"Not yet," said Sethral. Something had just dropped with a soft thump at the back of her cage. She felt her way over to it and smiled as her claw closed on the fish-leather strap of her satchel. Dusk on the cage-top was already gone. Sethral flipped open the satchel to find its contents untouched save for Dusk's scent and two missing items: her thistlecloth and one of her knives. "Scrap the thing about Phoenix; we just need ourselves and a boat. And I'm starting to get an idea."

Chapter 12

The next day was cooler than the last few. Instead of the sun and clear blue they had been getting used to, grey clouds brooded over the sky. The Coppertails were left in their cages. Sethral noted every motion and feature of the canyon with the intensity of far premature adrenaline, trying to map her plan onto the shifting reality of guards and tunnels and the swarms of bubble-creatures that seemed to have filled the canyon overnight. Spear-knocker was more distracted than usual. Sethral, Loki and Silversand were put away early, and Sethral was able to pirate an extra pair of maggots back to the cages without getting caught. She had Taz pass them to Ryatzi.

"The storm's coming," said Taz. He could hardly stop twitching. "Are you sure Dusk's going to take care of Phoenix?"

Sethral dug out the piece of bark she had hidden in her fur and tossed it to him. Dusk's scent still lingered on it, and its back was marked with an X cut by a knife. "He left that in the tunnel entrance we'd have to take to get Pheo. Unless I'm interpreting completely wrong, we're being told to stay out of it."

Taz turned the bark over several times, then sighed. "I trust him with that more than I trust myself, but I still don't like this. What if they get caught in our half of the plan?"

"Well, I left a snip of our plan where he left this, so with luck he'll figure it out and act accordingly. Also, we're going to be drawing a crowd before I set it off, so chances are that's when he'll make a break for it."

She climbed the cage vines and checked for the dozenth time that the shell bowl was ready. It was now stocked with a ball of tinder and a sheaf of dried herbs—the cataract grey knockout smoke mix they had robbed off the pair of would-be ship robbers Watersinger had encountered in the Lowlands. She had been carrying it around ever since, just in case.

"I'm really glad you're a hoarder," said Taz.

"I'm going to take that as a compliment." Sethral jumped to the ground as a white Watermouse appeared on the path by Silversand's cage. The creature just climbed the cages and ran up the wall. She had a bow at the ready.

"Buckthorn, what are the creatures here scared of up there?"

"Aria and Coppertails," said the big Saggitayria with a yawn. "They severed a major Canyonlander route when they set up this colony here, and the Coppertails have been fighting them for it for generations." He knocked a claw on the stone. "This ledge we're on right here used to be Coppertail territory."

"Why would Coppertails live in the canyons?"

"Because it's safer than the ground."

That was fair. Sethral checked for white Watermice again and meandered over to the cage wall she shared with Buckthorn. She tugged the vines gently, breaking the sap that had started to harden and seal their severed ends back together. In the far cages, Firebrand kept watch while Loki worked covertly on the last cage wall separating the renegades.

It started to get dark earlier than it should have. Loki got through the wall and passed Sethral's knife back. She had already picked the spot on the front of her cage: a more loosely woven section where a single severed vine would open a gap large enough for Whipper to get through. He wriggled into her cage just as the vine parted with a pop.

"You ready for this?" said Sethral.

"I think so."

She hugged him to test that statement, but he did feel ready. She handed him her tiny knife with its flint attached, and her tinder bag with the last of her tinder. "You remember where I told you to go?"

She heard him nod. He was a shadow in the darkness, dropping to a flowing slink as she pulled back the vine on the cage front. In a heartbeat he was gone. Sethral began to count heartbeats. No alarms were raised as a hundred passed, then two hundred. At three hundred, she smelled the smoke in the air. Someone in the canyon shouted, and the guards along the cage ledge disappeared.

"To me, now," hissed Sethral to Taz and Buckthorn. The message flew like a breeze. Whipper was back outside her cage, fiddling with the lock as renegades wriggled through the holes Ryatzi had bitten and she and Loki had cut. Silversand was last to arrive as the cage door sprang open. Sethral yanked her shell bowl down from the ceiling. She handed it to Whipper. "Don't get it wet."

He nodded and was gone again. Vines were creaking all over the canyon. Creatures shouted and buckets splashed. On the far wall, one cave entrance—the weapons storage room—glowed like a forge.

The renegades scrambled onto the cages and held still as a guard ran past. They snuck down the cage line until the cages ran out, braced themselves, and dropped back onto the path.

"Guards on the bridge!" gasped Silversand. She broke into a sprint. Sethral could hear the bounding pawsteps of the white Watermice as they hit the bridge, now a quarter of the way across, now halfway. Silversand reached the ledge end and dropped straight off it. She landed with a thump. Creatures piled after her to find a drop to a small lip of stone. With no time to jump, Sethral slung herself over the precipice and clung to the vines as white Watermice dashed off the bridge only paw-lengths away. They ran away up the ledge.

Sethral dropped down. Silversand was probing the stone around the alcove. She chirped. Then she was inching away along the wall along a ledge barely wide enough to fit her. Sethral felt it when it was her turn to follow. The stone was smooth and rippled from water and generations of Coppertail paws. The ledge ran for only a tail-length, then gave way to a series of long drops that took the renegades rapidly to the canyon bottom's nets.

"It's raining," said Silversand.

"Move faster," said Sethral.

The nets swarmed with creatures, but they were concentrated around the water holes. Nobody noticed as the escapees hugged the wall all the way down the canyon, then darted around the corner into the side shaft that held the boats. There were only two guards; they didn't have a chance to shout. Taz and Firebrand dropped them on a shadowed ledge. The boats were tied to long, thin vines running all the way up the shaft, so they could rise and fall with the floods. Sethral slashed the knots while Silversand and Loki wrestled with the gate blocking the exit into the river. Loki grabbed the Royal and pulled her back as lightning made the trees above the canyon sparkle. When the thunderclap rolled in, the Fisher dealt the gate a kick that snapped its main beam. They forced it open.

They could all fit in one boat if they squeezed. Buckthorn shoved the second boat out the gate empty; it was swept away. He jumped in last and the renegades propelled their boat out the gate. Everyone who could grabbed the vine nets above; already the water was high enough to leave them barely a copper-length of headroom. The current was rough and fast.

"There's a rope!" called Firebrand. She locked her tail onto it and pulled them over. It was a ferry rope, running straight across the cavern in the direction of the tunnel they needed to reach. Everyone who could hold on clung to it. The river folded around their boat and dragged it sideways. Paw by paw they pulled themselves across the canyon. The water's rise was accelerating. Buckets splashed at the water-holes in the nets, but the one ahead was silent.

"Hold your breaths," said Sethral.

A smoky haze hung over the water-hole just outside the tunnel. Sethral whistled Whipper's name, then took a deep breath and shut her mouth. As the boat passed under the hole, Whipper dropped down onto Firebrand. Downed bubble-creatures scattered the nets around the hole. In their light, Sethral could see the bodies of un-conscious white Watermice lying among them, some with buckets still clasped in their paws.

Her lungs ached, but the haze had seeped far and they were a tail-length up the tunnel before Sethral's eyes stopped stinging from the smoke. She risked a tiny breath. The air was fresh. "All clear!"

There were gasps around her as creatures let out their breaths. The tunnel was horizontal and visible from here to the canyon in the light of the bubble-creatures, but up ahead was blackness. The current was powerful. Sethral reached a paw up and yelped as it met the ceiling. "Push along the walls! Hurry, or we're going to get stuck!"

They gripped the walls with claws and braced against any knob they could find. The boat's high prow nearly scraped the roof by the time the roof gave way. They had emerged into a tiny cave. Ahead, the tunnel sloped sharply upwards. A stream cascaded down it towards them in a rushing torrent, soaking them with spray as they clung to the walls. It was all they could do to hold themselves in place until the canyon river rose enough to push them uphill.

'The way we came in is underwater!' tapped a paw on Sethral's back. It was Silversand. 'We're getting away!'

Shelha, that meant if they'd left even a hundred heartbeats later, they wouldn't have made it into the tunnel. The boat gave a jolt as it caught and pulled free of a rock. Sethral touched the wall and found it sliding past by paw-lengths a heartbeat. They were rising up the tunnel. Fast. A terrible thought struck her. What if the river's flood surge didn't push them far enough to get out? They couldn't walk up this tunnel; even Whipper wouldn't be able to cling to its slick, soaking walls. The flood would lift them as far as it rose, then simply recede again. It would take them right back down the canyon. There was no other way out by water; Buckthorn said the river was woven off with vine nets on either end of the colony.

Sethral was startled out of her horrifying revelation as the boat gave a heave and slid out onto open water, spinning slowly in the current. The swish of the water gushing up from the tunnel echoed off walls as far above them as Rockhall's main hall ceiling, and they drifted farther and farther across the pool. "Whipper?" said Sethral.

"We're going to land at a beach, I think." The Forester was perched on the prow. Sethral didn't know his seventh sense, object and void, could tell the difference between rock and a beach. Though maybe he was just detecting the slant of the shoreline.

The boat ground to a halt on rock. Everyone jumped ashore. "Ratty?" said Sethral.

'There's a tunnel this way.'

He led them away from the slowly rising pool and the continuation of the stream tunnel pouring downhill into the cavern's other side. Through a slot in the cavern wall there was indeed a tunnel, and Sethral didn't need Ryatzi's wind sensitivity to detect the breeze moving down it. A trickle of water flowed over their paws. They scrambled up the slick channel, over rocks and around baby rock teeth, until all of a sudden they were stepping onto soil, not stone. They were back in the forest.

"We're out!" said Loki. He and Silversand hugged each other, laughing. "We're out, we're out, we're out!"

"Tetch, where are Dusk and Pheo?" said Sethral.

The twins both did a scan. "They're coming!" said Taz.

"We're not safe yet," growled Buckthorn. He had grown only more tense since they had stepped off the boat. "We need to get off the ground!"

There were shouts in the distance.

"Come on, come on," whispered Taz. His paws tapped the soil.

"I'm not kidding!" said Buckthorn, starting into the forest. "We need to go now!"

"Phoenix!" Taz was gone in a flash. Phoenix collapsed against him and Dusk let got of his scruff. He had been holding it through the thistlecloth draped over the Pyrya's back.

"Come on, we need to keep going," said Taz, coaxing Phoenix back upright.

"Halo," panted Dusk.

There was a bird's chirp ahead. Halo took off into the forest, chirping steadily. They ran after her. Sethral heard Dusk stumble hard.

Firebrand caught him. "Hey, you're exhausted. Were you giving him your energy again?"

"Yes."

Taz was talking continuously to Phoenix, who was struggling just to stay on his paws. The sounds in the distance indicated their pursuers were closing the gap.

"Leave him behind," snarled Buckthorn. "If we're caught now, I will never forgive you all!"

There was a flurry of chirps up ahead, then chirrs in the forest, then suddenly there were sounds and breezes of motion all around them. Halo's voice shot into the air. Creatures fumbled after her to find a long, slender branch punched through the vine ceiling. They scrambled up it. Sethral gasped as Phoenix slipped and landed hard on the ground again, taking Taz with him. The Rocklander stifled a shriek.

"Taz, come up; they'll bring him!" called Ryatzi. His voice was back.

Taz leaped back. Something—several somethings—lifted Phoenix, still wrapped in the blanket. Taz bounded up the branch. The Pyrya was floated up after him, carried away from the hole and laid down on the flimsy, netlike ground. Halo chirped forcefully until the renegades had joined her beside him. The branch they had just come up was moving. The ground sagged as things leaped up and pulled back on its leafy top, levering its broken bottom off the forest floor. When it was horizontal, it was dragged back several tail-lengths. The path to the ground was gone.

Arrows whined by beneath them. White Watermice swarmed the place they had just been. Through chinks in the floor, Sethral could see creatures dancing backwards from one another. One lifted her bow and fired through the canopy. The arrow missed Silversand by claw-lengths. Bubble-creatures bobbed up close to the vine ceiling. Sethral realized the hole the renegades had come through had vanished under a convincing crisscross of loose vines.

Chapter 13

When their pursuers found no way to reach them—and maybe no way to prove where they had disappeared to—they darted away into the forest. Sethral put her head on her paws. There was no point in even trying to get up. She was too weak and shaky to stand. Taz had settled down with Phoenix curled against his flank. He startled so hard the vine floor shook. In the faint glow from Phoenix's fur, Sethral saw something move in the dark behind him. It must have touched him. There was a pause, then a Coppertail's head dipped into sight, held low, offering Taz a leaf.

It was beautiful. Its fur was so fine it feathered at the cheeks, dark and glossy. Its eyes were big like Halo's, and its muzzle was daintier than any Coppertail type Sethral knew. Taz took the leaf. As the Coppertail withdrew, its head dipped, and Sethral caught the silhouette of two short, pronged antlers curving off the top of its skull. Taz seemed to have forgotten what he was doing. He stared into the darkness where the Coppertail had vanished, until Phoenix whimpered. Taz curled tighter around him and offered him the leaf. Phoenix took it and snuggled down again.

"Do we have to move again yet?" said Ryatzi into the darkness.

Halo made a sound like two stones clicking and plopped down at his side.

"We can stay the night," said Ryatzi to the group at large.

"Good," said Firebrand. "This one's already asleep."

She had Dusk beside her. Sethral counted through each of the renegades. At Whipper, her heart plunged almost through the ground. "Tetch, we need to find Wing."

"Go to sleep," said Fletch.

He wasn't leaving an option in it. Sethral couldn't believe anyone could sleep right now. Wing was still out here. He had been out here, all this time they had been down in the canyon. Had he faced down Bluejay? Had he won? Escaped? What if he was hurt, or starving? He could hunt out here, but half the ground predators were most easily detected visually. They needed to find him. They needed to get back to him, and soon.

She must have been exhausted. There was sunlight overhead: just tiny chips of it, too small to even make spots on the ground. Sethral lifted her head. The second canopy stretched away around the renegades like a second forest floor, only more fragile, dipping like nets where vines and roots bridged the spaces between the flat-canopied trees. Through this rose the columns of this forest's giants. They hardly seemed living. Something this large could hardly be living. Their trunks towered up and up, into the deep green shadow through which the sunlight chips sparkled like stars. Vines and air plants and great, broad leaves curled up every trunk until each was a vertical forest in itself.

She wanted to move, but exhaustion heavier than a coat of mud wrapped her body. Everyone around her was sleeping. Everyone save for Halo, who sat at the edge of the group and just gazed into the forest. She was relaxed. She looked over and chirred softly as Sethral shifted positions. It was too much work. Sethral closed her eyes again.

Nobody got any white patches up here, though maybe the Forestairs just treated them while the renegades slept. Sethral wondered why they had taken such a liking to the group. There was food and water beside her each time she woke, and by the amount Phoenix slept, they probably brought medicines for him, too.

Sethral's thoughts came back to Wing every time she was awake. Sometimes it was immediate, other times she would get a short respite before she saw Whipper curled up hugging Firebrand or Fletch or Taz, and her memory reminded her that the mutt wasn't here. A deep heaviness rolled over her every time she remembered. She tried to pin down the source of it, but there didn't seem to be one.

She began to wake up in the heaviness, sometimes in a panic attack. Every day they spent here was another day Wing spent alone down in the forest. But with the heaviness came a helplessness bordering on lethargy, bordering on apathy. Sethral wanted to slap herself. It was like something had convinced her subconscious that looking for Wing would not do anything; that they were already too late, that he was already gone. She started to have nightmares of Bluejay walking through the forest towards the group, and Wing standing in front of them, unwilling or unable to get out of the way.

The nightmares got worse and worse until she woke up screaming to find Firebrand holding her, trying to calm her down. Sethral clung to her and sobbed. All the renegades and a Saggitayria she vaguely recognized were lying or sitting up or stirring around her.

"Where's Wing?" her own voice kept saying.

The Coppertails weren't meeting her eye. Taz was nervously grooming Phoenix and Fletch was trying to look anywhere else. Sethral looked past them and saw Dusk lying a ways apart from the group. He was looking at his paws.

He knew something.

Sethral struggled to her paws. "Dusk."

His body gave the slightest twitch of a flinch.

"Dusk, what happened with Wing and Bluejay?"

This time everyone flinched. Whipper clamped onto Firebrand, hyperventilating. Silversand was staring at her with something bordering on horror. A sickening feeling crept into Sethral's gut. She was not the only one the heaviness had struck.

"Dusk," she said again, louder.

His gaze was on his paws, but he wasn't looking at anything. He was blocking her out. He was blocking them all out. Suddenly, Sethral found herself up in his face, her claws gripping his chest fur, actually lifting him off the ground. "What happened," she said. She was shaking and her grip was white-knuckled, but she could hear her own voice and her voice was level. Nobody jumped up to stop her. Nobody moved at all. Dusk turned his head quickly to the side. Sethral drove her claws into his skin, but he didn't seem to notice. He was panting now. The emotion he was trying to hide from was leaking through, so raw Sethral could taste it. It was denial. And fear.

"What happened?!" she screamed, shaking him.

"He's dead."

She didn't realize her claws had gone loose until Dusk pulled back from them.

"He's dead," he repeated. His expression had sealed off. "He tried to talk to him. To Jay. Bluejay pounced on him and slit his throat. I watched him die."

He wasn't lying.

He wasn't lying.

Her body was backing away. She ran into Firebrand and kept trying to press back, like by moving she could escape what he was saying and make it not true. Firebrand just hugged her. She and the twins must have felt this already. Wing's seventh sense signature would have disappeared. They would have gone through the canyon forced to pick a belief in one of two impossible options: that Wing had been lost on the landscape beyond the range of their seventh senses, or that Bluejay's mission had never been to kill the whole group after all.

"Winter made Jay kill Wing," whispered Silversand. "No. She can't do this to him." Her face crumpled and suddenly she was sobbing. She sank to the ground. "She can't do this to Jay again!"

Sethral staggered as something shoved her away from Firebrand's back. Whipper's face was cold and stricken. "You're lying."

"I'm not."

"You're lying!"

"Dusk's not lying!"

He attacked her, but he was still weak from hunger. Sethral flung him off her. He curled into a ball on the ground and started to scream. Fletch ran forwards but Whipper kicked him off, screaming, "You're not Wing! Go away! You're not Wing!"

At the edge of her blurred vision, Sethral saw Ryatzi get up and walk away. Loki ran after him. Silversand was now rocking back and forth, sobbing too deeply for her body to handle. Fletch picked her up and let her burrow into his fur. Tears wet Taz's face and his breath kept catching, but he had curled tightly around Phoenix and he wasn't letting go. Phoenix was silent. He watched the renegades with eyes wider than usual and an expression Sethral couldn't read. Some part of her wondered if he understood what was going on.

Why had she thought she could keep Wing and Jay?

Suddenly, a calm settled over her. She had just lost both her parents for the second time. She was hurting because she had believed in the first place that parents were something she could keep. Drakons were a part of the world, and they always had been. So was war. War always came back, and it always took loved ones. She should have learned that the first time.

Whipper was now fighting Firebrand, but he didn't understand. There was nothing he could fight against.

"What are you thinking?" said a voice. It was the Saggitayria.

"That this forest is going to kill and there's nothing I can do about it."

"Oh? Now that's progress." He smiled. "I was starting to worry none of you would ever come around."

He had lived here for twenty years. He knew what he was talking about.

"Things in this forest die," said Buckthorn. "If you come here, you should expect that and stop trying to fight it. Anything that's weak here dies; anything that's strong survives if it doesn't get caught tangled up thinking it needs to protect the weak. If you want to live, the first step is to stop putting yourself in harm's way."

Wing had tried to talk to Bluejay. Why had he done that? Bluejay was an assassin. Wing should have known that trying to talk to him was useless.

Buckthorn's tone was comforting. "I know it's hard to let go of after being taught differently for all these years, but that's the way it has to be. It'll take some getting used to, but I think you've got a head start now. Do you think you're starting to understand?"

She nodded.

"Good. Now, where were you all trying to go?"

"After Radar."

"That's no good. He was going a long way into this forest, and he's much stronger and smarter here than most of you. If you want to live, you have to turn back."

"We have to find out how he kept his slave trade."

"Why is that your job?"

"It..."

There was suddenly no good answer. What was she doing here? They were not even half a moon into this forest and they had already lost Wing. And almost lost Taz. And if they were trying so hard to end Radar's slave trade, why had they diverted for a day and a half to chase Phoenix? He had left on his own. He had freed them to keep going, because he knew he was weak and that the weak didn't survive here. He had known he would just drag them down. But even after he had chosen to die, they had stayed with him and coaxed him back again. In doing so they had stalled long enough for Bluejay to catch up with them. If it hadn't been for Phoenix, Wing wouldn't have died.

"See? You're catching on." Buckthorn was truly smiling now. He looked pleased, even proud of her. He edged closer to her and leaned right in, murmuring, "This is a mess right now. How about we talk a little ways away?"

It was a mess. Loud and violent, and so unfounded. Sethral got up mutely and followed him away on the second canopy. Here, green light with no point source made shadows around the trees. It was much calmer. Peaceful.

Buckthorn turned to face her with a rippling body that spoke everything about his strength. He knew how to survive here. "Now. I'm glad I've got you, because I wasn't sure I was going to be able to get through to any of you. We've got to turn this journey around. You have nothing to gain from chasing after Radar, and most of you probably aren't going to survive it. And I want to get back to the Lowlands and the Far South Forest."

Maybe it was because it was the first time he had stated his motives, and because a large part of her still didn't trust him, even if he was right. But something about that statement felt out of place.

Sethral glanced up at him. "Why don't you just go, then?"

And for a moment, he fumbled. He recovered poorly. "I, well, you're all so young..." The statement was going a different direction and he turned it around again. "It would be a shame for you all to die out here. You deserve better."

"I thought you didn't care what happened to others." Sethral lifted her head. She felt like a fog was backing off again. "You only care about yourself."

His eyes darted and he licked his lips nervously. "You're not understanding. If we all go as a group, that's the best protection, right? More creatures means more creatures for predators to pick off first. Weakest first, and the strong make it back. You're strong. If we all go together, you'll have a chance to live."

"And why do you suddenly care about me?"

He lunged suddenly, and before Sethral could dodge, he had her back pressed to his chest with one of her own knives at her throat. "Let's talk this out," he said to the creatures who had suddenly surrounded him.

"I'm done talking to creatures who talk like my clan," said Ryatzi. "You only wanted to come with us so you could use us as a shield."

Silversand had her gauntlet on. Whipper was latched onto Firebrand's back with his face buried in her fur, but he wasn't fighting. Aside from Phoenix, Taz and Dusk, everyone was here. They were here for her. They were going to protect her. The knife pressed harder as she started to shiver. The fog was clearing and a slow horror crept up in its wake. What had Buckthorn been talking her into? And how had she been listening? She had agreed with him. She had thought for a moment like Ryatzi's clan, that her own life mattered enough to overshadow all other things, that those who protected others were weak, that the weak deserved to die.

She had thought Phoenix deserved to die.

"Sethral, this isn't your fault," said Ryatzi. "You're in shock and he's taking advantage of you."

"She agreed with me," said Buckthorn.

"Maybe. What counts is what someone actually chooses to do, not what they think when they're scared. Sethral, good job standing up to him. Buckthorn, let her go and we'll let you go. Now."

The blade was so tight against her throat now, she could feel a drop of blood running through her fur. "Hear me out," said Buckthorn.

The next moment his body went slack. The knife slipped from his claw and he crumpled to the ground. Dusk stood behind him, tails still upraised. The world was buzzing. Firebrand's scent wrapped her up, and Sethral felt herself being carried swiftly away, back to a spot that smelled like all the renegades, and like Taz and Phoenix, and sounded like Halo running anxious, twittering laps. Sethral was set down gently, tucked close against Firebrand's chest. Halo was attempting to groom all of her fur at once.

Wing was dead.

"I want to go home," said Sethral, and it came out in a whimper. "Fibes, I want to go home."

"We are home," murmured Firebrand. "We don't have a home anymore. Our home is each other."

"I want Wing."

But Wing wasn't here, and he was never going to be here again. He was gone. She was never going to hear his voice, or hug him, or be hugged by him. She was never going to guide him over another boulder field, or get told by him to go to bed, or see the love in his eyes as he looked around at his family. She was never going to get chided in his characteristic gentle way, or see him blushing when she teased him about Jay, or watch him calm Whipper when the Forester was crying again. Now Whipper had lost Wing, too. And Ryatzi, Silversand and Loki had just lost Jay.

Jay was going to die. And not quickly, like Wing had. He was going to die the long, slow, excruciating death of a bonded Coppertail whose bondmate was taken; he was going to waste away on the other side of the world, once again alone. And none of them would be there to ease the pain.

Firebrand was rocking her and she was crying, but she couldn't even feel the tears. She had never told Wing one last time that she loved him. She had hardly spoken to him since he had shut down. None of them had.

She had never said goodbye.

Chapter 14

Dusk, Ryatzi and Silversand never told Sethral what they had done to Buckthorn, and Sethral didn't ask. She just knew that Ryatzi had not been lying when he had ordered Buckthorn to let her go if he wanted to be let go, and that when Halo led them to a fallen tree and from there to a stream to drink, Silversand slipped away to wash her metal claws. When they were done at the stream, they went back to the canopy. Halo bounced about scuffing out their trail as they walked until Phoenix collapsed, which wasn't far. Taz found a secure dip in the ground and let the Pyrya cuddle up to   him again.

"I'll keep watch," said Silversand.

"Will you be watching?" said Loki. "You can't stop crying."

"I need something to do so I won't cry all the time!" Silversand burst into tears. "I don't see how you're not crying. Why are you getting mad at me?"

"I'm trying not to cry as well, okay? But not all of us dissolve into waterworks when we're still petrified of danger out in the forest."

"Guys," said Ryatzi.

"I'll take watch," said Loki.

"You can't just take it over from me like that!"

"You can both watch," said Fletch.

"He's saying I'm not good at watching," sobbed Silversand. "But I tried all of our year apart to be better, and I don't want to feel like I'm useless again."

"You're not useless, Silver."

"But I let Bluejay sneak up on us. I couldn't warn Wing."

"Silver, nobody could," said Taz shortly. "Stop putting the blame on yourself, watch if you're going to, and go hunt if you're not."

"Now you don't want me here either!"

Taz started to get up, but Phoenix grabbed him and started crying. He lay down again. Sethral pulled out her thistlecloth, but Phoenix screamed when touched and instantly devolved into a panic attack.

"Don't worry, Seth," said Taz quickly. "It's not you; it's everyone."

It was too late. Tears blurred her eyes as a scene replayed: the fear in Phoenix's eyes as he told the twins in every nonverbal way not to touch him. She should have known.

Taz had curled around the Pyrya and was trying to get him to breathe, but it was like something as sitting on Phoenix's chest. He couldn't move, and even the crying stopped as he struggled harder and harder to get air. Even Ryatzi didn't get attacks this bad. Silversand was curled up under another tree, sobbing. Loki was stone-faced, sitting on watch. Sethral's heart stopped dead. There was a Coppertail walking towards them through the forest.

She scrabbled for a knife, a stick; anything. The shadow was shorter than Firebrand but taller than Taz, and it moved with the steady footing of a killer. Sethral tried to scream, but her voice had frozen. Before her shaking claws could land on a weapon, the outline resolved itself into Dusk. He set a moth down beside Taz and left again.

There was a scream from across their camp as Whipper woke up. Sethral couldn't even move her legs. She willed someone, anyone, to intervene if the Forester started pummelling Firebrand again, but this wasn't one of those times. Whipper broke down and just wanted to be hugged instead.

"I want to go home," he said, over and over. "I want Wing. I want to go home."

It was too much. Hearing him say it was like standing in an echo-cave, sending her back the message in her own mind stronger and louder, until she couldn't take it anymore. Sethral started to cry again. She wanted to go home, but then it got tangled and 'home' meant the South Forest, not the Far South, and then having Wing became a necessary condition. Wing made a place 'home'. And the more she thought about it, the more she realized Jay did, too. How long had she thought this way? Even half a year ago, 'home' had still meant her clan.

Something moved in the forest again. Sethral's claw flew to her knife. It wasn't Dusk this time; it was too small. Before Sethral could move, Silversand had leaped to stand between it and Phoenix. The shadow kept flitting closer. It was too small to be a white Watermouse. Or maybe it was a small one. Whipper had gone deathly silent, clinging to Firebrand's back, and the Leslander and everyone else had joined Silversand. Sethral didn't remember seeing most of them move. She still couldn't make her legs get up. Silversand moved to protect her too.

It was a white Watermouse, but it got smaller the closer it came. It couldn't have been more than an older child.

'It's alone,' flicked Loki.

They stayed tense and silent as the creature reached the last tree and edged around it to face them, keeping the trunk at her back. She had something hugged to her chest. Sethral heard Firebrand gasp; it was her bag from Benty. Dusk had been unable to retrieve it when they had escaped from the canyon. He had not been able to find it.

Taz broke the silence. "Liebling?"

The white Watermouse that had stowed away on Watersinger hugged Firebrand's bag tighter. Then she dashed forwards, thrust it into Firebrand's paws and shot away up the tree. She was swallowed by the hazy shadows. With shaking paws and tail, Firebrand opened the bag. Everything was there, though her notebook looked more battered than Sethral had last seen it. She repacked the bag and slung it on again. "We need to go."

"No luck, Fibes," said Taz. Phoenix was limp against his side. The attack was over, but the Pyrya had been left so exhausted, Sethral could hardly see his breathing.

Firebrand looked ready to stamp the ground, but she probably knew that wouldn't get her anywhere. "Fine," she said. "Silver and Loki, stay on watch. If more follow her trail, we run." She lay back down and pulled out the notebook again. There was a leaf sticking from it midway through. Firebrand opened it to the spot and went still. She began to flip through the pages.

"Shelha," said Fletch.

This time, Sethral managed to convince herself to her paws. She joined them over the notebook. Partway through it, long ago, Firebrand had started a registry of sketches of edible things, a way of cataloguing jungle life for Benty while preserving the memories of what they had found by trial and error to be safe. When they had gone into the canyon, the sketches had covered a scant three pages. They now covered twenty-five.

"I've seen that before," exclaimed Fletch, pointing to one.

"These are beautiful," said Firebrand. She turned back the pages slowly. Each drawing was a minute masterpiece of delicate linework and perfect shading. Firebrand glanced at the forest again, then pulled out a jar and a small brush. The sketches had to be glossed to preserve them, each one painted over as lightly as possible, then held in a breeze and kept from touching anything while the gloss dried. Creatures took turns blowing on the pages.

Fletch was going through the bag again when he gave a cry. "Fibes, she had your haunting-whistle, too!"

Tucked in an inside pocket of the bag was the bone tube, its string wrapped neatly around it. Sethral fished it out for the Leslander. Its string had been retied with knots that slid when pulled, allowing the necklace to be adjusted. Firebrand dipped her head and Sethral slipped it back around her neck. They tightened it together.

"Shelha, we owe that little twerp," said Taz.

Fletch was taking a turn looking through the sketches. "She probably doesn't think so. These must have taken the entire time we were locked up."

"She probably felt like she owed us," said Silversand.

"So she was expecting us to get out?" said Taz skeptically.

"Who wouldn't, knowing us." Fletch shut the notebook. "Let's be honest here. We don't know when to give up."

"Wait, give me that." Firebrand grabbed the book again. She riffled through the pages. "I saw something right when you shut it. What in..."

She let the sentence hang unfinished and laid the notebook out in front of her. Tucked in amongst the back pages was another sketch, but this one wasn't a plant. Parallel lines snaked across the page. Short lines bridged them twice, marking off a section. In the corner of the page was a tiny, elongated x.

Firebrand flipped the page and everyone gasped. Taking up the full back of it was a beautifully rendered drawing of a ship. Sleeker than Watersinger, it had a sail patterned with what could only be a star map: small white points on a background just a shade lighter than black. Some of the constellations were even recognizable. There was only one ship in Simbra's registry that had had a night-sky sail.

"Salisetta?" said Sethral.

"And I think this is a map," said Firebrand, turning back to the previous page.

"What are the lines, then?" said Fletch.

"The canyon," said Sethral. She wasn't sure how she knew. Maybe their shape was familiar after so many days gazing up at the slot in the stone from below.

Firebrand tapped the part of the canyon blocked off by the shorter line segments. "This would be the colony, then. With the walls that Saggitayria mentioned at either end of it. I'm assuming the X represents the ship. But which way is it?"

"Well, I'll assume we can trust her drawing skills," said Loki. "It looks like she was really particular about the shape of the canyon. Maybe we can compare this to the real thing?"

Sethral closed her eyes. She could see the shape of the slot canyon in her mind, but the harder she thought about it, the less confident she was. "Where's Dusk?"

"Why?" said Loki.

"Because he's a Painter's Mind. He sometimes remembers things like he's seeing them again; that's how he identified Radar's Copper-tail vertebra. He says he can't do it voluntarily and it doesn't happen often, but he might remember the canyon."

She jumped in her skin as Dusk appeared behind her. He barely scanned the map, and flicked his tail at the forest. 'That way.'

"You remember!"

She got a dirty look. 'I always remember rocks.' He left another moth beside Taz and returned to the forest.

"I guess we all remember our home landscapes best," said Fire-brand quietly.

'He's still pretty mad at you, hey?' flicked Loki so only Sethral could see. 'Is this still about the Phoenix thing?'

'I don't want to talk about it.'

'Sorry.'

He meant the apology, but the reminder made the pain cut that much deeper. She would not be surprised if Dusk never forgave her for driving Phoenix away. She wanted to apologize to Phoenix, at least, but he had a long way to go before he was in any mental state to take it. Taz was teaching him to communicate his needs through Long Night taps, but they were starting from scratch. Compared to Phoenix, Jay had come into the renegades fully functional. Sethral didn't know what Taz could read in the Pyrya's body language, being that close. But after a rough day just out of the canyon, when Phoenix had cried at every touch and eventually fallen asleep exhausted, Taz had told the renegades he didn't think the Pyrya had ever been groomed before.

The others were still arguing over the map. Sethral got up and left the circle. Loki stopped Firebrand's attempt to stop her. He knew when she needed to be alone.

Unless they needed enough water to wash in, they didn't go back to the ground. Halo made them move every day, but they never went far. Sethral wondered how much energy Dusk had given Phoenix just to get him out of the canyon. The Pyrya remained fragile and so tightly glued to Taz, it was days before the Rocklander could leave to get a drink on his own. If left alone, Phoenix would panic.

Whipper never left Firebrand's back except when she went hunting, and then he didn't leave Fletch. He kept crying for days that he wanted to go home, that he didn't want to keep going. That eventually stopped. It must have sunk in that with Bluejay behind them, likely gone back to the South Forest, they had nowhere else to go.

Somewhere around the ninth or tenth day, Fletch returned from a foraging trip in a flurry of nerves. "Um, guys? Has nobody been paying attention to which way Halo's been moving us?"

"You're the one with the directional instinct," said Loki.

Firebrand was on her paws, immediately tense. "Why?"

Fletch beckoned all of them back the way he had come, then hesitated. "Actually, Taffles, you should probably stay here with Pheo and a guard. Or two."

Silversand planted herself on the ground. Ryatzi lay down, and Dusk was still off in the forest somewhere. Everyone else followed Fletch. He traced a winding path as the vine floor beneath their paws grew thinner and less reliable.

Firebrand stopped and frowned behind them. "Why does it look stretched?"

"What does?" said Loki.

"The vines. Look." She turned his head slightly with the tip of her tail.

Sethral mimicked the angle. Stretching away into the distance, the vine floor had taken on a directionality it had not possessed before, like some giant claw had pulled it towards the south. Sethral lifted a vine beneath her paws that matched the pattern. There was old scarring where it and the one beneath it met. She let it snap back into place. "Loki, which way is the canyon?"

He pointed back the way they had come. "We crossed it two days ago."

Two days ago would be several hundred tail-lengths. "I'll bet it was a flood."

They all stared at her.

"This high?" said Loki. "But it'd be going the wrong way, then. The river flows from the south. Floods don't move upstream."

Sethral shrugged. "Tell me anything else that can drag vines away from the river like this."

"That would explain what I found, at least," said Fletch. He led them a short ways further, then took a deep breath and closed his eyes. "Look up."

They did, and gasped.

Above them, suspended in vines, was a ship's mast. It was shattered at the base and at the top, just above the crossbar. The sail had been reduced to scraps of dark rag. Sethral grabbed a vine running down beside her and yanked it. More matted the airspace all the way up to the mast. She hauled herself up and started climbing. The mast, when she reached it, was more than twice the size of Watersinger's. Sethral wrapped her arms around it. Her claws did not meet on the other side. She sank them into the slimy wood. The angle was shallow enough to walk up, provided she went slowly to avoid losing traction. She reached the crossbar—itself as thick as Watersinger's mast—and edged out along it. The first sail scrap looked torn and waterlogged. Even beneath a growing colony of mosses, its colour was unmistakable. A white dot near its tip was not left by the jungle.

Chapter 15

A thorough investigation yielded nothing. There were no scars on the mast like there had been on the logbook box. Sethral wondered if the ship had lost the mast first and gotten stranded, easy prey for predators. What a horrible way to die. Suddenly struggling not to think about Bluejay again, Sethral pulled out one of her knives and carefully cut the sail scrap free. She nearly jumped back to the others, but remembered that she did not have wings to glide herself down. Shaking from the near miss, she descended the vines. She didn't need to say anything.

"Where's the rest of it, then?" said Firebrand.

"Shelha, Fibes," said Loki. "If just the mast is in this state, the rest of the ship is long gone. It's in pieces at the bottom of a river somewhere."

Sethral folded the sail scrap and passed it to the Leslander. Firebrand took it and kicked a vine. "I was hoping we'd be able to figure out how the crew died. Was there any sign of what might have killed them?"

"That was ambitious to start with," said Loki.

"No," said Sethral.

"We need to follow the river upstream, then," said Firebrand.

"The ship's gone, Fibes," said Loki. "Wood rots like paper in water this warm, and there are wood-eating worms here, too."

"I know. But before it was destroyed, the crew found Thaliar's Tree. If that mast came in on this river, the tree and where the crew was last seen is somewhere upstream."

"Firebrand," said Fletch. He rarely used her full name. "Don't you think you're getting a bit too wrapped up with Salisetta? We came here to find where Radar hid a body, not to chase a ship. I'm sorry, but solving the slave trade is far, far more important than this."

"But what if Radar went to the same place?" said Firebrand. "Then following the ship could keep us alive and take us where we need to go. Taz confirmed once already that Salisetta and Radar went the same way, and they still were when he passed this canyon. Radar left that asshole Saggitayria here, remember?"

"Did anyone ask him which way Radar went from there?"

Sethral gasped. "Fibes, get out your notebook. The map."

Firebrand obliged. Sethral blocked off all but the colony's section of the canyon with leaves to keep anything from swaying her judgement. She had asked Buckthorn which way Radar had gone. He had mocked her as an answer, pointing off into the pitch darkness knowing she couldn't see, but she remembered which wing he had used to point. She had heard it lift. He had been pointing at an angle towards the canyon wall.

Finding where, roughly, the cage line had been on the map, Sethral shut her eyes and oriented herself like she was back in her cage. She broke off a leaf stem and laid it on the map in the direction Buckthorn had pointed. Then she swept away the leaves.

Just upstream of the canyon colony, the river curved the exact same way her stem was pointing.

"So he was following the river," said Firebrand, and looked pointedly at Fletch.

Fletch picked up the notebook and snapped it shut. "Then we're following the river. But if we get so much as a whiff of whatever monster attacked Salisetta, we are retreating and coming up with a better plan."

"I thought you wanted to find out what killed them, too."

"I wanted to end the slave trade first, and after that, I wanted to find the ship so we could use the evidence to figure it out."

"Are we going back to the others, then?" said Loki. "If we've seen everything here."

"If this is all that's here, how did Liebling know what the ship looked like?" said Sethral. "I don't think that colony even had a writing system. And that ship left years ago. I seriously doubt Liebling's that old, given how much she grew between when we found her and now."

"The colony creatures told stories, though," said Loki. "Didn't you see them? It looked like dancing."

"But this?" Sethral took the notebook from Fletch and turned to the drawing of the ship. "Look at the detail on it. How do you describe this with that little backwards-stepping thing they did?"

Loki shrugged. "How does Halo talk at all, then?"

Sethral frowned. "Okay, fair." The drawing of the ship only got more incredible the longer she looked. Its rigging was near-perfect, and even the individual boards of the hull were visible. "If that's the case, this is seriously impressive."

Fletch took back the notebook and put it in Firebrand's bag. "We're going."

They retraced their steps. Sethral ran into Coppertail legs as Firebrand and Fletch pulled up short. They were back at the spot they had left the others, and it was empty.

Sethral couldn't move. Horrible scenes played across her mind: Bluejay returning, white Watermice with bows aimed at the group, an unknown predator with giant claws. She forced herself to look over the area again. There was no blood. She took a deep breath. There were no smells besides those of the renegades, so they had either left on their own or with Forestair assistance. Fletch and Firebrand were murmuring to each other. Fletch flicked towards the south. Taz must be okay. Then both Coppertails dropped their noses and searched the area.

"They covered their paws," said Firebrand at last. "But why? Dusk came back and nobody smells scared."

There was a chirr behind them.

"Halo!" said Loki. "Where are the others?"

She trotted a short distance and looked over her shoulder. They followed. After a couple hundred tail-lengths, Sethral began to smell the other renegades again. Then she could see them, clustered around a tree far ahead with Taz keeping watch off to the side. He got up and touched noses with Fletch when they arrived.

"There was a white Watermouse patrol about to pass us," he said in an undertone. "Halo didn't tell us until after; she just said she had found food so we would follow her away. But she also found food."

Phoenix lay at the base of a giant tree, watching it intently with his tail flicking like a hunter's. Silversand, Ryatzi, Whipper and Dusk all hopped and pounced around the trunk. Up the bark marched a fleet of alien-looking insects. They had hooked front legs and large, glassy eyes. Each was the size of the crabs that had flooded the renegades the night they had slept behind a waterfall back at the start of their journey. Silversand snatched one out from under Ryatzi's nose as he went to catch it. He startled violently, then tackled her.

"Keep it down, guys," said Taz.

"Sorry!"

Ryatzi smiled as he noticed the rest of them. "Hey Seth! You gotten over your aversion to giant bugs yet?"

"That happened a long time ago, buster." Sethral marched up to the trunk, snatched a bug and popped it in her mouth. It was a full bite in itself, and its surprisingly thin shell crumpled like paper. It tasted like the maggots from back in the canyon colony, but then again, most bugs did.

A particularly large bug escaped Phoenix, who was trying not to get up. Whipper snatched it and held it out. Phoenix just looked at him.

"It's for you," said Whipper. "I'm giving it to you."

Cautiously, the Pyrya took the offering.

"Good job, Whip," whispered Taz.

Dusk blocked part of the trunk with an enormous, glossy leaf in an attempt to funnel bugs towards Phoenix. Some cooperated, but most clustered under the blockage, trying to get over it. Dusk ran his tails through them and they tumbled to the ground. He piled them beside Phoenix.

"Wait, that works on bugs, too?" said Sethral.

Dusk poked the bug she was reaching for. It went limp and fell off the trunk. He added it to Phoenix's pile.

The march of bugs was inexhaustible. Everyone who could eat them stuffed themselves, then sat back and watched in amazement as the bugs just kept coming. Ryatzi yawned and started grooming. Phoenix looked at his paws. He was more transparent in his body language than Dusk, and that was saying something.

"You can ask, Pheo," said Taz. "You just have to look at me, remember? And I'll come right over."

Phoenix's gaze darted up, but he flinched and dropped it again before it met Taz's face. Taz sighed and came over. Phoenix flinched again when touched, but when Taz lay down and started grooming him, he shrank in close like he was starved for physical touch.

'He never asks,' flicked Fletch, concerned.

Sethral jumped as something twitched her satchel strap. Dusk had opened her bag, retrieved her thistlecloth and closed the flap again without her noticing. He fastened the toggle and stopped in front of the pair.

"Do you want the blanket?" said Taz. He got an affirmative tap. Dusk dropped the thistlecloth and caught it by the corner so it unravelled. He helped pull it over Phoenix.

'Aren't you hot?' flicked Fletch to his brother.

'No. He absorbs it all. He's freezing.' Taz switched to speaking and asked Phoenix, "What else do you need?"

Phoenix scrunched closer.

"It's okay," said Taz. "If you tell me, we can get it for you. It's not a problem."

He got a tap.

"Fofo, he's hurting."

Sethral handed Fletch her bag. If Pyrya retained their Dustlander traits, Phoenix was immune to many poisons, but it seemed to make painkillers wear off faster, too. And with his body still damaged from the Moonworms, it got worse after he ate.

"What else do you need?" said Taz. This time Phoenix hesitated for so long, Taz was about to ask again when the tap finally came. It was the smallest touch Phoenix could give and still be felt at all.

Taz's eyes widened. "Dusk, he wants you."

Phoenix hid his face in the blanket. He started to shiver as Dusk made his way towards them again. Dusk rested his muzzle on his forehead through the blanket—they could touch if it was between them—and murmured something, then lay down on Phoenix's blanketed side. Phoenix switched from Taz to him.

It was hard to say who was the most stunned. Fletch had his paw on the herbs he was folding into a pellet. He seemed to have forgotten about them. Taz hadn't realized he could get up now. Dusk flicked to Fletch, who hastily finished his task. Phoenix took the herbs straight from Dusk's teeth. Then he snuggled down and went to sleep. Dusk finished tucking the blanket over him.

Firebrand broke the silence. "I'm sorry, what just happened?"

"Exactly what you just saw, Fibes," said Taz weakly.

"I didn't know he trusted any of us this much."

"You haven't noticed the special treatment Dusk's been getting? This isn't new. I just didn't think it had gone this far already."

Sethral ran a mental list of all the times she had ever seen Phoenix picking on Dusk. She came up with a total of one.

Firebrand frowned. "That's true. Dusk, you're literally the only one I have never seen him hiss at. Like, ever. Well, there was the one time he hit you, but you'd barely met and I'm pretty sure he was panicking."

"Yeah, that was my fault," said Dusk. "And he felt awful after."

"He talks to you?" said Sethral.

"He doesn't need to. Have you ever just watched him?"

It was hard to admit, even to herself. She did watch Phoenix, but she had always ignored his signals.

Dusk put his head down. "I'm tired. If the rest of you want to keep talking, go somewhere else."

Phoenix was so calm the next morning, it was hard to tell he was even awake until Halo returned with a moth and Dusk passed it to him. The bugs swarming up the tree had disappeared overnight. Phoenix let himself be fed, then drifted off to sleep and stayed that way until midafternoon. Then he ate again and went back to sleep. Nobody drew the parallel Sethral knew they were all thinking of. Jay had responded exactly like this when he had first let Wing take care of him.

It was incredible how well Dusk could already read the Pyrya. He still made Phoenix tap for things for the practice, but if Phoenix was too tired, he'd just call those things himself. The requests ranged from food to a bathroom break to a block from the sun to a safer nest. Taz had never taught Phoenix words for half of them, but Dusk was always right. Moving on a daily basis went from a nerve-wracking ordeal to a non-issue. The hardest part of travel became keeping Phoenix awake for the duration of it. He slept for all but a sun's paw-length of each day, though Sethral often heard Dusk talking to him at night.

Sethral returned from the forest with a moth just in time to see Phoenix go limp again. Dusk stopped Firebrand, who had been grooming him.

"He's asleep," she said. "He won't know."

"Exactly."

She sat back. "Why didn't you do this earlier? Like, before he got sick."

"Because I didn't have his permission."

"Seriously? It's only that?"

"Yes," said Dusk, and curled up again.

Firebrand wasn't done yet. "Why don't you treat anyone else like that, then?"

"There's a reason, and I'm not going to tell you until everyone's here."

"Sethral, go find Silversand."

The cat had been missing since that morning. Since they had gotten the news about Wing, it had been normal for at least one renegade to be off in the forest alone at any given time.

"I don't need to," said Sethral.

Silversand was walking towards them through the forest. She looked like she'd been crying, but she wasn't anymore. She dropped a moth beside Dusk. "Why do you need to find me?"

Dusk was glaring at Firebrand, but the renegades were all here now for the first time in days. He checked that Phoenix was asleep. "Fine. Silver, Firebrand here asked why I make everyone get permission to touch Phoenix. Three things." He pulled the blanket's edge over Phoenix's head as the midmorning sawblade insect started up in the canopy above. "One: he's more sensitive than any of you except Whipper, so he startles really, really easily and that usually leads to a panic attack due to number two. He's got night vision like mine, he can feel an ant walking across the tips of his fur, and Whipper, you and him react to the same sounds. He also hides his nose every time one of you comes back smelling funny, so I'm willing to bet his sense of smell is pretty good, too."

All of that made sense for a nocturnal creature who hunted bugs in the quietest desert in the world. Phoenix's nose was in the blanket now; he had fallen asleep that way. Sethral sniffed the air surreptitiously. Ryatzi had tripped on a patch of off-scented flowers while hunting that morning. It still showed.

"Two," said Dusk. "He's been beaten up by Coppertails before, so that's his association with us. Other species haven't been much better, as you probably noticed at Linderward, and it hasn't just been in the south. Leading to number three." He pulled up the blanket's edge and used it to brush back Phoenix's fur. "Firebrand, permission is everything when someone's done this to you."

Across Phoenix's stomach was a scar as thick as two of Sethral's fingers and as long as her forearm. It wasn't old; it was still pink and puckered. A wound like that should have been lethal.

"This is why he won't let any of you touch his stomach," said Dusk. "He doesn't want anyone but me to know about it, but for safety's sake, I have to betray him a little on this." He smoothed Phoenix's fur down again and replaced the blanket. "From what I can tell, before he came south, he had a run-in with Iris's mate—that's who Rain is, that she's always rambling about. Rain gave him that wound. But somehow Rain died; Feefs thinks it's his fault, but I seriously doubt it. He's not a fighter and Rain was way stronger than he is. Anyway, Iris thinks it was him, too, and she chases him for that. He's also got this from about the same time."

Wrapping his tails in the blanket again, he uncovered one of Phoenix's paws and parted the fur just above it. Across Phoenix's foreleg was a scar from a knife cut, right across a vein. Dusk extended his own paw to reveal an identical one.

Fletch jumped up. "But you got that from—" He sat down again with a bump. "Dear Shelha."

"Exactly," said Dusk. He covered Phoenix's paw again. "I got that from Winter."

Silversand squeaked. She swallowed hard and sat back, extending her foreleg. Just above the cut Loki had once given her was a second scar. The two were nearly identical.

"Dammit," said Firebrand.

"Silver, when did you get that?" said Sethral.

"When she caught me. She was going to kill me after, but then she got the idea to use me as bait for the rest of you instead. I thought she was just going to use my blood for that."

"She took blood?" said Sethral.

Silversand nodded.

"What's up, Fibes?" said Taz.

Firebrand also had her gaze down. "I'm sorry, guys. Especially you, Taz. I never actually told you the truth about why I had to leave the army."

"What do you mean?" said Taz.

"Yeah, you were ranking pretty high up before you quit, weren't you?" said Sethral.

"I was. Winter didn't want to kill me because I had 'promise' as an official, but I couldn't stay after this happened." She extended her paw and revealed a scar just like the others. "I faked my name in the army back then. To Winter, at least. I was going by Rosethorn."

Chapter 16

Sethral shut her eyes against a horrible, sinking feeling. "Okay, I need to process this for a h e a r t - beat."

Dusk had just revealed more about Phoenix in a hundred heart-beats than she had known about him, total, and now the thought of him under Winter's paws made her sick. Firebrand was Rosethorn, the Leslander Wing had once seen chased by Winter's Drakons like Tornado had been. The renegades had at least five of 'them'.

"How many of her target creatures has she caught now, then?" she said. "That's four here, plus her first one—that was an Eastyren, right? I think that's what Bracken said. Then that Basilix that Whipper tried to save, too, and Naja-whoever's sister down in that place Whip and Loki got stuck together. That's seven. We know she's after Ratty, Tornado and Oakleaf, and she hasn't caught any of them yet. Seven of ten. Drakon shit, guys. We're losing this. We're losing badly. And we don't even know why she wants them yet."

"Well, she doesn't want us to have them," said Firebrand. "She's killed or tried to kill every single one of us after we got caught. The Eastyren's dead, and so are the Basilix and Naja's sister. Winter tried to kill me, tried to kill Dusk, was going to kill Silver, and..." She trailed off.

"Yeah, what about Phoenix?" said Loki.

Fletch seemed to have come to the same realization Sethral had, and Dusk looked like he already knew. Fletch's face creased. "The scars are the same age, Loki."

"I bet he got the wound on his stomach first," said Sethral. "Winter probably found him then, got what she needed and left him to die."

Dusk curled tighter around the sleeping Pyrya.

"But he didn't die," said Silversand.

"Yeah, what's with that?" said Firebrand. "An injury like that should have killed him. Dusk, has he told you that yet?"

"He hasn't 'told' me anything. I just figure out what he wants to tell me, then ask him questions and gauge the response. And no, I don't know how he survived. As far as I can tell, he doesn't know either."

"What about why he came south?" said Sethral. "If Winter caught him and Iris came here, he'd need a really good reason to follow them. Especially if the creeping winter hasn't hit his homeland yet."

"Same goes," said Dusk.

"What, he doesn't remember?"

"If he does, he's faking it really well, and one of those two is a far more likely option."

Sethral wiped her face with both claws. "So he doesn't remember. Maybe whoever saved him brought him here."

"But who else do we know who's come south?" said Taz. "Who else friendly, that is."

"Wasn't me," said Dusk.

"Dusk, what's the age of the scars?" said Fletch.

"Hm? I'd guess he got hurt over a year ago. Probably closer to a year and a half. It took a long time to heal."

"So it couldn't have been Jay, could it? He was out in the Western District by then."

"Yeah, Pheo wouldn't have survived out there. And it doesn't look like Jay's work. It was stitched."

"Since when are you a healer?" said Sethral.

Dusk raised an eyebrow. "You learn things when you're on your second war by my age."

"Your second—"

They were all staring at him now. All of them except Whipper.

Dusk groaned. "Whipper, you didn't tell them?"

There was a muffled, "I didn't have your permission," from Firebrand's shoulder.

Dusk put his forehead on his paws. "I fought in the North War. As a rebel."

Sethral leaped to her paws. "So you know what happened!"

"Winter tried to take over the northlands, pushed us into the mountains and accidentally set off a landslide that killed half her army and most of ours." He lifted his head again. "It should go on the record that I'm as petrified of landquakes and landslides as Jay is. Shelha, Whip, you didn't tell them anything?"

"You can tell them yourself."

Dusk swore under his breath, but it wasn't at Whipper. "Well, long story short, I'm bonded to the now-dead, quickly-revealed-to-be-asshole Coppertail who picked me up after that, I've betrayed more herds than Sethral's eaten bugs, and Whitewings and the creeping winter chased me south. So here I am."

"You're bonded?" said Fletch.

"I really don't want to talk about it."

"Shelha, Dusk, you're the healthiest broken-bond Coppertail I have seen in my life."

"Spite works wonders. He destroyed me once; I wasn't about to let him do it again."

"That's commitment," said Taz.

"You're incredible," said Fletch.

Dusk didn't look like he agreed much. "Thanks?" he said half-heartedly. "You really don't want to know what I did when I was messed up after that. Picture what I did to you guys, only following through, over and over and over again."

Whipper jumped to Dusk's back and hugged him. "I told you to tell them yourself, not beat yourself up again."

"I still don't deserve this."

Taz pointed. "Look at what you've got cuddled against you and I dare you to say that again."

Dusk glanced at Phoenix. "I don't deserve this either. I'm only not moving because he doesn't want me to."

"He trusts you."

"When the competition is Winter and Iris, that doesn't say much."

"Drakon shit, Dusk!" Taz stamped a paw. "Your competition is us! It's been me! You've fed him, stuck up for him when he didn't reciprocate, protected him, talked him back when he wanted to die, single-handedly freed him from that canyon colony, told us all off for doing things that were making his life worse, figured out what would make it better and taught us that, too, and now you're asking why he trusts you? You're not giving him credit, let alone yourself!"

Dusk hadn't moved his gaze from Phoenix. His eyes were getting damp.

"I told you," said Whipper into his fur.

Dusk took a shaky breath and curled up again. Disturbed by the motion, Phoenix nestled closer. He was still asleep.

"You would probably beat me in a fight," said Taz, "but if you want a stubbornness contest, try me." He turned away. "So? What's our plan?"

He was changing the subject. It was the first time someone had brought this up since they had learned about Wing's death, and everyone looked away. Sethral could tell the pain was still fresh for Taz, too, but he wasn't backing down. "I'm not going away until you guys talk to me."

"I want to keep going," said Ryatzi.

Silversand looked at the ground.

"I'm with Ratty," said Sethral.

"I know Phoenix doesn't care as long as he's with us," said Taz. "I'm in."

"Me too," said Fletch.

They went around the circle until it was down to Whipper, Dusk and Silversand.

"Dusk?" said Fletch. He got a limp but affirmative flick.

"Whipper?" said Firebrand.

Whipper had burrowed himself into Dusk's fur. He squeezed his paws and hid his face.

"Do we take a Coppertail yes from him?" said Firebrand.

"Yes," said Sethral.

All eyes turned to Silversand.

"Can we do this for Wing?" she said.

It was a sharp, hard ache. Sethral scrubbed her eyes, but the wetness she removed was already replaced. Most creatures didn't even bother to hide their tears.

"Yes," said Fletch.

"So we leave as soon as Phoenix is fit to," said Firebrand. "Dusk, any guesses how long that might be?"

There was no response. The Nightlock had fallen asleep.

Firebrand sighed. "I guess a broken bond explains why he's so tired all the time. Halo, are there any good hunting spots around here?"

Halo was making too-high-to-hear calls into the forest. She took a stance that Ryatzi translated into a direction, then went back to whatever conversation she was having. Phoenix twitched in discomfort. The kit glanced at him, chirred, and ran off. Sethral wondered if the second canopy was always this empty, or if the Forestairs had been keeping it this way. She had not seen them since the night of the escape, but she had a feeling they were never far away. They didn't seem enslaved like Halo's kind were. She wondered if they were helping free their South Forest kin.

Phoenix woke that night screaming. The brief respite brought on by exhaustion was ending. Dusk avoided a panicked bite and gave him space. He bolted. Sethral passed Dusk her blanket.

"I'll be back," he said, and followed the Pyrya.

"'Doesn't deserve it' my tail," grumbled Taz.

"He's not scared of much, is he," said Loki. "Dusk, I mean."

"Will he be okay?" said Silversand worriedly.

"I wonder if he's formally battle-trained," said Sethral. "Hey Whip. You've spent more time with Dusk than the rest of us. Can he fight?"

"He's scary," said Whipper, muffled by someone's fur.

"Hm. And you only saw him injured, too."

"Go to sleep," said Firebrand with a groan. "You can all argue over each other's fighting prowess when we're walking tomorrow."

'How did you catch that?' flicked Sethral. She yelped as Silversand dropped a worm as thick as a sapling on her tail. 'Hey!'

Silversand ignored her. 'Who's hungry?'

The jungle's morning chorus made tail-talk a necessity: a cacophony of buzzes, chirps, clicks, taps, hoots, pops, groans, and humming drowned out all other sound. Ryatzi and Loki were up in heartbeats. Firebrand flick-grumbled something about not being a bird, but she would still partake. Sethral looked around automatically for Wing and was rammed in the throat. She put her head down again. Half a moon had done nothing to tame the deep, gut-wrenching pain that came whenever she thought about Wing or Jay, and she thought about them often.

The canyon colony was behind them now; they had started moving only a day after deciding they were going to, and that had now been days ago. Phoenix was back on his paws, though you wouldn't know it by looking at him. He wouldn't walk anywhere unless Dusk or Taz was beside him.

Silversand flicked back a paw-sized ant that was investigating her catch, then ducked a butterfly the size of a Lowland dinner plate. It swooped back, apparently confused by her gleaming fur. She stepped out of the light.

'Do you eat butterflies?' flicked Ryatzi to Phoenix, who was awake and watching the worm hungrily. Phoenix's nose crinkled. Sethral leaped as a beetle dropped onto her wing like a gleaming blue river pebble. She snatched it off and tossed it away. A tiny bird darted after it.

Phoenix pulled the blanket over his head and headbutted Dusk. The Nightlock stirred. It took him a few heartbeats to take in the situation, and he nuzzled Phoenix's head. He could do that now without permission. 'Just ask,' he flicked. 'She brought it for sharing.'

Phoenix looked at him, puzzled.

'Like Whipper shares food with everyone, or Taz, Fletch and I always swap what we find,' flicked Dusk. 'It makes sure everyone always gets something to eat, especially if any of us are too tired or sick to find it ourselves.'

Phoenix looked down at the vines. Dusk pulled the blanket off his head. 'Go ahead. Ask.'

Phoenix glanced cautiously at Silversand, who was now divvying up the worm into meal-sized chunks. It would be enough to feed all of them. Phoenix chirped, a Coppertail sound for requesting food. Almost automatically, Silversand passed him a chunk, then went back to swatting Ryatzi and Loki's paws off the rest.

'See?' flicked Dusk.

Phoenix looked up at him, then looked back at Silversand and chirped again. This time she looked up, confused. She smiled and passed him another chunk. He dropped it in front of Dusk and started tugging bites off his own.

Firebrand got her tail stepped on for the half-dozenth time. She grabbed two worm-chunks. 'Go run,' she flicked, and hurled them as far as she could. Ryatzi and Loki sprinted after them. Ryatzi won, of course, and attempted to grab both pieces before Loki dove at him. Silversand had washed off the slime, but they were still too jiggly to hold. The Saberel lost his grip and Loki absconded with the food. He was tackled. Neither of them was laughing—it was play for honing footing and reflexes, not for fun—but it would give them good exercise.

Sethral glanced up as Silversand dropped a worm chunk in front of her. Nobody gave her much choice about eating these days. The cat took the smallest piece and walked over to Firebrand. Whipper was faking sleep on the Leslander's back. He had been completely devoid of energy since the canyon colony, and had started to shut off at mealtimes like this. That didn't fly with Silversand, of course. She would sit with him until he finished whatever she had brought, whether that took a hundred heartbeats or half a day.

'You too,' flicked Fletch, poking Sethral.

Sethral dragged herself up and prodded the worm chunk half-heartedly. Dusk had already finished and gone back to sleep. Phoenix was still nibbling. She didn't understand how they could still find an appetite. They were carrying on life like nothing had changed since the journey's beginning. She pushed away the food and put her head down again.

'Either you eat, or we do your exercises first,' flicked Fletch.

Eating suddenly became much more appealing. Sethral worked through the food as slowly as she could. She wanted her wings back, but putting in the work to get them there was far from fun. She made her bites smaller and smaller as she neared the end of the worm chunk. Fletch got up and started undoing the straps on her wing.

'You said you'd let me eat!'

'And what you're doing now has crossed the line from 'eating' to 'stalling', so it no longer counts.' He tossed the last strap aside and checked to make sure none of them had been chafing. 'Alright, spread it out.'

'What, are you my parent now?' grumbled Sethral, and immediately wished she hadn't.

'Yes, I'm filling the role, given that Fibes, Taz and I are next in the age and maturity order by a long shot. Out. Okay, how is it feeling?'

Sethral kept her mouth shut and her tail under her paw for the rest of the exercises. Had Whipper seen her say that? And Silversand had disappeared when she hadn't been paying attention. Was she out hunting again, or crying because Sethral had just gone and let her stupid mouth run off about parents again?

Ryatzi and Loki bounded up, panting. Ryatzi dropped a moth in front of Phoenix and sprinted away again, Loki hot on his tail. Phoenix watched them go, then stared at the moth for a good thirty heartbeats. Then he looked back after the pair.

'It's for you,' flicked Fletch. 'They're not coming back for it.'

Phoenix glanced at him, then just stared at his paws.

Sethral ripped a leaf off the vine floor, rolled it into a pellet and threw it at Dusk. It bounced off his nose.

'What,' he groaned.

'Feed your protege.'

Dusk lifted his head. He saw the moth lying untouched in front of Phoenix and sighed. 'If they give food to you like that, it's for you unless they tell you to save it for someone else. And nobody else here eats moths.'

Phoenix put his paw on the moth and looked up questioningly.

'Yes, you can eat it,' flicked Dusk.

Phoenix nipped off the wings and finished the moth. Dusk put his head back down. Phoenix glanced at him, then looked at his paws again. Dusk's tails lifted, pulled the blanket over his head and pulled him down. Phoenix snuggled against him and went to sleep.

Sethral tensed as a slight vibration in the vines indicated someone was approaching.

'It's Loki and Ryatzi,' flicked Fletch with a yawn. 'And Taz.'

The trio came trotting back again with the look of creatures with news to tell. 'Hey guys,' flicked Loki, first in common tail-talk, then Lesland. 'Did anyone else realize the ground down there flooded last night?'

Sethral, Firebrand and Fletch all jumped up. Taz tossed his brother a packet of leaves and other edibles.

'There's a hole back that way,' flicked Ryatzi, nodding behind him. 'Come see.'

Chapter 17

The morning chorus had waned enough to hear each other by the time they reached the place in question. The hole was a fairly large one for the second canopy; large enough that Whipper could have crawled through had he wanted to. Sethral took her turn poking her head down it. When her eyes adjusted to the gloom of the understory, she saw what the others had: the ground was slick, smooth and shiny, still wet and dotted with puddles. Mud had gathered at the bases of the trees; The water had been flowing with and   out   from   the   river   they   were f   o   l   l   o   w   - ing.

She pulled her head back. "Who here's got the best night vision?"

"Probably me," said Firebrand when Whipper on her back failed to respond.

"See how high the water got."

"I was already going to." Firebrand took her turn at the hole and pulled back with an expression of amazement. "Right up the trees. It must have been half a tail-length below us."

"And we didn't even hear it?" said Taz. "We've got Phoenix with us! What if it had made it all the way up here?"

"I didn't realize the ground had dropped this much these last few days," said Loki. "That rainstorm we had last night wasn't any stronger than the one we got out of the canyon colony on."

"The canyon here is narrower, though," said Firebrand. "The water would have risen farther than it did there."

"That doesn't fully explain 'right up the trees' silently enough that we didn't even hear it. I grew up in a river. Trust me."

"Well? Who wants to go down and explore?"

Taz stared at her. "You're kidding, right?"

"I'm not. Salisetta disappeared what... four years ago? If it sank and this river floods often, we might find debris stranded in the forest. Like the mast was."

"And if it floods again while you're down there?"

"It won't," said Ryatzi. "We've already had our rainstorm for the day."

"There are days when we get two."

"You don't have to come," said Firebrand. "But I want to go down."

Whipper got up and jumped from her back to Fletch's, where he curled up and buried his face again.

"I'll go too if it makes you feel better," said Loki.

Taz eased up, but only a little. "Be careful, dammit. Fibes, no excuses if Loki hears the water coming."

Firebrand smirked. "Yes, mom. Oh... sorry, Seth."

Sethral turned away before they could see the tears that had sprung up. "Have fun. Tell me what you find." Before they could answer, she walked back towards the group's camp.

"Nice going, Fibes," she heard Taz say behind her.

The walk was enough to stop the breakdown before it began. The forest was quiet and peaceful, with scraps of sun from a top canopy a little thinner than it had been before. Most of the trees here had stilted roots, great rods angled down and out from their trunks. Some of the stilts were so enormous, they punctured through the second canopy floor and connected to their trees up to a tail-length above. Sethral wondered what kind of force it would take to knock one of those trees down.

Dusk was awake and glaring at her when she got back. "Thanks for the guard."

"We figured you or Fifi would wake up if anything happened, and you're capable of defending both of you."

"Wake up? He's been comatose since morning and I sleep like a rock. We all know that."

"I didn't know rocks could sleep. And no, you don't anymore. You woke up when I threw a leaf pellet at you earlier, remember?"

"Then I wasn't fully asleep."

"You were out for the count, Blackfluff. Twitching and every-thing."

Dusk snarled. "Do not call me that."

She had a comeback all lined up, but her mouth took over and said, "Sorry," before it came out.

Dusk let his hackles go down. He curled up and went back to sleep. Silversand was still nowhere to be seen. She probably had seen Sethral's comment that morning. Sethral knew she would have to apologize to the Royal too, now. She slumped down to keep watch.

The exploration team was gone for most of the afternoon. Phoenix did not sleep well for the latter half of the day, and when the others got back, Dusk flicked, 'He's hungry,' to Taz and 'Next round,' to Fletch. Taz left to find moths and Sethral handed Fletch her bag.

"So, did you find anything?" she said.

Firebrand put her tail to her lips. When Fletch waved them off, she beckoned Sethral out of earshot. Loki and Ryatzi joined them.

"No parts of the ship," said Firebrand. "But two things. One, the ground down there is littered with these." She passed Sethral a large nut, already open. The two halves swung on their natural hinge, revealing a heart-shaped space inside.

"Thaliar's Tree," said Sethral. "What's the second thing?"

"We found a trail."

"I don't even want to know what made it," said Loki.

"A trail like what?" said Sethral.

Firebrand made a wavy motion. "Like a snake, but it left a double line down its middle like it had something on its belly."

"You're missing the most important part, Fibes," said Loki.

"It was as wide as I am tall," said Ryatzi.

Sethral looked at him blankly.

"It was definitely something living," said Firebrand. "We all agreed on that. But we don't know anything else. I wanted to follow it."

"And I shut that down," said Loki. "And I don't regret it."

"Also, it was going back to the river as far as we could tell, so we probably wouldn't have seen it anyways," said Ryatzi.

Sethral sat up straight. "Wait, back to the river? How do you know?"

"We found the trail twice," said Loki. "A washed-out one coming from the river and a really deep one going back. We assumed the direction based on what a snake trail would do, so it's not certain, but if it only came out when it flooded, chances are it lives in the water."

Sethral closed her eyes. "Okay. Who are we not telling about this?"

"Whipper," said Loki.

"Phoenix," said Firebrand. "And the only other two who don't know are Dusk and Silver, who are our two strongest fighters. So they have to know."

"Strongest?" said Sethral.

"Dusk we're assuming and Silver's beaten all of us," said Loki. "Without her gauntlet."

"No way. Ratty, were you using bites?"

"Yeah, I went all out. A bite isn't worth anything when I can't even touch her."

"What about Whip? He used to beat her all the time. He was faster."

"Not since she got back from her clan, no," said Loki. "Now she just lets him win."

Sethral groaned. "Of course she would. Well, wow. Yes. Please tell her and Dusk about this. And remind me not to pick fights with her."

"She wouldn't fight you anyway," said Ryatzi, smiling. "Your wing's still hurt."

Silversand returned shortly thereafter. She was dragging another enormous worm.

"Where are you finding these?" said Fletch. "The ground is a puddle."

"A rotten tree. They climb up inside it."

"Lots of them?"

"No. I've only seen two."

The worm's innards proved why it had been in the tree: it had been feasting on rotten wood.

"So they probably didn't ooze up there to escape," said Firebrand. "They must be flood-tolerant."

Phoenix leaped awake with a gasp and was suddenly on his paws, hissing. He backed away from the forest.

Dusk got up slowly and planted himself between the Pyrya and whatever he had detected. "Don't block him in," he said without turning around. "Fletch, I'm talking to you. Phoenix, stay here; I can protect you better if you're close."

Phoenix crouched down, panting. His eyes were wide.

"It's Halo," said Whipper. "And others."

"Pheo, they're safe." Dusk was about to turn back when something shifted in the forest. Phoenix bolted. Dusk closed his eyes. He took Sethral's proffered blanket and followed. When they were gone, Halo ran from the trees. She rarely made sounds they could hear anymore, and ran up to Whipper, then Sethral, dancing.

"They need our help," said Ryatzi. "Halo, can you show me?"

Halo took an affirmative stance and dashed back the way she had come. Ryatzi was back in a hundred heartbeats. "It's a hurt Forestair. Whip and Seth, can either of you remove arrows?"

"I can," said Whipper. He held out a paw for Sethral's satchel.

Halo came dancing back. In the shadows behind her, two Forestairs let themselves be seen. One had the dark, silken fur and short antlers of the second canopy subtype, but the one she was supporting was completely different. He was willowy and so fine-boned he was almost birdlike, with pale fur as long and wispy as bird's down. His antlers were even shorter than his companion's—just two single, back-pointing spikes. He was limping and the fur on his shoulder was matted.

"He got shot in the canyon," said Ryatzi, again translating from Halo. "While trying to... Shelha, Canyonlanders are Forestairs. Guys, these are Ampik and Shuria; Ampik's named after a bird, and Shuria I can't tell. He's from the Coppertails who've been trying to take back their travel route from the canyon colony."

Shuria shied back as Ampik guided him the last couple tail-lengths. Whipper met them in the darker shadows, where the Canyonlander was more comfortable. Halo was still dancing circles around Ryatzi.

"The wound's less than a day old," he said. "So we can catch it before it gets infected. He's already had something for the pain, and the Forestairs can take care of him as soon as the arrow is out. Halo, stop it, you're going to trip me. He's going to be okay."

"It didn't go deep," said Whipper, examining the arrow stub.

"Halo's saying they couldn't pull it out themselves."

"It might be barbed," said Fletch. "Whipper, be careful with it."

"I know." Whipper stoked Shuria's fur, then put his paw by the wound and looked up questioningly. Shuria put his head on Ampik's shoulder. Whipper withdrew his paw as she leaned over and began to groom away the blood herself. Halo ran back to them.

"Alright, leave them to it," said Ryatzi, steering creatures away. "There are already guards around, so they'll be safe. They'll let us know when we can come back."

"Fletch can stay," said Whipper. He had been having a conversation with all three Forestairs through various means of translation. "Fletch, they want you here. You know about arrows."

Fletch joined them and the other renegades retreated. Firebrand kept sneaking glances over her shoulder, which was probably half the reason Ryatzi took them out of view before letting them stop again.

"Don't," he said as the Leslander looked ready to sneak back again. "He only trusts us because we have Halo's recommendation. I don't want to spook him any more than he already is."

"Why is Ampik so chill, then?"

"Because we're already well-known in the second canopy circles." Ryatzi lay down with a yawn. "And they're closer to Halo's kind, I think. They've been helping her since she got here."

"Helping her? With what?"

"Well, food and water, and medicinal supplies for us, for starters. But she's also here for the same thing we are, so she's been trying to get directions."

They all stared at him.

He raised an eyebrow. "Oh, come on. Why else do you think a Forestair kit would show herself to regular creatures and follow us around?"

"Because... she likes us?" said Silversand weakly.

"Well, she does now. She likes Dusk, and the rest of us came after. But her end goal all along has just been to use us to find Firefly."

It was evening, and the sounds of the jungle were ramping up again; insects and birds, and the long, shrill hoots of something that didn't sound like either. The rich green of the forest filled the warm, darkening air.

'Keep talking,' flicked Sethral. 'You haven't explained yourself yet.'

'The skeleton.' Ryatzi looked tired. 'The one Radar has. She was a Forestair named Firefly. I can't tell if Halo wants to end the slave trade or just get her back to bury her properly, but it's probably both.'

'I'd guess more of the former.'

'I'd say the opposite. They change how they say a creature's name when that creature dies. They add something to it, and as far as I can tell, it's the forest—so a creature becomes themself plus the forest when they die. But everyone here and back home refers to Firefly like she's still alive.'

'She's a skeleton.'

'But she hasn't been buried.'

Loki and Silversand's eyes both widened.

'So she's not with the forest yet,' flicked the Fisher. 'Death to them isn't when someone dies; it's when they return to the forest... Shelha, that's beautiful.'

'But...' flicked Silversand. 'But then that means... that means they've been thinking Firefly was alive for the last more-than-twenty years.'

'Not just alive,' flicked Ryatzi. 'Radar's had her. To them, she's still alive and a prisoner. And Halo wants to set her free.'

Sethral could barely translate the last part for Firebrand. She could not bear to ask the question she most wanted—and didn't want—to ask. She wasn't sure she could even say it without breaking down. She looked up to find Ryatzi looking at her, and his expression ran a knife through her heart all over again. He knew.

'They changed Wing's name,' he flicked. 'And they call Jay entirely by Bluejay's now.'

Chapter 18

Whipper was sleeping back on top of Firebrand the next morning, and Fletch was curled up with Taz. Firebrand was awake but she clearly didn't want to shift Whipper to get up and hunt. She was also watching the for-est.

'Dusk and Phoenix aren't back yet,' she flicked when she saw Sethral lift her head.

Sethral sat up straight. 'What did Silversand say? Can you or Tetch detect them?'

'Nothing yet, and I can't, at least. But I also don't have much of a range with either of them.'

Sethral closed her eyes and made herself take a long, slow breath. The last time this had happened, she had completely broken down. If the group was going to need her to think in this situation, she couldn't do that again.

Phoenix bolted on an almost daily basis. Most times it was short-lived; Dusk would go after him and they'd be back within a sun's paw-length. The less frequent incidents were long ones. Those were the all-nighters Dusk would pull, following the Pyrya, taking the time it took to coax him down from whatever he had spiraled into. The difference between the two was what made Phoenix bolt. The short runs were usually triggered by something startling, so his panic would calm as soon as he was out of range. The long runs seemed to be more internal: a self-deprecating cycle, or the resurfacing of a fear of being rejected or being found.

Sethral kept her eyes closed and found the Drakon mandible in her bag. Twisting her claws over the hard, smooth shape and sharp points helped her focus. Phoenix had bolted yesterday because he had heard the Forestairs approaching, and because Halo hadn't warned them before she ran up. That should have been a short run. He could have heard something alarming in the calls that nobody else could hear, but then Whipper would have responded too. As for the distance, Taz would tell that for sure. Sethral reached out the Drakon mandible and poked him with it. He lifted his head.

'Where's Fifi?' she flicked. 'Is he in your range?'

Taz lifted his nose. He pointed. 'Barely. He's out of my range for Dusk, so I can't tell if they're together. But Dusk's bonded, so he can probably sense us.'

'Are they moving?'

'I can't tell. They're too far.'

'Should we be worried?'

He waited a long time before answering. 'I don't know.'

'Would that change if I said they should be back already?'

Taz got up and nudged Fletch, then gave her a muzzle tip to follow him. The three of them moved out of earshot.

'I want to get closer,' flicked Taz over the deafening whine of the morning insects. 'Fofo, something might be up with Feefs and Dusk.'

'I'll warn Firebrand,' flicked Fletch. While he crept back to their sleeping spot, Taz kept scanning the air.

'There's something weird about,' he flicked.

'About what?'

'Just... about.' He swished his tail. 'The signal feels funny.'

'Funny like what?'

'I don't know.'

Fletch returned, and the three of them made their way slowly towards the signal Taz could feel. Fletch tapped his back and Sethral jumped onto it. He knew she felt safer there.

They had gone some distance when Taz turned in an experimental circle, then shook his head like he had water in his ears. He stopped walking. 'I don't like it. Let's go back and get the others. I feel like there's something there that I can't detect.'

'Can you sense Fifi and Dusk better, though?' flicked Sethral.

'No. Worse. Pheo's signature keeps scrambling up and moving closer and farther faster than he can move. But it's like I'm not getting it properly, not like he's actually moving.' He shook his head again. 'It's weird, and it's freaking me out. Let's get the others.'

'I can't sense either of them at all,' flicked Fletch. 'Are you sure you're getting Pheo's signature?'

'Yes!'

He must have been really nervous, because Fletch left the argument at that and followed him back. They couldn't hide the elemental pair's absence from Whipper anymore, and he locked down on Firebrand's back, shivering. Silversand joined him.

'Ratty, can you be on sky-watch?' flicked Sethral. 'Silver, keep your ears out for anything out of place, and get Whip to as well if he can focus.'

'He can't. They're Coppertails, Seth; you know how he is about losing Coppertails.'

'I know. But without Phoenix, he's our only access to the high registers unless Halo shows up again, and I have a feeling she won't. And everyone, especially non-Coppertails, see if you can smell anything Taz can't.'

They cleaned up their camp and let Taz take the lead again. Sethral watched him this time, noting at what distance his paws started twitching again. He shook his head and whimpered. Sethral checked in with everyone, but nobody could smell anything strange.

Taz stopped again at about twice the distance he, Sethral and Fletch had first covered. 'It's jumping sideways too, now,' he flicked. 'I can't focus on it anymore or I'm going to be sick.'

'I'm getting it, too,' flicked Fletch weakly.

'Where's their trail?' flicked Sethral.

Silversand, Loki and Ryatzi spread out to search. They found the trail, as strong as if it had just been made on the damp second canopy floor. Phoenix had been running, and Dusk had followed at a more measured pace. The Pyrya had then slowed and Dusk had caught up to him.

'They lay down here,' flicked Silversand, finding a sheltered space among the stilts of a large tree. 'Pheo had your blanket, Seth. But... then they went this way.'

She followed the trail to demonstrate. After sheltering under the tree, the pair had gotten up and kept walking away from the renegades.

"Why?" murmured Sethral. She sniffed the trail herself. This had been after sunset; even Dusk would barely have been able to see. And the pair didn't smell scared. They were walking together, close enough that Phoenix had probably been leaning on Dusk like he liked to do.

Taz stopped with a yelp. 'It moved!' He pointed a shaky tail back the way they had come. 'I'm getting it from back there now...'

Fletch lifted his muzzle. 'I'm still getting it from up ahead. Fibes?'

Loki beat Sethral to translating for the Leslander. Firebrand slowly lifted her tail and pointed off to the side. All three Coppertails just looked at one another. Then Fletch flinched. He moved his tail a copper-length to the left. Taz moved his a tail-length in the opposite direction, returned it, then looked sick and put his forehead against a tree. 'Whatever you do, do not lose the scent trail.'

'Maybe they got scrambled, too,' flicked Silversand. She followed the trail as it took a broad curve to the left, then curved back the way it had been going. She stopped where Dusk had pulled Phoenix up short.

'Why didn't they just follow their own scents back?' flicked Firebrand. Loki beat Sethral again.

Silversand looked back at the trail. 'I think Dusk is a lot more used to using his seventh sense.'

"Thank Shelha," said Firebrand out loud—and not about Dusk—as the loudest species of the morning chorus stopped buzzing. "Silver, keep following the trail."

"Which way?"

"What do you mean, which way?"

The cat pointed at the ground. "There are two trails here. Maybe they went in a circle? "

Firebrand ran to her side. Sure enough, just past the place Dusk had stopped them, the pair's scents doubled into two identical trails. They moved apart from each other on their own straight courses.

"I do not like this," said Firebrand. "Sethral?"

Sethral moved to the second trail and repeated her check, but Phoenix and Dusk were both too light-pawed to scuff the vines, and only Wing could detect the trail of vegetation damage they would have left. There were no leaves to have been crushed either; the second canopy floor here was as smooth as if it had been mown by a herd of grazers. "I can't tell which way they went." She moved to the fork in the trails and peered down both of them. She pointed left. "Actually, go that way."

"Why?" said Firebrand.

"Let me test this first."

Silversand took them down the left-hand trail. In a hundred tail-lengths, it forked again. This time Silversand moved aside to let Sethral sit at the junction. Sethral sent Firebrand back to the last fork. He fur was barely visible through the trees when she stopped at it.

"I'll bet left again," said Sethral. "But give me a heartbeat. Silver, come with me."

She led the cat down the right-hand trail, then called Ryatzi along too when they were almost out of sight. He had scarcely reached them when Sethral saw what she wanted.

"I knew it. Okay, back to the others."

"Let me into your brain," said Firebrand, reaching the rest of the group at the same time as them.

"I think it's a scent mimic."

"Why?"

"Because Dusk always walks to give Phoenix the easiest trail, but this one"—she pointed to the path she was still standing on—"runs under a pair of really low vines farther along, and the other one

I avoided did too. I think it's something smaller than a Coppertail laying this. I sent you back to confirm that Dusk isn't going by scent; he's going in a straight line."

"If he was getting scrambled by the seventh-sense thing, he wouldn't be going straight," said Firebrand. "He'd be weaving, and he and Phoenix would probably be disagreeing by now."

Taz winced. "Actually, we don't think Pheo's seventh sense works."

"What do you mean, 'you don't think'?"

"He startles just as badly when a Coppertail walks up behind him as when anyone else does," said Fletch. "And he couldn't tell Iris from Dusk at a distance when Iris chased us at the Lowlands' edge. It would make sense if he grew up alone. It likely never developed properly."

"Okay, but that only solves the disagreement part of things," said Firebrand. "It still doesn't explain why Dusk is going in a straight line."

"Directional sense?" said Loki.

"Yeah, but why would he be following that?"

Everyone went silent as a faint whistle sounded through the forest. It was Silversand's Long Night name. Sethral was snatched off the ground. They ran, ignoring scent trails and seventh senses as they followed the sound. Something large filled the forest ahead. It was a huge stone outcrop, pale grey beneath a coat of moss and lichens. Dusk met them at its base. He went right to Firebrand's hug and put his face in her shoulder.

"Where's Phoenix?" said Taz.

Dusk flicked up the outcrop. 'Asleep. Don't wake him unless you brought food.'

Silversand bounded up the rock to guard the Pyrya.

"Have you not eaten since you left?" said Fletch.

Dusk shook his head. His breathing was shaky. Firebrand guided him to the ground and his legs nearly gave out on him.

"How did you find this?" asked the Leslander quietly. "Or do you not want to talk right now?"

"I found it yesterday. I guessed where we were lost last night and found it again."

"Wow," said Taz. "Your navigation is better than mine. So is your seventh sense scrambled, too?"

Dusk nodded. 'Phoenix says it's a smell. And he says it's on everything. He won't touch the bugs here.'

Sethral translated for Firebrand, who immediately began scanning the ground and rock for bugs.

"I'm hungry," said Dusk in a small voice.

"I'll bet." Fletch sighed and gave up scouring the rock face for anything they knew was edible. "Can Phoenix handle a trip before eating? We need to get out of here."

"I'll try." Dusk got up and bounded up the outcrop like it wasn't nearly vertical and as slick as mud.

Sethral struggled after him. She arrived just in time to see him wake Phoenix, who started crying, then freaked out and melted down into her blanket. Dusk managed to coax him to his paws. Something went wrong and the next moment, Phoenix had hissed and lashed out. He crumpled back to the rock. Dusk gave him a moment, then tried again. This time they made it down the outcrop, but the slippery journey scared Phoenix, who collapsed again. Sethral could hardly believe how much patience Dusk had for this. He lay in front of the Pyrya and talked to him until Phoenix calmed down enough to let Taz help him up and guide him.

They walked until the Coppertails' seventh senses worked again, and until Phoenix stopped hiding his nose in Taz's fur. The group camped again. Dusk was asleep in heartbeats, but Phoenix was too tired and hungry and in pain to work logically. He dissolved again. Silversand tapped Ryatzi and they sped off. They were back some time later, muddy-pawed and dragging a giant worm.

"You guys are lifesavers," said Sethral. She hugged them both while Firebrand divided the catch. Phoenix screech-hissed at Fletch, who was trying to give him a pellet of herbs. Taz took it and got bitten. Fletch took the pellet back, jammed it in a worm-chunk and shoved the chunk in front of Phoenix. Phoenix started crying. Sethral reached over to wake Dusk, but he was already up. He curled around the Pyrya. Phoenix sank down against him and completely lost it. A glance at Silversand, Loki and Ryatzi proved they were all thinking the same thing. Sethral tapped on Fletch's paw to excuse the four of them, and they slipped out together.

"I think the fewer creatures in camp right now, the better," said Loki. "Who's up for exploring?"

"Sure," said Ryatzi. Silversand shrugged.

Sethral pulled out one of her knives. "I'm down to find out what can mess up a Coppertail's seventh sense. What do we want our mark to be?"

"Something visible," said Loki.

Sethral slashed a nearby tree twice, cutting a long, pale V-notch through the moss on its bark. They started walking. She marked every tree they passed.

"They're doing it again," said Silversand.

They sniffed the ground. Their own scents stretched away ahead of them in a tidy trail, across ground none of them had walked on yet.

"That is freakishly accurate," said Loki. "They even got our walking positions right."

"But they're missing this," said Silversand. She flexed her metal claws. The scent of the metal also laced the fake trail, but the clawmarks Silversand was intentionally leaving weren't there.

"Well, now we know not to 'retrace our own scents'," said Sethral. "Shelha, I can't believe Dusk got out of this without even knowing what it was."

"Hey, there's double of us now!" said Loki as the trail split. "Imagine if that was actually another us. Wouldn't that be fun?"

"What?" said Sethral as all three of them looked at her.

"I think one's okay," said Silversand, and kept walking.

Chapter 19

They reached the outcrop, clearly marked which side of it they arrived on, and circled around it. Only a hundred tail-lengths later, the forest began to lighten. Sethral squinted as a gust of wind made sun gaps yawn in the canopy. The vine floor was also t   h   i   n - ning.

"Keep going or jump down?" said Ryatzi at last. They were standing on a perilous honeycomb of vines.

"Weather?" said Loki.

"Clear."

"Then I say yeah."

"Me too," said Silversand.

"Fine," said Sethral. "But I'm not walking first."

They found a way down. At ground level, the treetrunks were almost black, slimy with algae and caked with mud. The ground never seemed to dry between floods. It sucked at Sethral's claws like the bite of a toothless fish, and Silversand and Ryatzi were faring little better. Only Loki seemed at ease. His webbed paws carried him easily over the sodden surface, and he was trying to hide how much he enjoyed the mud.

"You miss your swampland?" said Ryatzi with a smile.

The Fisher fluffed a little and scrunched his claws. "The South Forest doesn't have enough of it. I sometimes make my own if I can find the right kind of stream, but it's not the same."

Silversand yelped as her paw hit a soft spot and plunged in up to her wrist. Sethral flicked over every nut she found. They were all Thaliar's Tree, and there were a lot of them. Everyone's heads twitched up as a breeze danced past. It had a very faint smell on it, weirdly familiar, like they had been smelling it already and this whiff was just a stronger version. It made her feel slightly dizzy.

"Loki, tell me a lie."

"I still want to kill Whipper."

"Good." He was lying. So her seventh sense still worked.

"Do you still think about that?" said Silversand quietly.

Loki picked at the ground. "Sometimes."

"Do you want to talk about it? Because I know we've never really talked seriously, but I'd like to. If you want to."

He shot her a fleeting smile. She smiled back and that was it.

"Light ahead," said Ryatzi.

They reached a wall of vegetation first. Light in the jungle was a resource plants competed for fiercely, and the edges of open spaces were always jammed. Sethral was thankful the four of them were small. Loki ploughed a path through the vines and ferns and shrubs and plants and dangling mosses, then broke through on the other side. He whistled.

"Well, let the rest of us through," said Ryatzi, shunting him sideways.

They emerged onto the pocked stone rim of a sinkhole over a shallow cave. Vines tumbled over its edges. Filling it was a pond, half green, half glassy blue. Floating plants packed themselves into a fringe that circled the water and encroached inwards, leaving only the middle clear. Each plant was a discrete unit of fat leaves and sumptuous purple flowers. The water they edged was a mirror of the sky.

"Those flowers are our Coppertail-scramblers, I'll bet," said Loki. "What are the grey things?"

"I think they're just the same plants folded up," said Ryatzi. Dotted about the fringe were soft grey spheres, each about the size of a plant and floating like the plants were.

"Back up," said Silversand.

They faded into the vegetation. Sethral was struck by a weird mix of fear and familiarity as the star-like silhouette of a Drakon became a Whitewing as it dropped closer and its pale wings materialized against the sky. It was circling the pond.

'Isn't it a long way from home?' flicked Loki.

'Not at Whitewing flying speed,' Sethral flicked back. 'But it does look a little lost.'

The hunter dropped sharply again, relieved to have found water, by the looks of it. It was searching for a place to land and drink. It braced itself, dipped below the sinkhole rim and skimmed the water under it. The plants bobbed in place when tapped. They must be anchored under the water. Establishing them as too flimsy to support its weight, the Whitewing cut a right angle and flew across the pond, trailing its mouthparts through the open water. It came back for another lap. At the pond's center, it was yanked out of sight with hardly a splash.

Sethral moved slowly after Silversand as the cat found their path and retreated along it. Ryatzi and Loki were right behind them. All four kept their pawsteps as soundless as they could in the mud, until their bridge to the second canopy loomed ahead and they fairly sprinted up it. Nobody stopped running until they were back at the rock outcrop where they had found Dusk and Phoenix.

Loki availed himself of several swearwords and dropped to the ground. "No, no, no, should not have gone there, not going back, and I am ready to be out of this forest. Who's with me?"

"Me and me," said Sethral.

"It just took a Whitewing like it was a snack," said Ryatzi. "What kind of monster does that?"

"Something large," said Loki.

"Thank you for your contribution," said Sethral. "I was hoping for information that would help me avoid whatever it is."

"Stay away from the water," said Loki. "That pond was connected to a cave system; there's probably water-tunnels all over this forest."

"So it could get anywhere."

"Stay away from all water."

Ryatzi took a dramatic leap away from a fountain-leaved plant. It was too much. Sethral dissolved into giggles. The others were quick to follow.

"I can't," said Loki. He wiped tears from his eyes. "How did this get so scary it's funny? Every time I think I've seen the worst this forest has to offer, it proceeds to take me like I just dared it to one-up itself."

"Remember when we used to be scared of Forestairs?" said Silver-sand.

"Shelha. Those were the days."

They jibed each other until they had all stopped shaking enough to stand up. Loki, though, stopped them before they made to leave.

"Wait," he said. "There's something else I wanted to talk to you guys about while it's just us here."

Ryatzi sat down again. Sethral saw Loki throw a glance at her and slowly returned to her seat.

"I was thinking about the Coppertails," said Loki. "I think Tetch, Firebrand and Dusk are all taking on a lot right now, and I think we can probably step up more than we are to help them. They're all exhausted. And I know we here have been having a rough time, but Whipper and Phoenix have it so much worse, and I know the others could probably use our support."

"Especially Dusk," said Silversand.

"He's doing the most, and he hides it really well, but he's been wearing himself out to keep up the amount of work he's been doing since we picked up Phoenix. I know I keep forgetting he's not even as old as Sethral or I."

"Has anyone asked what we can do to help?" said Ryatzi.

Silversand batted halfheartedly at a twig. "He's always grateful when I bring food."

"Well, let's bring some, then," said Sethral. "For all of them."

Silversand reminded them that Phoenix hadn't wanted to touch the bugs in range of the pond flowers' smell, so they marked the trees on a path to a new area. They spent the rest of the afternoon hunting and gathering.

"Thank you," said Fletch when they returned to the camp with their offerings. He was keeping watch while Taz slept and Firebrand talked to Whipper, who was sobbing again. Silversand and Loki went to help.

Sethral tried to stay quiet as she deposited a fresh stash of moths and other morsels beside Dusk. A slight breeze caught a moth wing and blew it into his whiskers before she could catch it. He startled awake. He saw the pile and flashed her a rare, if tired, smile. 'Thank you.'

Sethral scuffed a paw against the vine floor. 'We were talking... and I guess we're wondering what we can do to help you out more. Especially with Phoenix.'

Dusk pointed to the bug pile. 'This. I'm starting to suspect a lot of the issues we're having are just because of food. Getting those worms is good, but eating too much at once makes him sick and doesn't last, so smaller amounts more often is better. He's like Whipper.'

And he was healing still, constantly stressed, and seemingly stuck on high alert, like nowhere was safe. Of course food would be a pretty pressing need. 'How long is this much good for?'

'This should last him until tomorrow morning.' He caught her slight frown. 'He's nocturnal. He's up more at night.'

'Right.'

She looked up from the vines to find him smiling at her again. 'Thank you,' he flicked again. She had a feeling it was about more than just the food.

"Sethral, meet Lumpy. Lumpy, meet Seth."

Sethral blinked awake and screamed. The pair of feelers tapping across her face withdrew, as did the giant, mossy dome behind them. Sethral backpedaled until she hit Firebrand, who was laughing herself silly.

"What in Shelha's name is that?!"

Everyone was rolling in mirth save for Loki, who was still asleep, and Phoenix, who she had never seen so much as smile.

'Lumpy' moved like a scuttling rock, slowly and ponderously navigating the vine floor. It was as tall as Silversand and consisted of an overgrown, hard-looking, high-domed shell. The pair of feelers poked out from under its edge. Sethral dropped her head so her eye was level with the vine floor. She could see the silhouette of a number of crab-like legs under the shell.

The creature trundled in a direction that would take it straight to Loki, helped by strategic herding maneuvers from Taz and Silversand. It stopped when its feelers touched the Fisher. He yelped awake and leaped nearly a copper-length in the air. This time Sethral got to join the laughter. While Taz repeated the introduction, Firebrand poked her. "And now that you're awake, meet the rest of the herd."

All around the group, about a dozen mossy shells of varying sizes inched in patterns across the vines. They left trails of nipped-off leaves behind them, turning the vine floor from its fuzzy state to the smoothness it possessed everywhere else. Smaller shells, the size of Lowland bowls and under, grazed on their parents' backs.

Lumpy had escaped and rejoined its comrades with a disgruntled humming sound. They were all humming. Difficult to pick out under the scream of the morning chorus, they made short hums every few heartbeats when alone, and broke into continuous and varied streams of sound when they encountered each other and touched feelers. Phoenix's head kept twitching back and forth. Sethral suspected from the motions that the baby shells were humming too, in registers too high for the rest of them to hear.

A loud, wailing hum broke out from off to the side. A rat-like creature had pounced on a smaller shell and was trying to flip it over as it clamped down to protect itself. The other shells converged startlingly fast. In twenty heartbeats, the small shell was obscured behind a crowd of jostling domes. The rat-like creature managed to wriggle out between them, its tail crushed and bleeding. Silversand caught it. With the scare over, the small shell's wail stopped and the herd dispersed to continue their grazing.

Phoenix returned his nose to the blanket between him and Dusk. Sethral sniffed the air. A faint perfume lingered on it. She closed her eyes and traced a stronger thread of the smell. Her muzzle hit a vine. She gasped. The vines that webbed the second canopy's airspace had developed buds over the last quarter moon, but they had doubled in size overnight. Each was now fat and tipped with a translucence that revealed white below—flowers awaiting release from their green chrysalises.

"Are these edible?" said Taz, sniffing one.

Firebrand pulled out her notebook. Liebling's sketches were not arranged in any visible order, so it took some inspection to find the vine. Whipper sat up on Firebrand's back and grabbed a bud. When he peeled back the green outer casing, the smell wafted out, thick and floral. Whipper stuck his nose between the petals, yanked back and sneezed. He poked his tongue in instead. Yellow powder puffed from the cracks. The whole flower was loaded with pollen.

By the time Whipper had extracted as much pollen and nectar as he could from the bud, his whole muzzle was dusted yellow. He sneezed again, then swiped both paws down his face. A cloud of pollen swirled away on the intangible breeze. Fletch started laughing, and it wasn't at him.

"What?" said Taz. Lying upwind, he had found himself a bud and was eating it whole, entirely sparing himself Whipper's trouble.

"I love you," said Fletch. He grabbed a bud and plopped down beside his brother. "How are you doing this?"

"Just peel off the green stuff and bite it. It's like a fruit but with dust inside."

"You just made that sound so appealing," said Sethral.

"If it's food, I'm not complaining."

With only the sketches to trust, the twins had been relegated to the same handful of plant species since familiar plants had disappeared from the jungle. They were probably tired of them. And with even the sketch-plants often proving difficult to find, they were the most likely to go hungry on an average day.

"It looks like the buds are edible, but the vines aren't," said Firebrand, still peering at the sketch. "Make sure you don't eat the green layer."

Phoenix whined as a pall of dust blew over him.

"Sorry," said Whipper. He grabbed his new bud and jumped to the ground with it.

"It's gotten really breezy here these last few days," said Loki.

"Ratty?" said Sethral.

"Weather's clear," said Ryatzi with a shrug. "Maybe it's because of the landscape?"

Over the last few days, they had started to pass great stone hills like the ones now reduced to islands in the southern half of the Lowlands.

"Are you sure it's clear?" said Firebrand. She ran her tail down a huge, rolled-up leaf and gazed up the trunk its vine was growing on. "These were all unfurled yesterday."

"Ratty, you've got dirt on you."

Ryatzi sidestepped Sethral as she went to brush it off. It was all up and down his chest, right into his throat fur. It looked like someone had smeared mud on him. Sethral pulled back as she saw the nervous look flit in his eyes.

"It's clear from what I can tell," he said to Firebrand.

Phoenix had finally pulled his nose from the blanket and was sniffing the tree beside him. This time of morning brought bugs down from the upper canopy—night bugs, that hid lower in the trees by day and returned to the treetops at sundown. Phoenix pulled the blanket over his head and headbutted Dusk.

"There's nothing there?" said the Nightlock.

Phoenix poked the bark with his nose.

Dusk surveyed the mossy trunk. "It was a good one last night. Want to go hunting?"

Phoenix huddled down a little and put his forehead on Dusk's shoulder.

Dusk sighed. "Fletch? He's got a headache again."

"Pheo, are you drinking enough?"

"He doesn't need much," said Dusk. "And he finished the bowl last night."

"Has someone refilled it?"

"I did," said Silversand.

The water bowl was the deformed pitcher of some smaller version of the canyon colony's garden beds. Its waxy surface made it remarkably resistant to wilt; they had been using it for a quarter moon already and it was just as sturdy as the day they had found it. It got refilled with any fountain-plant water they found.

Fletch retrieved the bowl and handed it to Phoenix, but the Pyrya just dug himself farther into the blanket and started to cry. Sethral caught Dusk's meaningful look. She tossed her satchel to Fletch, tapped Silversand, Loki and Ryatzi, and retreated. The moths, they found, had crawled under leaves and bark slabs quite far up the trees, so they retrieved Whipper too. With his help, Phoenix was fed. He stopped crying, but he didn't change positions until they all got up to start the day's travel.

"Sethral," said Silversand.

Sethral turned to find that the cat had stopped walking. Wide-eyed, Silversand brought her eyes down from the canopy. She looked disturbed.

"I knew something was weird," she said. "We haven't had to use tail-talk all morning. The bugs are going quiet."

"Fibes?" said Sethral. "We need to get away from the river."

Chapter 20

Nobody questioned her. Sethral had never noticed how much they listened to her when she made a statement, and the realization made her decidedly uneasy. What if her gut feeling was wrong, the product of some mix of hunger and heat, or leftover anxiety from something totally unrelated? Why should her words be given so much power, especially when they took the group away from their only tangible lead to the ship and skeleton they were trying to find?

The forest only grew quieter as they drew away from the river. Lots of plants showed strange signs now, curling up or wilting like the heat had suddenly gotten to them. The air, once breezy, had gone still. It was not the same kind of still as before the last few days. It felt heavier. Sethral marked part of the feeling down to the silence and the humidity—even thicker than usual, if that were possible—but the rest she could not trace.

"Ratty?"

"Don't ask me. I don't trust it here anymore."

It flitted briefly across her mind that there might be a smell in the forest impacting his seventh sense now, but Phoenix wasn't hiding his nose and everyone else seemed fine. Restless, but fine. Jumpy, maybe, and a little nervous. Taz kept checking on Phoenix, who wasn't cueing in to the questions, and Silversand kept tripping on things. Loki looked equally distracted. Ryatzi's nervous tail-flick had started up again.

Okay, really not fine.

She didn't realize they had picked up pace until she had to break into a trot to keep up. It triggered the group. Firebrand swept her up and Loki jumped on Taz. Nobody could run without shaking the vine floor dangerously, but they kept up a fast canter until midafternoon. Then Firebrand tripped, spilling Sethral on the vines.

"Sorry," she panted.

It was almost too dark to see. "Up," said Ryatzi. "We need to get off the ground."

The trees of the forest were so old, many had damage and rotten hollows where branches used to be. The renegades fanned out to search. Silversand shouted for the group first. They found her beneath a behemoth of a tree. Sethral touched it and yelped as the bark came off under her claw. It was dead.

"We can't be in something too tall, or the lightning could get us," said Silversand. She leaped at the trunk and scooted up it on a network of vines. Sethral squinted past her. The canopy closed in above them here, but it was not from this tree; this one ended in a jagged point before it pierced the leaves.

"Up here!" called Silversand.

Sethral couldn't see her until she waved her tail. She was some four tail-lengths up the trunk in what looked like a rotten hollow.

Taz cast an eye over the thick vine lattice embracing the dead tree. "Fibes, can you manage this?"

"If I'm the one with the least chance of being able to, yes."

Taz started to climb, hopping between more jutting woody coils than Silversand had. They wobbled dangerously. Fletch bit his lip and didn't call whatever worried instruction he probably wanted to. Taz didn't fall, though, and finally vanished into the hollow with a flick of his tail.

"You know what, you guys go first," said Firebrand. "I'm going to take the longest, and this way if something comes, it'll be just me left instead of all of you."

Sethral had to bite her tongue to keep back her protest. Dusk nudged Phoenix towards the tree. The Pyrya made it up just as Taz had. Dusk took the vines like a staircase.

"I'm still jealous," whispered Firebrand.

Sethral managed a smile. It was her turn next, and it wasn't impossible, but her wings were even more of an obstruction than she had been getting used to. Silversand helped pull her over the edge of the hollow. The space was big. Past the hole was a drop of half a tail-length, to an floor of spiky, spongy wood penciled with worm trails and their gaping holes. Taz and Dusk were kicking off the points and filling the holes with them, smoothing the floor.

Loki dropped in beside Sethral. "Leave that one," he said. He indicated a worm hole at the bottom of the floor's slant. "We might want it for drainage."

Phoenix was curled up in as much of a corner as he had been able to find, his head under Sethral's blanket. Whipper was a ball of fluff in the fabric around his paws. Ryatzi landed in the hollow. Firebrand was alone outside now, and Sethral tried not to listen to Silversand guiding her up the vines on the trunk.

"Something's coming," whispered Ryatzi.

Sethral whipped around, but the Saberel wasn't focused on something alive. His head was up and his eyes were closed.

"What is it?" said Sethral.

"Nothing I know the patterns of."

Taz darted to hug Firebrand as she joined them in the tree hollow. "Don't make a habit of that." he said into her shoulder. "I hate that heroic 'leave me behind' shit."

"This coming from the hero who jumped in front of half of us when a mad Amasu once cornered us in the forest."

"Fibes..."

"I know. I'm sorry."

"Don't do it again."

"I promise to reserve it only for emergency situations."

That mad Amatsu had been Iris, after Jay at the time while the renegades were out following Pyrya tracks in the forest. The memory should have stung, but it had now become just one more moment in a long, long procession of moments when they had protected Jay for what would eventually be nothing. It was like her mind, exhausted from the pain, had collected all the moments into a fuzzy grey blob just insubstantial enough to slide past without stinging, and just large enough to settle like a rainy season's cloud cover over her sky.

Something floral cut through the gloom. Sethral lifted her head to find she was not the only one to have done so. A flower's perfume twined across the still air. It somehow failed to weaken as it diffused. Sethral followed Silversand to the door.

The vines that made and coated everything in the second canopy were moving. Fat buds split, and from them crawled skeins of flowers that unfolded in slow motion like froth building at the hem-corners of a waterfall. They were white, and the only thing more extravagant than their frilled petals and yellow, horn-like centers was their penetrating fragrance. Things flitted through the semi-darkness. When Sethral strained her eyes, she could see flickers of green light. All at once, fireflies—real ones—and the green lights interwove. The yellow signals turned into several shades. A blue light tumbled by. Each light and colour, none of them ever seeming to collide, swirled a different pattern though the sparkling dance.

The breeze that had lain dormant all afternoon sprang up again. A wave of air heaved upwards with a whoosh like the forest had stopped holding its breath. Clouds of pollen were propelled into the canopy. Sethral could picture them ballooning out through cracks into the sky. The forest took another breath. Sethral breathed in with it. She shut her mouth and eyes as a second, larger wind-wave swept up the trunk. She was enveloped in a yellow fog. Grit pelted her face. When she could open her eyes again, her fur had been coated like she had walked through a dust storm.

The forest breathed in again, and this time the pause was far, far longer than the first two. Sethral dove back into the hollow. The whole tree hummed like an instrument as the wind tore up it. It whistled over the open hole, blasted pollen into their hideout, and then hit the canopy hard enough to make the whole forest vibrate with a sound like a ship's bow wave. It subsided, but this time it was not silence that replaced it. The breathing had woken a storm breeze, and a shivering rustle dashed through the canopy.

Something tapped her shoulder. Fletch was below her in the hollow. "Whatever happens, don't act scared," he said quietly.

Behind him against the opposite wall, Sethral could see Phoenix curled up against a patch of nothingness, all that Dusk became in the darkness. The Pyrya was panting.

"Just stress," said Fletch. "He's never been in a summer storm and there's no way to explain it that makes it any better. We're trying to stay calm so it doesn't make it worse."

The coal-like glow of Phoenix's fur was dim again. It had been recovering slowly since they had treated him for Moonworm, but even at its best now, it was still a far cry from when they had first met him. A firefly next to a Lowland lantern. Sethral's heart twisted as she realized she could see the light through patches of her blanket. That blanket had to last this journey. If it fell apart, Phoenix and Dusk would lose their only physical contact and the Pyrya would completely disintegrate.

"Sethral!" Silversand's whisper brought her back to the view outside. The cat's voice was shaky. "I found out what made that big wind from down there."

"Well, fill me in, catface. I can't see in the dark."

"It's not dark yet."

"It's dark enough."

"It's flooded." Silversand pointed down the trunk. "There's water over the second canopy floor. It must have pushed up that wind when it came in."

"Is it still rising?"

"I think it is."

"How fast?"

Silversand peered down at it for a while. "Not very."

A bloom of pale colour caught Sethral's attention. The water had reached a pillow of white flowers, and pollen swirled out across it like a comet's tail.

"Tetch?"

Only Taz looked over.

"Which way is southeast?" said Sethral.

He pointed, and the chill up the back of her neck spread through her whole body. "Silver? It's flowing upstream."

"What is?"

"The water." Sethral pointed the way Taz had. "The river was going that way when we left it." She pointed the way the pollen was going. The two were a near-perfect reverse.

"Let me up," said Loki. Sethral and Silversand squished together to make room for him. He took one look and spun to Sethral. "Salisetta. Seth, the mast, remember? And the stretched vine floor. They were both angled to match a flow like this."

"What if it switches?" said a quiet voice. Firebrand put her paws up on the wall and peered over their shoulders. "What if the flow we saw until now was just the dry-season direction, and it flips when the season changes? Sethral, it's almost the end of the dry season in your clan's forest. What if that's why Salisetta never found a way home?"

Sethral was going to just say it, but as the words formed, the ones from the logbook overlapped them and came out instead. "Because 'no rivers here flow northwest',"

"And then after the attack, the river goes through another cycle and brings parts of the ship downstream," said Loki. "The mast doesn't get far enough, and the wet season hits again. It ends up in the trees."

"But the logbook box eventually makes it back to the Lowlands," said Firebrand. "Three years after the ship disappeared."

The water had risen a little more and then stopped, and pollen drew smoke-ribbons across the flow. It was completely silent. The trees shook their leaves at another breathy gust of wind. When it died, Sethral could have convinced herself that the forest was peaceful. That the bugs, frogs, birds and other creatures that normally made up here as deafening as a Lowland mob were simply asleep, and that the heavy clouds rendering everything an evening shade were just blankets like those now giving the South Forest a North Moon sky year-round. The air was cool.

Another wind came through. Its tail lingered and kept playing in the leaves, and the silence filled once again with a soothing rustle. The storm, if they were getting one at all, was taking its time. Sethral dropped back into the hollow. The Coppertails besides Firebrand had made a pile, as Taz joined Dusk in making a nest for Phoenix, and Fletch ended up on Taz. Ryatzi had found himself a cosy spot between somebody's paws; it was hard to tell in the dark. The remaining renegades groomed pollen from their fur and fitted themselves into nooks and crannies. They fell asleep one by one as the rustle in the trees outside came and went, came and went.

Sethral bolted awake as someone seized her scruff and flung her against the wall. Something was thundering like they were behind a waterfall. Creatures leaped around the hollow, shouting and lashing out at something in the dark. Someone screamed. Something whipped across Sethral's side. It was big and as heavy as Loki, cold, smooth and wet. Steely coils tangled in her wings before Silversand got a grip on it and dragged it off her. A chain lightning bolt froze the scene.

An eel the length of a Scythe looped around their hideout. Ryatzi, Silversand, Firebrand and Taz were trying to corner it, and Loki was poised in the doorway. Through the madness, Sethral saw him yell and kick something away. The eel found a wall and then suddenly it wasn't on the floor anymore. Silversand screamed for Loki to let it past. Another lightning flash saw it silhouetted midway out the top of the door.

"They're not trying to come in!" shouted Loki over a thundering Sethral realized was a torrential downpour outside. Loki snarled and lashed out at something below the doorway. Lightning illuminated another eel as it worked its way up the trunk around the hole. It moved with a mix of motions, half wave-like like a caterpillar, half folding itself around vines like a snake. Squinting as another sheet of rain blasted him, Loki peered out into the forest.

"What's it like?" shouted Firebrand.

"Infested! I can't see where they stop, but they keep dropping down all over. I think they're up in the branches!"

Sethral wanted so badly to see, but right now she was dry and the deluge was so solid, the world outside was a white wall when lightning lit it. Loki staggered as another gust hit him.

Firebrand pulled him down off the edge of the hole. "Don't fall, or we'll never find you again."

"Don't," said Sethral as he went automatically to shake off.

"Sorry."

Dusk lowered the blanket he had whipped up to protect Phoenix's flank. The Pyrya was motionless. Either he had calmed, or he was stressed out of reasonable limits and had shut down.

Sethral found Dusk's flank in the darkness. 'How is he?'

'You don't want to know.'

'Is there anything I can do to help?'

'Don't touch him.'

She couldn't even see Phoenix's face; Dusk had wrapped the blanket around it to dampen the lightning, thunder, pounding rain and screaming wind. Fletch sat in front of them to block the spray. The tree swayed as another wind gust ripped through.

Sethral found Loki by smell. 'How high is the flood?'

'About a tail-length and a half below us. That's as high as it's getting though, I think.'

I think wasn't particularly reassuring, but Loki also knew water and Sethral had decided to trust other renegades when they spoke on their areas of expertise. She found Ryatzi next, but he was asleep. How he could fall back asleep so fast in this was a mystery. She poked him. "How long is this set to last?'

He sprang awake and relaxed when he realized it was only her. 'I can't tell the end, but I also can't really read it, so I can't really say.'

'Helpful.' She considered the hollow, with its smells of renegades and the wet wood of the drainage hole swallowing the rain that got inside. 'Ratty, what are the chances we could catch one of those eels?'

Loki leaped up as another long, steely thing plunked into the hollow. The eel found the wall and got out before they could jump on it.

"Hey Loki!" shouted Sethral. "Try and catch the next one!"

Chapter 21

A third eel tumbled into the hollow. In a heartbeat, Loki blocked the exit, Whipper blocked the wall, Silversand had her claws on, and both Sethral and Ryatzi were circling the snake-like fish. Sethral could not see it outside of the lightning flashes, but she could hear the rotten wood it broke when it writhed, and Silversand was about to make it writhe. The cat attacked first and pinned the creature long enough for Sethral to grab hold. Between them they slowed it. Ryatzi got his teeth in behind its head a split heartbeat before it broke Sethral and Silversand's grips, and then it was whipping around, its tail smacking the walls with a sound like splitting ice, its needle teeth gaping. Whipper got hit and tumbled half a tail-length. Loki darted in, but the tail smacked him until he had to retreat again. Ryatzi was taking the brunt of the blows. Unable to hold on, he dropped the creature. It roiled for the exit, but Loki was back in the hole and kicked it inside again. Firebrand joined the battle. She got Ryatzi's hold on the eel again, and she was large enough to keep it. The eel's tail smacked her too, then whipped around her neck.

"Get it, quick!" she gasped through her bite.

Loki did, and got a solid grip on the creature's tail-tip. Sethral twinned his hold and they circled Firebrand, dragging it off her neck. The eel's middle coils were so powerful they could twist into knots supported by nothing more than their holds on its neck and tail. Sethral and Loki backed up and Firebrand went the other way. It was like trying to stretch a giant spring. The eel jerked them towards each other again. Then Whipper leaped onto it and it convulsed and went limp. They set it down. Whipper still clutched the knife hilt protruding from the back of its neck. The blade, sunk its full length into eel, barely pierced the other side.

"That is one strong fish," said Loki, panting.

"It's huge," said Silversand. "What's that on its belly?"

They flipped it over. On the eel's underside were two sets of fins, each fused together into something resembling a long, muscular sucker. One was closer to its head, the other over halfway down its body. Both were equipped with tiny hooks.

"So that's how they climb," said Loki.

"Who's hungry?" said Silversand.

Dismembering the eel gave them another surprise. Sethral yelped as something scampered over her claws. She fixed her eyes where it landed and waited for the next lightning strike. The flash revealed a smooth, shiny marble caught in the floor.

"It's full of eggs!" said Silversand.

Sethral picked up the marble cautiously. Most fish eggs were edible.

She was distracted by another whoop. "Hey guys, we know what this is!" said Loki. "Remember those eel eggs Dusk and Silver found on a branch here once? This tastes the same. I'll bet that's why these things are all headed up the trees!"

Sethral popped the egg in her mouth. Bugs all tasted the same to her, but fish did not. Loki was right.

"Hey Dusk," said Firebrand. "Do you think fish eggs would be close enough to bugs for him?"

"The question is whether he'll eat anything at this point, but I'll give it a try."

"Give him some and save the rest," said Firebrand. "If they were ready to be laid, they'll stay alive and last as long as we need them to, and we don't know how long this storm will last. Eat the rest of the thing first."

Loki and Silversand loaded the eggs into the water bowl—they barely fit—and divided up the best parts of the fish. Sethral found another egg that had escaped them and passed it surreptitiously to Whipper.

The frenzied eel migration eventually slowed to a trickle, letting the renegades relax again. The storm itself showed no sign of letting up. By the time Sethral woke up hungry again, she could see around the hollow; it was some time of day, though she couldn't really tell when. Most creatures were asleep. Phoenix had curled up and managed to fit himself entirely under the blanket. Sethral checked his water bowl, then wandered over to the remains of the fish and helped herself to a piece. She snuck a couple eggs and dropped them beside where she could only guess Phoenix's head was.

The tree rocked as another powerful gust sent spray in the door. Rain hammered up the trunk in waves as the wind blasted it. Sethral startled as something moved beside Dusk. A nose poked out from under the blanket and sniffed the eggs. It took one and withdrew. Sethral scooped up another handful and added them to the pile.

There was nothing to do and she wasn't tired, so Sethral groomed out her fur and wings, then undid the strap on the sprained one. She lifted it slowly. It was stiff and sore, but she could move it slowly and not feel like she had torn something. She did her exercises at a leisurely pace. The storm, of course, hadn't changed by the time she was done, so she found Firebrand and set about purloining the Leslander's notebook without waking her. Well, one of her notebooks. She had three. The delicate operation was successful. Sethral moved to the brightest part of the hollow and set the book down. As she did almost every day, she paged through the plant sketches, then flipped to the map and laid it out on the floor. She wasn't sure what she was still looking for. The map was the same as it had ever been: two lines for the canyon, two lines marking off the colony, and what she now knew was a miniature picture of Salisetta's mast off in the corner.

It took her some time to realize Phoenix was watching the drawing, too. He had lifted his head with the blanket still draped over it. He glanced at her, then looked back at the notebook. The eel eggs were gone.

'Want more?' flicked Sethral.

He glanced at her. It felt like a yes, so it probably was. Sethral got him another handful, then went back to the map. She sighed and flipped the page. She had been over every detail of the ship drawing; every star on the sail and rope in the rigging. She had found no further clues.

"What's that?"

Sethral startled so badly, the notebook leaped in her claws. Whipper had come up behind her and was peeking over her shoulder. She flipped to the ship drawing again. "Salisetta."

"No, not that one. The next page."

"You mean the map?"

"No, the other direction." He reached out and flipped to a blank page. "That."

"It's blank?"

"No it's not." Whipper traced one finger in some design across it. "It's really faint, but it looks like Radar."

Sethral lifted the notebook to catch more of the nonexistent light. There was nothing on the page.

"Phoenix, can you see it?" said Whipper.

Sethral held the notebook out to Phoenix. He nodded. It was the most normal thing she had seen him do since before he'd gone down sick.

"See?" said Whipper.

"Can you two see things that we can't?" said Sethral. Nobody else had remarked on anything on the pages after the ship, and they had all seen it... all of them except these two. "Is there anything else drawn like that? Really faintly, I mean."

"Go through the pages."

She did.

"There's one," said Whipper when they were halfway through the plant sketches. He pointed to a drawing of the flowers that had just bloomed outside. "The lines on their petals are the same."

"Show me."

He ran a claw from the tip of each frilled petal to its centre. As far as Sethral could tell, the petals in both the drawing and in real life were white. But what Whipper was tracing was a very common marking, followed by insects to find the nectar a flower offered.

"Keep flipping," he said.

Two more plants and a fungus had hidden markings. Sethral scrolled through blank pages while Whipper watched them for more drawings. At the map, his paw shot out. "There."

"Where?"

"A line." He touched a claw to the canyon colony and drew an almost-straight line away from it, parallel to the river. It passed close to the mast, but did not visit it.

Sethral flipped past the map to the page Whipper had seen Radar on. "Would you say that and this are drawn in the same ink?"

He nodded. They went quickly through the rest of the pages, but there were no more drawings of either kind. They woke the rest of the renegades.

"Fibes, Liebling told us which way Radar went," said Sethral.

The Leslander was on her feet with a gasp that made Phoenix flinch. "Where?"

"The same way we're going."

Whipper got a drawing stick from Firebrand's bag and carefully traced over the line so the rest of them could see it.

"But why would she do that in a different ink?" said Firebrand.

"Maybe in case it was found? I dunno. Creatures here are really wary of Radar, but if we were supposed to see this, I don't know who wouldn't be."

"Don't even say it," said Fletch.

"I wasn't going to," said Firebrand. "I will just rest in the satisfaction that I was right."

"But doesn't that mean we're on a collision course with whatever attacked Salisetta?" said Taz.

A wind gusted through and they all had to stop talking as the rain hammered their tree too loudly to be heard over.

"Is it just me, or is it easing up a little out there?" said Loki when the wind ceased. "I can actually hear you guys."

"It is," said Ryatzi. "But only a little."

Firebrand sat down. "You guys are probably going to hate me for saying this, but what if Radar was going to the same place Salisetta found?"

"He could have just been following the river," said Loki.

"But why this river? Radar couldn't have reached the Daemon's Outback at the same place we did; Ives said it was a lake even before the floods. And if we assume the skeleton Benty found was actually Firefly, Radar would have to have fetched her before coming here. Benty said the skeleton was past the Lowland basin's southern edge. If you follow that edge, you can get to this forest by land. Why would Radar have gotten the skeleton, then come halfway around the basin to reach this river and then follow it? And ask for directions, too. Directions to what? If he just wanted a secluded place to hide Firefly, he could have gone anywhere. Why make his life so much harder?"

"What if that skeleton Benty found wasn't Firefly?" said Fletch. "What if Radar killed her somewhere else?"

"Same goes. Why would he have crossed the Lowlands and gotten someone to boat him out here across the lake, when he could have just travelled around by the north or south basin edge?"

"Because it's easier to catch food in the Lowlands?" said Ryatzi with a shrug.

"Whipper, what—" said Sethral. The words stopped halfway out her throat.

"Tracing it," said Whipper. He was halfway through the drawing only he and Phoenix could see. There wasn't a shred of doubt what it was.

"He came here twenty years ago," said Sethral. "That is freakishly accurate. What's he carrying?"

"I don't know. I'm just tracing it."

"Fibes?"

Firebrand came over as the package over picture-Radar's back took shape. It was a backpack, drawstring-topped and remodeled to fit a Coppertail. The straps were tied off to shorten them for his smaller frame. Sensing their interest, Whipper left the rest of the tracing unfinished and focused on the pack. The drawing was as detailed as the one of the ship. Wrinkles and lumps folded the backpack's fabric.

Firebrand pointed to two knobs jutting out opposite each other. "That's a bone. Upper leg, Coppertail-sized."

"So the canyon colony probably knew what he was carrying, if they replicated that in their stories across twenty years," said Sethral. "Shelha, I like those creature less and less the farther I get from them."

Loki eyed her. "I mean... they also keep slaves and helped Radar in return for a Saggitayria whose wings they then clipped. That was a pretty low bar to start with."

"And it just keeps getting lower."

The last word was drowned out as the rain ramped up again. The question, 'Keep talking when it lets up?' was passed around by taps, and creatures returned to their respective corners.

They rationed the eel eggs thinner and thinner, then finally ran out. Creatures slept as much as they could to conserve energy. Taz and Fletch, the only ones unable to eat the eggs, stripped the closest flowering vine of its battered flowers. In the dark and the endless lack of things to do, time became as meaningless as the endless sheets of rain still sweeping down outside.

It ended as suddenly as it had begun. Sethral opened her eyes in the pitch black to find the forest silent. Her hearing was manufacturing the rain sounds she had grown so used to. She got up shakily. With the rain gone, she could go outside to find food. She felt her way to the exit, which she could somehow see in the dark, and looked outside.

The canopy had been battered thin. Between broken branches and folded leaves was a sky so full of stars, it looked painted in luminescent ink. There was no moon in sight. Was it a new moon? They had parted ways with Iverae on an almost-full moon, and it had been more than half a moon ago... it must have been a moon and a half. She nearly fell off her perch as something moved on the trunk below her. Whipper clicked his name in the darkness. He slipped over the doorway's rim and vanished into the hollow in a trail of floral scent. When he appeared again, it was all over his fur. Sethral hugged him and he hugged her back.

'Feeling better?' she tapped on his shoulder.

'Not really. But I wanted to help the Coppertails.'

He must be collecting flowers for Taz and Fletch. Sethral pulled back and put her claws on his shoulders. 'I thought you didn't like being out at night.'

'It helps me think.'

'Do you want to talk with anyone about what you're thinking?'

He scuffed his paws and looked down. 'Yes, but not really you. I'm sorry.'

'Don't apologize. As long as it's not no one, I'm happy.'

'It's not no one. It's Dusk. And I think Phoenix listens.'

Sethral struggled not to show her surprise. She shouldn't be that surprised. Dusk and Whipper had spent a lot of time together in Dusk's darker days, and from the snippets of his background she knew, they had some things in common. She found herself glad Phoenix listened in when they talked, whatever they talked about.

By the next morning, they could leave the hollow to find food. The vine floor was a mess, covered in mud, detritus, and Thaliar's Tree nuts washed up from below.

"So why didn't we see any of these up here before, if this happens every year?" said Firebrand, frustrated.

"Maybe they rot?" said Sethral. "Or something eats them. Or it doesn't happen every year."

"I thought they were rot resistant."

"They grow," said Loki. They rounded on him to find him holding up a nut split by a fat, white root-tip. Loki returned it to its divot and picked up several more. They were all splitting open. The quickest already had rootlets out, twining into the mud.

"But what grows up h—" Firebrand stopped. She and Sethral stared at each other.

"We're screwed," said Sethral. "We're never going to find anything."

"Care to share the revelation?" said Taz.

Sethral pointed to the vines all around them. The vines that made up the vine floor, that wound up the trunks and webbed the spaces between them, that rooted in mats to the soil below. The vines that had flowered just days before. "These are all Thaliar's Tree."

Chapter 22

"You have got to be kidding me," said Taz.

"We're not," said Firebrand. "But Sethral, we're not screwed. Look at these." She grabbed the wilted base of what had once been a flower cluster. "They're already rotting. None of these vines are going to make any nuts, and the nuts so far have all washed in from upstream. These were pollen flowers, not fruiting ones."

"There's a difference?" said Taz helplessly.

"Most flowers are both. Some are one or the other."

"So we need to find the fruiting ones," said Sethral. "The other half of the species."

"That's where all the nuts are coming from. And that is the thing nobody has ever seen."

"Except maybe Salisetta's crew."

Fletch coughed lightly.

Firebrand closed her eyes. "The skeleton. I get it."

Fletch turned serenely and started walking. Firebrand loosened the shells off several sprouting nuts and jammed them in her bag. She and Sethral followed the other renegades.

The Thaliar's Tree vines grew like nothing Sethral had ever seen. By the time the mud on the vine floor dried, the fastest had roots halfway down to the forest floor. The nut shells—and everything else left behind by the storm—were consumed by a network of white tendrils. The jungle's resumed canopy chorus ceased halfway through the afternoon. The renegades ran for shelter before the storm broke. The downpour was violent but short. Very short.

"Back to normal," said Loki. Even the flood was nearly gone, and the river seemed to have resumed its regular flow. "I guess this explains why it still took three years for Salisetta's logbook to get back to the Lowlands. I wonder if this place gets a storm like that more than once a year."

Sethral poked the residual mud. "I doubt it. The winds completely change when my clan's forest goes into the wet season, and then switch back in the dry season again. That storm was probably what happens here when it goes dry to wet. They probably get something else for the other way around."

"You lost me at winds changing."

"What, that doesn't happen in the North Forest?"

"There's no wind in the understory."

"Ryatzi, what's up?" called Fletch.

The Saberel had stopped some ways ahead. Slowly, he lifted his head. "Fibes? And Loki. You might want to come look at this."

They joined him. He had found a hole in the vines, large enough to provide a clear view of the forest floor. In the mud there was a slender trail. It could have been made by a snake, but there was a gouge down its center.

"That's the same as the giant one we found," said Firebrand. "Did you see what made it?"

"One of those eels."

Whipper jumped on Firebrand's back and clung there like the group was going to attacked at any moment. Sethal saw Loki swallow hard, and turned a pointed gaze on him.

"I... thought I was dreaming," he said.

"About what?" said Firebrand.

"A few nights after we got here, we camped behind that waterfall, remember? I woke up in the middle of that night, and there was... something in the water outside."

Everyone backed away from the hole.

"What was it doing?" said Firebrand.

"I think it was trying to get to us." Loki glanced at Phoenix. "Feefs held it off. Then it left."

Phoenix looked nervously at a vine as eyes pivoted to him.

"Sethral?" said Firebrand.

"What, you think Loki's lying? Because he's not."

"Phoenix, how in Shelha's name..."

'It didn't like fire,' flicked Phoenix.

Loki translated.

"And you held it off alone?" said Firebrand. "Drakon shit, Phoen ix... I don't think I'd have that much courage."

Phoenix glanced at Dusk, who murmured something to him. Phoenix went slightly fluffy. He shrugged.

"No, seriously," said Firebrand.

'It wasn't going to touch me.'

Loki translated again.

"But you can't have known that for sure."

'Nothing ever does.'

Sethral opened her mouth, but the words fizzled away. Birds and bubble creatures, a giant snake and Daemon's Outback Aria; those creatures had targeted Phoenix when he had been sick and weakened. When the coal-like rippling of his fur was gone.

Other images replaced them. A flood of Forestairs cut as if by a knife when Phoenix had circled the renegades. Hollows flying in panic. Firebrand saying the Pyrya could chase off Whitewings. Dirt on Watersinger's deck and the sound of a mob in the distance on Linderward. Phoenix couldn't have been stealing from their gardens. If he had been, he would only have taken what they didn't want—the bugs on the leaves of their precious plants.

Even Halo had ducked and crackled when asked if she had gotten close to the Pyrya. Sethral lifted her heavy head to find that Dusk had draped her blanket over Phoenix and pulled him into a hug. Nobody else was moving.

"Can we get away from the river?" said Loki pleadingly.

The second canopy dissolved that evening.

It had been thinning all day, as the land rose and the vegetation underwent a dramatic shape-shift. No longer flooded, the forest floor filled with plants. The short, flat-canopied trees that formed the structure of the vine floor became interspersed with taller, bushier species. The vines themselves did not care, and the second canopy warped accordingly until it could no longer hold the angles it was being forced to assume. The vines split into capes around the trees.

The dissolution of the vine floor revealed that the trees themselves had reverted from stilted trunks to shapes more familiar to the first part of the Daemon's Outback. Buttresses cradled camp-sized hollows. The ground was more roots than soil, the air more vines and hanging moss than empty space. Sethral climbed a mound of giant, tortured roots and squinted into the gloom. She could not see more than ten tail-lengths ahead.

Down on the forest floor, everything loomed. The air pricked with tiny sounds: clicks and rustles that never seemed to come from a discernible direction. Whipper and Phoenix fixated on the side of a buttress as tall as a Rockhall cave. Phoenix lifted one paw and tapped it delicately. A white insect the size of a nut kernel scuttled from a patch of moss. Whipper snatched and ate it. Fletch watched the ground nervously. He had not touched the soil yet, but hopped from root to root as the last renegades found their way down from the second canopy.

"We're probably safe," said Firebrand. "I'd be surprised if anything big found space to live underground here."

"I'm not taking chances."

A layer of sound left the ringing buzz far, far overhead. A species had left the chorus for night. Sethral tipped her head back. Layers of vegetation blocked all the the rarest glimmers of light through the canopy. Whipper giggled as he and Phoenix found another bug. Phoenix wrinkled his nose at it, so Whipper ate it again. Phoenix snatched a layer off the bark. It was a camouflaged moth. He held it for a heartbeat, then cautiously offered it to Whipper. Whipper split it and gave half back. Another moth danced towards the Pyrya's glowing fur.

They followed Loki's seventh sense to water, a clear, clean stream nestled in a rocky channel. Its banks were soft with moss. Fletch lay down and started the nightly grooming circle. Whipper was restless. He finished combing over Firebrand's back, hesitated, then hopped down and approached Dusk and Phoenix. Phoenix startled violently as he shuffled his paws.

Whipper fluffed. "Sorry. Um... can I groom you?"

Phoenix glanced at Dusk, but the Nightlock was sound asleep. 'Why?'

"It's still hard for you to do yourself, right? And I like your fur. I think it's pretty... and it looks soft. And I know you don't usually like creatures touching it, so it's okay if you say no."

Sethral could tell he had more to say. After a few heartbeats, he scuffed his paws again. "And... I'm still scared of fire. After the one in the North Forest. But I don't want to be scared of you. And I know you're not fire, but I think it would help me convince myself if I could feel it and not just see it."

Phoenix eyed him for a long moment, and Whipper kept his gaze turned down. At last Phoenix lowered his head and shifted so the blanket could be pulled off his back. He closed his eyes as Whipper ran both paws through his fur.

Whipper smiled. "You are soft." He stuck one paw in Dusk's fur to compare. "I think you're almost as soft as him. You recovered fast."

"It's been over a moon since the Moonworm," said Fletch.

"That's still fast." Whipper returned both paws to Phoenix, then hugged him. "I don't think you're scary. You don't even smell like fire. If anyone's scared of you, they've never been in a real fire."

Phoenix buried his nose in the blanket against Dusk's shoulder. Whipper went through all of his fur and picked out the bugs, then tapped him lightly. "Can I stay here?"

Phoenix didn't reply, so Whipper pulled the blanket back over him and curled up on Dusk's back instead. Sethral edged around until she could see Phoenix's half-hidden face. There was a faint, dark line down his cheek.

Even before the forest lightened the next morning, the change in climate introduced itself like a blanket of hot, wet fur. Sethral groaned and rolled over. The air stuck to her face like a cloth. She heaved a breath and it padded her lungs instead. She sat up. Of all the renegades, only Phoenix was still tucked up. Silversand was flat on her back. Dusk was stretched out like a cat on a sun-warmed rock, and only the twins' paws were touching each other. Even Ryatzi, who never slept in anything but a tight ball or a tidy loaf, was half-uncurled.

If she was the only one up, it was too early to be awake yet. Sethral picked her way down the bank and waded into the stream. She dipped her belly cautiously, then straight-up lay down. The water was landscapes cooler than the air. Sethral stuck her head underwater, yanked it back and shook it off. She returned to her sleeping spot much cooler.

Giggling woke her again. It took an effort just to move. It was so humid out, even her dry fur stuck to itself in spikes. Her wet fur hadn't dried at all. Feeling about to suffocate if she stayed down, Sethral hauled herself upright to find Loki, Ryatzi, Firebrand and Fletch all in the stream. The Leslander had no head. She yanked it from the water and shook it furiously. She had what looked like a rock in her mouth. She passed this to Ryatzi and went back under. The rock was a shellfish of sorts. Ryatzi chipped its edge with a bite and passed it to Whipper, who was perched on the bank with his belly fur wet. Whipper jammed a broken branch into the chip and levered the shell open. He splashed the water. Loki appeared downstream and swam back.

"Your turn," said Whipper, and passed him the opened shell.

Firebrand yelped and leaped back. She lost her footing and went in up to her neck in the deeper water, where she stayed. "Loki?"

"Hm?" The Fisher stuck his last bite in his mouth and paddled over.

"Are rocks supposed to shoot off other rocks and roll away?"

"Sounds like Springfish." He dove under and disappeared. Firebrand passed Ryatzi another shellfish.

Sethral eyed a spider's web the size of splayed-out Silversand at the water's edge. The spider seemed content where it was, though it jiggled violently when the waves shook its web. Loki went by underwater in a shadow of grey. Disturbed by the motion, several tiny fish leaped from the water, one straight into the web. The spider was on it in a heartbeat.

Whipper had been unable to crack the latest shell. He held it out for Ryatzi again, but the Saberel gave him a pleading look and didn't move. He was up to his back in the water, and only his face and scruff weren't wet. His fur was curling in the soggy air. Whipper hopped into the shallows and passed him the shell. He cracked it again and passed it back.

Sethral was struck by a sudden urge she had never felt before. She was already wet. What was there to dislike in getting wetter? She crouched on the bank and waited for Ryatzi to turn away. A pounce plowed her straight into him, straight into the water.

It was a full-blown water fight in an instant. Loki ambushed them both underwater. Sethral found Firebrand's leg and bit it. She was lifted by the scruff. Firebrand flung her in the deep water and plunged after Loki, who fled. Sethral barely grabbed a breath as Ryatzi snuck up and yanked her under by her tail. They were attacked by Taz, who was attacked by Fletch and dunked. Fletch lost his footing. Taz dragged him under, dunked him back and escaped.

Firebrand cornered Loki in a stream bend. Ryatzi went to Fletch's rescue, so Sethral paddled towards the Leslander, intending to ambush her from behind. She was beaten to the prize. There was a blur of shadow and something knocked Firebrand clean off her paws with a terrific splash. Dusk slipped through her bite and bolted, giggling. The twins converged on him. Dusk was fast, but his fur dragged him down in the water; he fell prey to the attack and dove under to escape it. Two against one wasn't fair, so Firebrand switched sides. Taz leaped up on a high knob of bank and readied to pounce. Firebrand crept up behind him.

"I've always wanted to do this," she said, and got a delightful shriek as she shoved him off the drop.

Silversand had joined the fray. She, Loki and Ryatzi were a wild tumble, which suddenly un-tumbled itself and vanished underwater. There was a five-heartbeat pause, then all four Coppertails screamed and lost their footing. Dusk got his back first. He nabbed Silversand and tossed her in the deep water, shrieked and was sent under. Loki leaped off him to cannon into Fletch. Dusk grabbed Taz's leg and yanked it out from under him. He resurfaced and tried to flee, but the twin also had good footing and could run faster. They tumbled into the water again, laughing.

Silversand escaped a fight with Ryatzi and sprinted up the other bank. The Saberel pulled up short and retreated quickly so only his head was above water. Sethral climbed the bank and pounced on him again. She tried to drag him into the shallows, but the moment she did, he abandoned the fight and dove deeper. Loki ambushed him underwater. They cavorted away down the river's main channel, trying to swat each other's faces.

When everyone was too wiped to take another bound in the water, attention turned back to food. The riverbed was slick rock with a thin strip of sediment down its bottom. Dotting the crevices along the banks were shellfish of all kinds, from crabs with pincers the size of Whipper's paw to mussels larger than Sethral's. There had once been Springfish, but these had long since escaped.

The twins and Dusk scoured the riverbanks for plants while the others joined the mussel-cracking initiative. Loki explored the stream for more treasures. At one point he got a crab to clamp onto a stick long enough to bring it back, but nobody figured out how to get around its claws in time, so it escaped. The Fisher also found a Stonecutter large enough to serve as a Lowland anvil, but it was too large to even lift from the water, let alone crack. He released it again. Red worms poking from the river bottom yanked out of sight as it jetted slowly away.

"Are those edible?" said Loki, resurfacing.

"You'd know that better than us, Fishface."

They took turns diving under to try and catch a worm, but none of them were quick enough. Sethral checked on Whipper and Phoenix, back on the bank. Whipper had taken the Pyrya under his wing again, and the two were catching bugs.

The plant-hunters returned successful. Taz was fluffy in the face and getting ribbed by his brother on one side and Dusk on the other.

Firebrand saw the scene and gave an evil grin. "Hey Dusk!"

"If you say a single word, I will kill you!" shouted Taz.

"You asking him about—"

Taz tackled her with the force of a small Whitewing.

"About what?" said Sethral when they resurfaced.

Taz spiked his already spiky fur and growled.

Firebrand smirked. "Nothing."

"Wait, you know?" said Dusk.

"Tell us!" said Fletch.

"I know nothing," said Firebrand loftily, lying with every inch of her being.

"I swear you will wake up with nectar in your fur and an ant's nest crawling though it if you say a word," said Taz. He hopped delicately onto the bank and plopped down to groom his fur.

Chapter 23

One by one, creatures left the water. Sethral stopped grooming as Ryatzi began to climb the bank, then caught himself and sank back down in the water. Loki shook his head as Sethral started to get up. He pulled Ryatzi away downstream. When they returned, the Saberel had mud on his chest again.

Silversand shrieked as she stepped on a rock that turned out to be squishy. Several prods revealed it to be a plant-creature with a round body the same consistency as a Pitt-web. Its top was opaque, fading down to a translucent underside suckered firmly to the rocks. It had no visible mouth or organs. Silversand abandoned it to investigate instead a paw-sized, perfectly circular hole in the rock beside it. She whipped her paws back. Firebrand pulled out her sketchbook. A pair of adorably large eyes peered back at them from the burrow.

"Don't touch it," said the Leslander as Silversand extended her paw again. "It probably bored that hole. I've been seeing them all over."

A yelp up the bank came the moment before Phoenix dissolved in tears.

Taz hurried over. 'What happened?'

'He can't use the grooming request on me,' Dusk flicked back.

Taz went stock-still. 'Wait, he used a grooming request?' He dropped down beside them. "Shh, Phoenix, this isn't your fault. That's a good thing to do. It just won't work with you and Dusk."

Phoenix was completely inconsolable. He screeched when Taz tried to come closer, then buried his face and body against Dusk's side and sobbed. Dusk wrapped both tails around him and hugged him close.

"That's rough," murmured Loki.

"Did he try and ask?" said Sethral.

"Yeah. Did it automatically, I think, but it burned Dusk like it always does when they actually touch."

Something about the whole situation tripped a wire in Sethral, and suddenly the flood of grief was back. She ran into the forest. The strongest expletive she could think of escaped her, and she spun around and punched a tree. How was any of this fair? How was it fair to Phoenix, who had trusted Wing, and who Wing had abandoned with nothing but Dusk, who he couldn't even touch? How was it fair that Wing and Jay had been able to groom each other, when Dusk and Phoenix would never be able to?

Why did elementals have to exist? If they didn't, Phoenix would not be crying right now, Dusk would be able to properly look after him, and Jay would not have gone through moons of pain before he got his wings. Winter would not be able to chain them now to keep hurting him. Elemental powers did nothing but hurt.

The obvious advantages tried to force their way into her consciousness, but Sethral forced them out again. They didn't count in the face of this.

She wanted Wing to come home.

And the tears were back. They never seemed to let her go. Buckthorn's words kept circling back to haunt her: why had Wing tried to face down Bluejay? He should have known better. If he hadn't been so reckless, he might still be alive.

"Leave me alone," she sobbed.

Fletch sighed and lay down beneath the next tree. "I'm sorry. You shouldn't be alone out here."

"Go away. I can look after myself."

He put his head down and closed his eyes. Sethral knew he was right. She had anticipated at least having the fight to shout at him properly, but her own body was betraying her. She wanted a hug. She ran up to Fletch and flung her arms around him. His chin rested over her shoulder as he hugged her back. For once, nothing interrupted the moment. Sethral let it stretch until the immediate need was fulfilled, then just curled up against Fletch's chest. They stayed that way for most of the rest of the morning.

Crying had chilled her body, but as the midday heat climbed and she calmed, the air's presence returned, hot and muggy. Splashes indicated that others were back in the stream.

"Fletch, we need to keep walking."

He at least seemed comfortable in the heat. He had not moved his chin from her back. "We're not going anywhere for now. Feefs is asleep and it's probably better if we keep it that way."

She frowned. "How can you tell?"

"Because I can sense Taz and Taz is cuddling him."

"Good." Sethral sank her forehead into his chest fur. It was too hot. "I want to go swimming again."

"Go for it." He released her. "Just don't run off alone again, okay? I know it's hard, but we need to stay together."

They napped and paddled for most of the day. Sethral pulled herself from the water again come evening to find several creatures grooming like they were getting ready to start moving.

"Are we travelling at night?"

Taz, Firebrand and Silversand all looked at each other. Loki guiltily popped a limpet in his mouth.

"Did we decide that without even talking?" said Sethral with a laugh. This happened a lot now, though it rarely reached the consensus this appeared to have without a word being spoken.

"I mean, it'll be a lot cooler," said Taz. "And we get a bit of moonlight down here now, so some of us at least should be able to see."

Phoenix was lying half on Dusk's back, watching something in the forest. Dusk was monitoring him closely.

"What're you seeing, Feefs?" said Taz.

Phoenix startled, glanced at him, and looked back at the forest. Dusk poked him.

'A trail,' flicked the Pyrya.

Firebrand and Taz jumped up. "Where?" said Taz.

Phoenix pointed into the unbroken vegetation.

Taz frowned. "Where do you see a trail?"

'The bugs are following it.'

"Which bugs?"

'The glowing ones.'

Sethral mimicked Taz's squint. There were no bugs that she could see, and certainly no glowing ones. Phoenix started to look unsure of himself. His eyes flicked to Whipper for support.

"The little green ones," said Whipper. "Can't you see them?"

Firebrand blew out a sigh. "I think we've confirmed you two can see things in some colour or something the rest of us can't. I believe you. Phoenix, which way does the trail go?"

Phoenix tipped his head to peek into the vegetation. He pointed again.

"I'm willing to bet," said Dusk, "that that's a Forestair trail."

Whipper hopped up, his eyes bright. "Can we follow it? Will they get mad at us?"

"No and yes," said Sethral. "Don't even go close to that thing."

Whipper pouted. "But Forestairs here are nice. And even the ones in the South Forest let me and Dusk follow their trails."

"Yeah, and almost killed Dusk, Ratty, Neptune's patrol and I for following another."

"You were following one of them, not their trail."

"Ratty?"

Ryatzi flinched. "Whipper's right."

"And then they stopped when we ran? That was giving up pretty easily, don't you think?"

Ryatzi got to his paws. "Look, I don't know. I don't know everything about them, and sometimes they make just as little sense to me as they do to you. I just know that the ones in the South Forest are not out to get us, so the only reason they would have attacked you then is because you were following one of them and the rest panicked. When you ran away, they let you go."

"Oh, they're not out to get us, are they? Then I've got a few things to ask you about, if you're talking." Sethral lifted her claw to tick them off on her claws. "One: chased Wing, Silver and I in the forest at the edge of Winter's territory."

"That sounded like protection to me. I'd guess there was something in the forest they wanted to get you away from. They didn't try to catch you, right?"

"No. Okay. Two: attacked us all in the forest, injuring several of us and kidnapping Silver."

"Winter's orders. They can't disobey."

"Three: chased Dusk into Winter's territory so a patrol would spot him."

Ryatzi gave her a dirty look. "You don't need me to tell you that one."

"Planting Dusk. Fine. Four: tried to drown Dusk in the Rockhall pool."

"Come back to that one."

"Okay." She needed both claws now. "Five: ordered Kastar and Rose's herd to prevent Loki and Flitter from coming back to us."

"Wait, what?"

"Yeah."

"Who ordered that?"

"The Ghost. Who, as far as we can tell, is a Forestair."

Ryatzi put his head against a treetrunk. "Then it's probably the same one that's been following us, that Halo won't tell us about. And given that it sounds like it's gone rogue like she has, it's probably the same one that tried to drown Dusk."

"How do those things connect?"

"I was a spy, Seth," said Dusk. "And the Forestairs knew what Winter wanted from me. Anyone trying to protect you guys would have wanted to get rid of me, and if it was the Ghost, it wouldn't have wanted me to find out about the herd through Loki or Flitter."

Phoenix chirred and looked at him.

"You're seeing my stable side," said Dusk. "I got into this group as an infiltrator for Winter."

Phoenix froze.

"After she caught you in a new moon hunt, starved you half to death and set Drakon and Forestair tails on you," said Firebrand. "If you're going to tell him like that, at least give him the context."

Phoenix started to back away, half ready to abandon Dusk and run to another of them.

Dusk caught the look and crumbled. "I'm not working for Winter. Don't worry."

Whipper landed on his back and tugged both of their fur. "Up. Firebrand, can we leave in a bit?"

"Whenever you're done," said Firebrand, and lay down again.

Whipper pulled until both Dusk and Phoenix were on their feet. Phoenix kept his distance from the Nightlock. Dusk didn't look at him.

Whipper steered Dusk away. "Find a place you want to talk. You're going to tell him everything. You can't just leave it at that."

They left together.

"That kid is a gem," said Taz. "I hope he can make them talk."

"For Phoenix's sake, if nothing else," said Firebrand. "Shelha. Self-sabotage aside, he can't just pull the leaves out from under the poor kid like that."

Whipper seemed satisfied when he brought the pair back after dark. Phoenix still wasn't standing close to Dusk, but he no longer looked scared. Dusk had clearly been crying. He left to get a drink at the stream alone.

"Success?" said Taz as Whipper jumped to his back.

Whipper nodded and hugged him. "Are we following Forestair trails now?"

"If Phoenix is willing to," said Firebrand.

Whipper jumped to the Pyrya's back. They talked for a bit, and Phoenix finally nodded. He and Whipper led the way down the hidden path into the vegetation.

Chapter 24

T he parallel came without prompting. As the forest phased from overgrown to eerily tidy, Sethral was transported back to the moment Dusk had stepped into the lead of the Darkwood search, moons before. How that forest too had darkened. How a trail then too had materialized from nowhere, winding away into the gloom.

Dusk reappeared and joined Phoenix in the lead. They did not stand as close as before, but Phoenix at least did not draw away. They seemed to have developed an unspoken language. At some turns, Dusk would defer to the Pyrya to decipher where the trail would reappear. At others, it was the reverse. Whipper retreated to Firebrand's back, unneeded.

By the time the last light had left the sky, the passage of bugs Phoenix had seen was visible to all of them. Sethral still could not make out the green ones he had identified, but fireflies, their yellow lights like candle flickers in the dark, drifted past like a scattered river whose current they were riding. Firebrand gasped as a moth's wings flashed like a mirage. A pair of green lights lingered where it had been. Sethral felt the breeze as feather-light wings investigated the group. The moth flashed again and flew away, leaving its afterglow to hang like a ghost in the air.

A firefly gave a spastic burst of flashes and spun a loop in the air. A second light darkened to orange and pulled away. The first pursued it. Their flashes synchronized into a game of call-and-answer as they danced away up the trail. Sethral jumped as a coloured light flickered close to the ground. Phoenix had just made a tiny flame run down his tail-tip. He was looking at Dusk. The Nightlock reached out a careful paw to bat him, but Phoenix hopped back. He made the tiny light again. Dusk hopped after him; he hopped back again. This time the flame scampered down the full length of his tail.

Was he asking Dusk to play?

This time when Dusk extended his paw, he went for the light. Phoenix almost let him tap it, then bounded ahead. Red fur and black shadow circled each other on the trail. Dusk pounced, and this time the light shot out of reach. Phoenix dove back into the group in a glowing blur. Dusk pulled up short as he found Taz between them, and Phoenix giggled.

Actually giggled.

Sethral found Firebrand's paw in the dark and squeezed it. Dusk was trying to find a way through the group without cornering Phoenix, who proved adept at evading such a situation. The light flashed again. Dusk dropped to his belly and scooted after it, and Phoenix bolted. They wound up behind the group, then whizzed through it again, now both giggling. Fireflies scattered off the trail as they pulled up. Phoenix landed a solid bat to Dusk's face and ducked a return one, but got hit on the recoil. The blows were no more than taps—Phoenix was still too underconfident to swat harder, and Dusk was matching him—but the speed was level with that of the twins.

A moth distracted both Coppertails. It flashed its wings again and fluttered away along the trail. The two looked at each other, then back at the rest of the renegades, who hurried to catch up.

The trail had changed. The trees around it were larger than ever, and the path they were on began to take them through arches of roots and soft, moss-and-fern hollows cradled by giant buttresses. Fireflies were thick in the air. Glowing moths flashed their wings like signals, and smaller things sparkled in the spaces between. A frog trilled. It hopped off its root and was swallowed by a swath of downy sedges somehow visible in the dark. Fletch tripped on a head-sized puffball mushroom, which discharged a smoky plume. Several creatures sneezed. Phoenix darted towards Dusk, caught himself and whined. He went to Taz and put his nose in the Rocklander's fur.

"No," moaned Dusk as Sethral offered him her blanket. "I can't handle that when I'm moving around."

"It's cooled down now."

"You can say that when your fur is as thick as my guard hairs."

That was fair. Sethral found his leg in the dark and switched to Long Night taps. 'Phoenix likes it, though.'

'Yeah, and he's as close to overheating as I am. He's just too stubborn to let that stop him.'

Something plucked the blanket from Sethral's claw. Phoenix stood with it in his mouth and looked at Dusk. Dusk pulled it over his shoulder. Phoenix headbutted him through it and bounded away.

Dusk pulled the blanket off and gave it back to Sethral. "Hide it, or I swear I'll tie you up in it so you can see how it feels."

"You have to admit that was cute."

"Whose side are you on?"

Phoenix returned with a very large leaf in his mouth. He laid it carefully on Dusk's shoulder, heatbutted him again and left. He was back moments later. This time he had something else in his mouth. Dusk cocked his head questioningly. Phoenix dropped the thing in front of him and ran. Dusk picked it up. It was a twig of edible berries.

"Good job, Whip!" whispered Sethral into the darkness.

"Hm?" The Forester lifted his head on Firebrand's back. "What?"

"Fifi just brought a present for Dusk."

"That wasn't me."

Dusk was staring after the Pyrya. "Did he remember I liked these, or was that just fluke?"

"You don't give him enough credit."

Dusk looked about to reply, then closed his mouth again. He passed Sethral and Whipper each a berry and finished the rest.

Phoenix darted back from up ahead with an almost-trill Sethral had never heard from a Coppertail before. The renegades followed him under a root arch, then through a passageway under a fallen log as wide as a Coppertail was tall. When they emerged on the other side, there was a light through the canopy ahead.

Sethral nearly tripped herself as something long and stringy caught her claws. She had stumbled into a patch of mushrooms before it managed to register that the strings were not trying to bind her claws. A grass-like substance blanketed the ground. The renegades all gasped as a shadow bounded past them. It made no sound, and left no smell. Two more shapes bounded after it, one leaping clear over the renegades' heads. There was a chirp from ahead.

"Halo!" cried Silversand.

Halo was not a kit anymore. In a moon and a half she had grown as tall as Ryatzi, and her antler-bumps were proper antler-bases now. When they stopped in front of her, she bowed a greeting. Ryatzi returned it. The Forestair invited them after her and led the way under a last fallen log into a clearing.

Above stretched the canopy of a tree with leaves as luminous as half-moons. Clouds of fireflies, moths, and other flashing or glimmering things made a swirling mist that filled its branches, from which a gentle rain fell. Thick, lush grass carpeted the ground. Taz yelped as a drop hit his haunch. Whipper jumped to his back and they both sniffed it.

"It's nectar," said Whipper, and they all turned their gazes upwards.

Almost invisible at first, flowers like fluted vases curled down from the twigs of the tree. The scent from them rivaled the Thaliar's Tree vines. Phoenix startled as a droplet hit his shoulder. Dusk removed it with a quick lick. Sethral had just wondered where the Forestairs had gone when a shake of the branches sent down a rain of nectar. Shadows leaped across the shining backdrop. Delicate muzzles probed blooms large enough to admit them. There was a rustle in the forest. A new herd materialized and bounded up knobs into the trees with the lightness of pawed breezes.

The longer Sethral watched, the more she realized it was not only Forestairs in the tree. A pair of creatures with fish-like scales but paws like gliding mice scampered after each other up the trunk. A lizard perched on a vine and lunged at passing fireflies. Something larger than a moth flapped overhead and vanished into the canopy. Phoenix froze as a snake uncoiled from a high branch. Taz took his scruff and pulled him out of sight of it. He unfroze again. Whipper was now hopping between the Coppertails, grooming each as the nectar left spots on their backs.

"Are we waiting for something?" said Sethral. When nobody had an answer, she forged into the grass. It was sticky with nectar. Sethral ran her fingers up a blade and licked them. The sweetness flooded her mouth and wrapped her senses in a delightful floral perfume.

Whipper appeared beside her and the two of them romped about, trying to find the areas with the heaviest nectar fall. Whipper dragged his paw up a sheaf of grass and held his palm up for Phoenix, who licked it tentatively, then licked it clean. Halo appeared down the tree with a flower in her mouth. It was as long as her head and neck and then some, with a curling stem and a bulbous body that dipped in the middle to hold what turned out to be a reservoir of nectar. The renegades took turns mining this, then shared the pollen, too. Then they groomed each other's faces.

A Forestair herd—Sethral was starting to wonder if 'flock' was a more appropriate term—trickled down the trunk. Phoenix shied back and dove between Taz and Firebrand as the boldest creatures came right up to sniff the renegades' paws. Halo danced through the group. She wound up beside an older creature, with whom she bounded a lap around the tree. They broke off in a tight spiral. Several more Forestairs joined this, and all together trotted in a circle for over twenty heartbeats before they dispersed again. Halo returned to the renegades and touched noses with Ryatzi, then Dusk.

"What's she saying?" said Firebrand.

"Introducing us," said Ryatzi. "And sharing news, but most of that's out of my league. No wait, there. That's something about Firefly."

Halo was going in another circle with a Forestair her age.

"She moves too fast," said Ryatzi. "Hey Halo, who's your friend?"

Both small females stopped and bounced. The one that wasn't Halo twittered.

"Another bird," said Ryatzi with a smile. "Figures. Okay, you two keep talking. Sorry."

They went back to trotting in a circle.

"Now it's just teenage gossip," said Ryatzi. "Sorry. I missed the important part."

"Sorry?" said Loki. "Shelha, Spitfire. It's impressive enough already that you understand it at all."

"It's not hard if they go slower. They're literalists, so any motion they make is going to be close to what they're communicating. If you overthink it, you're going to get stuck."

"What," said Sethral as several pairs of eyes strayed to her.

"It's okay, I have the same problem," said Firebrand, patting her back.

Phoenix and Dusk flew through the group again. The sugary nectar was getting to them, and Phoenix was proving the faster one. It probably helped that Dusk snatched nectar drops off him every time they stopped.

"If you collapse tonight, I'm not carrying you," called Firebrand as they whizzed by on another lap. Dusk, if he heard, ignored her.

Silversand shrieked as something long and stringy reached from the canopy of a nearby tree. A second string followed the first and attached to a different twig. When whatever it was had secured itself by six different strings, it moved slowly out of the canopy. To Sethral it vaguely resembled the seed snow from back in Costar, blown up to the size of a Coppertail. Its body was small, hardly larger than her splayed claw, but from it radiated dozens of long, thin tentacles fine enough to wave in the breeze as they sought holds. She could not see eyes or any other feature that might mark head from tail, but then again, she wasn't quite sure where she should be looking.

The thing, luckily, did not seem interested in anything but the tree, and climbed out of sight once it reached the glowing canopy. The Forestairs did not seem disturbed by its presence. Halo returned to the tree as the flock on the ground departed. The renegades played and caught nectar drops and licked the grass and found things to eat in the clearing by the light of the leaves. Sethral lost track of time. At last a tug on her satchel stopped her long enough to realize how tired she was getting. Dusk smiled and flipped open the flap as her foggy brain failed to process what he wanted. He took her thistlecloth and returned to a hollow among the tree roots, where Phoenix was already asleep. Creatures drifted to join them.

There was something cool and heavy draped over her head. Sethral tried to shake it off, then reached up a claw. It met a wilted petal. What she lifted from her face was the limp, deflated fabric of a flower as long as her arm. Its smell brought back the memories of the night before. The ground was barren dirt, scattered with broken twigs and dead flowers like discarded bandages. The soil was full of tiny holes where the "grass" had retreated. The canopy overhead was a light, battered green.

Sethral removed a flower leaking nectar into Taz's fur and tossed it away with her own. Ryatzi, Firebrand and Silversand's scents tracked away across the dirt together, likely gone hunting. Fletch was picking over an edible vine on the other side of the clearing. Phoenix, the last early riser of the group, was either asleep uncharacteristically late or else an exceptionally good fake. Dusk beneath him was panting in his sleep. Sethral removed the straps on her wing and used her exercises as an excuse to fan them both.

When the hunters returned, Ryatzi and Silversand went back to sleep. Firebrand talked with the twins for a while, then sat down at the edge of the clearing and pulled out her sketchbook. Sethral found enough food to make her stomach stop quivering. Slicing open flowers for a final treat revealed residual pockets of nectar, but they were crawling with ants, tiny insects, and things like moving pollen grains. Climbing the tree felt like too monumental a task for the heat. She rejoined the nap corner.

When the sun went down, they roused themselves and gathered at the southeast corner of the clearing. Phoenix and Whipper had found another trail. The glowing green bugs, it seemed, liked to congregate on the threads of open space nobody else could see. The trail wound through the lumpy, root-mounded understory with the characteristic ease of the species that made it. If ground-dwelling predators even existed here, Sethral doubted a Forestair trail would cross paths with them.

Chapter 25

The soothing darkness, throb of the night chorus, warm air, and rich, damp smells of the jungle blended together. In the daytime, when the forest was too loud and the heat and humidity too oppressive to do anything but sleep, the group did not try to fight it. At night they found trails and followed them. It did not rain once, and Sethral began to wonder if her clan's wet season was this one's dry time. Like they traded the rain. As the rainless days continued, this seemed more and more plausible. Sethral considered trying to figure out the winds that might make it that way, but directions had all become a blur. She had no idea if they were even still going the right way.

"Are you sure we haven't overshot it?" she murmured into Firebrand's fur.

"We'll be reaching it tomorrow or the day after."

Sethral sat bolt upright. "What?"

"We haven't just been walking blindly, Sethral. Loki's been tracking the river, and Tetch are holding the direction. Calculating by our average travel speed compared to Salisetta's, we're getting close."

Sleep had suddenly deserted her. Now she felt stupid—if they had been relying on her to get them anywhere, she would have failed them long ago.

Firebrand pushed her back down. "Go to sleep. We're handling this."

"I'm sorry." Sethral put her face back in the Leslander's fur. "I've been leaving this all to you guys..."

"No, we've taken it from you. You don't have to carry everything. Go to sleep."

She couldn't even fight that. In the aftermath of Wing's death, it had been good to have time to think about things other than a mission to end a slave trade whose own perpetrators were themselves slaves.

Shelha, it sounded bad when she put it like that.

Even the fact that they might be reaching Salisetta's resting place tomorrow was rapidly losing its shock value. Sethral felt like nothing could shock her anymore. Though maybe that was just the heat. "Fibes, what are we going to do with the skeleton if we find it?"

"Give it back to the Forestairs. I imagine Halo will take it."

"But it's still missing a bone. And an antler."

"We can think about that once we get the rest."

"Okay." Sethral rolled over. The canopy, built of layers and layers of leaves, sparkled prettily, like chips of sunlight on distant water. "Fibes?"

"Go to sleep."

"What are we going to do when the war's over? If we make it out alive."

This time, Firebrand didn't reply.

Taz rolled over. "I'm ready to plant ourselves somewhere and just live in peace. Can we all live together? Like back in the Rockhall days?"

Whipper landed on his back and stuck to it like a burr. "Yes."

Taz ruffled his head.

"I thought that was obvious," said Silversand, confused. "Was anyone thinking of leaving?"

"They better not be," said Loki, muffled. Ryatzi beside him yawned, half-uncurled, and went back to sleep.

"No," said Taz. "Just wondering what we're going to do."

"Of course we're going to live together," said Silversand. "Whipper and Loki and Ratty have nowhere to go, I'm not going back the Royals, and... well, Sethral, I guess you could go back to your clan. And Fletch and Taz, you could go back to your range in the Rocklands, if the Drakons leave it again."

"But I don't want to leave you guys," said Taz. "And I actually think the forest is growing on me. Fofo?"

"I don't have a preference anymore," said Fletch with a smile. "It's a bit weird. I try not to think about it. I assumed we were sticking together."

"Seth?" said Taz.

Sethral wiggled one claw in a hole in a nearby trunk. It met something squishy. She withdrew the claw. "Well..."

Even the simple word caught in her throat. Before she could catch them, tears had blurred her vision. "I was going to ask my clan if Jay and Wing could adopt me. There's a whole next-of-kin thing I'd have to go through, given that I don't quite count as an adult yet, and obligations to the clan and stuff. But now that I've been here a few years... there's a chance they would have agreed. I was going to ask Talin about it when we were there, but I never got the chance."

Firebrand curled around her. "Would they agree if it was the herdmates of your parents asking?"

Sethral flung her arms around the Leslander's neck.

"They can try and say no," said Taz. "I dare them."

Laughter struggled through the tears and Sethral couldn't really tell which was which. "Don't beat up Kite, please. He's nice. And Talin takes fights as challenges."

"Screw him. So do I."

"Sethral, we want to keep you," said Fletch. "Even if they say no and you need to run away again to make it work, we'll back you up."

"Thank you."

"We already know Dusk is staying." Taz rolled over again and poked Phoenix. "What about you, redfluff? Want to live with us after we beat Winter and all this shit is over?"

Phoenix had been faking. He opened his eyes and just stared at the Rocklander like he couldn't tell if he was being taunted.

"I'm serious," said Taz. "Do you want to stay with us?"

Phoenix turned to Dusk with a mildly panicked chirr. He shoved his paws under the Nightlock's.

Dusk blinked awake. "What?"

"Tell him that staying with us is as easy as saying he wants to," said Taz.

Dusk rolled onto his back and smiled up at Phoenix. "Just say yes. We'll look after you."

"That looks like a meltdown coming," said Taz. He got up and pulled Phoenix off Dusk as the Pyrya started to tremble. "You know what? We're going to make that a yes until proven otherwise, and screaming at us in the middle of a bad day doesn't count. You're staying, Feefs. Fofo, help me here."

Fletch stepped in while Dusk sat up and groomed down his fur.

"No stream?" he said, glancing around.

"Nope. If there was, I'd be swimming." Loki had given up on sleep. He tickled one of Ryatzi's paws, narrowly avoided a bite, and rolled upright. "I'm hungry."

"Sorry, but could you guys clear out for a bit?" said Firebrand. "This is going to be a long one."

Phoenix had now started crying. Sethral yanked Ryatzi's tail, pulled away an anxious Silversand, and followed Loki and Whipper out of the clearing. Ryatzi trailed after them, yawning. Together they located a streamlet and found creative ways to soak themselves in its paw-deep water.

Fletch finally came to find them as the buzz of the morning chorus settled into its throbbing midday tone. "You're good to come back."

Sethral prodded Ryatzi and turned to find Silversand standing frozen, staring into a bush. Very carefully, the cat extended a paw and hooked a feather-fletched arrow from the branches. They all dropped to the ground.

"It's not new," said the cat.

Creatures slowly un-crouched again. Sethral took the arrow and turned it over. It was green with mold, and fine webs of fungi threaded the fletching. Its tip was stone, bound in place with a remarkably rot-resistant twine.

"That's the same as the one Shuria got shot with," said Whipper.

Sethral ran her fingertip along the sharp barbs chipped into the tail of the arrowhead. "The canyon colony's arrows weren't barbed."

Ryatzi closed his eyes. Loki poked him.

"Spit it out, Ratface," said Sethral.

"Back during that storm," said Ryatzi. "When we were all talking about why Radar came here, I had a question I never asked. Two, actually. I've been wondering how Radar survived the Forestairs in this forest, and why he picked the Outback of all places to hide Firefly. I had thought there were parts of it that were pretty uninhabited, but the Canyonlander thing kind of disproved that. There are Forestairs everywhere. And everyone here knows about them."

"And?"

"I think he picked this forest because creatures here know about them. Look at the canyon colony. They're been holding Forestair territory for generations. And Shuria got shot by whatever lives in this area. What if Radar asked the canyon colony for a place safe from Forestairs, and they pointed him here?"

"And what if that's why other creatures in this forest are so suspicious of Radar?" said Loki. "If Coppertails and Watermice are fighting each other and Radar sided with the Watermice, of course the Coppertails would see him as a threat."

"Hold it," said Fletch. "We have no proof for any of this."

"Not 'no' proof," said Sethral. "We know it's weird Radar chose this forest, that Coppertails like those Lowlanders Taz met when he got sick are wary of him, and that he specifically found the canyon colony and traded Buckthorn for directions. After he got directions, he kept going the same way Salisetta went. We also know that the canyon colony at least has a war with Forestairs, and that something here hates Forestairs enough, and has enough skills, to shoot one. We're theorizing because we've always been good at that, and I frankly think it sounds legitimate."

Loki took the arrow from Sethral's claw and pointed it at her. "What if whatever lives here killed Salisetta's crew?"

Fletch frowned. "But it would take something Whitewing-sized at least to leave those marks on the logbook box."

"We know something like that. It even lives in the water."

"That thing wouldn't need help to kill a ship's crew and sink a ship," said Ryatzi. "I saw that trail it left."

"I saw the thing itself, Spitfire."

"But then why," said Sethral, "would the ship captain's last words be 'Thaliar's Tree'?"

They all looked at each other.

"Shelha, Moldywings," said Loki. "Way to make me less nervous about tomorrow."

Phoenix was asleep, or pretending to be, when they got back to the others. Sethral was surprised to find him still present, until she actually thought about it and realized that the time he and Dusk had nearly lost the rest of them had been the last time Phoenix bolted. She wondered if the two things were related.

They had scarcely lain down to nap the rest of the day away when Silversand jumped so fast, Whipper screamed. The cat bounded off a treetrunk a tail-length up and landed again with something floppy and translucent in her mouth. She dropped the freshly killed bubble-creature.

"Spies," said Firebrand.

In a heartbeat they painted themselves into the forest. Sethral crouched in a loose spot among the bushes, Dusk and Phoenix behind her. She willed the Pyrya not to freak out. He looked about to. She did not realize Silversand had never left the clearing until a paler patch of root shifted. As soundless as a Forestair, the cat glided whisker by whisker towards a second bubble-creature now bobbing where the first one had been snatched from. There was another blur, and the limp sack on the ground doubled. Silversand returned to camouflage.

A third bubble-creature appeared. There was little chance this one had seen any of them, so Silversand remained hidden until it bobbed away. Sethral panicked as her mind flew to the two dead bubbles on the ground. Her eyes followed, to find that the pair had faded into a mound of leaves Silversand had somehow kicked up to cover them. When had that happened?

A faint whine nearly made her panic again. Phoenix was shivering, in a clear struggle not to press his forehead to Dusk's shoulder to calm himself. Sethral teased open her satchel and drew out her thistlecloth. There was a blackish smudge along one edge of it. She fingered the cloth, but it felt damp all over, with no difference on the stain. Dusk took the blanket and draped it over his shoulder.

The renegades lay still and tried to breathe quietly for what felt like a sun's paw-length, not daring to move lest anything following the bubble-creatures was listening. At last, Silversand rose. She was gone before Sethral could flick her a question, so they lay in silence again until she returned.

"They're gone," she said.

A cold hand clutched Sethral's chest. "They were here?"

"Two of them. They smelled like the white Watermice; I think they're the same species. They stopped back that way and waited for a little bit, then went away."

They extracted themselves from the vegetation. Fletch lay down in front of Whipper and bit his tongue as the Forester pulled stinging ants from his fur. They were big, each half the length of Whipper's claw, but not as big as the bugs so far had been.

"Loki, river?" said Firebrand.

Loki pointed the same way Silversand had when she had indicated where the creatures had been.

"Phoenix, any trails?"

Phoenix still had his face turned into Dusk's shoulder. The blanket now covered his whole head and he was curled up as close as he could get without touching fur. He didn't move.

'Dusk?' flicked Taz.

'He's awake.' The Nightlock looked weary. 'He doesn't feel like answering.'

Loki was on the hunt for water, so Sethral translated for Firebrand.

The Leslander closed her eyes as though willing patience to come to her. Apparently it did. "Can anyone else spot Forestair trails now?" she said.

Silversand and Ryatzi exchanged a glance.

"Um... I think we both can," said Silversand.

"Where do they go from here?"

"I think Sethral's sitting on one?"

Sethral leaped like something had bitten her backside. Behind her were the loose bushes she, Dusk and Phoenix had hidden in. She had parked herself in front of them again in case the need to hide returned. She wiggled a finger at both elementals. "Which of us found that first?"

Dusk pointed at Phoenix. Of course it wouldn't be that easy. Well, at least they had Ryatzi and Silversand now.

"Let's follow them," said Firebrand.

"Fibes," groaned Taz.

"It's the same way as the river, and if they have a trail, it'll be a safe one."

"Safe? Fibes, they shoot Forestairs! We should be more worried about the creatures that made the trails than whatever it helps us avoid."

They went silent as Ryatzi crouched. A small Aria was perched far up a tree above them, its head cocked as it watched them curiously.

Ryatzi had a hungry look in his eye. 'Can someone bait it down?' he flicked.

Sethral opened her pouch. She had many shiny things in it, from her knives to a mirror shard to the three coloured gems she had once stolen from the same Drakon's pouch that had once held the broken caradel stone Winter blackmailed Dusk for. She found the mirror first, but the smooth crystal face was dulled with the same sooty colour as the edge of her blanket. The gems at least were clean. The Aria perked right up at the blue gemstone's sparkle. It crept down the trunk, oblivious to Whipper sneaking up the other side. He shoved it off.

"Please don't dismember that here," said Dusk as the Saberel dropped the corpse on the ground.

"What, are you squeamish?" said Sethral.

"Remember Arling?"

"I'd rather not. Wait... are you saying you are squeamish?"

Dusk closed his eyes. "If we could not talk about this, I'd appreciate it."

"Sorry. I just thought... well, someone like you..."

"You mean a rebel? Yeah, I was fine until they all died in front of me."

Sethral swallowed hard. "Sorry."

"Don't follow me," said Dusk, and it took Sethral a heartbeat to realize he was talking to Phoenix. He got up and stalked away.

Phoenix remained glued to the ground behind him. His gaze flicked between the other renegades and the bushes where Dusk had vanished, like he wasn't sure which emotion was the appropriate one but had several ready to take over. Whipper landed in front of him and took hold of his fur. Sethral entertained the idea of asking if someone was going to follow the Nightlock, then realized Silversand was already gone.

But then Silversand was back in a flurry and Dusk was still gone. The cat had her gauntlet on. "Firebrand?" she more squeaked than said. "The ship's here."

Chapter 26

Taz had to grab Firebrand's tail to keep her from deserting them. "Where's Dusk?"

"He sent me back. I think he's spying."

"Are there creatures to spy on?"

"I—" Instinct. So probably yes. "He didn't say what he was doing. But it felt like spying."

"Then he's probably spying," said Sethral. "That idiot. If there are creatures about, we need him back here, now."

"Please don't," pleaded Whipper. His voice had been too low to hear up until now. He had both forepaws knotted in Phoenix's fur.

Phoenix's breathing was like butterfly wings, almost too fast to follow. His paws were pressed to the ground so hard they made divots. Something snapped in the forest and Whipper was flung back; there was a red blur, a click, and the Pyrya went statue-still.

'Sorry, Phoenix,' flicked Silversand. On her outstretched paw, her gauntlet had been clipped to snake form.

Taz cautiously approached the frozen Pyrya and touched him. He didn't move, and when Taz took his scruff and pulled him down again, he went with the motion as if molded from clay. Everyone else sank slowly with them.

Everyone except Whipper, who had disappeared.

Sethral knew she had moved a bit too quickly as she jerked her head around. Suddenly, there was no sign of Firebrand either. Her eyes returned to find a gap where Ryatzi had been. She was about to freak out when a Long Night hiss behind her said, 'Here, now.' Her body obeyed so fast she felt like smoke. Dusk left her and spirited the rest of the renegades into the bushes. They regathered in a Forestair clearing.

'Silver, let him go,' flicked Dusk.

'No. He'll bolt.'

Dusk shot Taz a look. The Rocklander got a hold on the relaxing muscle in Phoenix's scruff, and the Pyrya's legs gave out on him. Silversand un-snaked her gauntlet. Phoenix started to cry softly. He was trembling.

Dusk scanned the forest again, then started pointing to each of them. 'Taz, stay with him here. Fletch, help keep Feefs calm. Loki, Ryatzi, on guard. Whipper, find a tree and hide; if they get attacked, come find us. Silver, Sethral, Firebrand, you're with me.'

'Where are we going?' flicked Sethral.

'To find Firefly.'

Sethral planted her paws. 'Explain.'

'The forest around us right now is swarming with Forestairs. Halo's here, and she and the others keep milling back and forth like there's something here they want us to find. I want you and Firebrand because you're our two smartest observers, and Silver because she and I are the only ones who stand a chance against bows if we're found first.'

'By who?'

'I don't know.'

'Trust read, Sethral?' flicked Firebrand, dropping her bag on Fletch for safekeeping.

'If I'm getting the Forestairs, which I probably am, I don't think they're trying to trap us. I don't like this place at all, though.'

'It's too quiet,' flicked Silversand.

There was nothing quiet about the jungle. The heat seemed to soften Sethral's body, letting the penetrating whine of the sunhigh chorus run strings through her head and her hearing and her suddenly throbbing wing. The sound changed depending on which way she turned her head. Firebrand nodded to Dusk, who slid down a Forestair trail like a shadow.

The soupy air clung to Sethral as she struggled to keep up. Already she felt dizzy, and she could feel a headache budding between her eyes like a malignant tumour. The air felt too thick and too thin. It escaped her, leaving its humidity in its stead, so her lungs felt empty before she even breathed out. Dusk had wet his fur in a stream somewhere, and Sethral wished with every fibre of her being that she could do the same. They stopped abruptly and she swayed on her paws. Now the forest was rushing, whining and ringing.

There was something through the trees ahead. Paw by paw, Dusk took them to the forest fringe. It was the canyon fringe. They were back above the river in its deep stone trough, and Sethral woke up as a cool mist brushed her face. The rushing wasn't the forest. It grew louder as she refocused, then louder still, until she was standing on the cool, damp soil with the smell of spray in her mouth. The brightness ahead resolved, and she gasped.

The canyon here was a dead end ship-lengths broad. To their right, the river swept in almost at the surface and lost the ground beneath it. The cataclysm parted around natural teeth in the stone and jetted down like many walls of water into a steamy mist. At the waterfall's center, a ship floated in midair. Salisetta was every bit as grand as the pictures. It hung with a grace that taunted the ten tail-length drop beneath it, its curled railings corroded, snapped mast defiantly upheld, sweeping prow green with damp, and a javelin of stone skewered through both flanks as cleanly as a Forestair kill.

'When the river reversed,' flicked Firebrand. Her frown bordered on a glare as it pivoted upstream. 'So where in Shelha's name is Thaliar's Tree?'

'They saw it,' flicked Sethral. 'We need to go where they were.'

'It's so exposed. It'll be dangerous.'

'Care to let us in on the conversation?' flicked Dusk in Sethral's other tail-talk.

'Calm down,' flicked Sethral, though her own heart was dancing its own rendition of Flicker in the Hollow. 'We were saying we need to go where the crew's last view was. On the ship.'

She tugged the straps on her wing, but Dusk just turned and started up the bank.

Sethral ran to catch up with him. 'Hey, warn us before you take off! Where are you going?'

'To the ship, smartass.'

Firebrand caught his tail and he whirled with a snarl. She dropped it again. "Dusk, take a breath. Taking it out on Sethral isn't going to help our teamwork."

"What's your problem?" said Sethral.

"None of your business."

"It is, actually, given that we're trying to stay together here and you're acting like you'd rather ditch us and take on this forest yourself."

Dusk stormed off again, but Firebrand blocked him in a bound. The way he jerked aside said that something was wrong.

"Hey," said Firebrand.

Before Sethral could take a step, the Leslander had her chin over Dusk's shoulder and her tail over his back. Something gave out in him, and he slumped into the hug.

Dusk let himself be held for only a heartbeat. When he pulled away, he resumed his path towards the waterfall. Firebrand followed before Sethral could get close enough to ask her what that had been about.

The top of the waterfall was disconcertingly silent for the amount of water stampeding over it. As they passed it, the roar of its collision with the river below was cut by two-thirds, replaced by the rush of rapids. The river above the falls was a mess of rocks and rock arches. There were many routes to the ship. Dusk paused only to scan the full river, then jumped down onto an arch. Sethral finished taking the straps off her wing before following.

Silversand set paw on the ship first. As the best one at taking falls should the rock break, she probed every corner, bounced on the weak spots, and finally announced the rock's hold to be sound. They joined her warily. Sethral moved to the downriver side of the deck and shielded her eyes in the sun. She blinked, scrubbed them, and squinted hard. The canyon walls continued all the way down the river. In the heat, humidity and rising mist, however, the distance blurred as if half erased before a hundred tail-lengths had elapsed.

Sethral bounded to the stump of the mast and climbed that instead. With the extra tail-length of elevation, the view was a little better, but the canyon banks remained resolutely uninteresting.

Sethral looked for Firebrand, to find the deck empty. She hurried to the open hatch. The trapdoor was missing, and the holes where its hinges had once been were rotted to pits in the deck. Dusk, Silversand and Firebrand were all below.

"Find anything?" she called down.

Silversand appeared in the murky shadows and jumped back to the deck. "There's nothing there. No bodies or anything."

Sethral dropped through the hatch. She landed with a thump on a barren floor whose wood flaked when she dug her claws into it. When her eyes adjusted, she saw Firebrand at one end, sniffing walls whose only features were fluffy fungal growths mounded about like the aftermath of a snowball fight. Dusk she could only spot by smell. He appeared briefly by the light beneath the hatch, then returned to the shadows and was lost again.

Firebrand finally noticed Sethral's presence and trotted over. "Any sign of it?"

"Lots of trees, but nothing special. The ship must have been washed pretty far downstream before it got caught here."

There was a faint cry from the deck. "Caves!"

Sethral turned to the hatch and was struck by a feeling of stupidity. There was no ladder, and the jump was too far for her to make. Firebrand crouched to let her on her back. Only from there could she get to the deck. Silversand had her head through the railing where Sethral had been standing only moments before. She pointed them to the canyon walls. Barely visible through the mist were dark blots on the stone, which seemed to grow more numerous towards the canyon bottom.

"No," whispered Dusk.

They lifted their heads. Figures lined the riverbanks. White Watermice stood as if carved from stone, their bows drawn on the renegades. More made a half moon across the river rocks. Closest of all, a tight knot blocked the spit that ended at the ship and the spike that gutted it.

"Sethral?" said Dusk. He was right in the line of fire. Sethral could see every detail of his outline, which in a heartbeat would be shot full of arrows. "Give me the bell."

Her throat was like paper. "What?"

"The metal thing you make fires in."

"The dish."

"It's not a dish."

Sethral moved like she was reaching out to touch a sleeping Hyenar. No arrows fell as she eased open the flap of her satchel. The metal dish was tucked where she could grab it easily. Dusk had found a pebble on the deck and curled it tightly in one tail. He moved the other close to her, and Sethral eased the dish into it. Dusk flipped it over and tapped it with the stone. A ringing note fired out across the river. Bowstrings jerked back, but none released as Dusk tapped the dish again. Sethral did not realize he had taken a step with the sound until he had done it thrice more and was standing on the upstream side of the ship. She could see his paws shaking.

"Get below," he said. "As soon as I hit it."

He laid the dish upside-down on the rock spike. As the first arrow left its bow, the pebble swung down and split, it struck the metal so hard. The air rent. Sethral screamed as the soundwave passed through her skull and her vision blacked; she hit the floor of the hold without a memory of falling. A body thudded beside her. The ship lurched. Something was banging, like rocks to the Rockhall floor. It lurched again. Then the rock spike snapped and her stomach sailed up as the ship came free.

They fell.

Nothing in a dream was as dreamlike as the falling. It lasted forever, long heartbeats without a floor or a touch of breeze, and Sethral closed her eyes and imagined she was floating. The air was warm, like a bed. She reached for the hatch, but time had slowed and her body moved as if caressed by sleep, too slow to get out and fly in time, too aware that she would never make it.

She did not feel the impact with the water, but regained consciousness on her back as the walls fragmented around her. The deck split, and a bright peal of sunlight washed the water that swallowed her in a heave as warm as her body. There was no breath in her lungs. The surface sparkled, sinking upwards so that its patterns became stars and the stars webbed together in a broader and more beautiful spread. Bubbles sliced deep where the waterfall met the water, and resurfaced in flocks to join the flow that tugged her now away from the roiling water, into a safer, quieter, slowly darkening place. The surface was quite far away now. The stump of the mast fell across it and bobbed indignantly.

Something closed on her scruff and revealed that she could feel almost nothing. Sethral closed her eyes and the floating returned, only this time it came with tingles in her paws and tail that she wished would go away. Something compressed her lungs until they hurt. The air was still ringing. Or was it the water?

No, it was the air. The compression came again and Sethral vomited water. Shouts around her cut short with a splash muffled through the ringing. She reached out and touched something warm. The ringing was her own head. She tried to sit up and the ground made loops. No matter which way she moved, it was always against her. The shouting returned. Something dropped to the ground beside her. Sethral reached out. This one was also warm. Was it the same thing, or a new one?

"Sethral! Sethral! Can you hear me?"

A slap to her face doubled the ringing. Dusk had slapped her once. Dusk.

Dusk.

Sethral bolted upright and was smacked by the ground again. Strong paws held her steady as she flailed, until she realized she was too weak to do anything.

"Can you hear me?" said Loki again. "Sethral, answer me. Can you hear me?"

"Yes." It came out more a gasp than a voice.

"Thank Shelha. Spitfire?"

"She's up," came Ryatzi's voice. It was hard to tell distances with the ringing. A frantic babble marked 'she' as Silversand.

"Where's Dusk?" Sethral tried to say, but it came out jumbled and she had to try again to make sense.

"We got you all out," said Loki. He had not let go of her forearms, Sethral realized, as she tried and failed again to rise. "Lie still. You're still stunned."

That made sense, so Sethral closed her eyes. She was plunged deep into the floating again.

Chapter 27

It was black. Sethral scrubbed frantically at her eyes, but it did nothing to remove the plastering blackness that cloaked everything right down to the claw in front of her face. She couldn't see the claw in front of her face. This was the ringing. Something had broken, and now she couldn't see. She whimpered and scrambled upright, pawing and pawing her face. Something caught her claws and she screamed.

"Sethral, shhh. It's okay. It's me."

"I can't see. Loki, I can't see."

"It's night. We're in a cave. I can't see either."

Sethral let her claws fall limp. "Do we have a light?"

He let go of one of her claws and pulled something across the floor towards him. After a moment, he let go of her other claw, too. The tink of flint on metal brought a burst of sparks in the dark. Sethral's body went weak.

Loki returned the items to her bag and fastened the flap again. "How's your hearing?"

"The ringing's almost gone. I think we made it into the ship before it did anything permanent." Her stomach seized. "Dusk and Firebrand! Where—"

Loki caught her claw again and fixed a paw over her mouth. "Asleep. You're all here. Relax."

"Where are the others?"

There was a sigh in the dark. "Don't freak out. They got caught."

She wanted this journey to be over. She wanted to go home. Before someone else died. Now they were caught again, and they still hadn't found Firefly. Sethral swallowed back sudden tears and pressed her palms to her eyes. If the others were caught, she had to calm down. They needed her calm. "Where?"

"We don't know."

"Is everyone here okay?"

His silence lasted too long.

"Who's hurt?" said Sethral.

"Fibes broke a leg when the ship fell, and Dusk's been unconscious since we got him out of the water. The Watermice that fell in with you got... taken."

"Taken by what?" said Sethral, though deep in her gut, she already knew.

"Don't make me answer that, please."

Sethral found him in the dark and hugged him. His breath shuddered like he had been holding it in.

"What was that bell thing?" he said into her shoulder.

"That metal dish I had in my bag. Dusk broke the rock with it so the ship would fall."

"That almost killed you guys."

"It was that or get shot."

Loki slumped down, and his voice cracked. "I don't know what to do, Seth. We can't fight bows. And we can't go back to the river or that thing will get us. We barely got you guys in here before it found our first cave. It was butting against the tunnel we took..." he shuddered hard and Sethral hugged him tighter.

"Don't think about it for now," she said. "If you found a connecting cave, there's going to be more. There's a good chance we can get out of here without going back to the river."

"Fibes can't walk. And if we don't have her, we can't move Dusk."

"Then we wait for him to wake up."

"He's really out, Seth. I think the bell or the fall did something to him. He's got a fever."

"Where is he?"

Loki reluctantly left the hug and pulled her a few paces to the cave's other side. Firebrand was asleep with one leg stretched out on the cool stone. Sethral ran a claw down it, but it felt like Loki or Ryatzi had already set the bone. Dusk was curled in the crook of the Leslander's flank. Sethral could hear his breathing in the dark, shallow and irregular. His fur was dry from the heat beneath it. He jumped when she touched it. Sethral rested a claw on his forehead, but he was still out cold.

"You guys are up?" said a voice in the darkness. Silversand found her way to their side.

Sethral jumped as a lick on the forehead accompanied Ryatzi's scent. She hugged him. "Can you navigate around here?"

She got a tapped 'mostly'.

"How rested are we all?"

"More than Phoenix, Tetch and Whipper," said Silversand.

Sethral shook Firebrand until the Leslander stirred. "Which way are Tetch and Pheo?"

A tail drew a line down her flank in the direction she had expected. So they were still alive, then.

"Okay, good." She gave Firebrand a final hug. "Stay here with Dusk. We're going to find a way out."

Firebrand tapped an affirmative and put her head back down. Sethral found all the herb packets in her satchel and left them beside her. Everything smelled wet and she couldn't see the packet colours in the dark, but Firebrand was more familiar with the herbs than she was.

'Ready?' clicked Ryatzi in the dark.

"Yeah. Let's go."

Ryatzi had found the next wriggle-hole. Their scents would stay for moons on the cool, damp stone, so Sethral did not bother leaving marks as they felt their way slowly to the next cave. Here there was a hole in the ceiling. They helped each other up. Sethral scrambled last over the edge and nearly ran into Ryatzi, who was gazing down a tunnel.

'It's long,' he clicked. 'Do we want to follow it?'

"It's downstream, right?"

"Yeah," said Loki.

"Then yes."

Silversand gasped suddenly. "Look!"

They bounded together, but the tunnel was empty.

"At what?" said Sethral.

"You... right there. Can't you..." Silversand stepped ahead of them and called down the tunnel, "Hello?"

Loki found Sethral's wing in the dark. 'There's nothing there,' he tapped.

"She wants us to follow her," said Silversand.

"Who?" said Sethral. She was getting a strange feeling. Loki's seventh sense detected creatures; he would know better than any of them if something was or was not present. But somehow the tunnel didn't feel empty to her either.

"A Coppertail. A Forestair." Silversand took another step. "You want us to come?"

'Do we follow her?' tapped Sethral on Ryatzi's shoulder.

He wavered, then tapped back, 'Mark the trail.'

"Lead the way, Silver."

Silversand trotted fearlessly down the long tunnel. Fur brushed Sethral's shoulder as Ryatzi swapped places with her to take up the rear.

By the end of what must have been a moon's paw-length or more, Sethral doubted she would be able to retrace their trail with or without markings. The caves linked and bubbled like syrup dribbled into snow. The renegades climbed and dropped, wormed through holes so narrow they had to pull each other through, scaled walls only Silversand seemed able to see the pawholds of, and skidded down inclines so slick they might as well have been iced. Nobody spoke.

Sethral had just started to wonder how much farther she could go without food when Silversand slowed. She held out her tail to stop them and crept forwards alone. Something blocked the tunnel ahead. Silversand put her paws up and kneaded her claws into something softer than stone. The thick aroma of damp bark filled the cave.

Sethral approached cautiously. What she found was a living wall, curved so gently it must have been a tail-length broad. The bark Silversand had scratched came away in filaments from a green underlayer that was not quite wood, not quite plantflesh, tough but not hard. Whatever the growth was occupied the whole tunnel. It was vertical, sunk from the ceiling down through the floor, and where the tunnel did not accommodate it, the rock cracked to make room.

Silversand gave a cry and ran to one side. They ran after her to find her hindquarters disappearing through a narrow gap between the thing and the wall. They squeezed through one by one. On the other side, Silversand had fallen to a crouch. "I don't like it," she whispered.

Here a long tunnel dipped downwards. Sethral clicked her tongue into the darkness and was met by echoes off a myriad facets of rock; the clear passageway dissolved into caves and other formations ahead. She took a step and skidded. Slime covered the floor, green-smelling and fresh. Sethral held a claw in it long enough to feel which way it oozed. It was coming from the growth they had just crawled past.

"Get back to the other side," said Silversand.

"But—" said Loki, but the cat whimpered.

"Something's coming, get back, now, go!"

They were back through the crevice in half the time. Silversand came last and crouched by the gap. Sethral crouched beside her. From somewhere far away, deep in the caves, came a long, slow scrape. There was a pause of twenty heartbeats, then the sound resumed in a faint hiss that grew back into the scrape and elongated, coarsened, then tapered off again. Like a sanding tool the size of a ship drawn over a shipside. Like a snake over stone.

"Where is she?" breathed Sethral. "The Forestair."

"Back here with us. But she wants us to go through there."

The scrape had stopped. They held bated breaths until their lungs ached and their limbs fell asleep. Sethral flinched as the sound resumed. This time it retreated, one long, slow hiss at a time.

"Water," said Silversand.

"Where?"

"No. It went back in the water. Right at the end."

Sethral wiped her slimy claws and and put them on the cat's shoulders. "Listen, Silver. I believe you, and I think there's something on the other side of this plant-thing that we're supposed to find. And it kills me to say this, but I don't think I'm going to be any help getting it. If that thing comes back, I'm not going to make it back through here in time. Are you okay going without me?"

"I was going to say I should probably go alone." Silversand's voice gave her away as she looked at the ground. "I was hoping you wouldn't force yourself along."

For some absurd reason, that drew a smile to Sethral's face. Maybe it was because the cat was right, and she could see it now. "Silver? You know, I'm really sorry I didn't start trusting you sooner. Because you're really the most capable of any of us, and I'd probably have screwed up a lot fewer things if I'd said so moons ago." She hugged the cat. "Come back if you need anything."

The cat nodded and was gone. Ryatzi started to groom himself nervously. Loki edged into it, and they groomed each other. It could only have been another hundred heartbeats before near-silent paws bounded back up the tunnel. Silversand tumbled through the gap all in a rush. "Sethral! There's a lock and it's too rusty to pick. Do you have a file?"

She did. She actually did. She had picked it up at the dump on Ridia and Firekyle. It was an old, rusted metal piece that had lost its handle and been bent into a curlicue, half-melted like it had fallen into a Lowland forge. Damp items spilled from her satchel as she dug for it, hoping against hope she hadn't lost it in the waterfall. She had not. Silversand took it and was back through the gap before another breath had passed. In another hundred heartbeats, the rasp of a file echoed faintly up from a lower cave. Files were loud. Sethral tensed more and more until she heard exactly the sound she was dreading. The rasp stopped immediately, and Silversand dashed back. Once again they waited, the cat panting, until another scrape heralded the massive eel's return to the water.

"If you do this too many times, it'll get suspicious," whispered Sethral.

"I know."

Silversand left again. This time, the rasp was muffled when it started. She must have found a way to dampen it.

The scrape returned with a sharp heave, but before it had left the water, there was a ping and the splitting bang of stone on stone. Silversand sprinted up the tunnel with something that clattered and swept along the floor. A cloth bag filled with oddly shaped pieces piled through the gap and the cat tumbled after it. The scraping surged up the tunnel. The rock that had banged was swept aside.

"Run!" cried Silversand.

Sethral slung the bag over her shoulder. Something the weight of a tree struck the plant mass hard enough to make the tunnel tremble. The scrape began to jerk back and forth.

"It's been chewing the other side," panted Silversand as they stumbled frantically back along their own trail. "It's almost through. We need to lose it."

'Small cave!' clicked Ryatzi. They doubled back and tumbled through the crack in the rock. The tunnel on the other side sloped upwards, then down again. Sethral hissed as Ryatzi stopped at the top of the rise.

'There's another way here,' he clicked.

Loki braced himself and let the Saberel leap off his back. The hole was large enough to jump through. Silversand went next, and she and Ryatzi pulled Sethral up using the bag straps. Loki sprang up on his own. Already Ryatzi had found another passageway, small again and leading upwards. Or maybe he was just picking the upwards ones. With the manic energy of fear, they slipped and slid through the caves until fresh air made them all stop dead. The cave they were in had a hole in the side of it. The draft left no doubts that the tunnel led straight outside.

The ground trembled again.

"I think it got through," whispered Silversand. "It's down in the caves."

'There's no way into here big enough for it to take,' clicked Ryatzi, halfway around the cave. They relaxed, but only a little.

"I'm just as worried about what's up above," said Loki. "We're only protected from half the danger here."

Ryatzi jumped down from a ledge at the top of the cave. 'Don't touch the top of the slope here. It's a rockfall waiting to happen. Do you want to check outside so we know how close we are to anything dangerous?'

"No," said Loki, but Silversand tugged his fur. She was on her way to the tunnel.

"We're both the same colour as the rock," she said. "We scout first."

When they were gone, Ryatzi found Sethral and crawled under her wing, shivering.

She hugged him tightly. "Stay behind me if they shoot at you, okay?"

He nodded. Sethral wasn't sure where he had gotten his fear of arrows. Probably in the Lowlands after he escaped from Radar. It was not uncommon for villages south of the Valkenland to arm themselves in ways the north side would not even think of, and what those creatures didn't recognize, they shot at.

Realizing she was still holding the bag Silversand had returned with, Sethral let it slide to the ground. Her file was jammed in the top, slimy with plant sap. Sethral wiped and pocketed it, then ran her claws down the bag. The cloth was tough, nearly waterproof, and rotting only in tiny areas. It was fitted to a small, Coppertail-like frame.

'It's the one,' clicked Ryatzi quietly. He removed his paw from the cloth. 'Radar's.'

Sethral tightened the drawstring and hugged the bag. A bone inside jabbed her ribs. Until they returned it to its rightful guardians, she had to be ready to protect this with her life.

Silversand and Loki returned at a slink. "I think you need to come see this," said the Fisher.

The tunnel was padded with soil and overgrown by the time they drifted like moonshadows up to the exit. This slanted slightly to give a breathtaking view of the night sky. Stars laid more thickly than sand gathered in ribbons around pockets of darker darkness. Were the stars themselves different here, or was it something about the air between them and the ground that made them look this way? Sethral looked for the moon to confirm it, and caught her breath.

The moon was a sicle blade, creamy and in its rightful place in the sky. But mirrored across the inky circle its orb would fill when full was another crescent. It was thinner than the first, a suture needle to a rib bone, and smaller, too. More curved. I was the same colour the normal moon had been behind a pall of Rock Flat dust.

"'The moon...'" murmured Sethral. The rest of the sentence in Salisetta's logbook had not been legible, or maybe it had never been written. The moon.

Loki tugged her fur, a finger to his lips. Silversand had crept out on top of the cave entrance, and had just signaled the coast clear. Mounting the rise proved them close to the river; not ten tail-lengths away, the ground pitched over the cliff of the canyon. The water was quiet. Far away upstream, the waterfall was a thin, white line, soundless with distance and visible in the cooler, less humid night air. Loki turned her around. There was a rocky protrusion down-stream. At first she saw nothing around it but the strangely barren, grassy ground. But the longer she peered into the moon-washed darkness, the more she thought there was something wrong with the hill.

Its sides didn't jut upwards like they were supposed to. They bulged, but only here and there, like the stone was marred by strange tumors. And its top seemed to be missing. Where pale surfaces would normally reflect the moonlight, this hill simply faded into the night, and the stars above it were strangely spotty. The shading on the rest of it was far from uniform. Sethral let Silversand lead her off the cavetop into the shadows. When she opened her eyes again, she could see.

A half-vine, half-tree with a trunk thirty paces across grasped the outcrop. It looked to Sethral like a spider, the rock a prey-creature locked in its embrace. 'Branches' scarcely thinner than the main stem tangled over each other and replaced the top of the hill in a tall pile. Their ends radiated towards the sky. Both the branches and the trunk were covered in bulges like the galls on late Mist Moon flower stems. Each could have filled her room in Rockhall.

"I think something lives in it," said Silversand, who had the best night vision among them. "There are holes all over the bumps. Like burrows."

Sethral pulled Radar's bag tighter across her back. "Ratty, are there Forestairs around? Or Silver, where's your friend?"

"She's not here," said Silversand.

Ryatzi didn't answer. Before Sethral could ask again, shapes appeared around their perch. She gasped and clutched the bag. But the shapes weren't Watermice. The dark, feathery fur of the second canopy Forestairs made them look assembled from the graceful threads of the grass shadows. It took a second, then third pass around their circle to realize that the gap among them was not empty. Halo's fur had a silver cast in the moonlight, painted with the same brush as the grass. She stepped into the circle and bowed.

Sethral pushed the bag onto her back again and came slowly down the outcrop. Halo had grown again. She had been Ryatzi's height when they had last seen her; now she stood a paw's length taller. Sethral pulled off the bag and held it in her arms for a last moment, then offered it to the Forestair. Halo let her fasten it to her back. It needed only a little tightening. When it was secure, one of the dark

Forestairs threw back her head and gave a shrill, singing call into the night. Their pelts flashed and were gone.

"We did it," said Loki hoarsely.

"Not yet," said Sethral. "Benty has one of her antlers. And Winter still has the last bone."

The twin crescent moons floated higher now than the moon ever did back home. One bright star looked about to be pinched between their tips. Sethral lost herself in it for all of a heartbeat when a crack of stone sounded in the distance.

Chapter 28

The image of the monster from the water breaking to the surface paralyzed her. Around her, her friends didn't dare move as the sound came again, then was answered by a smaller crack. The first returned. For a few heartbeats everything went silent, then the first began a steady beat. It was not natural rock breaking. This was someone hitting rocks together. The higher tone overlaid itself on the first in a mesmerizing rhythm. The rock beneath the renegades shuddered.

A Coppertail's screech sent ice through Sethral's body. It was followed by the creak of many bows. It snarled, then fell silent with a whimper. The sound carried so far on the still air, they might as well have been tail-lengths from the dark parade that had materialized in front of the behemoth vine-tree. A wide ring of creatures flickered with the glint of moonlight off glossed bowstrings. At their center was a smaller clump. Sethral grabbed Loki's arm. One of the creatures was glowing.

The rock-sounds had not moved. They were at the edge of the river, on a spit jutting from the canyon's edge. Creatures there looked out into the canyon, and the rocks tied to the bottoms of the staves they carried maintained the steady clattering at their feet. One stepped past them and gave a shout that echoed up and down the canyon.

"Negrilaw!"

The rock under Sethral's claws shuddered again. A deep scrape vibrated the air from the cave beneath them, and the monster butted the rock again. Why didn't it turn around and return to the water and the creatures that were calling it? Had it gotten trapped?

Already the procession had reached the base of the spit. The rock-drumming intensified.

"They can't jump!" squeaked Silversand. "It'll kill Phoenix!"

There was no time to think. Sethral seized Loki's arm and sprinted back into the cave, up to the ledge where Ryatzi had warned of a rockslide. The biggest boulder was on unsteady footing. She hurled her weight against it. Loki caught on as it rocked, and though he must have thought her crazy, he doubled her impact when the boulder swung towards the incline again. This time pebbles skittered and the buildup gave way. The boulder thundered down the cave, and though Sethral and Loki were halfway to the surface when it connected with the back wall, the boom shook them off their paws. Loki dragged Sethral up again. Rocks tinkled and crackled. Something slammed against the other side of the wall, and the entire back of the cave crumbled.

"Run!" screamed Sethral.

Ryatzi and Silversand were with them as they fled the cave. Ryatzi took them straight to the forest. Sethral could not look back until they had plunged among trunks and found one rough enough for all but Ryatzi to climb.

"I can outrun it," he said when they hesitated. They scrambled up the trunk.

Out on the field, the hummock with the cave entrance was silent and still. Sethral nearly lost her grip, her claws were shaking so hard. She sank them into the bark beneath her. A narrow wedge of shadow poked from the cave in the field. Across the grass, the creatures on the spit had halted, and half their bows now pointed this way. The Coppertails were still hemmed in. The drumming had stopped.

The wedge elongated and began to grow. Bigger and bigger it got, until it leveled out to precede a snakelike body as thick as Ryatzi was tall out of the cave. It had sensed the creatures across the field. The grass parted in a vee as it began to stalk them, its motion half a slither, half a crawl. From above, it looked for all the world like a rivulet of dark blood through the moonlit grass. A piercing whistle sounded from the vine-tree. At once, every bow was trained in the direction of the monster they could not see. Could the guard not tell what it was? Bows would be useless against this thing.

"Run," whispered Loki. "Shelha, why aren't they running?"

"They'll still be shot." One of Sethral's claw-tips broke. She tried to relax her grip, but it was like prying hardened metal. The eel paused and readjusted its course. It was headed for the center of the parade. On a quiet or unspoken signal, the white Watermice bundled together and forced the Coppertails and Whipper—Sethral could see a dark blob on Taz's back—out in front of them.

"Sethral," said Silversand, alarmed.

"It's okay," said Sethral. She could not tell if she was lying to herself or not. Please don't freeze. I'm counting on you. Please.

The eel lunged and fire lit up the parade. The monster recoiled. White Watermice at the back bolted. Those in the front could not turn their backs. Phoenix was brighter than Sethral had ever seen him, the flames on his body more orange and white than red. He darted forwards with a screech that rivaled a Whitewing's. The eel pulled back, then shot at him like a spring. He leaped clear and returned the charge. He pressed closer, seemingly fearless, and the eel took an awkward hunched coil back into the grass. Phoenix leaped at it again. He was within striking range. Sethral could see the monster's teeth in the firelight. It jerked suddenly, and its silhouette revealed an arrow lodged in its nose-tip. White Watermice had marshalled themselves in a line behind the Pyrya and were pouring arrows past him. Few seemed to harm the eel, but at last one struck home. The monster's body writhed back. A shot had found its eye in the dark. It whipped around and crossed the field in heartbeats, to vanish back down the cave.

The Watermouse crowd reappeared like they had only gone for ammunition, and suddenly the Coppertails were surrounded again. A bow drew on Taz and Fletch, but Phoenix leaped between them. It was hastily fired skywards. On the other side, another replaced it, and the Pyrya darted out along the spit. He made a mock run at its end and Sethral nearly had a heart attack. A shout lowered the bow. He was threatening them. Threatening to throw himself into the river if they harmed the others. Taz and Fletch fell under ropes, not arrows, and the bows turned on Phoenix. Before they could shoot, his fires went out, and he collapsed on the rock.

Sethral had just pried her claws from the branch when Ryatzi screamed. With a shout there were creatures all around the tree. Bows pointed up into the branches and down at the Saberel, who was on the ground. Sethral smelled blood.

"Ratty!"

Ryatzi snapped at a creature who ventured closer, and was shot again. Silversand climbed slowly down the tree. A creature shouted again and jerked its bow at Sethral and Loki.

'They've got us,' flicked Silversand from near the ground. 'Obey them or they'll kill him.'

A moment later she was jumped and wrestled down. Ropes bound her muzzle and paws. Loki squeezed Sethral's claw. They descended together and were similarly taken. Sethral could hear Ryatzi panting nearby. He whimpered as someone kicked him. Please, let the shots not be lethal. They couldn't have shot him somewhere lethal. She wanted to run to his side, but she was trussed up like an Aria's prey. She wanted to say even one thing to him, but if she got shot too, they would be in double the danger. She tried to flick in the dark, but she got no reply.

Please be okay. Please be okay.

He was kicked again, and the whimper this time was weaker. Something ran down Sethral's face, and when she took a breath, it hitched so hard her shoulders shook. She had lost Wing and Jay. She couldn't lose Ryatzi, too. She couldn't. Please. Please!

There was a light sigh and the bowcreature standing over her slumped among the tree roots. The base of the tree had gone silent. The last white Watermouse spun with bow upraised, then also relaxed. The bow fell to the ground, its owner crumpled on top of it. Sethral could have cried.

"Where's Firebrand?" said Silversand's anxious voice.

Sethral's bonds slackened like they had come undone themselves. She turned to see a pale, willowy Forestair lift Ryatzi's body onto the back of another, who sped away. Dusk had not answered the question. He and a strangely familiar Canyonlander stood side by side among the fallen Watermice. Their heads were dipped towards one another, but they made no sound save for the occasional twitches of paws in leaves. The Canyonlander lifted its head to gaze out across the field.

It was Shuria. The Forestair Whipper and Fletch had once treated for an arrow wound now walked without a limp, and he held himself with a regality Sethral had long ago learned to associate with a warrior. He paid no attention to the other Canyonlanders that flitted about him. Loki sat up and started rubbing life back into his wrists, and Silversand helped a strong-looking female chew through the last of her bonds. Sethral's mind kept replaying Ryatzi's limp body, and her heart had not slowed a beat from when she had first heard him scream. He had to be okay. They had taken him away to be treated. He was going to be okay.

What could only be a scout bounded in from the field's edge. This time Shuria and Dusk broke off and both paid attention as the creature danced, so lightly her paws were nearly soundless. When she was done, Shuria shifted his, and the scout was gone again. Dusk turned, and Sethral's heart skipped half a dozen beats as he walked towards her. She kicked herself for fearing a friend, but there was something about the Nightlock that sent shivers down both her wings.

"We need you to burn it," he said.

"Burn... what?"

"The tree." He flicked one tail towards the vine-tree where it hunched on its rocky hill. "I don't care how, as long as we see that thing in flames."

Sethral swallowed hard. "Not the whole thing. It's their home. There could be children in there."

He bared his teeth. "Do I look like I care?"

Maybe it was her idiotic mind that made her so reckless, or maybe it was the memory of that orange glow over Nova's forest. "I don't care. Pick a part of it if you have to. I'm not going to burn the whole thing."

She flinched as Dusk's paws shifted, but he was only translating for Shuria. The Forestair remained expressionless. He stepped up beside Dusk and doubled the gaze on Sethral. She held her ground.

"He says the creatures there once caught a Canyonlander kit," said Dusk. "They put her on a rope and let their children poke her with sticks, then fed her to the Negrilaw."

"I don't care," repeated Sethral. The steadiness of her own voice surprised her; her claws were now shaking. "I'm not going to be like them, then." Three final words nearly made it out, but she caught them. She looked up and met Dusk's dead black gaze, and decided to say them anyway. "Or like you."

He hit her so hard, she was flat on her back before the world stopped spinning. There was no air in her lungs. She filled them with a painful gasp.

Dusk's voice cut like ice shards. "Ryatzi is dying."

Sethral rolled over painfully and let the tears fall unhindered. "I know." It came from somewhere she had no control over. "But I'm not going to be like them. And you. What would Phoenix say if he saw you doing this?"

His paw whipped back, but it caught on an invisible string before he snapped it over her head again. He swore out loud. "I'm doing this for him. They're going to use him to control that thing; why do you think they wouldn't let him kill himself? Don't you dare bring him into this."

"Then make me stop." She stepped into his striking range. "I dare you."

They faced each other down, Dusk's paw upraised, Sethral with her tear-lined face lifted, defiant.

At last, slowly, Dusk lowered his paw. "What do you suggest, then?"

She had not had a plan, but one came to her mind without prompting. Like it had been there all along. "What do they value besides the tree?"

Dusk passed this to Shuria, who passed an answer back. It brought a sharp look to Dusk's eye.

"The Mother seed," he said. He glanced at her, translating from Shuria. "This is the tree that makes all those nuts. It drops them in the river all wet season, then when the river turns, they're all washed downstream. But those only grow into vines. To make another copy of itself, it makes a Mother seed. It's big, like the head of the Negrilaw but round, and it hangs over the river on its own stem. The creatures who live here take care of it. Besides themselves and their home, it's the thing they defend most viciously."

"Its own stem?" Sethral peered across the moonlit field. Against the shadow of the canyon, faintly moonlit, she could see it if she looked hard enough. It appeared to be listing. "Ask him if it's more tilted than it should be."

Dusk frowned, but did so. Shuria cocked his head, and suddenly he and she were sharing something Dusk was not.

"Yes," said Dusk, turning back to Sethral.

"Then that stem is already dead."

Silversand gasped. "That's the one the eel chewed through!"

"I thought it was weird when I saw the tree on the surface," said Sethral. "I'd thought we were closer to the canyon when we ran into that root-thing underground, and the tree's too big for it, too. And it would have been at too weird an angle. It must grow up from below."

"So if we were to add weight to it somehow, we could topple it," said Loki.

"Not add weight. We'd have to be aboveground for that, and we'd probably get shot. I say we push it from below."

"But the eel's down there," said Silversand.

Sethral plucked a branch from the ground. Dry season. Even the moss up the tree had crackled beneath her claws. "That eel is afraid of fire."

Chapter 29

Shuria dispatched his scout again the moment she returned. The strong female that Silversand had made friends with was also sent off, with slightly longer instructions. The rest, on translated orders from Sethral, began to gather fuel and pile it at the forest's edge. The scout returned. Thaliar's Tree was quiet, locked down with guards at every entrance. Taz, Fletch and Whipper had been thrown back in a prison pit with no guards. Clearly the colony trusted they would not escape, and did not see the worst that could happen as such a bad thing.

"So they're bait," said Loki sourly.

"All the better for us," said Sethral. "Are we clear to move into the cave?"

She got 'Waiting on it' from Dusk and returned to organizing the fire material by size. Tinder was going to be the limiting factor. "Dusk, ask if there are any Aria webs around."

He did, and soon tinder was no longer the limiting factor. They now had enough for a balanced fire. Whether it would last as long as they needed it to was the riskiest question.

The scout—her name was Piili, Sethral leaned—bounded back with an all-clear on the cave. She was not even out of breath. She joined the other Forestairs in shuttling the firewood belowground, through the tunnels to a safe space down-tunnel from the severed stem. Sethral accepted a ride and was brought down to choose the best place for the fire. It would need vertical space to keep the smoke out of the most important tunnel, and lots of ventilation. The Negrilaw's beach proved the best candidate. With Piili on watch, her paws in the water like she could feel the eel coming that way, the fire was assembled, then lit.

Aboveground, the strong female—Zeena—had returned, and she had not returned alone. Half the Canyonlanders she had brought were assigned to Sethral to help with the underground portion of the plan. The other half remained above.

"You two are with Seth," said Dusk to Loki and Silversand. He left no question in it, and even Silversand did not complain.

All too soon came the whistle that meant everything was in place. Sethral and her group waited tense and silent, straining their ears for any trace of sound that meant things had gone awry. In under three hundred heartbeats, Piili dashed down the tunnels. The prisoners in the pit were free.

"Go," said Sethral.

She and her creatures flung their might against the leaking stem bottom. Greased at the edges by its own juice, it groaned, then slid almost imperceptibly upwards. Sethral speed-taught how to do things on a count, and on a count they pushed again. Then again. Inch by inch the stem was thrust upwards through the rock. Groans became creaks, then shuddering screeches, until Sethral felt the whole thing start to tip.

"Get back!" she cried, and ran for the lower tunnels.

Rocks cracked and thick juice splattered down as the back of the stem was dragged up the wall. The Mother seed hung over the river must have weighed as much as all of them combined. With a last, long groan, the stem accelerated, popped free and was flipped into the river. The hole let the screams of white Watermice pour in. Fear of the Negrilaw abandoned, they flooded from Thaliar's Tree and ran to the river, then along it, following the fallen stem. More flocked around the hole. One tried to descend, but was forced back by the slick walls. Sethral and her team faded into the tunnels.

Sethral would have been first back to the surface had the Forestairs not been so light-footed. When they reached the cave entrance, she was swept off the ground. She landed on a Forestair's back and clung to the creature's long fur as he flew after the others, away from Thaliar's Tree. They leaped straight off the edge of the canyon. Her ride hit a ledge tail-lengths down and jumped again without even a jolt of landing. Above, below, in front and behind them, Canyonlanders sprang along the vertical rocks like neither they nor the renegades weighed more than air. The moment the canyon narrowed, Piili took a soaring leap across it. She landed on a ledge near the bottom and zigzagged to the canyon top. Here she paused to check behind them before sailing back again.

Sethral closed her eyes and let the silky night air and sweeping jumps carry her. She was physically exhausted, but her body was so far from sleep, she felt ready to stay awake for days. Something painful nudged the bottom of her consciousness and she wondered vaguely what it was. She must have shoved it down there to focus on the rescue. She didn't feel like bringing it up again.

They travelled farther than Sethral could process in her half-asleep, half-wakeful state. The crescent moons slid down the sky and dawn crept up to replace them, and still they were flying. The Canyon-landers showed no sign of fatigue. Sethral did not realize she had fallen asleep until a bump brought her back to consciousness. The canyon had disappeared. They were in the forest, winding single file up a steep, overgrown hill whose carved stones poked like bones from the moss. Her ride still stepped like that moss was mist, but he had tripped on a root. He must be more tired than he appeared.

Sethral sat up and looked for her friends. Loki was asleep on a female Forestair farther downslope. In the other direction, Silversand sat still and silent on Zeena's back at the head of the line. Sethral watched her and tried to puzzle out why this felt wrong. What did Silversand usually do?

She usually drove the Coppertail she was riding half-bonkers trying to hunt leaves, lean out to catch sights or sounds, or find a comfier position. At very least, she looked around. The buried thing in Sethral's mind surged upwards as the realization about Silversand collided with her check for her last friend. It was a punch in the chest. A punch harder than Dusk's blow, which had left a headache she could barely register.

Ryatzi's whimper, weak and in pain. His thin, still body lifted and whisked away on a Forestair's back. Sethral tapped the Forestair she was riding. "Where's the other one? My friend?"

He looked back at her, uncomprehending. Sethral clawed back the threatening tears and tried to imitate Ryatzi's posture, or body language, or anything, but the unchanged, tired gaze that met hers showed she was not getting through. Of course she couldn't speak Forestair. She had never been able to understand them, much less imitate their beautiful dance of a language. She didn't know why she had tried. She hugged herself and tried to rock away the fear and the terrified tears. It didn't work.

Her Forestair glanced at her again, then chirred softly to the one in front of him. She let him by. He trotted quickly to the front of the line and fell into step with Zeena. They had a quick exchange.

"She doesn't know," said Silversand. Her eyes moved briefly to Sethral's face. "You were asking about Ryatzi, right?"

Sethral nodded, sniffled, and sank her face in her claws. Her Forestair returned to the line behind Zeena.

"His name's Tante, by the way," said Silversand, returning her gaze to the forest ahead. "The one you're riding. Just so you know."

"Tante?" said Sethral. He looked at her more quickly, and she managed a smile. She hugged his neck. "Thanks anyway."

He wouldn't understand, but she hoped he got the gist. He chirped softly and licked her on the head.

The trail continued to climb, rougher and rockier the higher they rose. At last the forest broke. Sethral caught her breath. They were up a mountain in a range of green, broad-sided mountains. At this elevation, the forest thinned and the canopy dropped. Smaller, scruffier trees replaced the giant ones of the lush lowland they had left below. It was only when the scrubby trees too had thinned into dry alpine scrub and a smattering of tall brush that the trail turned sideways along the slope. They circled the peak and suddenly arrived where Sethral immediately knew they had been headed.

A cirque carved from the mountainside grew thick with a carpet of tan grass, edged with plants made of thick, spiny pads linked together at the long ends. Canyonlander kits flocked from nowhere to swarm the returning convoy. Sethral nearly lost her balance as one popped up on Tante's back. The wee creature was the size of a Royal kit, and so delicate she was worried it might break if she touched it. It sniffed her paws, chirped almost out of her hearing range and waved its tail happily. Then it was suddenly on the rocks up the side of the cirque. It followed the adults from half a tail-length above.

At the back of the cirque, they entered a wide cave entrance into an even wider cave. The floor had been ringed with grass mats where Forestairs slept and groomed each other, and kits flowed constantly to and from a tunnel at the back. Sethral slid to the ground as Tante crouched. She was immediately set upon by kits. They leaped back when she moved, then crept forwards again. Something tickled her tail. She swished it and a kit hopped away. Another sniffed her wing. As they established that she wasn't a threat, she was suddenly awash in tiny muzzles.

Silversand sat down nearby to make their investigation easier. The kits were already giving her fur experimental licks. "I think this is how they find out where someone is from," she said.

"How, tasting us?" said Loki. He was trying to keep his more ticklish spots away from the kits. It wasn't working.

"It gives them a stronger smell read."

"We must be the most different creatures they've ever smelled..."

Both of Sethral's wings were now on the floor, swamped with kits. None of the adults made any motion to stop them. A couple even joined in. They always touched their muzzles to anything they sniffed.

Tante stopped by a now-clear grass bed at the edge of the cave and looked back at her. Sethral extracted her wings with less difficulty than she had expected; the kits weighed as little as birds, and were so nimble they hopped clean over her feathers if she so much as brushed their paws. Loki and Silversand trailed after her. They curled up together on the grass and were again beset by kits. Sethral vowed not to cry in front of the colony here. She fell asleep to the moth's wings of Canyonlander kit grooming.

By the next morning, the journey from Thaliar's Tree to the Canyonlander colony had faded to a misty smudge. Sethral sat at the edge of the cirque and watched the distant, sunlit rim of the canyon gradually burn clear of fog. The river was filled to the brim with grey.

"No sign of them yet?" said Loki.

She shook her head as he found a seat beside her. A kit trotted after him. It got distracted by Sethral's wing and set about sniffing her.

"We're still a novelty, huh?" said Loki.

"She's probably a new one."

"Has Tante been looking after you?"

"Mhm. Yours?"

"Yeah."

The Forestairs that had given them rides here continued to host them, bringing food and finding them beds in the hall where nobody seemed to have their own sleeping space. Loki had wanted to help fish or forage, but Silversand had told him not to offer. Besides the fact that any Canyonlanders could find in a sun's paw-length what any of them could in a day, it didn't seem polite.

"Any news?" managed Sethral at last.

"Not that Silver can tell. I think she's still trying to figure out where they took him."

Silversand emerged from the cave with a flock of kits trotting dutifully at her heel. She had acclimatized fastest to being constantly shadowed. She stopped to stretch in the sun—several kits looked curious, then copied—and padded over to join them.

"Taz and Fletch are on their way," she said. "With Whipper. Firebrand's staying back until her leg heals enough to travel, I think, and Dusk and Phoenix are hiding in the forest with Shuria and the others."

"Why?" said Loki.

"I don't know. I didn't understand."

"Probably Phoenix losing his shit," said Sethral. She fingered the loose side of her bag. Dusk had stolen her blanket at some point between arriving with the Forestairs and leaving to attack Thaliar's Tree. She still couldn't figure out when.

Loki fiddled nervously with a grass blade. "And what about..."

Silversand shook her head.

"I trust them," said Sethral, more forcefully than intended. "If Forestairs healed Wing when Corsair cut his eye, they can handle this."

Her friends stayed silent. Silversand had tried to ask about Ryatzi yesterday and today, but each time she imitated him, the Forestairs looked at her like they didn't understand. Her acting of anyone else had drawn immediate recognition. Silversand's ears pricked up suddenly. Downslope, a small flock of birds with strangely shaped beaks rose squawking from the trees. Someone was making their way up the mountain.

Taz and Fletch arrived with a small convoy of Canyonlanders originally from Shuria's squad. Whipper practically fell off Taz's back onto Silversand. Taz looked at the expectant pool of kits at his paws and waded resignedly through them to hug Sethral and Loki.

"We can't understand anything they're saying and Whipper won't talk," he said. "Where are the others?"

They told him the scant little they knew, then the fact that they had found and returned the skeleton. Not much else seemed worth the energy of speaking right now. Taz sank down beside them with half a groan. Sethral rubbed his shoulder.

"We need to get home," he said.

The jungle stretched away for days. Moons. Jungle all the way to the horizon. Even from this vantage point, Sethral could not even make out the waterfall it had taken them two and a half moons to reach. Shelha knew how much farther they were now.

"Do we have to go back across all of that?" said Loki in a voice that broke even as he tried to steady it.

Taz didn't reply. Sethral touched his shoulder and found he had fallen asleep. She curled up against him.

The Canyonlanders' hospitality did not seem to have a limit. Rather, as the days wore on, Sethral felt more like the renegades were being accepted into the colony. Dusk and Phoenix arrived, both nonverbal, and were given a cave somewhere in the tunnels the rest of them had not been taken to. Then two more Canyonlanders returned with Firebrand. The dry season brought cool, dry days to the top of the mountain. Sethral found herself lying in the hot sun as often as Silversand. There was a part of her, deep inside, that never seemed to get warm.

She was napping on one such day when a sound froze her awake with her eyes still closed. Someone had just said Ryatzi's Forestair name. Sethral stayed still with her hearing suddenly as sharp as if she was still in the caves with the Negrilaw. There was a long silence that somehow felt like two Canyonlanders talking, then one repeated the chirp and added another sound to the end of it.

Ryatzi had once said that understanding the Forestair language was as much about instinct as interpretation. Perhaps even more so. He had called it that Silversand and Dusk would be the first to understand it, and Whipper simply because it was closer to how Whipper had engaged with his own clan. Sethral sometimes understood—or thought she did—random words of a conversation. Usually when her mind lapsed and she ended up analyzing less than she usually did.

No, this was not a lapse. Sethral forcibly relaxed her wings again. She was paying too much attention to have understood that sound. She was about to slide back into sleep when it was repeated again. It was not a product of her imagination. The sliding rustle after the chirp made her unremitting chill feel like a warm blanket by comparison. Something about the word, whatever it was, was more potent than any sound she had ever heard a Forestair make. Suddenly shivering, she opened her eyes and risked a glance over her shoulder.

Dusk had come out on the cirque without her realizing. He was walking in a circle with Shai, one of the flock's older members. Dusk watched intently as the sleek female dipped and pranced ever so slightly. Occasionally he would give an affirmative in reply. They broke apart before Sethral realized the conversation was over. She scrambled to intercept Dusk as he made for the cave again.

"What did she say?" she said.

'Go ask Tante to show you.'

"Show me what?"

He met her eye for just a heartbeat, and there was no emotion in his gaze. 'Where they buried him.'

Chapter 30

The stone turned to liquid under Sethral's paws. She was on the ground without realizing she had fallen.

Dusk stepped past her. 'He's not dead. Ask Tante to show you.'

"But... that... was the forest." Dusk stopped walking, his back still to her. Sethral fumbled for the words. "What he said after Ratty's name. That was the forest. That was what they add when someone dies."

She could almost taste the exquisite patience Dusk was using on her. 'Go ask,' he flicked, and walked away.

"I don't know how!" she cried after him. She sank down on the grass with tears tracing hot tracks down her face. Never had she felt so helpless, or scared, or confused. Like the world was disintegrating into threads, and every time she grabbed one, it broke or slid out of her claws. She gave a shuddering sob and hugged herself. What did he mean, 'he's not dead'? Shai had used the word for death. Used it on Ryatzi's name. It made sense now why nobody here responded when Silversand asked about the Saberel. To them, a creature ceased to be when they became something else. Ryatzi on his own no longer existed.

She jerked violently as something nudged her back. Shuria—arrow-catcher, the fastest warrior in the flock—had been following the Nightlock. He cocked his head. Sethral no longer cared enough to dry her face as she met those big, brown eyes. "What happened to him?" she whispered.

Shuria watched her for a long time. Sethral's heart sank back to the lake bottom it had settled on. Of course he wouldn't understand. It had been a moon; she had to stop expecting creatures here to know her language. Fur brushed her side. It took her a soft chirr from the Forestair to realize that Shuria had crouched to offer her his back. She got on shakily and in a moment they were descending the trail down the mountain. It took half a sun's paw-length just to get to the bottom, but like all of his kind, the Canyonlander was as fresh when he reached the lowland as if they had just left.

Strange sights flashed by as they spent the rest of the morning and half the afternoon running along trails that didn't exist until Shuria walked on them. They passed wetlands in open clearings, and dark, shadowed hollows where fungi grey as tall as Silversand. The chill in Sethral's body intensified, so she huddled down on Shuria's back and closed her eyes. The sounds, smells, and light patterns melded together into a background hum.

In a flashback to the journey up the mountain, she was awakened again by a jolt of feeling. It was not a stumble, though. Shuria was no longer walking, and had poked her with his tail in a gesture so startlingly Coppertail-like, for a moment it distracted Sethral entirely from the grove they were standing in. When she finally did notice, the line between dream, memory and reality blurred. Around her, the trees were white. Sethral touched a shaky claw to the bark of an evergreen. Unlike the white grove in the South Forest, there were many species here. Their bark colours and textures varied, but their leaves were all as stripped of hue as if they had grown under the soil for a moon.

When she removed her claw, Shuria moved through the trees with utmost respect. He stopped beneath a young tree with leaves so finely divided they looked like feathers. White feathers. The soil beneath it was disturbed. Shuria looked back at Sethral and repeated what Shai had, Ryatzi's name and the forest, but there was a matter-of-factness about it that did not fit at all with the situation.

"He's... there?" said Sethral. She pointed to the ground.

She got an affirmative. Shuria was not letting her down, so she gripped his fur to stifle the shudder in her claws. "He's alive?"

He repeated the name and forest, then cocked his head at the ground. After a moment, he tapped his paws—digging—and added a papery crackle. He looked back at her.

Sethral hugged his neck and murmured, "I don't understand."

Their "death" was a return to the forest. Could that mean buried but still alive, too? But why bury a creature who was still alive?

Shuria shifted posture in what Sethral felt immediately was a sigh. They left the grove and began the long trip back to the mountain. The sun was halfway down the sky. How long had it taken to get here? How far gone had Ryatzi been by the time the creature carrying him had arrived? Sethral stayed only half awake on the return journey. Tante accosted them at the cirque's entrance after moonrise and scolded Shuria roundly for the apparent infraction of making off with another Forestair's guest. He took Sethral back and brought her to where the other renegades minus Phoenix and Dusk were asleep in a pile in the cave. Sethral slid out of consciousness the moment she was laid down.

Firebrand was limping around the cave having a cheerful argument with the healer Ninik—if a 'healer' could even be distinguished in a full clan of healers—through a complete language barrier when Piili flew into the cave in a flurry of insect sounds. She dashed a circle around the whole place before Zeena, Shai and Shuria arrived, then skidded into a circle-trot with them. It fell apart as the overactive scout outpaced the others and ended up just running around them. Sethral shot up straight as she heard the same crackle Shuria had made when he had taken her to the ghost grove.

Shuria's gaze went to the renegades. Zeena sent Piili into the back caves. The scout was re-ejected a heartbeat later. She dashed to Taz and returned to the caves with him. In another heartbeat she was back again. Dusk had replaced Taz. The Nightlock's expression was deadpan as he stopped beside Shuria and matched the Canyonlander's gaze over the renegades. "Sethral," he said. It was the first she had heard him speak out loud since Thaliar's Tree.

A convoy had materialized in the cave entrance: Shai and Zeena, Ninik, Piili, and two more creatures Sethral couldn't remember the names of.

"Are you coming or not?" said Dusk, jolting her from her reverie.

Sethral's face went hot. She bounded to join them, and Zeena crouched to offer her back. Then they were once again down the mountain trail. The trip to the grove seemed much shorter this time. Maybe because Zeena was half again Shuria's size, and probably much less bothered by carrying a heavy Saggitayria through the forest for half a day.

When they reached the grove, it was to find the ground beneath the feather-leaved tree spotted with grey. Mushrooms, mist-coloured and lifting sturdy round caps, grew thick on the ground in an area a little smaller than a curled-up Coppertail. Piili was digging before the rest had caught a breath. Ninik joined her, and Shai, Dusk and the two Sethral didn't know vanished into the forest. Shuria took each mushroom the diggers uprooted and dropped it carefully somewhere else in the grove.

The hole seemed to melt into the forest floor. Within forty heartbeats, Piili skipped back. Ninik carefully shifted a last few paw-lengths of dirt. Beneath them was a papery surface. Piili excavated around it until a husk like a dried flower had been half unearthed. Ninik slit it open. Sethral gasped as she lifted Ryatzi out by his scruff. He was curled in a limp ball and seemed unconscious. Carefully, Ninik backed out of the hole. She chirped at Zeena, who lay down and made a nest with her body.

Sethral didn't know what to do. She could hardly stay perched on Zeena's flank, but was stepping on the ground here permitted? Had they brought her to help with this? Why else would Dusk have picked her? Then Ninik turned and Sethral forgot everything with a terrified sob. Ryatzi wasn't healed. His whole chest was red, soaked with blood. She scrambled to his side as he was rested in the crook of Zeena's flank. Ryatzi looked too fragile to touch, thin again and pale around the lips. On his side were two symmetrical white splotches each the size of a Coppertail's paw. Those hadn't been there before. Sethral searched his chest fur, but she found only the scars he'd had before.

She slowed halfway through a second search. There was no blood. His fur was soft, if a little coarse from a lack of grooming, but not stiff or sticky. Slowly, she ran her claw down it. The red started at his throat and strengthened to flare across his chest, evenly distributed and blending back to copper at the edges. For the last moon, Ryatzi had rubbed mud across his chest.

Her laugh came out choked, and she wanted to hug him but she didn't dare. She would have to hug him later. Spring colours this strong would have attracted attention from males and females back in his clan, and from what she knew of him, he wanted nothing to do with either. Whether he hid the colours now out of fear of competition or embarrassment at their strength hardly mattered.

Ryatzi's body shifted, and Sethral clued in for the first time that Zeena had been grooming him this whole time. She used quick, strong strokes like a mother might use to warm a newborn, and the Saberel had started to shiver almost imperceptibly. Sethral didn't seem expected to help, so she buried her fingers in Ryatzi's chest fur again and steadied herself in the feel of his heartbeat easing from faint and irregular to something resembling normal. Well, normal for a still deeply unconscious creature who hadn't eaten in over a moon.

She repeated that as it sank in. Over a moon. He shouldn't even be alive after that. She returned to the hole. The digging Coppertails had joined Shuria in dispersing mushrooms, and the papery husk was for now left untouched. Sethral touched it, then broke off a piece. On close examination, it proved to be made entirely of filaments, layered closely together and adhered with a weak natural glue. The husk's inside was smooth save for two places where it gathered inwards into a thick cone broken off before it reached a tip.

Or... maybe it was the husk that grew outwards from the cones. Sethral hurried back to Ryatzi. The two white spots on his side matched the shape of the cone-tops precisely. Like they had been attached to his side. Jay would—

No. No now.

Sethral locked her eyes on the white spots until Zeena's muzzle covered one briefly and broke the gaze. She returned her claws to Ryatzi's fur and fixated on them instead. She leaped in her skin as he coughed. Zeena stopped grooming and slid her tail under his chest. Ryatzi was lifted so he wouldn't choke as the coughing grew into a fit, then died away. It seemed to be what the Forestairs were waiting for. Zeena lifted the Saberel to Shuria's back.

They were back at the cirque come nightfall. Sethral felt ready to fall over the moment the warm air of the cave washed over her. Silversand, Loki and Fletch all ran forwards with a cry when they saw Ryatzi. Sethral let Fletch handle it. She stumbled to the space the three had come from and slumped to the grass.

"Told you," said a voice behind her.

She was too done to even talk back. "Thanks."

Something shifted beside Dusk, and a murmur made Sethral spin around. Phoenix was here, his head on Dusk's shoulder. Dusk said something back and got a half-headbutt too tired to commit to itself. Whipper on Dusk's back shifted in his sleep.

"Where's Taz?" said Sethral.

"Probably flirting somewhere."

She gave him the dirtiest look she could muster. Taz didn't flirt.

'He's with Firebrand,' flicked Phoenix, almost imperceptibly.

Sethral had to stifle a smile. Dusk gave her a suspicious look, then frowned down at Phoenix. Phoenix managed to maintain a perfect illusion of sleep.

Sethral wanted to shut her eyes right then and there, but she had lately developed a compulsion to see each of the renegades before she went down for the night. Right now it was particularly strong. She dragged herself to her paws and wandered outside. Taz and Firebrand were chatting quietly in the corner where Firebrand usually exercised. Both smiled when they saw her.

"Going to bed?" said Firebrand.

"Yeah." Sethral hugged each of them in turn. "Goodnight. Love you."

"Love you, too," said Taz. "Sleep well."

Something had changed about the main cave when Sethral returned to it. She looked around foggily and gradually processed that every kit she knew—most of them now two paw-lengths taller than they had been when the renegades had first arrived—was gathered inside. In roughly the same end of the cave, too. That was unheard of. Scanning further to determine what the source of interest might be, Sethral perked up as Shai stepped through the crowd of youngsters. They actually parted to admit her. A moment later, half of them stuck their little butts to the ground. Sitting? Canyonlander kits never sat.

Fletch was curled around Ryatzi in the renegades' sleeping spot, and both Dusk and Phoenix were now asleep or faking it. Silversand had sat up with every rapt muscle as restrained as the kits' were. She too was watching Shai, who had started to dance.

"Stories?" said Sethral.

The cat nodded.

Sethral lost her next words in a yawn. "Can you understand?"

"A little. She's going a bit slower for the kits. It's... I think it's about us. There, that's Thaliar's Tree. We're splitting up, and there's someone stalking both groups... half of us on the ship, exploring..."

Sethral saw herself and each of the others briefly in Shai's body language, then white Watermice. She would know white Watermice anywhere.

"Getting surrounded, and..." Silversand glanced at Dusk and switched to tail-talk. 'Dusk setting off the bell and all of us going down. Fletch heard it and sent Loki and Ratty off just before they got ambushed. And...'

Several kits leaped up and dashed in tiny circles as the Negrilaw arrived. Sethral shuddered. The eel smashed the ship—she wasn't quite sure how she knew it was a ship—and took the white Watermice that had fallen while Loki and Ryatzi swam the renegades to safety. Sethral suddenly understood why Dusk had told them to get back in the ship before he set off the bell. Besides saving their hearing, he had gotten them far enough underwater in a thick enough swirl of debris that the eel probably hadn't noticed them.

She had missed what happened to the other group, but now Taz, Fletch, Whipper and Phoenix were in a hole in the ground and the rest of them were in a hole in the caves. That must have been the cave entrance, Sethral realized, as Halo's distinctive bow appeared and her own acted self handed over Radar's bag. The scene switched back to Dusk and Firebrand—or just Dusk? It was just Dusk, and he was in the forest. He must have left Firebrand and gone looking for help. He found it... in the story, a group of Canyonlanders had just arrived.

"It was Shuria," breathed Silversand. "Seth... he saw us split up to explore the ship, and he knew we were in trouble, so he ran to get help. Dusk ran into him when he came back with the others."

Shuria and those 'others' merged with Dusk's character as Sethral's released the Negrilaw—the kits were now hopping like a pan of pop-seeds—and arrived just as Ryatzi got shot. Dusk wiped out the white Watermice almost single-handedly before they realized their companions had fallen. The fastest Canyonlander ran Ryatzi away, while Sethral... Sethral was jolted to real life by a tidal wave of kits suddenly popping and dashing circles around her. One step from Shai brought the overexcited crowd back to the proper side of the room.

Silversand giggled. "You're a hero."

"I didn't do that much. Dusk's the one that stormed the Tree to get Phoenix back."

"Shai's saying it wasn't that hard. Apparently all the Watermice went after the seed. None of the Forestairs even got shot at."

Sethral flushed and was glad of the semi-darkness that hid it. "That was just lucky."

The story did not make the rescue seem any more dramatic than Silversand described. That made sense again, Sethral supposed, for a clan of literalists. If they told stories like this, she wondered how long they could accurately preserve history.

"It's a new story now," said Silversand. She frowned. "It's us again. In the canyon colony this time."

"They saw that? What's their explanation for not helping us, then?"

"They couldn't even get close." Silversand's face was serious. "The colony's a pretty serious enemy for them. She's acting like it's amazing that we got out."

Sethral fiddled a claw uncomfortably in her bedding. That plan had succeeded on so many flukes, it could hardly be called a plan at all. It still chilled her to recall reaching up to find the tunnel ceiling just above her head. A hundred heartbeats had made the difference between escape and recapture. Or worse.

"I don't think they travel that far usually," said Silversand. "They don't have anything on us after that... just when we were near the canyon. Now it's a different story again."

This one was all about jungle creatures: Forestairs and white Watermice, and what looked like Aria and a giant bird. Sethral had let herself fall half asleep when Silversand gasped.

"It's Radar!"

Chapter 31

Heat burned up through Sethral's body. For a moment, she could see the Vipra in Shai's body, and even the chill she couldn't rid her body of was temporarily alleviated. There was something choppy about the story, making it harder to understand than the last ones.

"I think it's second-hand," said Silversand. "She's telling what she heard from the second canopy Forestairs. Their dances are a little different. Can a dance have an accent?"

"Well, it's a language, so I don't see why not."

Silversand frowned at the progressing story. "Radar's doing pretty much what we guessed. And they really hate him. But they're also scared of him... I think Radar's probably the only creature from outside that they're actually scared of. It's really spooking them that he had a Forestair skeleton."

"So why can't he control them, then?"

"Because there's nothing he can do to them by revealing them. Nobody survives coming here, and even if they did, they wouldn't find Forestairs that didn't want to be found. It's not like the South Forest... those ones have a lot less to hide in. They're trapped by the winter weather on the Western Shield and the dry season in the Far South, and they're really close to the Lowlands. It's the Lowland creatures that would come after them if they knew they were real."

Silversand did not seem to realize how sophisticated that reasoning was, so Sethral just smiled at her for a time while she continued to watch the story. She supposed Silversand did have all the pieces to put that together. She had lived in the Western Shield, the Lowlands and the South Forest, and had visited the Far South, too. And now she knew Forestairs. This was not the clumsy, daft creature who had first joined the renegades.

"Silver?"

"Yeah?" The cat glanced over.

"I'm really glad to have you around."

Silversand looked surprised for a moment, then smiled back, then got distracted by the story again. "Oh! He's reached here... he used fire, too, Seth. To hold back the Negrilaw while he locked up the skeleton. And then the Forestairs couldn't get it back without breaking the lock, and they couldn't break the lock without warning the Negrilaw, and the they couldn't hold back the Negrilaw without fire, and they can't make fire. That's why they needed us."

"All that for fire."

"Well, and breaking locks. They're not very good at that either. And it was a big one. Oh, it's another story again. I think... it's Winter arriving south. It's in the South Forest Forestair accent now. I wonder if they all pass stories around."

Sethral half listened for the interest of hearing the story from a Forestair perspective, though it was much the same as it would have been from hers. There was even the same amount of focus on Radar. Radar terrified everyone equally, it seemed.

"The Ghost is a Forestair," said Silversand. "He got shot."

Sethral opened her eyes. "What?"

"He got shot." Silversand was staring wide-eyed at Shai. "Bringing a letter to the herd... just before..." Her voice quavered. "Seth, that's why we never heard about the creatures who took Jay. They had allies stationed outside the fort, and they shot the Ghost. He had to run, and he followed us and helped look after us instead, but he got sick... Whipper!"

Whipper jumped awake.

Silversand rounded on him. "You treated a Forestair in that cave Halo turned us away from?"

Whipper's eyes were big. "He didn't want me to tell anyone."

Silversand sat down. "That was the Ghost."

"Watch what she's saying, Silver," said Sethral.

Silversand spun back to the story. "It's stopped following us. And... oh, it's changed again."

"Who was the Ghost?"

"He and Halo worked together. I think... I think they were both looking for a group to come find Firefly. Halo found it first."

The next story was another Forestair one, so they repeated what they had found to Whipper, then tuned in for a brief account of the Drakon winter that had overtaken Sethral's clan.

"They're going back in time," said Loki, who was also awake and watching now.

"Winter was there?" said Sethral. "During the Drakon winter?"

"Not there," said Silversand. "Just in the south at the same time. She found something in the South Forest, and then went to the Lowlands, I think. They don't have anything on what she was doing, but I think it's because they can't follow her into the Lowlands."

"It was before the end of the North War, Seth," said Loki. "Way before the fire and the creeping winter and everything else going weird."

"It still seems awfully coincidental."

They argued through several more stories, then watched one that seemed to show the first time white Watermice settled in the Daemon's Outback. Their presence shunted Canyonlanders to far reaches of the forest and caused widespread migration changes for all the Forestairs. When that story ended, Silversand frowned at Shai. "She's repeating the war story."

"I thought she was going back in time," said Sethral.

"It's the same. Look. That's the creeping winter."

It was something that felt cold, though Sethral wasn't sure how Shai was managing to portray cold.

"And the forest is dying in circles," said Silversand.

Sethral locked onto what would have to be Winter, but the figure changed before she could confirm it. Then it changed again. It was still performing the same action. "Silver, I don't think that's Winter. It keeps switching species."

"Nothing can change species," said Loki.

"Nyasi!" gasped Silversand. "That was one thing creatures in the Lowlands thought their power was... imitating other species! Sethral, it's changing, but they're all Coppertails. I think that's a Nyasi."

"So what's she telling? Did she start the war story again where she left off before?"

Before anyone else could answer, the frown drained from Silversand's face. Her mouth hung slightly open, like she had been about to say something that now lay forgotten. "Royals," she whispered.

"She's showing Royals... and they're running away because the forest is dying."

Sethral forgot how to move.

"The Forestairs... had to leave," said Silversand. She was narrating now. "They ran to the Western Shield, but it got cold in winter, and in summer it burned. Some ran to the Highlands... but there were... Whitewings. There were Whitewings. And some of them got desperate and even ran to the Lowlands, but..."

"The Lowlands flooded?" said Loki hoarsely.

Shai cut a twirl as the Nyasi returned. Storms. Big storms. Then bigger ones. Very quietly, Whipper began to sing Flicker in the Hollow. The story grew more fantastic, out of reach of what Sethral could understand. By Silversand's face, she could no longer follow it either. Sethral turned to wake Dusk, to find the Nightlock already watching quietly. He shook his head. Some climax occurred, and suddenly Shai stopped and just stood. Silence fell over the cave. Deafening silence.

Silversand flicked with a certainty that came from somewhere beyond the story. 'The Nyasi won.'

"So are we leaving?" said Loki as Dusk and Fletch turned from their hushed conversation with Zeena. Dusk walked past him and Sethral like they didn't exist.

"They have a way home for us, but apparently it's late," said Fletch. "Something to do with the weather."

"Late?" said Sethral. "What is it?"

"Good question." Fletch let slip a look of exasperation.

"So he doesn't listen to you anymore either?"

"Sethral..." He looked ready to chide her, then thought twice and dropped the peacekeeper act. "You know what? No. No, he doesn't."

Firebrand appeared in the cave entrance and made her way through the kit-laden grass towards them. Her limp was evident and she still couldn't run, but she could stay on her paws for most of the day now. "Fletch, did you get the news on our ride?"

"No, I got cold-shouldered by an attitudinal teenage Coppertail who hasn't spoken to Taz or I since yesterday for no apparent reason. Did you?"

Firebrand smiled weakly. "He told me it'll be here today."

Fletch looked ready to bite something. He closed his eyes and took a deep breath. "Alright. I'll ask Ninik if we need anything." He spun on his heel and stalked away.

"I hope Dusk's not treating Phoenix like this," said Sethral.

"Doesn't seem to be," said Firebrand. "Are you two ready to go?"

Sethral's claw went automatically to her satchel. She restrained it and nodded. She had triple-checked already this morning. "I'm going to find Tante," she said, and left before they could hear the sudden lump in her throat.

A cry went up as the sun passed its zenith. Sethral ran outside as a rushing like a mighty wind beat the mountain without a wind to accompany it. In the valley pulsed a green, shifting blob more liquid than mist. Beneath it was a strange sight: the forest was raining upwards into the cloud. Sethral stared at it for more than a few heartbeats before she realized it was an insect swarm of a scale about to pass the largest she had ever seen.

The blob elongated towards the mountain with the same rushing, re-coalesced, and stretched in another direction. Already it was half again the size it had started at. The 'rain' was more insects from below. Every Canyonlander in the flock had now gathered in the cirque, from the tiniest late-season kits to Shai and the other older warriors. The Forestairs bobbed and danced excited conversations. Another cry made them run forwards, but it was a false alarm: the bug swarm returned to the valley again.

And still it continued to grow. Sethral had expected the blob to level out when it could fill most of the valley's center, but now it was that size and rather than slowing down, the upwards rain had accelerated. The gush of wings was so loud, she could no longer hear the chirps of the Forestairs around her. Again someone sounded the alert. This time the edge of the swarm extended overhead, and Sethral leaped as something large and sharp pelted her on the back. Dead, dying and disoriented bugs rained from the thundering cloud. The Canyonlanders skittered about snapping them up like kits in a honey-ant nest. Sethral picked one up. It was as long as her whole foreclaw, and tough-bodied, with wings like grass blades. Far from the first thing she would have considered edible. She tossed it to a Forestair.

The cloud edge retreated. Already the ground had been picked clean of bugs, and Canyonlanders had taken to the mountainsides to keep gleaning. Sethral heard a giggle behind her. Phoenix had a bug in his mouth. He darted forwards and attempted to poke Dusk with its still-moving legs. The Nightlock escaped with a very undignified backwards hop. He snatched a bug himself and fended off the Pyrya with it.

A roar of wings made Sethral fling herself to the ground amidst vivid images of Whitewings. A shadow blocked the sun. From over the mountain came a creature so massive it could not possibly be alive. Feathered wings each as broad as the Canyonlander cave sent a hurricane rolling down the mountain as the Draygon soared overhead. Its tail was as thick as a South Forest tree. It kept coming and coming. Two Basilix coasted on its slipstream. Then it was past, the massive fin on its tail swooping down as it plunged in slow motion into the valley. Just before it entered the bug cloud, Sethral saw its mouth open.

A second roar found its way around the mountain. The bug cloud had parted around the first Draygon like minnows around a Scythe, and now the cataclysm of a million bug wings filled the sky over the cirque again. The second Draygon intercepted it overhead. Its mouth was lizard-like and apparently toothless, so wide, Sethral could have stood up inside it. A fringe rimmed it and tufted like whiskers at its corners. The Draygon plunged down through the swarm in the valley and broke out the bottom of it, turned, opened its mouth again, and surged up from below. The first passed it in the other direction. They were as beautiful as aquatic snakes weaving a dance through the liquid cloud. They twined around one another. They paired up and flew in each other's bow waves. They turned their immense, graceful wings on end and circled the cloud like ship's sails, then folded and plunged through the condensed bugs. Their Basilix darted about below in the midst of the upwards rain, even their clicking wings obscured by the massive noise of their food source.

And still the bug cloud grew.

Now the Draygons began to arrive in numbers. Soon there were five, then eight, then at least ten; after that, the bugs and the breathtaking aerial dance removed Sethral's ability to count them. The bugs never seemed to thin. The valley was still thick with them as the sun sank and the Draygon numbers began to dwindle again. So thick the other mountains disappeared and the air turned to fire in the setting sun.

A piercing whistle disrupted the dance. Draygons circled around to pass the mountain and see what made it. Sethral squinted up the slope. There was a silhouetted Forestair at the very top of the mountain. Zeena. She whistled again, and the way the Draygons reacted made Sethral wonder if it was a name. Most turned back and resumed their feeding. One, though, broke away and circled the mountain. Zeena crouched to the ground to avoid being blown away. Closer and closer the magnificent creature came, and for the first time Sethral saw a pair of lizard-like arms on it. They looked small against that barrel chest, though each was as long as Zeena was tall.

The Draygon's tail touched stone and it coiled down backwards onto the mountaintop with a final, plant-flattening gale. It folded its wings. Even without them, Sethral doubted it would have found much room to turn around in Rockhall's main hall. Zeena appeared again near its head. Did Draygons have a language? Could they understand one from down here? To even see one on the ground was unheard of in any story Sethral had ever been told.

After a long time, Zeena left the Draygon and appeared at the top of the slope. Forestairs did not have a tail-talk, and she whistled down much like she had called the Draygon. Tante trotted over and nudged Sethral. All the renegades' host Forestairs gathered around them. Those who could offered rides. Sethral climbed on Tante's back for what she knew would be the last time and hugged him tightly.

The Draygon was even larger up close than it had been from below. Long-lashed and soft brown, eyes as big as Fletch's head watched the new arrivals with what could have been a friendly smile had the creature had a face that could smile. Fur-like down grew between its scales. It was not snake-like at all. Sethral held out a claw as its massive head extended towards her. It sniffed her gently. One puff of breath could have knocked her off Tante's back, but it was so careful, she wasn't even afraid.

Zeena jumped up on the Draygon's back, and just like that, a row of long plates like giant scales there lifted. In a hop, Tante was beside his flockmate. The plates had uncovered a row of soft patches of the Draygon's back, downy skin folded in long wrinkles. In flight, anything here would be shielded from the wind by the slanted plates.

"They carry their babies there," said Silversand. She patted the Forestair she was riding. The creature hopped up too, and the cat dropped off her back. Almost immediately, her paws began kneading in the soft down. Sethral slid down beside her. She was startled to find that the Draygon's back was warm, even where the skin faded to scales.

"Sethral?" said Fletch from the foremost soft patch.

Sethral picked her way carefully to reach him. It had been three days since the Forestairs had retrieved Ryatzi from the ghost grove. He had not woken up yet, but faded between un- and semi-conscious states that sometimes brought tremors she was best at quelling. Fletch had tucked him under the base of the plate between the Draygon's wings. There was just enough room for Sethral and Loki to join him. Fletch stationed himself with his brother behind them, and Dusk and Phoenix went behind them. The plates began to decrease in size after that, so Firebrand took her own patch, and Silversand and Whipper occupied the second-last one. Sethral had to get up one last time to hug Tante. She missed him already, and they hadn't even left yet. She was never going to see these creatures again.

Nobody rushed her, and several more of the renegades got up to say goodbyes. Then they were all settled at last. Sethral ducked her head as the plate lowered above her. The Draygon's great body uncoiled, a softer sound than the Negrilaw on the stone. Then it recoiled again, gathering into a spiral, then up in a pile like the snake that had once stalked Phoenix. All the plates pressed down as the Draygon surged up. Sethral clung to the folds of its back. They gained altitude with terrifying force and speed. They were airborne. Almost immediately they leveled out and banked around the mountain. The Forestairs had turned to tiny figurines on the rocky peak and the scoop of the cirque. They bobbed goodbyes. Sethral waved back. With a final lap, the Draygon cruised away. Its wings barely beat, but the mountain shrank behind them like the world was sliding in the opposite direction as they flew.

Chapter 32

The upper air was cold. When the mountains had been lost from view, the Draygon dropped in altitude, but it did little to stay the chill that crept in around the plates, stirred off those great wings, and whisked away the microcosm of warmth Sethral tried to huddle into as quickly as it formed. She and Loki did what they could to shield Ryatzi.

When the sun went down, Sethral finally worked up the nerve to sit up and look over the surge of the Draygon's shoulder. Swept with shadow and brushes of orange light, the forest was as soft from here as the cloud filaments that lingered where they formed about the treetops. A river canyon curled away like a penciled line. Sethral had not realized how much it dallied. It had seemed straight from the ground. It too was filling with mist. Sethral imagined mist fish that would swim through the full mist waters. When the orange receded and finally left the dark trees, a sparkle caught her eye. Moving up the river ahead was a flock of cool, blue-white lights. It was hard to tell as the Draygon quickly gained on them and passed them by, but they didn't seem fast. Not like flying. Maybe there were mist-fish after all.

She finally got too cold and tired to watch any longer, and returned to the haven of the soft patch. It was still much warmer than the air outside. Loki had fallen asleep. Sethral wedged herself in beside him.

They did not touch down. When they got thirsty, the Draygon rose into low clouds or dropped into mist and channeled the water that gathered on its mouth fringe into channels down its scales. The Canyonlanders had left small stashes of food at the bases of the plates they were sheltered under. It was little but nutrient-dense: seeds and bugs, and small fruits with hard shells and tangy-sweet jelly inside. Sethral choked on the memory of Tante teaching her how to crack those. She couldn't touch them until hunger drove her to it on the fourth day. Ryatzi awoke confused and scared, and was coaxed by Loki to eat and drink something. He drifted back to sleep with the Fisher holding his paw.

With nothing to do but stay warm and conserve energy, the days became more dream than waking. Sethral had a hard time watching the forest below. It was so harmless from here. It glided by so easily. Nothing stopped them. Nothing stalked them. Nothing needed to protect them but the giant of the sky that nothing would touch. From here, the jungle was not hot or humid. They could sleep without worry of needing someone on watch. The Draygon slept with only one eye at a time.

Sethral tried to keep out the bitterness, but it crept through the cracks and twisted her heart until it brought tears to her eyes. Why couldn't they have travelled into the Outback like this? They could have escaped every scare and harrowing ordeal; the canyon colony and the Aria and the earthbound predators that had nearly taken

Fletch. The sickness that had nearly taken Taz. If they had travelled like this, Wing might still be alive. Why hadn't the Forestairs gotten them this ride before?

By the end of the sixth day, they could see the Lowland lake. Sethral was ready to do anything but keep riding. As the Draygon descended at last in a long, slow spiral, she tried to shake functionality into the stiff limbs she would have to walk on again the moment they reached the ground. The Draygon's back tilted as its tail touched down first. In a reverse of its take-off, it coiled down into a pile, then a spiral, then half-sprawled across the stone. Fletch navigated gingerly to its head to thank it. Sethral stayed with Ryatzi until Firebrand came to get him, then joined everyone else on the ground. They took shelter in the forest until the gale of the Draygon's departure stopped shredding the trees.

Firebrand dug a bone tube from her chest fur. The three-note tune of the haunting-whistle echoed faintly off the forest's edge. They listened into the silence that followed, but nothing replied. Visions of walking moons more around the edge of the Lowland basin were disrupted by Firebrand's statement.

"Let's start walking."

"Which way?" said Fletch.

Nobody had an answer to that. Well, nobody until Phoenix lifted a tentative tail and pointed north.

'The bugs aren't right,' he flicked. 'We were farther that way.'

A breeze ruffled the forest edge. Sethral shivered, but the shiver caught and made her whole body shudder. She edged up against Taz's paws. "It's cold."

"We've gotten used to the heat," said Firebrand.

But it was more than that. The sky was blue, but the blue had a pale, chilly tone to it. It was Thunder Moon unless her time sense had deserted her. The start of the storm season. This place had been warmer back in the early growing season when they had left. Sethral shifted as Taz's leg began to burn a stripe down her shoulder. "You're hot."

She wasn't sure if he was ignoring her, or if he really hadn't heard. He looked up over the lake as another wind blew through, and they both shivered. Steely waves slapped the cliff base.

"Let's get back in the forest," said Firebrand. She led the way and they followed mutely.

Darkness fell quickly without any sign of Watersinger, so they found a place to curl up together and spent the night. Sethral stayed close to Taz. She was no longer sure if it was him who had the fever or herself, or both. Small chills scampered down her body at the slightest breeze. She buried herself in the fur pile until her body burned and she had to crawl out again, but the outside air was freezing. She returned to the pile. She still couldn't get warm.

Taz started to shiver alarmingly the next day. Through chattering teeth he insisted he could walk and refused to back down to Fletch, so they struck out again parallel to the cliffs. Firebrand kept them just inside the forest's edge where the wind was less. Ryatzi, wrapped in Sethral's blanket on the Leslander's back, did not wake up that day or the next, though he twitched when she blew the haunting-whistle.

Sethral started to cry when they stopped that evening. They were going to walk forever. They were probably half a moon from Iverae or Watersinger, and they were going to have to travel that distance before they could rest. She just wanted it to be over. She turned to the closest creature—Silversand—and put her face in the cat's shoulder to find that Silversand too was shivering. Her fur was hot in the cool air.

A new fear took up the mantle. What if the sickness wasn't curable? They already had to stop periodically so Taz could lean against a tree to regain his footing. Sometimes the dizziness tripped him, and Fletch had to help him up again. If it overtook any of them before they got to safety, they were going to have to start leaving creatures behind. Leaving them one by one while the rest pressed frantically on, trying to find Iverae in time to come back and get the ones who could no longer walk on their own.

Firebrand blew the whistle one last time. Phoenix's head shot up. He scrambled to his paws. 'I heard something.'

They held deathly still. When Phoenix stayed immobile, Firebrand lifted the whistle and blew it again. The forest returned to silence.

'It's her!' Phoenix dashed back and hopped over Dusk, then poked his muzzle close to the Nightlock's.

"Feefs can hear Iverae," said Firebrand when Dusk stirred awake.

The Nightlock dragged himself up and they stumbled and tripped through the darkening forest in the direction of the whistle none of the rest of them could hear. Firebrand stopped them some time later and blew again. This time the call rebounded like an echo.

Iverae nearly collided with them as they broke out onto the stone clifftop. Mixed laughter and whimpers of relief were punched through when Silversand sniffled. Iverae crouched down and hugged her, and the cat dissolved into hysterical sobbing.

"Shhh, it's okay," said the Watermouse. She rubbed Silversand's back. "You're safe. You lot look exhausted. And where's..."

Wing was gone.

Gone.

"Oh no," murmured Iverae as she saw their faces. "Okay. Let's get you back to the ship."

It was well after dark by the time the familiar crash of waves up the rock crack softened the night. Iverae returned from the hold with a lantern and blankets while they helped each other down onto the deck. Fletch unwound the dirty thistlecloth from around Ryatzi. Iverae was beside them with a clean, warm replacement. Sethral located Dusk and Phoenix, but when she picked up the thistlecloth, the piece she had grabbed came off.

Sethral stared at the grey rag in her claw, uncomprehending. Slowly, she found the edges of the blanket and lifted them, but the bottom half flopped to the deck when the top left the ground. She dropped it. It was a rip, right? She could mend it. She found the rag again. It didn't feel torn. She fingered one edge and found herself with a clawful of fluff. Her other claw spasmed. Her claws went right through the fabric. She took the rag in both claws again and it parted gently down the middle. Unsalvageable.

Sethral sat quietly on the deck, numb, in front of the remains of her blanket. The blanket that had been her constant companion since before she had run away from home; that had helped her gain Ryatzi's trust, helped save his life after a Vipra bite, helped pull Dusk from hypothermia when he had nearly drowned, and given he and Phoenix their only way of touching each other. Now they had lost it. She waited in dread for the little trill Phoenix now made when he wanted it. For the slow, crushing reality to sink in.

Iverae had gotten up and crossed the deck. Sethral closed her eyes as she heard the trill, but it was followed immediately by the soft purr of a blanket given. Iverae had draped her quilt over Phoenix—it completely covered him—and he had made himself a tent of it. Dusk managed a smile. He took the pawed blanket and led it away to Iverae's cabin.

Iverae returned, saw the disintegrated thistlecloth and gave Sethral a hug. She pulled back in concern. "You, too?" One paw touched Sethral's forehead. "Looks like I need to get you all back to the Valkenland. Come. The others are setting up beds."

Sethral let herself be supported down to the hold. It was narrower than she remembered. Taz and Silversand were already asleep, and Firebrand and Fletch had just put the finishing touches on a nest for Ryatzi, who Loki and Whipper were keeping warm. Sethral started to join them, but was gently blocked by Fletch.

"Not until we know you're not contagious," he said. "You're beside Taz."

Something scraped the side of the ship. Iverae had returned to the deck, and her pawsteps moved back and forth, accompanied by scraping and the occasional shudder. She flung her weight against something and the ship dropped half a paw-length.

"Hold tight!" she called down.

She yanked something and the ship came free. Sethral had never thought she would be in a falling ship twice in her life. Watersinger hit the water with an almighty crash. Small things screeched and clattered against its sides. It was flung back into the crack by a wave. Something buffered the collision with the stone. When the water recoiled, the ship was sucked out with it. Sails snapped. Watersinger lurched forwards, and by the next time the wave came, they were past the wave line and out onto the open water.

Sethral did not remember the ship being this fast. The snapping continued until Iverae yanked something. Their speed jumped up even further. Sethral fell asleep to the creak of the ship and the back-and-forth padding of the Watermouse's paws.

The journey became such a blur, Sethral began to wonder if it was the speed of the ship or her own failing memory as the fever slowly took over her body. Or maybe even the speed was her imagination. Watersinger had been with the wind on the way to the cliffs, and sailing against it was supposed to be much, much slower. Yet she heard the creak of bowstrings at Etho on what felt like only the next day. Iverae talked sharply to the creatures there. When they did not comply, she flung the mooring rope back on the deck and swung them away so quickly Sethral knew the ship's speed at least was real. Watersinger did not move like it used to. She wondered what Iverae had done to it during her repairs.

When they were underway again, the Watermouse poked her head below deck. "They wouldn't give us food or medical supplies, so I'll have to land us at an island to stock up. How are things?"

Someone rested a paw on Sethral's forehead. Whipper, she thought vaguely. His words fogged as he said something to Iverae about a fever. Why could she only hear Iverae? She supposed the Watermouse had a pretty strong voice. Especially compared to Whipper. Someone made her drink. The water tasted bitter, like Fletch had put something in it.

Two nights later they bobbed in the shallows off a small, deserted island. Sethral tracked Phoenix's paws as he darted back and forth on deck. Catching moths. There was a faint splash off the side of the ship. A heartbeat later, the darkness condensed like the air had been sucked out of it. Sethral found herself bolt upright. "Fletch!" she tried to cry, but it came out in a whisper. Panic surged through her body, and this time her voice came to life. "Fletch!"

Paws that were not Phoenix's landed on deck. Fletch flew for the hatch, but it slammed shut and locked. He smashed the bolt from the wood. Before he could gain the deck, there was a piercing scream and a thunderous splash. The floor hit Sethral's shoulder. She tried to get up, but no matter which way she turned, she couldn't leave her bed behind. She sank her claws into the wood. Renegades were bolting up the ladder. Loki plunged into the lake after Phoenix, but the water was quiet. Nothing splashed. Nobody screamed.

The ladder was suddenly in front of her. Sethral dragged herself up it and fell on deck. She pushed herself into a sitting position against the mast. Then the lake surface erupted.

"Take him!" shouted Loki.

Iverae dove off the railing. There was a wild snarling, then a scream that sent a knife through Sethral's chest. Something flailed out on the water. Iris choked, resurfaced and screamed again. She was dragged back under. The water around her began to churn. A Scythe tail smacked the surface. Iverae shouted from the bank. Fletch and Dusk were gone. By the railing, Whipper was wrapped around Firebrand's neck, hysterical and screaming. Fletch reappeared and plunged into the hold, back again moments later with a blanket and lantern. He returned to shore. Sethral made it to the railing just in time to see Dusk grab someone's scruff and drag them up the bank.

"Dusk!" shouted Fletch.

Dusk lifted his hackles and snarled. He stumbled back again, dragging the creature with him. The lantern sparked to life, and a cry tore from Sethral's throat. Phoenix lay motionless on the grass. His fur, soaked through, was black. Not even red, like when its light faded. Black. Dusk pulled him another step, then staggered and fell to the ground. Phoenix couldn't be dead. He wouldn't be draining Dusk's power if he was dead. Sethral's claws gripped the railing so tightly they went numb. Dusk tried to get up again as Fletch approached him, but he slumped sideways, hyperventilating now. He had to let go. He was going to kill himself if he didn't let go.

Phoenix's body jerked like someone had shot him. His muzzle opened in a gasp. Fletch pounced and dragged Dusk off him, already unconscious. Sethral slumped to the deck. Phoenix was breathing. He was breathing. She barely registered the nauseating scent of blood wafting off the water. Loki must have injured Iris. Scythes attacked anything that bled.

Fletch held Phoenix so he could breathe while Iverae rubbed him down with the blanket. Firebrand had left the deck without Sethral realizing. She checked on Dusk, then lay down in front of Loki on the bank and put her paws on his. The Fisher was in shock. Whipper clamped onto him and sobbed into his dripping fur. Eventually Firebrand brought them both back to the ship. Iverae stood on the bank and shouted instructions while the Leslander let out... when had Watersinger gotten a triangular sail? The same red sun snapped at its center, but the black corners had swooped to the ends of a long, graceful rod slanted crosswise across the stump of the mast. Firebrand hauled up the anchor and the wind drove the ship aground. Dusk and Phoenix were lifted aboard. Iverae was right back at the ropes. Before Fletch and Firebrand had moved the elementals to her cabin, Watersinger was flying across the lake like Sethral had never thought a ship could fly.

"What are you doing up?"

Firebrand was behind her on the deck again. Sethral kept her forehead on her claws. She was too weak to move. Firebrand lifted her by the scruff and carried her back to her bed in the hold. The bedding shifted as the Leslander lay down beside her.

"Did you see all that?" she said quietly.

Sethral nodded. She did not realize how much she wanted a hug until Firebrand pulled her into one.

"It's going to be okay," murmured the Leslander. "We're almost at the Valkenland."

They stayed together as the ship rose and fell like a bird over waves taller than Sethral remembered. Then as those waves gradually died. The sail was hauled suddenly and Watersinger's bow wave failed as the ship skimmed to a halt. Iverae blew a different haunting-whistle into the night. A small boat bumped against Watersinger's side. The two knocked together gently as creatures scaled the rope Iverae tossed them, and hushed voices moved across the deck. A single creature returned to the boat and sped away.

Chapter 33

Sickness wrapped like a stifling cloak, at once cold as winter and hot as burning coals. Eyes too heavy to open revealed only scraps of light when dragged up to show a crack of the outside world. It was hard to breathe. Sometimes she was puking, but the bitter coat it left in her mouth never seemed to go away. Everything ached so hard, it hurt when anyone's icy fingers touched her fragile skin.

Sometimes there were sharp things needling her flank, other times sour liquids forced down her throat. Why couldn't creatures treat her gently? Weren't they supposed to treat the sick gently? Or maybe she had been caught by Ryatzi's clan. Or Winter. What if the sickness was from Winter? Was this how she treated Jay? Had Wing been sick when he died? Was that the reason he couldn't run away?

Fevered scenes followed one another: a sneering Bluejay ripped out Wing's throat, Winter cackled over Silversand's dead body, then Dusk's. Phoenix screamed and screamed as Iris slit his stomach open, then Winter came when he couldn't move anymore. Phoenix became Wing. Had he still been alive when the rest of them got taken? Had they left him to die? They had never gotten to bury

Wing. They would never be able to visit his grave. They would never even know where it was.

Hot tears matted her cheeks. Someone tried to wipe them, but it wasn't someone she knew. What if this was all a dream and she woke up back in the canyon colony, never having escaped at all? What if she had gotten heatstroke like Loki and dreamed the whole thing? Spear-knocker's spear banged against the vine bars. He shouted at her, but then he was speaking Forestair and she couldn't understand Forestair. He lifted a bow and shot Ryatzi. Then he shot Silversand. Loki ran towards Sethral with terror on his face. His body was suddenly full of arrows, dead before he hit the ground. The vine walls became the disintegrating walls of Salisetta, then a shattered Watersinger as it fell... fell...

She landed in Rockhall. But Winter was there, too, approaching with her army. The fort was already surrounded. She ran for the main tunnel to find a Whitewing filling the air in front of it, Taz dead in its claws. Behind it in the tunnel she saw all the other renegades scattered across the ground. Motionless. Tante was there too, and Talin. She spun in horror. All her clanmates' bodies littered the main hall floor. She searched for her parents and found them beside Wing and Jay, sightless eyes still fixed on her. Accusing her. Even as she ran towards them, they faded and disappeared. She ran to Talin, but he was gone. Bodies were winking out one by one. She ran to Ryatzi, but the red on his chest was blood and he didn't have a heartbeat. Dusk and Radar stood side by side in front of her and fixed her with cold, emotionless eyes.

"He's dead," said Dusk. "Get over it."

"Seth?"

The scene sped into a whirl of green jungle and red walls, then the grey-white stone of the Canyonlander colony, and the orange of the Darkwood. Everything was dying. Everything she tried to hold onto died.

"Seth!"

She was shaking, but it wasn't herself. It stopped but kept going, and something bit her tail, hard. Sethral screamed and bolted back. The world vanished in a tangle of blankets. No, that was her face in the blankets. She didn't want to lift it for fear of what she would find. Everyone was dead. She didn't want to open her eyes to find the leering skeleton of a dead renegade talking to her.

"Seth..." Silversand shook her again, pleading. "You were dreaming. Wake up."

Dreaming?

Sethral slowly tipped her face out of the blankets. Silversand sat beside her, worry etched in every crease of her fur. She didn't look hurt.

"Oh, good, you're awake." The cat dropped to the mattress. "You've been screaming for two days and none of us could get you to wake up. Fontie, she's awake!"

Sethral's throat wouldn't open for fear of the answer she would get to the question she most needed to ask. Who was 'us'? Who was left?

"You're the last one up," continued Silversand. "We were all scared about you."

Sethral managed to activate her own voice. It sounded like she hadn't used it in days. "Who..."

Silversand opened her mouth, then finally noticed the fear that clung to Sethral's body like Aria's web. Her face softened. "Everyone's fine."

Before Sethral could answer, a lean Rivrit housewife in a neat apron bustled into the room with a tray in her paws. "Well, it's about time. Questions later, dearie. First, you need some proper food in you. A creature can't ask proper questions on half a moon without proper food." Whatever was in the bowl on the tray steamed gently as it was set down. Fontie dusted her paws. "I'll be in the kitchen when she's done," she said to Silversand, and took her leave with a wink.

Sethral glared at the cat.

"We know you," said Silversand. "Nobody's answering anything else until you eat."

Sethral pulled herself towards the tray and sniffed the bowl tentatively. She had no appetite, but she wanted answers.

The food was delicious. Sethral's stomach gurgled a little as she ate, like it threatened to reject the input, but it kept it down. When she was done, she licked the drops off her whiskers and looked at her roommate.

"Ryatzi wants to see you," said Silversand.

Sethral tangled herself in the blankets in her haste to sit up. It didn't register how weak she was until Silversand darted to catch her.

"Slowly," said the cat. "You were sicker than Drakon fever until two days ago."

"Where's Ratty?"

"I'll take you there."

Silversand guided her off the bed. The room had two more mattresses in it. Taz was out cold on one beneath a blanket that bore

Fletch and Firebrand's scent, and the other renegades' smells clung to the other. The window over it wafted in a chill breeze that did not quite dispel the taint of sickness that still thickened the air. Outside the room was a hallway with a wood floor. One end smelled like a kitchen. At the other was a door. Silversand took them to the kitchen end, where they found Fontie clattering about with pots on a metal-topped fire.

"She ate," said Silversand.

Fontie had a lovely, kind smile. "Ah, so I can sto' makin' myself not-presen' fer questions, then? Thank'ee kindly, love. Sethral, is i'? Your frien's been askin' fer you, won' take any calmin' otherwise. Come now." She wiped her paws on a towel and took them back to the hallway, to a door just around the corner from the kitchen. She knocked twice before easing it open. "Ryatzi, love? She's 'ere teh see you."

Sethral's legs gave out at Ryatzi's small cry. Fontie slipped into the room and sat on the mattress with a paw extended to hold him back. Silversand got Sethral on her paws again. Fontie lowered her barrier when they reached the bed. Ryatzi more fell than stumbled across it; he was so weak he could barely manage his paws. Sethral caught him as he collapsed into her arms. He curled up and started to cry.

Fontie made a soft noise. "Oh, poor thing."

Sethral closed her eyes. Fontie pulled the blanket around her and Ryatzi and nestled a pillow between her and the wall. There was quiet talking in the room, then the Rivrit left. Silversand lay down on the other end of the mattress. It was hard to imagine, now, any feeling that could compare to finding someone alive and well when she had last seen them far from it. Sethral could think of two more creatures she needed to find like that, but right now that didn't matter. Right now nothing else mattered. She wanted to tell Ryatzi to stop nearly dying on her, but this time she had a quieting suspicion it had gone the other way, too. She had never seen him so upset.

Ryatzi cried himself out, then simply huddled in her arms and shivered. Sethral found a second blanket on the bed and pulled it over him too. Part of his chest was exposed, so she covered it for good measure. He relaxed a little.

'How bad was it?' she flicked to Silversand.

'You?'

'Yeah.'

'The healers said we almost lost you. Taz, too.'

'Weren't you sick, too?'

'We all were. But you two had something else.'

Sethral stroked a claw down Ryatzi's back. He shuddered when it drew near his arrow scars, so she withdrew it and returned it to the hug.

Someone tapped Fletch's Long Night name on the door. Fletch cracked it open and poked his head in. "Silver, is Seth—oh, you are here. You're up! Welcome back." He came in and shut the door quietly, then switched to tail-talk. 'How is he?'

'A bit of a mess.' Sethral managed a weak smile. 'Can't you tell?'

'Dusk and Phoenix are both okay, by the way.'

She had not removed that from this moment so thoroughly after all. Sethral folded both wings around Ryatzi as her limbs went so weak she almost lost her hold on him. She hid her face in his fur. Both okay. Everyone was okay.

"The creatures at Etho knew about Iris," said Fletch quietly. "But they didn't warn Ives. She told the Valkenland guards about the attack, and Ridia and Firekyle has shut down all exchange with the border islands. They think Wasp might have taken over there without them noticing."

"But what about Post?"

"Post is dead. The Pitt-web took over."

What a horrible way to die. Ryatzi went limp and Sethral glanced down. He had fallen asleep. "How's Taz?"

It was Fletch's turn to smile. "Recovering, still entirely reliant on Fibes and I, and about as uptight about it as you'd expect."

Sethral didn't particularly feel like letting go of Ryatzi, but now every part of her was knotting up in an anxious ball until she could go see Dusk and Phoenix. Just to confirm they were okay. 'Can you hold him?'

Fletch stepped in and took her place. "They're in the room beside this one. Dusk might be awake, so just knock before you go in."

"Thanks."

Silversand guided her to the other door. Sethral tapped her Long Night name as Fletch had, then pushed the door open a crack when there was no reply. The curtains were drawn in the room beyond. Empty shelves cast long, slanted shadows across the walls, and an empty desk backed two mattresses on the far side of the floor. Dusk was asleep on one, his paws tucked in a way that indicated he had put them there himself. Phoenix, though, was also on his side. He never took that position on his own. His fur was still dark. Red, not black, but missing even the faintest trace of a glow.

'Are the healers sure he's okay?' flicked Sethral.

Silversand nodded. 'They're not sure why he's still like that, but they say he's recovering fine. Fletch thinks it might be because Dusk saved him.'

Could water kill a Pyrya's powers, even if it didn't kill the creature itself? Sethral suspected Phoenix wouldn't care even if that was the case, but...

But what? But he would lose his moth-catching ability? That wasn't true; he had managed alright in the Daemon's Outback even when his glow was faded. Sethral felt the warm fingers of shame creep across her face. But the renegades would lose the protection that his fire gave? Why did she care? Did she still believe there was any possibility of him leaving if he was no longer useful like that?

Sethral turned more quickly than she had intended, prompting Silversand to caution her again to slow down. She returned to Ryatzi's room in a messy haze, curled up with him again and lost all worries to the dreamless bed of sleep.

Chapter 34

The house turned out to be the same one where Taz, Fletch and Firebrand had spent the renegades' year apart. When Sethral could walk, she left Ryatzi sleeping and explored as much as she felt was polite. She found Firebrand and an older Rivrit outside, sitting together on the grass in a pile of books.

Firebrand looked up and grinned as the door creaked shut. "You're up! Seth, this is Benty. Benty, Sethral, our resident war planner and mystery solver."

Sethral picked her way down the cold stone steps. "War planner? That's Dusk. I lit a fire and shoved a plant out a hole."

Firebrand cleared a space among the books. Behind the pair was a garden, only half kempt.

Benty waved a paw at it. "Help yourself to anything you find here. The greens need eating, and goodness knows there's probably more things in there that we haven't found yet. Haven't had much time to keep up with it, unfortunately."

"Didn't this area got taken over by Leslanders after you and Tetch came home?" said Sethral.

"They've switched sides," said Firebrand. She glanced at Benty, who rubbed the cover of an old, battered book.

"The floods have broadened the lake in the northern Lowlands," he said, "and the Far South Forest has been overtaken by Aria and Whitewings. Winter's army can no longer reach us here. The Leslanders that were left behind or refused to leave have gradually come to trust the locals, so they let us shelter here when we explained our situation."

"Where's my clan?" said Sethral.

"The non-clan group Saggitayrii all relocated to the Lowlands south of here," said Firebrand. "In the wilder part. After they declared war on Winter, the clan groups apparently held a line against the Aria until those other members were safe, then disappeared. Nobody's gotten close enough to their camp to see if it was planned, but knowing your clan..."

Sethral felt surprisingly calm about that. It had likely been planned. The clan groups had relocated in the Drakon winter, too, and this time they would have had much more time to get away. And they would not have left to fight Aria unless the non-warriors were somewhere safe first.

Firebrand eyed her sidelong. "You think they're okay?"

She nodded.

"Any idea where?"

"No. If they're not in the Lowlands... no, I don't know. How far are the Aria?"

"Up to the north end of Nova territory," said Benty. "They seem to have stopped there, and I suspect it is because of the weather." When Sethral didn't understand, he continued, "You have probably noticed how cold it is here for storm season. It only gets colder the farther north you go. Growing season this year did not come at all in the South Forest, and as you can see, storm season has hardly come either."

"Is Winter still in the South Forest?"

"We can only assume so. We have no news from anywhere farther than the edge of the Lowlands and a little ways past. Flitter has made it a day into the forest there before the storms and the Whitewings drove him back."

Sethral sat up. "Storms?"

"Constant ones." Benty shook his head. "Back when the Saggi-tayrii still came to visit our towns, they said they could stand at their territory's edge and see nothing but a grey wall on the horizon."

Sethral met Firebrand's eye. Storm clouds pinned. How far had Flicker in the Hollow—the Silence—progressed while they had been away? And what would the forest look like beneath it? Sethral leaned against the Leslander's side and tapped surreptitiously, 'You said he had a Forestair antler here. Does he still have it?'

Firebrand's tail curled around her. 'No, he gave it back before the Aria took over the Far South Forest. I asked him about it, and I'm confident the Forestairs took it.'

A weight lifted. 'Good.' Sethral curled up against the Leslander. A breeze, cold like nipping teeth, nibbled her wings. She was debating going back inside when Fontie appeared at the door.

"Ah, there you are." The housewife bustled out with a downy bundle in her arms. It was a dark brown comforter as thick and soft as three thistlecloths. She tucked it around Sethral. "All of you the same; can' stay still fer more than three shakes of a goo' broom. You're still recoverin', dearie; a' leas' try teh stay warm. Is this alrigh'?"

Sethral snuggled down. "It's perfect. Thank you."

Fontie's eyes softened. "Come fin' me if you ever nee' anythin' else. I'll be righ' inside. Dad, the two in your study jus' woke up, if you wan' teh ge' your pen."

Benty waved a paw without looking up from his book. "Ah, thank you, my love. But I got it already."

Fontie crossed her arms. "I tol' you no' teh disturb 'em."

"The black one said it was okay."

That sounded awfully charitable for Dusk. Sethral pulled the blanket tighter. If Dusk was awake, the thought of visiting that room suddenly sank her nerves.

But Firebrand had already shifted. "I'm going to go see Feefs. Coming?"

"Can I ride?"

"Sure."

Sethral pulled herself onto the Leslander's back and tried to keep as low as possible as they ducked into the house. Firebrand also used her Long Night name when she knocked on the study door.

"Come in," came a quiet call.

Firebrand pushed open the door and Sethral's claws locked in her fur. Firebrand gasped. "Dusk, you—"

He was going to kill himself again.

"Look what we can do now," said Dusk with a sparkle in his eye. Phoenix was huddled against his side, head tucked into his shoulder and neck like the curl of a small fern. There was no blanket between them.

Firebrand dropped to the ground as her legs gave out on her. "Shelha, Dusk, don't do that to me."

A subtle look of mischief hinted that that might have been the point. Dusk licked Phoenix's cheek and got a shiver.

'Is he... okay?' flicked Sethral.

'Nope. This is just a really quiet meltdown.' Dusk dragged the blanket off Phoenix's bed and added it to his own. He seemed awfully cheerful, given the circumstances. "Fibes, can we get some food in here? We're both starving."

Sethral held on again as Firebrand got up. They ran into Fontie on the other side of the door. She had a full tray in her paws, and smiled at them both as Firebrand held the door open for her.

"She misses having Coppertails around," said the Leslander as they headed back outside. "Just watch; she'll feed Phoenix half to death now that he's awake. She thinks he and Dusk are too skinny."

"They are."

"I know. Especially Feefs, though. Benty said they should be about the same weight when they're healthy."

"The Pyrya?" said Benty without looking up. "Yes, he's a strong little thing. Dustlander build. Probably quite speedy, too."

"What?" said Firebrand when Sethral had to muffle her sudden laughter.

Sethral was spared having to say how alike they were by the Rivrit, who adjusted a final map in the overlapping spread he had assembled on the grass.

"Is this what you were looking for?" he said.

Sethral peered over Firebrand's shoulder and knew immediately what the Leslander had asked for. Pinned against the wind with rocks, the maps covered the South Forest and surrounding area, textured to show forest types and other landscapes. Vaguely visible across them was a huge circle, cut halfwise by the South Cliffs and snipped by the mountains in the east. Its edges were a little crooked, like Benty had not noticed it was there.

The South Forest's trees were all equal-age inside that semicircle. Like something had wiped them all out some three hundred years ago, prompting them all to grow back at once.

'Dead circle,' tapped Sethral.

Firebrand nodded. "Benty, it's perfect. Thank you."

"I suspect this is something I'm not to know about, given that you haven't told me?" said the Rivrit.

"It's probably safer if you didn't know."

He sighed and gathered up the maps again. "With your family, I suppose most things are."

Firebrand twitched a little at the word 'family', but it was past before Sethral could question it. "And did you find the book?"

"Indeed I did." He handed her a slender volume in red-edged leather. "In a fitting colour, no less. I'm afraid some of the descriptions are a little insensitive, but the author spoke to nobody but migrating herds, so the information should be accurate."

Firebrand flipped open the book and sighed. 'Western District' was the title on the second page. Beneath it, 'Flatlanders' was underscored by the subtext 'Leslanders of the North'. Firebrand skimmed the page faster than Sethral could read, turned to the next and skimmed that, too. "It's kind of accurate," she said. "I'll give them that."

The handwriting on the page was cramped and curly. Sethral gave up reading. "How?"

"Strong hierarchy, unstable pack structures, land division by social status... but they're not even territorial. They just walk all over everyone else's territories like they don't exist." She curled her lip at the next page. "And they kill their kits."

"What?"

"If they catch them." The pages ruffled. "Here... 'Kits age to maturity in southern landscapes to gain the speed and strength necessary to evade adults on the tundra.' Shelha, those aren't Coppertails. More like Hyenars."

Sethral wrapped both arms around Firebrand's neck. "Well, I'm glad they don't live here, then."

"They do. That's what Theo and Altera are."

Sethral stared at her.

"The two that took Jay," said the Leslander. "I'm guessing the third was a Western District Northlander, same as Jay."

"Jay's a Raindai." Just saying it made Sethral's throat ache. 'Is' a Raindai, or 'was' one?

"They're basically the same thing. Only Sabletine are really a separate group. I mean, look at Nyasi. They're basically Western District Flatlanders; you can get Nyasi kits from normal parents."

That was just wrong. Bracken couldn't be the same as that tall, cruel male or blue-spotted female.

"And then just throw in water elementals and you've got the whole clan," said Firebrand distastefully. "Well, they're successful, you've got to give them that. Sadistic, but successful. Dominate Northlanders in their range, Western District included... no weaknesses, no pack or partner loyalties. Shelha, is there any way to defeat these guys?" She reached the end of the chapter and looked disgusted. "Fine."

The next chapter was about Northlanders. Firebrand skipped most of it and stopped at another heading. "Longlanders," it read. "Extinct".

"What were they?" murmured Sethral. The blanket was cozy and she was half falling asleep, but Longlanders was a name she hadn't heard before.

"The ancestor of Nightlock and Sabletine. Probably looked like Highlanders, but nobody's ever seen one. This guy's just guessing they existed."

Species history was much less interesting than Silence history, and it reminded Sethral of Arling's classes. She curled up and napped until a shout from the laneway brought Silversand, Fletch and Fontie tumbling out of the house. Iverae sauntered up the path with a bag slung over her shoulder and a grin on her face. Whipper and Loki bounded on either side of her. A young Rivrit with a family resemblance to Benty sprinted ahead of them to fling himself into Fontie's arms. Iverae saw Sethral on Firebrand's back and tipped her a wave.

Fontie sat down to listen to the young Rivrit trip over his own tongue in an excited approbation of ships. Sethral saw Iverae flick, 'Is the kid awake?' to Fletch and Silversand. She got a yes and got into a laughing traffic jam at the door as she, Fletch and Whipper all attempted to enter. Silversand picked up a prey trail and beetled away into the forest.

Loki wandered over to the book pile. "Hi Seth. Fibes, you're still here? Find anything interesting?"

Firebrand was too deep in her book to hear. She groaned as Sethral shifted to make room for Loki on her back.

Sethral patted her shoulder. "You're big and strong. You can hold us."

"You two are heavy. And Loki, your paws are freezing."

He lay on them and grinned at Sethral. "You should see what it's like out on the lake. You think this is cold and windy? It feels like North Moon on the Plains out there. There's whitecaps all over the water."

"Remind me not to go."

"Fibes, when are we leaving?"

"When Taz and Feefs can walk."

Loki grimaced. "Right... we have to get Feefs on a boat again."

"Well, we killed Iris, so he doesn't have to worry about that at least."

Sethral stopped Loki before he shot back. 'She's in book mode,' she flicked. 'Not worth it.'

Loki shot the Leslander a dirty look and shifted his paws deeper into her fur. Sethral wanted to tell him about Phoenix and Dusk, but her mind had circled back to Jay and she no longer felt like talking much about anything. She pulled the blanket over her head.

"Nothing helpful about Pyrya," said Firebrand. The book thumped shut. "Whatever happened to his fur, we're on our own."

"Shame," said Benty.

Their talking lowered again, muffled through the blanket. Loki rested his chin on Sethral's back and went to sleep. She was about to drift off too when Firebrand snapped, "They're not my kids."

It sounded like it came out more sharply than intended. There was a long silence, then Benty asked something Sethral could not hear.

Firebrand's shoulders shifted. "He's the one who abandoned them," she said bitterly. "You can't just adopt kids and then leave them like that."

Benty's sigh wilted, like he agreed but hated to admit it. Sethral told herself otherwise, but the words echoed over her as she quieted her breathing to maintain the illusion of sleep.

Chapter 35

"Not even a fight?" said Taz.

"He's going anywhere Dusk is." Fletch tucked a last blanket over Ryatzi on Firebrand's back. Silversand hopped down the house steps with Dusk behind her. The Nightlock waited at the bottom until Phoenix had rejoined him and returned his forehead to his shoulder.

"C'mere," said Iverae. When Dusk curled his tails around Phoenix and pulled him over, she took a blanket from a pile and cast it over both their backs like her sister cast fish nets. Dusk flashed her a smile.

The main street of the village ran through a ghost town. Houses boarded up against the weather were missing shingles. Shutters were blown askew. Overgrown gardens made thickets between the buildings, where the detritus of a once-thriving ship-building community slowly deteriorated. Dead leaves skittered across the road. The forest was calmer, and the river where they found Watersinger anchored shivered only slightly in the breeze. The ship's profile was nothing like Sethral remembered. It was slimmer than before, and Iverae had been inventing again. Fixed to the top of a shortened mast, a long, graceful spar kissed the prow and rose back over the deck, ready to carry a triangular sail like a lifted crest. The sail's third corner was affixed to the deckside, so the whole canvas would arch like an canopy over the ship when the wind filled it.

The ship bore other signs of its time at the edge of the Daemon's Outback. Its new ropes were made of an unfamiliar material, thin, green, and devoid of loose fibers. Reconstructed from a patchwork of boards, the shipsides were scarred from being wedged in the rock crack, and from the branch-woven basket Iverae had encased it in to soften the drop from the cliff. Sun exposure had left the stern bleached, so that the ship's wood now ranged from white at the back to a spray-darkened gold patched with black. The railings were still warped. Sethral wondered if Iverae planned to leave them that way.

Iverae directed them on board and tasked Fletch with making everyone comfortable while she pulled ropes and half-raised the new sail. She did not even haul anchor until the distribution of blankets was complete, and those still sensitive to the cold were stowed below. Whipper, undeterred by Silversand's loneliness, joined Dusk and Phoenix in Iverae's cabin.

The wind picked up as they got closer to the lake. Iverae stowed her punting pole and hoisted the sail the rest of the way. Sethral watched in awe as it rose above her. It tugged into the wind, drawing the ship with it. She had never seen a ship so large sail so easily into the wind. The gush of Watersinger's bow wave intensified as they accelerated, towards the lake, into still stronger wind. When the overcast sky opened up and the first slate-grey wave smacked across their prow, Watersinger cut through it like it was mist.

Wind howled across the lake, and the ropes from the sail to the deck whined and sang. Iverae wrestled them with a grim deter-mination. White-capped waves kicked up cold spray where they shattered against the ship's sides. When she had soaked up enough of the view and nearly soaked herself, Sethral dove below deck. The strangulation of the wind cut the chill like she had walked from outside into Fontie's kitchen. She pulled the hatch shut behind her.

"Nasty out there, hey?" said Loki.

"Yeah. Whew." She shook herself violently and bounded down the ladder to plunge into a blanket. It was toasty enough to make her frozen claws tingle. "Did you heat these?"

"Nope, it's just that cold out."

"Weird." Sethral sank her claws in the blanket again, and they tingled harder. She had never felt a temperature difference like this with anything other than another creature on the warm end. She picked up the blanket and cast an eye around for someone to curl up with.

"No," said Ryatzi.

"I carried you here," said Firebrand at the same time. "You owe me."

Everyone else laughed. Sethral did her best to look hurt. "Heartless mudsuckers."

Fletch pulled his blanket off a warm nook beside him. Sethral took the spot and reciprocated by not burying her now-burning claws in his fur. She could groom him in thanks when her body temperature had recovered.

The ship pitched again, making the lantern strung between the ceiling and the floor spin in tight circles. Sethral did not notice the tension in her body until it started to ease. As it became apparent that Watersinger was equipped to handle the rough water, she settled back and pulled her satchel out from beside her. She had been forced to jettison many items in the Daemon's Outback. The notebook she had once drawn a map of Costar in had been reduced to pulp when Salisetta had fallen in the water. The Sequoia Mouse skeleton and its bag had rotted, and even her tiny knife had needed its handle stripped and re-bound. Ryatzi was curled up in her new thistlecloth, a gift from Fontie. His chest was dyed brown, also courtesy of the Rivrit couple. The colour change had calmed him a lot.

Firebrand looked up as Iverae jumped through the hatch. The trapdoor banged shut, and she locked it with a new bolt on the inside. She grinned at them. "Warm down here! Toss me a blanket there, Rocklander."

Fletch did. The Watermouse wrapped herself in it, plopped down and blew on her paws. "It's too stormy out there to make it across the open water, so I've dropped anchor. We'll keep going when it passes."

"I thought it had died down," said Firebrand.

"Nope. We're just behind an island."

Everyone tensed.

"They're safe," said Iverae. "There's a Hyenar-strength bolt in the cabin hatch, and I showed the Nightlock how to use it."

"You—" Firebrand frowned. "It was a smaller one before. And you could unlock it from outside. Did you change it for us?"

Iverae threw an herb stem at her. "After what happened to the kid? Of course I did. What do you take me for?" She looked about to say more, but was halted as Silversand walked up and hugged her. She smiled and hugged back. "I like you guys. If you ever need something from me, just ask."

The next morning, Watersinger rose and fell quietly on swells that tugged it towards shore. Sethral poked her head above deck to find that Iverae had actually anchored quite far from land. The sky was a flat, heavy grey. The nub end of a rope slapped Sethral's head, and she yelped. She spun around to find Iverae re-coiling the rope for another go.

"I know that look," said the Watermouse. "I'm told you're supposed to be staying out of the cold."

Sethral scowled. She had been monitoring the wind to decide when best to dash to the railing and see the waves. She pulled back so only the top of her head and her eyes were higher than the trapdoor, far enough to see, but low enough to duck if Iverae sent the rope at her again.

The cabin hatch clunked and swung open, and Dusk hopped on deck with a bucket in his mouth. He stopped at the sight of Sethral. She pulled lower. Dusk sent her a look of mild warning and padded to the side of the ship, where another rope lay coiled. This one had a metal clip on its end. Dusk secured it to the bucket handle and fed it overboard, half-filled the bucket and was back down the hatch in a heartbeat.

"Get down," said Iverae.

Sethral bounded down the ladder. The Watermouse leaped in after her, grabbed the hatch and yanked it mostly shut. She peeked through the crack. She suddenly had a knife in her paw.

"Can I see?" said Sethral

Iverae tipped her head at the crack. Sethral crept up beside her. For a heartbeat she was certain her eyes were playing tricks on her. Soundless, the silhouette of a Whitewing shifted in the low clouds. It was swallowed again, but another appeared to its left. Ahead of both, a third entered a thinner patch of cloud, to reveal that the three were part of a flight of at least twenty. Each had six white wings, and cruised faster than Drakon flight without a wingbeat between them. To be so visible at their altitude, and so unbothered by the wind, they must each have had a wingspan of at least the length of Watersinger.

"Whitewaters," said Iverae.

Just one of those could overturn Watersinger if it took the mast and pulled. It could tear the sail off a ship. Rip the roof off a house and fish out the inhabitants inside.

Iverae leaned back and resheathed her knife. "They don't bother us, thank Shelha. It's rare to even see them this low."

"What do they eat, then?"

The Watermouse gave her a mirthless smile.

"Great," said Sethral. "Does that at least keep the Whitewing populations down?"

"Not in the slightest."

Something thumped the ship bottom. Sethral decided against asking how large Scythes had gotten now, too. Iverae at least seemed unbothered, and returned to the deck as soon as the Whitewaters were gone. Soon the creak of the mast heralded a slow turn around the island, back into the wind.

The near-Valkenland islands, grey and winter-pressed as they were, soon seemed lush against the ones farther north. Wind like Whitewing song ripped spray from whitecaps and tore at what few leaves still clutched the barren twigs. Vegetation on the ground was permanently flattened. Waves lashed stony, eroded shores, where bushes that had sprung up in warmer moons were now reduced to ragged mats of flotsam and foam.

A log pitched on the water as Iverae finally steered Watersinger past the last island behind and onto the open lake. Almost immediately, the ship heaved upwards. The drop sent stomachs airborne. Sethral ducked as the trapdoor slammed shut. She locked it and marveled at the lantern in the hold, which spun and spun, strung as it was, but never once spilled a drop of oil. It must be a new design. She gripped the ladder as the ship pitched again.

"Seth, over here!" called Loki. He and the other renegades were piled at the back of the hold. Sethral was flung off her paws as she tried to join them. Silversand, gauntlet on, helped her the rest of the way. Sethral could understand now why Iverae had put Phoenix in her cabin when she discovered he got watersick. Here at the center of the ship, the roll of the water lost its nauseating edge. Fletch passed around snacks.

"Somebody's got to be miserable," said Loki quietly, tapping the wall. He glanced up as a cold draft leaked down. Firebrand passed him a charcoal stick. He gave her a look. "I'm not that tall."

She closed her book with a groan and got up so he could stand on her back and mark the crack in the deck for Iverae. He stopped with his paws on the deck boards.

"Hurry up," grumbled Firebrand.

Sethral scrambled to her paws. "Loki, what is it?"

"There's something else on deck."

Silversand's gauntlet pinged. She was up the ladder before anyone could move, and eased back the lock. With her head, she pushed the trapdoor up just enough to peek outside. The door banged as she pounced. A gonging screech louder than a Drakon's rolled across the deck and smashed against the railing. Something was flung overboard with a splash audible even though the wind.

"Get up here!" shouted Silversand. "Anyone who can fight!"

Sethral was grabbed by the scruff and tossed back with Ryatzi. She hissed, yanked a knife from her bag and nearly caught Firebrand's tail as the Leslander, Fletch and Loki bounded on deck. Fat black birds the size of Whipper perched on the railings and made a row up the ship's long spar. Silversand stood bloodied in the middle of the deck, lips pulled back in a snarl. Iverae had one paw on the tiller and her knife extended in the other. While the birds locked their attention on the new arrivals, she slid a rope around the tiller and ducked across the deck. She straightened up back-to-back with the renegades and swung the heavy clip of the bucket-rope in a slow, menacing wheel. It struck like a snake. A bird cartwheeled from the railing. Silversand raced up the spar; Fletch drove the rest of the flock off the railing. Sethral caught a bird mid-flight and drove her knife into its chest. Firebrand flung a corpse overboard. She ducked as a Loki took the mast in a leap and intercepted another bird three tail-lengths in the air. They hit the waves in a cataclysmic splash. A bird whipped across the deck on Iverae's rope. She smashed it into the railing. Fletch grabbed it and dumped it in the water.

"Heads!"

Sethral ducked. Loki sprang off the railing, cleared the deck and took another bird with him into the water again. Sethral snatched Iverae's knife from the Watermouse's belt. She ambushed two birds that had cornered Silversand. Both fell dead. Sethral yanked the knives free; Silversand shook a splatter of blood off her gauntlet. Loki heaved himself over the railing again and fell to the deck as something enormous hit the hull like a swung log. Fletch and Firebrand grabbed opposite wings of the last bird and ran it into the mast. They threw it overboard and ducked as a tail-smack sent a fountain of spray two tail-lengths in the air.

"Did you have to go in the water?" said Fletch.

Loki tried to evade him, but the Rocklander was having none of it. Loki was pinned and only released again when Fletch had confirmed a lack of Scythe bites.

"That was reckless," said the Rocklander. "Don't do it again."

Loki shook himself off. "I'm more nimble than they are. I just gave them the birds, and they took them."

"And I'm sure you're just shaking from the cold."

"Sethral, I thought I told you to stay in the hold," said Firebrand.

"What, and let the rest of you fight? I'm not that weak anymore."

Iverae slid down against the railing and smoothed both paws back over her ears. "You lot just fought off a flock of those things and now you're bickering about it?" She dropped her paws. "Cool. Who do I get to nag?"

There was a clunk as Silversand dragged back the hatch bolt with her tail, her only appendage not soaked with Hollow blood. She poked her head down. "We're all okay. Oh no. Seth?"

Sethral tipped a knife at Loki. "You're least contaminated."

"I'm wet."

"I don't think he cares."

"Can one of you just go down?" said Silversand. "Please?"

Loki padded past her and dropped down the ladder. Left alone in an enclosed space... it wasn't a fear Ryatzi had had before. Sethral shuddered away the suspicion she had harbored since the Canyonlander colony, but it slithered in regardless. Did Ryatzi have memories of being buried?

Firebrand rapped her name on the cabin hatch.

"No," came a muffled reply from below.

"We need your bucket."

"Get your own."

Firebrand turned her eyes skyward, but was spared by the grate of a bolt. Whipper passed the bucket out the trapdoor with a smile that said he intended to make full use of Dusk's inability to get up and stop him. Iverae was soon hauling water to wash the stains off the deck and everyone on it. Sethral had to grit her teeth as the icy water sloshed over her claws. They went numb almost immediately.

"Alright, you can groom the rest." Iverae set the bucket aside. "You're all shivering like grass in a landquake; for Shelha's sake, go get back in the hold."

Sethral wished vines and rich green jungle over the scenery, then squelched the vision so violently it drove her claws into the deck. We would not wish for the landscape Wing had died in. A prod nearly sent her nose over wingtips onto the boards.

"Hold," said Fletch. "Go."

Sethral dragged her suddenly leaden paws to the trapdoor. She couldn't cry again. Not after Iverae had nearly gotten attacked by Hollows and Loki nearly eaten by Scythes. She had cried so many times over Wing and Jay, she now felt more exhaustion than self-pity when the pain twisted its dagger into her heart again.

"Them again?" said Firebrand quietly.

She nodded. Admitting it tipped the feeling over the edge. Firebrand pulled her back to her nest and curled around her to let her rock out the pain. It hurt. It still hurt so much. It had been five moons since Wing had died, and the ache still would not go away.

"When we find your clan," said Firebrand, "I'm asking them about you first thing. And if they say no, you don't listen."

Sethral wasn't sure how that made things feel better, but it did. She hugged the Leslander. "But what if they need me?"

"Then you say we need you more. And that you need us. You're a renegade, Seth, and you're the best analyst we have. If we're going into another Great Silence and anyone wants us to do anything about it, they can't stop us."

www.ingramcontent.com/pod-product-compliance
Lightning Source LLC
Chambersburg PA
CBHW070423170726
48291CB00002B/331